If There Be Pain

Other Titles by Gloria Mallette

If There Be Pain

GLORIA MALLETTE

KENSINGTON PUBLISHING CORP.
http://www.kensingtonbooks.com

DAFINA BOOKS are published by

Kensington Publishing Corp.
850 Third Avenue
New York, NY 10022

ISBN 0-7582-1159-7

First Kensington Trade Paperback Printing: December 2006
10 9 8 7 6 5 4 3 2 1

Printed in the United States of America

For my husband, Arnold, who listens to me gripe, who rejoices when I'm jubilant, who gives me advice that I rarely take, and who, after all these years, still sits and engages in hours of conversation with me.

For my son, Jared, who thanks me for cooking his favorite foods—chicken wings and broccoli, who kisses and hugs me daily, who still wants to marry me even after I've scolded him, and who brightens my day and gives me hope for the future of mankind.

And last but certainly not least, for God Almighty who blesses me each and every day I get to share my life with Arnold and Jared.

IF THERE BE PAIN

At Mama's knee, life's lessons can't be learned;
only in life's journey can our stripes be earned.
While some are wary where they tread,
others rush unwittingly straight ahead.

For those who do not heed an elder's plea,
they are surely guaranteed to pay a hefty fee.
Arrogantly they believe, what's worth a gain
can't come without inflicted pain.

They care not about the hearts they crucify;
their ultimate goal is to self-satisfy.
How they treat their many lovers
is often kept beneath the covers.

They are not concerned that which goes around,
perhaps will unexpectedly come around.
In time they will face a mighty reckoning rain
and not realize it's due to a poor soul's pain.

—*Gloria Mallette*

Prologue

Scratch . . . scratch . . . scratch . . .

Eight-year-old Kyle Lawson's eyes slowly opened, but they closed again as he fell back to sleep.

Scratch . . . scratch . . . scratch . . . scratch.

Again, Kyle opened his eyes. Something woke him, he just didn't know what. Groggily, he raised his head and looked around the room he slept in whenever he spent the night at his grandfather's. Everything—the dresser, the television, the chair, his big stuffed Dalmatian sitting on the chair his grandfather won for him out at Coney Island—had an eery shadowy look to it. Kyle looked toward the window. There was no daylight seeping through the blinds, a clear sign that it wasn't time to get up yet. Turning over, Kyle pulled the cover up over his head and nestled deep in the warmth and coziness of his bed.

SCRATCH . . . SCRATCH . . . SCRATCH!

Kyle bolted upright in bed, throwing the cover off. He heard it. Something was in his bedroom. Something—

SCRATCH . . . SCRATCH . . . SCRATCH!

His heart pounding, Kyle's eyes darted toward the closed closet door on the other side of the room near the door to his room.

Something was in his closet. Something was scratching to get out.

SCRATCH . . . SCRATCH . . . SCRATCH!

"Granddad! Granddad!" Kyle kept his eyes on the closet door.

SCRATCH . . . SCRATCH . . . SCRATCH!

"Granddad! Granddad!"

There was dead silence. No one was coming. Kyle cut his eyes from the bedroom door back to the closet door and back again to the bedroom door. The doors weren't that far apart, but maybe he could—

The click of the closet doorknob turning and opening shot chills up Kyle's back. He gasped. Unable to move, his eyes wide, his breath caught in his throat, Kyle gawked as the door slowly opened, revealing the blackness within. Still unable to move, his heart pounding rapidly in his chest, Kyle looked hard at the black hole that opened up in his room that seemed to grow wider and blacker with each passing second, seemingly engulfing the whole room, engulfing him. He wanted to scream, he wanted to cry out, but he could make not a sound.

Then . . . eyes! Big . . . green . . . scary eyes shot out of the blackness right in Kyle's face, just inches away! Teeth . . . big . . . long . . . sharp teeth . . .

"Aaaaaaaaaah!"

"Kyle . . . Kyle . . . Kyle, wake up! Wake up!" Granddad Preston shook Kyle harder and harder, trying to wake him up. "Kyle!" He pulled on the cover Kyle had wrapped himself up tight in until he could see Kyle's face and his eyes squeezed shut.

"Boy, you're having a nightmare. Wake up!"

Kyle, breathing hard, woke up and, seeing his grandfather in his brightly lit bedroom, threw his slim little arms around his neck and again squeezed his eyes shut.

"Granddad, Granddad, the monster's in my room! He's gonna get me, he's gonna eat me!"

"Son, you had a nightmare. There's no monster here. Look."

Kyle refused to let go of his grandfather or to even look around his room.

"There is, Granddad. I saw him. He has big green eyes and big sharp teeth. He's gonna eat me."

Granddad Preston peeled Kyle's arms from around his neck, but he held him close. Kyle buried his face against his grandfather's broad chest.

"Look, Kyle. Look around. There's no monster here."

Kyle didn't open his eyes. He couldn't, he was too scared. "He went back in the closet, Granddad. That's where he came from."

Kyle began to whimper. His eight-year-old mind told him that the monster had to still be hiding in the closet.

"There . . . there," Granddad Preston said, patting Kyle gently on the back. "Let's go open the closet door and make that big, bad monster go away."

"No! You make him go away."

Granddad Preston got up off the bed, leaving Kyle with his hands covering his face. At the closet door, Granddad Preston struck the door hard with the palm of his hand, startling Kyle. Kyle screeched and hid his face in his pillow.

"Monster, be gone!" Granddad Preston bellowed. "Leave my grandson alone forever!"

Striking the door again for good measure, Granddad Preston opened the closet door wide. He made a show of searching the closet. "He's gone, Kyle. Look. Look, Kyle. The monster's gone forever."

Sheepishly, Kyle peeked through his fingers at the closet.

"See?" Granddad Preston said. "He's gone."

Kyle timidly lowered his hands. "Forever?"

"Forever," Granddad Preston said, coming back to the bed. He took Kyle up onto his lap and folded him in his arms. "That monster was real scary, huh?"

"Uh-huh," Kyle said in a little voice.

"But the monster didn't get you, did he?"

"Uh-uh."

"That's because Granddad's here. I wouldn't let no big, bad monster eat my favorite grandson, would I?"

"Uh-uh." Kyle always felt safe in his grandfather's arms. "I don't like nightmares, Granddad. I don't wanna ever have another nightmare again."

"You won't."

"You promise?"

"I promise." Granddad Preston loosened his hold on Kyle. "In fact, to make sure of it, I'm gonna let you wear my special turtle."

Now Kyle was interested. He'd always liked the little gold turtle hanging around his grandfather's neck.

Granddad Preston unhooked the gold chain from around his

neck and put it on his grandson, just as his grandfather had done to his father.

"My father gave me this turtle. It came from your great, great-grandmother."

"I know," Kyle said as he held the turtle in his hand and looked at it.

"The turtle is a powerful symbol of protection, of long life and of good health. Our people—"

"The Tuscarora people, right, Granddad?"

"Yes, the Tuscarora nation. Years ago, our people always gave new babies turtle amulets to keep with them throughout their lives."

"What's an amulet, Granddad?"

"A necklace, son. Like this one, except it wasn't gold. Back then, it was made out of wood or stone or rawhide. Your great-grandmother had this one made out of gold. She said it looked better."

Kyle turned the turtle over and looked at his great-grandmother's name, Idell, etched on its underbelly. He'd seen it so many times before. He turned it again and looked at its ruby red eyes.

"You take care of this turtle, Kyle, and it'll take care of you."

Kyle asked in awe, "I can have it, Granddad?"

"Yes, you can have it. But you have to take care of it. You have to protect it from harm so it can protect you from harm."

"I will."

"You can't lose it, Kyle. And you can't let your friends play with it; you can't even let your friends see it. It has to stay under your shirt so no one will see it and want to take it from you. You understand me?"

"Yes, Granddad. I understand."

"Good. 'Cause if you let someone take it from you, you'll have bad dreams again, and you don't want that, do you?"

"Oh, no, Granddad. I don't ever wanna have another bad dream again."

"Then don't ever take it off. The power of the turtle won't be able to protect you if you take it off."

Chapter
1

If Kyle Lawson had to admit to a weakness, it would be a weakness for the sweet, intoxicating scent of a beautiful woman. Admittedly, he'd be lying if he said every woman who smelled good was a beautiful woman to behold—that was too far from real to be believed. In the real world, every beautiful woman just doesn't smell good. Oh, she might wear some nice perfume, perhaps she spent a hefty dollar for it, but the real deal is, her perfume might not complement her own natural scent, which might ooze from her pores like an odoriferous gas clinging to her skin for those within ten feet of her to smell and gag from. A bad-smelling woman, pretty or not, was a serious turnoff. So Kyle had had his share of ugly women, and at times, women twice his age, and double his 175-pound frame, because they smelled good. He was a sucker for a woman whose perfumes and body splashes enhanced her own natural scent, but he liked just as much a woman who didn't have to wear perfume to smell good. That's the woman he was especially drawn to, but he'd come across that woman so rarely that when he did, he made sure he got his fill of her, for his mind would not rest for fantasizing about wanting to get that woman into his bed. Hell, it didn't even have to be his bed. Her bed was preferable; but in the end, it didn't matter where as long as he made love to her. With that in mind, the first thing Kyle said to a good-smelling woman after he'd made her acquaintance was, "I must say, you smell as good as you look." As corny as that line was, Kyle had yet to meet a woman he'd said that to who wasn't flattered and had given him the warmest, most appreciative smile that said, "Thanks for noticing." Too bad most men didn't realize all they had to do was compliment a woman on her style, her perfume, and even on her smile. It did the trick for Kyle; he never had to worry about being turned down. Not even by his own employees.

Of the five women currently working for him in his medical transcription service, he had only slept with three, and that was because Nadine always smelled like boiled cabbage, and the fifth employee was his mother. He couldn't very well sleep with his own mother, but giving credit where it's due, his mother was the one who introduced his nose to the heady scent of a woman. He could remember lying with his face nestled in the curve of her neck, smelling her sweet perfume and falling asleep knowing that the arms that held him would always comfort him. He loved the perfumes his mother dabbed behind her ears and onto her wrists, and from the age of ten, for any occasion, he always gave her gifts of perfume, which started him on his lifelong gift-giving odyssey of finding the right perfume for the women in his life. Although admittedly, at one time, he gave the women who were closest to him whom he permitted into his bedroom the same perfume so none would pick up on the scent of another woman on the sheets. He stopped doing that when he realized that no one perfume smelled the same on any two women. Changing sheets was easier than stomaching the scent of a perfume that stank when a woman's passion heated her skin and changed the scent of the perfume she wore. Now, he always gave different perfumes to the women in his office, but he never had sex with them in his bed-room. He kept what went on between them down in his basement office, two floors below his bedroom. The ones he chose to sleep with seemed satisfied with that arrangement, that is, until he hired Grace. Grace had been with him a little over a year and was his best transcriber. He'd slept with her more times than he could count, and she was always trying to sweet talk him into taking her up to his bedroom. He never would—she was an employee, after all, and keeping her downstairs was paramount; he didn't want her to have access to him during and after business hours. Which was why, two months ago, he put a stop to their in-office sexcapades. But earlier tonight, the visibility of Grace's ample cleavage, the thigh-high skirt that exposed her firm thighs clad in black tights only inches below her panty line, not to mention the sweet, enticing scent of J'adore that kept wafting up his nostrils every time Grace came near, killed Kyle's resolve to not sleep with her again.

While the printer churned out the medical reports Grace had worked overtime to get out, Kyle sat submissively behind his desk as Grace, her skirt hiked up around her waist, her black tights and black panties dropped to the floor, straddled him for an intimate lap dance that mature, consenting adults had every right to enjoy, but that employee and employer had no business indulging in. Of course, he knew better and had, from the beginning, told Grace nothing would ever come of their illicit romps in the office, but when she and the others kept putting their assets up in his face, he couldn't help himself. Hell, a good-smelling woman was hard to resist.

Chapter
2

As was his norm, Kyle was awake even before his clock radio went off at 5:30 A.M. He'd gotten his five hours of sleep, which was about all he ever got. He had awakened only once after he'd had that weird dream. He'd dreamed that he'd gone to the bathroom, and while he stood at ease with a heavy stream emptying from his body, to his surprise, a woman's unblemished hand with long, lacquered red nails snaked up out of the hole in the toilet and began to lovingly massage him, giving him the kind of pleasure that made his eyes roll back in his head and speed up his breathing while lifting him off his feet as his body tensed and began to quake in anticipation of the surge that would surely give him relief. But that's not what happened. He remembered that his breath caught in his throat as he was being squeezed in a viselike grip by the hand that was no longer massaging him, but was painfully strangling him, making his eyes pop out of their sockets as he gasped for air and struggled to free himself of the death grip on his most prized body part. He felt as if it were being torn from his body—the pain radiated up his spine and down his thighs and legs into his toes. As hard as he pulled back, all the harder the hand pulled, dropping him down onto his knees. Petrified, he started to scream, and that's when he awakened, shaken and drenched with sweat. As soon as his eyes relayed to his brain that he wasn't in the bathroom but was in his bed, he was able to bring his breathing under control and lie back down. He'd had weird dreams before, but he never had any idea as to what they meant and never cared to find out. And this dream was no different. Bad dreams had haunted him all his life, he was used to them, they were like old girlfriends who refused to go away. Kyle touched the gold trinket on his chest. So much for a symbolic gold turtle protecting him.

At five-thirty in the morning, Kyle had more to worry about than a bad dream. He was teetering on the edge of bankruptcy and no one knew, not even his mother—his bookkeeper and office manager. She would have a stroke if she knew that his extensive personal spending had been pulling on his business income. Business was good, but more money was going out than coming in. He had huge credit card debt, thanks to his women, and he had to do something about that. He sat on the side of his bed staring inwardly at the "to do" list etched on his brain, and like always, he put items in their order of importance. First thing, before his appointment at the bank, he had to have his mother call the messenger service and have them deliver the transcribed medical reports to Dr. Seymour out at Coney Island Hospital and to Dr. Wittman out at Lutheran Medical Center. Then she needed to get a repairman from Computer World to come out to service the six-month-old Canon laser printer, which broke down last night while Grace was printing Dr. Wittman's reports. Drs. Seymour and Wittman both were steady, big money paying clients. Kyle couldn't afford to miss a deadline with either one. Thank goodness for the trusty old, antiquated IBM 4019E. It was a dinosaur, and Kyle had wanted to trash it when he purchased the Canon, but Grace insisted on holding on to the IBM because she was comfortable with it. Dr. Wittman's reports would be delivered on time, thanks to Grace, but then again, thanks to Grace his third chore was to advertise for a new medical transcriptionist.

Grace quit on him last night, and Kyle could blame no one but himself. He knew how Grace felt about him; she had professed her love more times than he wanted to hear, which is why he stopped having sex with her. Grace wanted a committed relationship that he wasn't open to. For one thing, he didn't love her. If he loved anyone, or rather, if he was close to loving anyone, it was Audrey—and that was a big if. Grace? She was his employee, he was her boss, and he saw no reason for that to change. Of course, in hindsight, he should have kept their relationship strictly business, but when a woman puts her body in a man's face every day in a way that says, "Look at me! Don't you want some of this?" It's hard for a man to turn a blind eye. And Grace's low-cut tops and up-to-her-ass skirts revealing her tight, muscular thighs heightened his interest on a daily basis. Then when he overheard Grace telling the other women in the office about her workout routine with her elliptical machine and Billy Blanks' kickboxing tapes, Kyle wondered how those powerful thighs would feel wrapped around his body. Just thinking about it heightened his senses around her. He smelled her, he brushed up against her, he watched her every move with cool distraction, yet he felt like a wolf lying in wait.

It took four long months for the wondering to be answered, and although Kyle later wondered if he seduced Grace or if she seduced him, when they ended up horizontal on the love seat in his office after work, he partook of her as if he were a man finally freed after a year in jail. Neither he nor Grace gave a second thought to Grace's live-in boyfriend or her two children at home. From that night on, every time she stayed after work and they got it on, he didn't mind paying her overtime whether there was legitimate work done or not. Everything was working out just fine, that is, until just before Christmas when Grace let it be known that she wanted more, and that's when he let her know that maybe they shouldn't indulge in their extracurricular romps anymore— it was bad for business.

"So, what am I supposed to do, Kyle? Keep working for you and forget we ever had sex?"

"You don't have to forget, I won't. It's just best for business if we go back to having a purely professional relationship."

"I can't do that, Kyle. I'm in love with you. I got rid of my man for you."

"I didn't ask you to do that."

"But you—"

"Grace, I told you I didn't have time to invest in a relationship because I have a business to run. That's why I'm divorced in the first place." Even when he said it, Kyle knew it was a lie. His marriage ended because he never stopped seeing other women, and at this very moment in time, he was seeing three other women pretty regularly who Grace knew nothing about.

"But I could help you in your business, Kyle. I already work for you. I could do even more."

He shook his head. "I'm not looking for a partner. I'm sorry if you thought—"

"I thought you loved me, Kyle. You said—"

"No, I said I loved having sex with you. It's not the same as saying, 'I love you.' "

Grace turned away from Kyle and, with her hand over her nose and mouth, tried to muffle the sniffle that escaped her.

Kyle knew that he should put his arms around Grace and console her, but keeping his distance felt right. "I'll always care for you, Grace. You're a valued employee."

That painfully hurt look on Grace's face said everything that her tongue didn't. She simply walked out, leaving Kyle relieved that she was gone. She showed up at work the next day dressed in a black turtleneck sweater and black pants, and she wasted no time leaving when the five o'clock hour chimed, but she still wore the same perfume. That was two months ago, and since Christmas, Grace had remained the consummate professional. That is, until the printer broke down last night. Grace smelled good, she looked good, and using the excuse that he was kissing her on the cheek for staying behind to help him get the work out, before he knew it, they were in a lip-lock that couldn't be broken with a crowbar. When it was all said and done, Grace walked out, leaving him hot to go another round with her, and annoyed that before him lay the task of having to fill her vacant slot. He wasn't going to beg Grace to stay when he couldn't give her what she wanted—himself.

So, moving on, this morning while his mother looked for another transcriber, Kyle planned on keeping his appointment with the bank. He was going to refinance his mortgage and, hopefully, end up with monthly payments that were more manageable so he'd have more available cash to pay on his credit cards. That debt alone was strangling him, not to mention the car notes—his and Lorna's. Lorna was great in bed, but how she had talked him into paying her car note for a year he didn't know. He was sorry now that he let her talk him into leasing that damn car. That was another four hundred out-of-pocket every month, which will end in three months, and he had no intention of renewing. Adding that expense to all of his credit cards, personal and business, he was embarrassingly overlimit to the tune of $27,000. How stupid was he to have given major credit cards to three shopaholic divas who weren't paying him any mind when he asked them to curtail their spending? Neither of the three knew about the other, yet they all thought he was a bottomless pit of dollars. They were going to bankrupt him if he didn't stop their spending, but he didn't know how to get the cards back without letting them know that he wasn't rolling in dough.

The chirping of the radio alarm clock broke Kyle's pensive mood. That's about all he used his alarm clock for—to snap him out of his ritual of sitting on the side of his bed and getting lost in the minutiae of annoying money and people problems. He shut off the alarm with a solid tap on the button on top of the clock. It was six, time to get started. After a quick twenty-minute walk on his treadmill and an even quicker twenty minutes of weight lifting, he got cleaned up and headed next door to his parents' house for breakfast. Working from home in his basement office was great, but it was even sweeter to live next door to his mother, who happened to make the best buttermilk pancakes in the world. Twice a week, she made them especially for him. Breakfast on other days of the week weren't bad either—hash browns, sausage, bacon, eggs, and thick, buttery grits to comfort his Southern soul. But this morning, explaining to his mother that Grace had quit was sure to spoil a great stack of pancakes.

Chapter
3

Kyle almost laughed when he saw his father standing at the top of the stairs, his hands stuffed in his pockets and only one button buttoned at the neck on his heavy wool jacket. The grim, hooded look in Marvin Lawson's eyes said it all—Kyle was in trouble. That look took Kyle back to his teen years whenever he broke curfew or had committed any other juvenile infraction that his father would be waiting on the stoop to confront him with when he got home. But Kyle never sweated it. Getting past his father had always been a breeze—a ten-minute lecture about his wrongs and admonishments to not do it again was light stuff. His father was cool. He was never one to grab him up by his collar and threaten him; it was his mother who did that. When he was a kid, his mother would deprive him of something he most wanted or treasured, but always there was a smack or two upside the head—clear up till he was nineteen years old.

"Dad."

"Son." Marvin looked off down Prospect Place toward Flatbush Avenue where he could see the steady stream of bumper-to-bumper rush-hour traffic snaking its way toward the Brooklyn and Manhattan bridges.

Standing alongside his father, Kyle began to feel the late February chill through his silk sweater. He quickly regretted coming out of the house without a jacket—although he'd walked only about twenty feet.

"So, Dad, what's up?"

Marvin continued looking up the street. "Grace called fifteen minutes ago."

Be cool. "Yeah, well, Mom is the office manager."

Giving Kyle a disgusted look, Marvin asked, "When you gonna get a handle on that thing, boy?"

Kyle shoved his cold hands into his pockets. "Look, I didn't force myself on Grace or beg her to spread eagle on top of my desk."

"That's not the point. Haven't you learned yet to screw with some discretion? How many times have I told you—"

"I know. Don't shit where I eat."

"Then why the hell do you keep doing it?"

Still maintaining his cool, Kyle let out a low, soft breath. He was no longer a kid and didn't have to stand there and allow himself to be browbeaten.

"Look, it's cold out here. Can we go inside and—"

"Son, even an alley cat knows better than to do that, that's why they roam. Why in the world—"

"Okay! Damn." Kyle shoved his hands deeper inside his pockets and hunched his shoulders up to his ears. "Stop lecturing me, Dad. I'm thirty-four years old. I—"

"Then you should know better, Kyle. It's very distressing to your mother that you're still running around humping everything in sight, like you're a teenage boy who just discovered you could use that damn thing for something other than peeing. Mature men have better control than that."

"Hey, I didn't do it alone. Grace had a hell of a lot of say in what we did—together. She bailed when I wouldn't give her what she wanted, and that was probably a ring, which I never promised her. Grace was a good worker; I'll miss her. But you know something? I'm not worried. I can get another transcriber in place within a few days. If Mom won't handle it, I'll do it myself. Right now, I'm going back inside my own house to eat breakfast. I don't need this crap this morning."

"Kyle!" Marvin roared, stopping Kyle before he could start down the stairs. "Calling yourself a man don't give you license to disrespect me or your mother."

"What about you respecting me? I'm a grown man, Dad. I pay my own bills, I have my own home. I don't need you or Mom lecturing me or checking on me. I don't need a nod from either one of you as to whom I can and can't sleep with."

"Yeah, you might be past the age of consent, but you have a ways to go to get past the age of stupid."

Stunned, Kyle gawked at his father. He couldn't believe—

"That's right, I said it—stupid. Kyle, you act like you have no sense, like you're still a boy who just discovered how to use his own dick."

"Dad—"

"Dammit, Kyle, you need to grow up! You need to put yourself in check and start acting like you got the good sense God gave you, before you get yourself some disease that'll kill you. Hell, the way you're treating women like they're disposable razors, one of them might turn around and use a razor on you."

"That'll never happen. I—"

"You don't know that, Kyle! Some women don't play. Look, how would you feel if some man treated your daughter or your sister the way you treat women?"

"Humph. Anyone mess over my daughter, he better pray I don't find him, and I don't think I'll ever have to worry about some man messing over Carole. She's gay, remember?"

Marvin leveled a disgusted look on Kyle.

On the other side of the unlocked, slightly ajar door, Betty Lawson eased closer so that she could hear better.

"Oh, I forgot. You don't like hearing that Carole's a lesbian. Still can't deal with that, huh?"

Marvin narrowed his gaze and stepped closer to Kyle. "You have a smart-ass mouth, boy. One of these days, you're gonna have to answer to somebody."

"For what, Dad?" Kyle had had enough, and he certainly no longer felt the cold.

"What am I doing that's so damn wrong? I'm not forcing anyone to be with me. Grace is a grown-ass woman. It was up to her to keep her damn thighs closed. If there was any disrespect, it wasn't on my part. She's the one who told my business to you and Mom."

Stepping back from Kyle, Marvin shook his head. "I'm done talking to you. You're on your own."

"Isn't that what you told Carole when she told you she was a lesbian?"

Marvin cut his eyes at Kyle, glaring threateningly.

Betty closed her eyes and pressed her lips tight to keep from saying anything.

Kyle felt the back of his neck heat up. He had tread dangerously close to his father's breaking point. He glanced at his father's hand to see if he had balled up his fist—he had. This time, he stepped back.

"Okay. Look, Dad. What's the big deal? I like women, they like me. Unfortunately, I got with Grace, and perhaps that was a mistake. I admit that. But who did I really hurt? Me. I lost a good employee."

Marvin chuckled drily. He stuffed his fists inside his pockets. "You're selfish, Kyle. You don't give a damn about anyone but yourself."

Inside the house, Betty nodded in agreement.

"Oh, well," Kyle said. "No matter what I say, I'll be wrong. I'm going home." He started to step off the stoop.

"Kyle," Marvin said again, stopping Kyle before he started down the stairs, but Kyle didn't turn around.

"Son, you're using women and that's not right."

"Dad—"

"Just listen a minute, Kyle. Just hear me out."

Kyle folded his arms high and tight across his chest. He fixed his eyes on the red door across the street. He could remember when Mrs. Becker painted that door that bright-ass red three years ago. He hated it then, he hated it now.

"Son, being with all those women don't make you a man . . ."

Kyle groaned.

"The measure of a man is not in how many women he can bed, but in the love he can give to one woman, one special woman, alone."

Betty listened to her husband's words with a cynical smirk on her lips. *He should talk.* His own infidelity twelve years ago was still very painful to her.

Kyle's better sense told him to let his father's remark go un-challenged, but his vindictive voice said, *Hit him where it hurts.*

"Dad, why don't you help me understand why it is that your wife wasn't that one woman for you . . ."

Marvin's face dropped.

A soft gasp escaped from Betty.

". . . when you had that three-year affair with Noreen Clayson? By the way, you still seeing her?"

Betty couldn't believe Kyle's blatancy. She opened the door.

Stunned but a second, Marvin grabbed Kyle by the front of his sweater and yanked him from his six-foot height down to his own five-foot-nine eye level. He growled, "Boy, I will put your ass six feet under. You don't talk to me like that!"

"Marvin," Betty said, "come inside."

His father's threat put no fear in Kyle's heart. If anything, he was annoyed that his father had his hands on him, yet in turn, he didn't put his hands on him. He dropped his eyes and reminded himself to stay calm. The last thing he wanted to do was have a fight with his father out there on the front stoop or anywhere for that matter.

"Let go of me, Dad."

As Betty eased her hand on her husband's upper arm, she glanced around at her neighbors' houses to see if anyone was visible. "Marvin," she said again, "come inside."

Still holding on to Kyle's sweater with one hand, Marvin gri-maced and pressed the ball of his hand into his right side, ignor-ing Betty.

"You listen to me, boy. Your mother is the only one I had to an-swer to. You, I don't owe an explanation. You talk to me like that again"—Marvin pushed off on Kyle's chest, releasing him—"I'll end your life. You deal with your dogging around before some woman takes a blade to what you treasure most."

Kyle cooly smoothed out his sweater. "Can't you tell, Dad?" He looked his father in the eye. "I'm real scared."

"Go home, Kyle," Betty said, trying to gently pull Marvin in-side the house.

But Marvin had more to say to Kyle. "That's your problem. You think nothing can hurt you."

Kyle started down the stairs but had more to say himself. "Were you so different from me when you were a young man, Dad? Were you a saint?"

"That's enough Kyle," Betty said, "Go home. Marvin, y'all need to stop this."

"Boy, I never disrespected women the way you do, nor did I ever disrespect my parents in any way."

"Aw, man. Dad, I'm not trying to disrespect you or Mom, or any of the women I see. I don't put their business out in the street or up in each other's faces."

"Oh, yes, you do, Kyle. A few months ago, you had three women show up at your house at the same time because you couldn't remember that you'd made a date with all three for the same evening. You call that respect?"

"I had a senior moment, so sue me—they didn't. In fact, two of them hung around and we had a damn good time. They weren't hurting too badly."

"Boy—"

"Kyle," Betty said, stepping forward, "you're trifling! I'm ashamed of you. I can't believe the ignorant things that are coming out of your mouth."

Kyle huffed and looked off up the street. *Goddamn! This must be fuck with Kyle day!*

Betty continued, "You run around here like a dog in heat, listening to no one, doing whatever the hell you feel like doing. You act like you're an addict—"

"So now I'm an addict? I don't do drugs."

"You're a sex addict, Kyle. And it's too damn bad they don't give lobotomies for that."

"The boy's stupid," Marvin said.

"Oh, sh—" Kyle went on down the stairs. "I'm going home."

"Your father's right, Kyle. You are stupid. One of these days, somebody is going to hurt you real bad for messing with her feelings."

At the bottom of the steps, Kyle looked back. "Well, like we used to say in football, 'If there be pain, hey, I can handle it. I'm a man.'"

"Betty wasn't impressed. "Kyle, a man never has to say that he's a man. He only has to act like one."

"Betty, don't say any more to him. Kyle's a hard head, and a hard head makes for a soft ass."

"A real soft ass," Betty reiterated.

Kyle took one long pause before turning back. "Mom, why don't you take the day off. I don't need you." Kyle left his parents staring after him, not caring what they were thinking. He no longer lived under their roof, so he wasn't about to sit like a schoolboy with his hands folded in his lap while they scolded him. Where did they get off telling him not to have sex with whomever he wanted, as often as he wanted, and with as many women as he wanted? He wasn't having it. Not today, not any day. He paid well to have his choice of any woman he wanted. Isn't that what being a man of means was all about?

Chapter
4

It took Kyle only minutes to make himself a palatable breakfast of scrambled eggs, dried bacon bits, and onion. It wasn't a meal that could touch his mother's fluffy buttermilk pancakes, but it was food that sated his empty stomach and gave him the energy he needed to get his workday started. The clinking of Betty's keys as she entered the basement office alerted Kyle to be ready for her mouth. It was just like her to show up when he'd told her not to come in. It was still early yet—8:30. Lucille, Nadine, and Diane wouldn't be in until 9:00, but this was his mother's usual time to show up for work. Sitting at Grace's desk, Kyle began flipping through the Rolodex to find the number for the messenger service.

Betty quietly hung her jacket on a hook on the brass clothes tree. Kyle made it a point not to raise his eyes to look at his mother as she headed for her own little office in the back. It was times like this that he hated that he had hired his own mother to work for him. When she retired from her thirty-one-year position as a high school math teacher with the Department of Education and offered to help him with the bookkeeping, he had not hesitated in hiring her on. Who else would be more trustworthy than his own mother? And the fact that she lived next door in the landmark limestone on Prospect Place in the Prospect Heights neighborhood he grew up in was a plus. She would always be on time, and she was. Three days a week his mother worked until two in the afternoon. Kyle couldn't have asked for a better employee. He started his medical transcription business four years ago, transcribing the tapes himself. With the vast number of hospitals and clinics throughout Brooklyn and Queens, his business grew quickly. After a year, he added medical billing to his services and hired on four transcribers, freeing himself to go out to market and publicize his service in person. Kyle spent his time visiting hospitals and clinics drumming up new clients. Right now he had forty-seven steady doctors on his roster of clients and fifty who used his service on a "need to" basis. But he was always looking to add more doctors, especially now that he desperately needed the money. He had money troubles that his mother didn't know about—he didn't allow her to see his personal credit card statements and household expenses, just the income and expenditures for the business. She knew about the $11,000 he owed on the business credit card and was always haranguing him about paying it. Man, if she knew about the car he was leasing for Lorna or about the money his women spent on his personal credit cards, she'd have him committed.

"Kyle," Betty called from her office.

Kyle dropped his head. *Damn.*

"I know you heard me, Kyle. Come in here."

"I'm about to call the messenger service. You'll have to wait."

"The call can wait. Get in here."

Damn! There it was, that tone, that demanding, obey me tone that she always used when she was upset with him. While he wanted to say, *I'm not a damn kid. I don't have to jump because you say so,* he didn't—he took his time. By the time he sat in the chair across from his mother, his office manager, Kyle felt as if he had been called on the carpet for picking his nose and farting in church. This was the down side of having his mother work for him—she had easy access to him and wasn't a bit shy about telling him where he messed up.

Betty stared at her middle child, her second-born son. She couldn't figure out where she'd gone wrong in bringing him up for him to have such disrespect for himself and for the women he was using.

His mother's disappointment was clear in her eyes, but Kyle

had nothing to be ashamed of—he owned his own home, his own business; he called his own shots. He didn't have to answer to anyone.

"Kyle, why—"

"Mom, don't start." Kyle stood

"Why Grace, Kyle? Grace was the best transcriber in the office. It'll be a miracle if you can find anyone as good as her again. Why can't you control yourself?"

Kyle tightened his jaw. First his father, now his mother. He wasn't having it.

"Why do you have to sleep with every woman who crosses your path?"

"Not every woman, Mom. I haven't slept with you."

Betty gasped. Her hand to her breast, she gawked at Kyle.

"Damn, Mom. It was a joke."

"Why would you say such a vile thing, Kyle? I'm your mother. You don't joke with me like that. Are you crazy? Why would you even say such a thing?"

"It seemed fitting, Mom. It was a dumb-ass quip to a stupid-ass question."

Again gasping, Betty's eyes fluttered. "My God, Kyle. How are you talking to me? You've never—"

"How are you talking to me, Mom? I'm not a kid. You have no right to question me about my sex life."

"Boy, I'm your office manager. I have a responsibility to question you about goings-on in this office, and that includes you sleeping with the women in your employ. Boy, don't you know any one of those women could bring a sexual harassment suit against you?"

"They won't. It's always been consensual."

"Says you, but that may not be what they say later. What Grace might say later."

"Mom, you're worrying for nothing. There will be no suits from Grace or anyone."

Shaking her head in disbelief, Betty sat back.

"I have to go," Kyle said, about to turn away from his mother.

"Kyle, I can't understand how a man as intelligent as you, with so much going for him, would let his sexual needs rule his better sense. Do you know if you were a woman, you'd be called a whore?"

Kyle exhaled his annoyance. "You think a lot of me, don't you, Mom? I appreciate your vote of confidence."

Betty ignored the sarcasm. "Well, Kyle, you don't act like you have good sense. Personally, I just can't believe how stupid and irresponsible you've been."

"The Small Business Association didn't think I was stupid or irresponsible when they presented me the Small Business of the Year award last year."

"Do you think you would have gotten that award if they knew that you slept with your employees?"

"Maybe if they had known, they might've given me an award for that."

"Keep being a wise ass, Kyle, you'll end up losing this business. You're much smarter than this, but no one would know it by your actions. Everyone around you isn't blind, Kyle. I've known for a while that you were sleeping with Grace, and I suspect you've slept with Diane and Nadine, too."

"You must be kidding. Nadine? Mom, the woman wears rubber bands on her wrist like they're the finest in gold bracelets. She has a dour face, a boxy linebacker figure that's probably never worn silk, and she smells sour. I'd have to be dead drunk and stranded on top of Mount Everest for a month to even think about touching her."

"Then why did you give her perfume for Christmas, which you also gave Diane and every other woman you know? Are you gonna lie and say you didn't sleep with Diane either?"

Kyle looked sheepishly at his mother. Maybe he had better change his *modus operandi*. By now, anyone close to him had to know about his predilection for giving perfume as gifts.

"In case you didn't know it, Mom, perfume's the easiest gift to give a woman. Most women wear perfume. And for your information, I gave Nadine perfume hoping that it would do something for her sour-ass disposition, not to mention her—"

"Don't say it, Kyle. You shouldn't have your nose close enough to Nadine to smell her in the first place."

"Mom, my nose could be in the Bahamas and I'd still be able to smell Nadine. As office manager, you should speak to her about her body odor."

"Don't be ridiculous. The woman doesn't smell, you just don't like her."

"You hired her. I never would've."

"We're off the subject, Kyle. The question is why do you have to sleep with the women who work for you? You have all those other women; you meet women all the time. Why sleep with women you have no godly intention of marrying or being with once you've gotten your fill of them? They're your employees, for god's sake."

"I'm not raping these women, Mom."

"I didn't say you were, and you didn't answer my question."

"Look. Plain and simple. I like women. It's as plain and simple as that. At times, I spend most of my day with the women who work for me. They want me, just like I want them. We're adults, it happens. The problem comes in when they, on their own, expect something more than I'm willing to give. I promise no one anything."

"That's not true, Kyle. The minute you sleep with a woman, especially more than once, it's implied that you're serious about her. In a woman's mind, that's damn near a promise of commitment."

"Women think like that, men don't. And you know why that is, Mom. Men need variety, women need a provider. Y'all look at every man as a potential cash cow."

Betty just looked at Kyle.

"Well, it's the truth. Why else do women start planning their weddings two seconds after meeting a man with a job?"

"Kyle," Betty said, "I didn't realize how warped you were. I didn't raise you like this. How—"

"Oh, I guess I'm the only man on earth who thinks the way I do? Like I believe that."

Betty could see that she was wasting her time. "Look, Kyle. The bottom line, you're playing with fire. You keep bedding your employees, you won't have a business. One of these women will sue you one day, and you'll lose everything, including this house."

"That'll never happen."

"Oh, believe me, that and much worse can happen. Kyle, you keep leading women on, you just might lose your life."

"You and Dad have been watching too many of those stupid crime shows. There isn't a woman out there that can take me out."

"You're stupid if you believe that."

"What am I supposed to do, sit still while some woman kills me because I won't marry her?"

Betty shook her head sadly. "Too bad you didn't grow up in the South, you'd know better than to be this naive."

Kyle flipped his hand at Betty, dismissing her remark. "I'm not even gonna ask what the hell that means. I don't wanna know."

"There's a warning women in the South say to the men in their lives who've wronged them."

"Mom—"

" 'Don't go to sleep.' That's what women down South used to say. Because sleep is when a man is most vulnerable. That's when a woman can get even with him."

"Well, you know something, Mom? If a woman I sleep with is capable of doing something to me while I'm asleep, then I would be right not to marry her. But I grant you this, Mom, I will stop sleeping with my employees—it's too much of a hassle."

"Oh, is that all it is, a hassle? Kyle, it's more than that. It's very unprofessional, and it's quite immoral. Your brother would never do anything like that."

Kyle wondered when she'd throw Preston up in his face. His big brother, Preston, the doctor, would never do anything wrong. All Kyle's life, he always heard, "Why aren't you like Preston? He's an A student; he's so well-behaved. He's so special." Granted Preston was a very good urologist; his famous clients could attest to that. Well, kudos to Preston, he made their parents proud. But then Preston's path was set from the time he was born. Betty and Marvin expected the best of their firstborn and invested a lot of time and a lot of money in his education. They didn't do the same for Kyle, especially when they realized he didn't have a mind for science. In high school, biology and chemistry were like foreign languages to him. He was good at math, but he was better on the football field, that is, until he tore the hell out of his right knee on a line-drive tackle playing college ball. His NFL dreams were derailed, and he barely made it out of college with a liberal arts degree. He always felt like he disappointed his parents. They used Preston and his achievements as the benchmark Kyle fell way short of, and at times, he felt like they were right.

"Preston has a successful practice, a beautiful home, a lovely family—"

"I'd appreciate it if you wouldn't shove Preston's life down my throat."

"I'm just trying to point out to you that you can do just as well as Preston."

"I am doing as well as Preston! Or haven't you noticed, Mom? It seems what you're saying is that I'm a nothing. That—"

"I'm not saying that, Kyle! It's just that you keep messing up when you sleep—"

"Forget it!" He flipped his hand disgustedly at his mother. "I have a business to run."

"Kyle, I'm not through."

"Well, I am." He stepped out of her office.

"Kyle!"

He whirled around. "I'm done. I'm not discussing my sex life or why you feel I should be more like Preston a second longer."

"Fine, but you will stay put until I'm finished talking."

"You're treating me like a kid. I'm a man who happens to be your boss."

Betty planted her hands flat on her desk and pushed herself up out of her chair. "Get this, Mr. Boss Man. I'm your mother for life. Your title as my boss can end in the blink of an eye."

Neither blinked, neither said a word as the only sound in the room was that of the ticking clock on the wall over Kyle's right shoulder. The reproachful look in his mother's eyes made him feel as he did when he was ten years old and had gotten caught throwing spitballs in the school cafeteria.

"You need God in your life, Kyle. You're—"

"Aw, man." He had to get out of there.

"—really out of control."

"Mom, I have an appointment. I have to go."

"Fine, Kyle, you go ahead. But remember this. A hard—"

"I know, a hard head makes for a soft ass."

"That's right, and some lessons are hard learned. You could get hurt—"

"Yeah, well, if there be pain. Mom, please. I have to go. Are you finished?"

Deeply exhaling her disgust at her son, Betty picked up a piece of paper from her desk. "Okay, Mr. Lawson."

Kyle rolled his eyes. He couldn't believe how hard his mother was riding him. He wished he could fire her ass.

"There's a problem with Dr. Seymour's and Dr. Wittman's medical reports."

"What about them?"

"Haven't you noticed every time one doctor submits a report to transcribe on a patient, at the same time the other doctor submits the same report on the same patient going to two different insurance companies?"

"Actually, I haven't, but I'm not the one transcribing, so I wouldn't know who the patients are in the reports."

"Well, I'm not transcribing either, but when I do the billing, I take note of the patient names. Kyle, there's something not right going on here between these two doctors. I've been meaning to talk to you about it. I've read several of the previous reports just to see if I was right, and if I read the ones completed yesterday, I'm sure I'll find the same situation—identical reports. It seems to me these two doctors are either sharing patients, or by some weird trick, it's the same doctor with a different name. Either way, something's not right."

"Mom, a patient can see more than one doctor, and usually a doctor, a primary doctor, refers his patients to a specialist. Both Dr. Seymour and Dr. Wittman are surgeons. They are not the same doctor. Maybe the patient got a second opinion. You—"

"And a second surgery that was exactly the same as performed by the first doctor."

"Mom, you're fishing. Just do your billing and nothing more."

"Kyle, I'm looking at what could be medical fraud."

"Mom, we're hired to transcribe the medical reports and the billings, that's all. We're not watchdogs for insurance companies. Is that it?"

"I just thought you needed to be aware of this. It's reported all the time about medical insurance fraud. It affects everyone's insurance cost, including yours and mine. Kyle, you should—"

"Mom, I have to go."

"But, Kyle—"

"Look, when I get some time, I'll look over the reports, and if I see something suspicious, I'll . . ." Kyle shrugged, knowing that he'd do nothing. "I don't know. Look, I have to get going. I have an appointment at Downstate." His mother didn't need to know about his appointment with the bank. "Please see if you can get the employment agency to send over a new girl. Also, the printer needs servicing. And don't forget to messenger those reports to Dr. Seymour and Dr. Wittman. I'll call in after Downstate."

"One more thing, Kyle."

"What now?"

"Don't talk to me in that tone."

"But, Mom, I have to go."

"And you will, in a minute."

Kyle wanted to punch the wall.

Betty could care less about the look of agitation on Kyle's face. "I see you have an appointment Friday afternoon at Brooklyn Jewish."

"Yeah, and?"

"Kyle, your grandfather is right across the street at—"

"Mom, I know Granddad's in the nursing home across the street from the hospital. If I get a chance, I'll stop by."

"You said that how many times before?"

"Mom, you more than anyone know how busy I am. I have—"

"I don't wanna hear it, Kyle. . . .

Damn! Here we go again.

"You can't tell me in more than a year and a half, you haven't been able to find thirty measly minutes, in your extremely busy life, to go visit your grandfather. You're lying, Kyle, and you're selfish. You don't know how long your grandfather is going to be with us."

"That could be said for any one of us."

"That's right, including you. So you need to find time to visit your grandfather. You don't seem to have a problem finding time for all the women you're screwing. It takes time to be a whore, Kyle. You seem to have plenty of time for that."

Wham! Kyle felt like he was just hit across the face with a two-by-four. His mother was really on his ass over Grace walking out. She wasn't holding anything back. He had better get in the wind before the words between them got any uglier.

"I'm outta here."

"Kyle, go see your grandfather. He's talking about seeing his great-grandfather sitting on top of a white horse holding out a medicine bag to him. He thinks his great-grandfather is handing his power over to him in the afterworld. You know what that means, Kyle?"

"I said I'll go!"

"It means that my father's ancestors are calling him over. It means—"

"That's hogwash. That's Indian folklore. I don't believe in it."

"Well, Daddy believes in it, and that's all that matters, but I believe it myself."

"That's not my problem."

"It may not be your problem, Kyle, but Daddy's been asking for you, and you will go see him."

"I said I would, Mom. Damn."

Betty gave Kyle a warning glare. Kyle huffed softly and looked away.

"Your grandfather thinks the world of you, Kyle. Go see him. I'm tired of making excuses for you."

"Then don't. Tell him the truth—I'm busy. He probably wouldn't know me if I visited him, anyway."

"He's not senile, Kyle. He has bladder cancer. His mind is just fine."

"Not with all the medications he's on. He's like a zombie."

"Well, he needs that medication for the pain. But when he's alert, Kyle, he knows you're out here whoring around like—"

"I'm not whoring around, Mom! And why would you tell him something like that, anyway?"

"Because I don't lie to my father, like you're lying to yourself and me."

Kyle pressed his lips tight to keep from saying something he'd regret.

"If you're ashamed of something you're doing that you don't want your grandfather to know about, then cut it the hell out. But the reality is, I'm not telling him anything he doesn't already know."

Still pressing his lips together, Kyle glared intently at his mother.

"Oh!" Betty said as an afterthought. "But I'm not supposed to talk about your sex life, am I? Excuse me. Kyle, if you can't find half a minute for your grandfather, shame on you. What if your father and I ended up in a nursing home? Do you plan on ignoring us, too?"

"Damn, Mom! Get up off my back. I told you, I'll go see Granddad on Friday. In fact, I'll make it my damn business to visit him. Can I *please* go now?" Kyle again started out of the office.

"Well . . .

"Aw, damn!"

"Your father wants you to go with him to your brother's Friday night to help him move his piano up from that room on the parlor floor to the second floor. He and Donna are remodeling their brownstone."

"Can't. I'm busy." Kyle hurried out of his mother's office before she could browbeat him into changing his plans, which he wasn't about to. He had paid out of his pocket $2,000 to escort Audrey Copelin to the $1,000-a-plate dinner for Assemblywoman Heloise Horton. It was a fund-raiser for her upcoming race in the fall to retain her seat. Kyle couldn't miss this dinner, it was important to mingle with and be seen by people who could make a difference with a single phone call. And the call he needed was to the mayor. Audrey was trying to get appointed to the bench in Brooklyn's Family Court. She was tired of prosecuting child negligence cases and deadbeat dads. She wanted to make a difference in a big way as a Family Court judge, and he was going to help her. Who knows? She just might be the one he ended up marrying.

Chapter
5

As hungry as he was, Kyle had to remind himself not to touch the dinner rolls until the salad was served to every single person at his table—which hadn't happened yet. If he had not been running late, he might have had time to eat lunch, but his first two appointments at Kingsbrook Medical Center ran over, backing up the rest of his day. By the time he made it to his third appointment at Brooklyn Jewish Hospital, he had come within inches of ramming into the back of an SUV, had run three red lights and an unmentionable number of stop signs, and still, he had missed the doctor by twenty-five minutes and had to reschedule. His perilous drive over to Prospect Place in the up-and-coming neighborhood of Crown Heights was a waste of time and pissed him off. He hated being late for appointments as much as he hated missing appointments. Adding new doctors to his client list was his bread and butter and more important than ever.

Wednesday, after his meeting at the bank about refinancing his mortgage, he needed as many new accounts as possible. Refinancing was not an option for him—he needed cash in hand. He ended up applying for a home equity line of credit of $100,000 in order to pay off his outstanding debt. The bank officer warned Kyle, upon closing, all of his credit cards would be seized and the accounts closed out. Kyle didn't know how he was going to tell Audrey, Dalia, or Lorna that they had to give back their credit cards. On Friday night, he'd see Audrey and would broach the subject with her.

On Friday afternoon, determined to be on time for his next appointment, Kyle was back in his car about to pull out when he caught a glimpse of an elderly man being escorted by a male nurse into the Jewish Hospital Nursing Home across the street. *Damn!* He flat-handed his steering wheel—*Damn!* He almost forgot. The illuminated clock on the dash flashed the time at 2:11 P.M. His next appointment was at 3:00 downtown at the Brooklyn Hospital Center on DeKalb Avenue—a good fifteen-minute drive away with traffic. He didn't want to waste a minute getting downtown when he might have a problem getting a parking spot near the hospital. But if he didn't run across to the nursing home to visit his grandfather, his mother was going to be even angrier at him than she already was. Not that he was afraid of her, he just didn't want her nagging him about it. On the other hand, he didn't know if her nagging was any worse than seeing his grandfather slobber his oatmeal down his chin onto his pajamas.

Sure, Kyle loved his grandfather and had, at one time, been fairly close to him, but two years ago, when Preston Howell turned ninety and started urinating on himself and getting that shake in his hands, Kyle couldn't bear to be around him. His mother had agonized over having to put her father in a nursing home, but she had no choice—changing the diaper of a 90-year-old, 130 pound old man was nothing like changing the diaper of a 90-day-old baby. In the end, it was a family decision, but his mother still lived with the feeling that she betrayed her father on her sleeve. She was the only one who felt that way, but then, she was his child—the youngest of three.

Staring at the dashboard clock certainly didn't stop time. Already Kyle had wasted two minutes trying to decide if he'd visit his grandfather or not.

"Hey, man," a pony-tailed, dreadlocked young man double-parked next to Kyle said. "Are you pulling out?"

"Yes . . . ah, actually no." He cut the engine and quickly got out of the car and sprinted across the street, oblivious to the string of curse words hurled at his back by the dreadocked young man.

The only thing on his mind was the time. *Ten minutes. That's all the time I can spare.*

Within minutes Kyle was hurriedly entering his grandfather's room, only to find him asleep on his side facing the window. *Damn, I could've saved myself the effort.* Looking around the room, Kyle could see that nothing had changed—except maybe the plant with leafy vines that now snaked to the floor from the window ledge it sat on. The few personal items his grandfather had did nothing to make the room inviting, and it was funny how his grandfather fussed about not wanting to be in the hospital, yet his room looked every bit like a hospital room—he was in a hospital bed with the railings up; there was a wheelchair near his bed; there was a plastic cup and water pitcher on the tan, metal night table; and there was a curtain that could be pulled around his bed to give him privacy. Hell, it even smelled like a hospital room, but the whole floor did. Kyle didn't see what the difference was. But his mother and his grandfather's doctor agreed if being in the nursing home across from the hospital gave him the around-the-clock care he needed, then the nursing home it was.

On the wall over his grandfather's head was the round bear shield his grandfather had inherited from his father, who'd received it from a long line of forefathers who were all shamans—medicine men. As old as that shield was, its colors—reds, whites, and black—never seemed to fade. That shield always fascinated Kyle and maybe that was because his grandfather took care of it and talked about it like it was the Holy Grail.

Kyle eased closer to the bed to get a better look at the shield. The black bear and the five paw prints signifying physical strength and spiritual power were most central. The bear was supposed to be a fearsome fighter and a wise healer, or so his grandfather said. The bear being black was supposed to mean intense spiritual devotion and great victory. The wise healer part Kyle never understood, not when bears were destroyers, but his grandfather explained that the bear was the protector of his family while also being its healer. He said that's why the shield was encircled in red, because red was bear medicine, strong medicine. Red was the color of long life, and the owner of the shield was obligated to walk the road of righteousness throughout his life. The fact that his grandfather had owned that shield as far back as Kyle could remember was certainly testimony to the kind of man he was—definitely righteous. The white feathers hanging from the bottom of the shield supposedly represented the spirit world, a world Kyle never believed in, but his grandfather did. As a boy, Kyle sat for hours listening to his grandfather tell tales about the shield and its powers, and the battles it had been in. It was the one thing he had that was a legacy to the people he came from—the Tuscaroras. His grandfather was proud of his Indian heritage, despite the fact that he came from a tribe that had been run off its land in North Carolina by white settlers long before he was born. Whatever powers the shield was supposed to have, they didn't work back then.

Pulling his eyes off the shield, Kyle again looked at his grandfather—still asleep. Kyle watched him sleep. The blanket that covered him up to his chest was as flat as if no one was under it. The thin, bony face looked like no one Kyle knew, certainly not his grandfather. His illness had robbed him of his robust 180 pounds, his strong good looks, and had stolen from Kyle the grandfather he used to wrestle with and play ball with for hours on end. It wasn't fair to his grandfather to have lived all these years just to be reduced to a shell of himself. Kyle sniffled and quickly realized that he was tearing. He wiped his eyes dry. He couldn't stay. He had to get out of there, but he wanted his grandfather to know that he had been there. From his inside jacket pocket he pulled out his pen and began looking around for a piece of paper. He started from the room to see if he could get a piece from someone on staff.

"Leaving already?" Granddad Preston asked, his back still to Kyle.

Stopping immediately, Kyle dropped his head. He almost got away. Halfheartedly, he turned back to see that his grandfather hadn't even turned over yet, but that didn't surprise Kyle that his grandfather didn't have to see him to know that he was there. He'd always had a sixth sense and seemed to inexplicably know things.

Kyle went back to the foot of the bed. "Hey, Granddad, I thought you were asleep."

"Just resting my eyes." Granddad Preston slowly turned onto his back, and then gripping the side railings, tried to push himself higher up in the bed. His strained effort was futile, he barely moved an inch.

"Let me help you." Kyle hurried to the head of his grandfather's bed and, getting a hold of him under the arms—immediately feeling the puniness of his frail body, which repulsed him—pulled him higher up in the bed.

Granddad Preston grunted painfully.

"You okay?"

Closing his eyes, Granddad Preston took slow, determined swigs of breath to help him deal with the sharp pain that racked his body.

Kyle could see his grandfather's bony chest rising and dropping. "Should I get a nurse?"

"No," he said weakly, "I'll be all right after a while. Just give me a minute."

Kyle quickly checked his watch—2:23. He had to get out of there—now.

"Busy man, huh?"

"Actually, Granddad, I do have to leave. I have a meeting downtown at three. But next time I come I'll stay longer."

His eyes closed again, but Granddad Preston said weakly, "Next time. Maybe I won't be here next time."

"Grandad, don't talk like that. You'll outlive all of us."

"No, sonny boy. It's time for me to cross over. The ancestors are waiting for me. The great shaman himself, the old Indian, is waiting for me." Granddad Preston smiled.

Kyle knew that his grandfather was referring to his own grandfather, the great shaman of his youth.

"That's a great honor, huh, Granddad?" Granddad Preston didn't respond. After several slow ticking seconds crept by, and Granddad Preston didn't stir or open his eyes again, Kyle began to back away, hoping to slip out without waking him. Old age was a joke—a bad joke played on once virile people who had only death to look forward to.

"Kyle."

"Yeah, Granddad." Kyle took one giant step back to his grandfather's side.

"My death song. You have it, don't you?"

"Yes, Granddad, I still have it." Kyle had to think for a minute where he had put it. It had been about five years since he'd last seen the testament to his grandfather's life. He'd written it himself when his grandfather was in the hospital six years ago with pneumonia and the doctors thought then that he wasn't going to make it. Three years before, his grandfather had written a death song to Grandma Lucy—they'd been married for fifty-five years when she died nine years ago.

"The death song is tradition," Granddad Preston said at the time. "It's a tribute to your loved one when she starts on her journey to the other side. Those left behind must honor the life that's no more."

Kyle remembered that Granddad Preston's death song to Grandma Lucy was like a beautiful poem of the love he had for her, and when Granddad Preston thought he was going to die, he'd asked Kyle to write his death song, and Kyle surprised himself, he wrote what he thought was a beautiful tribute to his grandfather. Now if he could just put his hands on it, he wouldn't have to write another. Perhaps it was somewhere in the back of his desk.

Granddad Preston looked as if he had again fallen off to sleep, and again, Kyle thought it was safe to leave. He started to turn—

"Read my death song, Kyle," Granddad Preston said, his eyes still closed. "I don't want anyone else to read it."

"Sure, Granddad, I'll read it. I'm gonna go now. I'll come back tomorrow."

"All right, knucklehead. You be careful."

Knucklehead? Kyle chuckled. His grandfather hadn't called him that in years. He used to call him knucklehead whenever he didn't listen and got himself in trouble.

"Don't climb too far up in that tree, you hear me?" Granddad Preston's voice grew stronger, but his eyes remained closed. "You gon hurt yourself one day."

Now this was freaky. Kyle stared at his grandfather. It was like someone flicked a switch. That quick, his grandfather thought

Kyle was still a kid climbing the tree in his backyard. Kyle did fall out of that tree when he was ten. He could have seriously hurt himself, but his grandfather was spotting him and caught him in midair. As strong as his grandfather was back then, he still sprained his back, but he did catch him.

"You hear me, boy? You stay outta that tree."

"I will, Granddad. Don't worry about me."

"I want you to stop upsettin' those little girls, too. They don't like boys who make them cry."

"Okay, Granddad, I will." Now Kyle knew for sure that his grandfather had gone back. He used to tell him about upsetting little girls when he was a kid putting worms down their blouses in the park.

"I gotta go, Granddad. I'll come back to see you another time when you're stronger." Behind him his grandfather was still talking, about what, Kyle didn't know. He wasn't hanging around to witness his grandfather's journey back in time. The clock was no longer going forward, it was going backward, taking his grandfather to a time he was probably most comfortable in.

After his last meeting, by the time Kyle got home, he had just enough time to shower and dress in the black tux he left hanging outside his closet before rushing out to pick up Audrey. He had all but forgotten about his visit to the nursing home. Thankfully, Audrey lived in Clinton Hill, two miles away on a direct path to the Brooklyn Bridge. Light traffic and valet parking at the Ritz Carlton got them seated at their table five minutes before the first speaker stepped up to the podium. Kyle wasn't one to put on airs, but he sure as heck was one who was in his element amongst the political power brokers of New York City. Looking around the room, he recognized many of the politicians seated around him— he was an avid Sunday morning watcher of all the political talk shows, often verbalizing his own opinion at speakers he agreed and disagreed with. Perhaps his father had been right, maybe he should have gone to law school so that he could have embarked on a political path that could have, possibly, made him the feted at this expensive-ass dinner.

Audrey leaned closer to Kyle and with her eyes told him to look to his left.

Catching a whiff of Audrey's heady Tresor perfume—lilacs and apricots—Kyle followed her eye direction to where Bill and Hillary Clinton were about to sit on the podium. This was the first time he'd seen Bill or Hillary in person. Already, he felt like he'd gotten his money's worth. Bill Clinton was *the* man, in office or not. He never faulted Clinton for touching up that intern—a man of power had to be sucked off more often than the average man, or else he'd bust a nut from all that heady testosterone filling his sacks every time he made an executive decision, or every time a world leader kissed his ass. Hillary understood that, she wasn't stupid, that's why she stayed married to Billy Boy after he humiliated her in the eyes of the world. Kyle could respect Hillary for standing by her man, although she had to be kicking his ass behind closed doors. That's what she was supposed to do, but still she showed the world that she didn't care what they thought, that's why she became a senator and might well surprise everyone and become the first female President. Guts. The woman had guts. That's the kind of woman Kyle wanted. Because if he had been president, God knows how many interns he would have had jerking him off—probably the whole damn roster. Now that's a thought.

Under the table, Audrey nudged Kyle with the toe of her shoe and arched her brow.

That's when Kyle realized that he had been smiling. Audrey wouldn't understand, it's a man thing.

Finally! The waiter was serving salad to each of the six people at his table. It was about time. Then as if someone had given a signal, everyone picked up their forks. Frankly, Kyle could do without the rabbit greens, he needed some real food, but he didn't have a choice. He dug into his salad of romaine lettuce and cherry tomatoes sparsely sprinkled with a few crunchy croutons and a smattering of Italian dressing. Like everyone else at the table, Kyle ate like he had manners, and not like he was hungry. He topped off his salad with two heavily buttered rolls—they weren't big enough to fill up a three-year-old.

"Quite tasty," the bejeweled older woman to Kyle's left said.

"Yes," he agreed. They had nodded earlier when he and Audrey sat at the table. Right away, he had noticed the older woman's perfume—light but richly fragrant, smelling like a garden of wild orchids. The old girl probably had a whole lot of heat left in her oven.

"I'm Kyle Lawson and this is Audrey Copelin."

"I'm Phyllis Schecter, and this is my husband, Ira."

They were getting ready to eat so no one shook hands, a slight nod and a quiet hello was all that was needed.

"We met, Mrs. Schecter," Audrey said, "at the Children's Society Annual Dinner last year in Chelsea."

"Yes, I do recall. You're a prosecutor in Family Court, if I'm not mistaken."

"Yes, I am."

"How is it going?"

"Everyday's a struggle to get agencies to understand their responsibility to the children under their guardianship. They need to better police the families they're choosing to house their children in order to better protect them from abuse. They can't keep taking any individual who applies to foster these children without doing a thorough investigation."

"I agree," Mr. Schecter said. "But aren't agencies hard-pressed to find appropriate families who are of the caliber that would be best suited to temporarily parent children?"

"Yes, that is a dilemma; but even the families who make it onto an agency's foster parent list should be reined in every few months for remedial parenting courses, thereby reinforcing their parenting skills, which, in turn, would eliminate any possible harm to a child in their care."

"Isn't there a program currently in place?" Mrs. Schecter asked.

"Unfortunately, no. There is the initial ten-week parenting course that every perspective foster parent or preadoptive parent is required to attend, but that's it."

"And that's not enough?"

"By no means. Which is why I'm currently preparing a proposal to present to the State's Bureau of Child Welfare."

"That's a great idea," Mrs. Schecter said.

"Actually, Audrey has many ideas on how the system can be fixed," Kyle volunteered. "Which is why she's seeking an appointment to the bench in Family Court, as well as a position at the Bureau of Child Welfare."

"How ambitious," Mrs. Schecter said. "My dear, you would certainly be an asset in either position. You know the courts and could very well make a difference."

"A huge difference," Kyle said. "Audrey cares about what happens to every child who comes before her. I believe Audrey could save the lives of many children in the system."

"Mr. Lawson, you're such a supportive man," Mrs. Schecter said. "Miss Copelin is so lucky to have you in her corner."

Audrey's eyes twinkled. Kyle pushed his salad plate away and picked up his wine glass. "We're both lucky," he said, meaning it. Audrey was the kind of woman any man would want. She smelled good; she was good in bed; she was intelligent, educated, and was on a political career tract. He needed a woman like her on his arm.

"Ah," Mr. Schecter said, "our dinner."

Kyle had already noticed the waiters removing the salad plates and replacing them with larger plates of steamed asparagus shoots, a kid-size helping of wild rice, and half of some sort of herb-seasoned chicken breast. He was ready to eat, but damn, they could have given him the whole chicken breast. He was starving.

Mrs. Schecter tasted first her chicken. "Lovely flavor. I always so enjoy my meals here at the Ritz. The chef is magnificent. Wouldn't you agree, Mr. Lawson?"

"The best," Kyle said, biting into his own tender, melt-in-your-mouth chicken. He had never eaten at the Ritz Carlton before and had not a single clue who the chef was, but Mrs. Schecter didn't have to know that. He gave Audrey, who was looking at him, a sly little smile. As far as he knew, she had never eaten there either.

By the time the table was cleared of the dinner dishes and more bottles of white wine were emptied and mouth-watering cherry syrup–laced cheese cake was being eaten and savored, Kyle and Audrey were on a first-name basis with Ira and Phyllis Schecter. They never did get to converse with the other dinner guests at their table, but that was all right. Ira and Phyllis were on a first-name basis with Mayor Bloomberg and magnanimously offered to introduce Audrey to the mayor.

"Michael is always available to meet intelligent, progressive Black people such as yourself."

That's what Ira said—progressive Black people. Kyle almost said "Oh, shit" out loud, but caught himself. Instead, this time, he was the one to nudge Audrey. By the unreadable look on her face, he didn't know what she was thinking, but he knew she was going to do just as he did—bite her tongue. Audrey wanted that position, and if the means to the end was in tempering her words, then she would. She and the Schecters exchanged business cards while Kyle kept his in his pocket. He was glad that the conversation never turned his way. Not that he wasn't proud of his home-based business, in this circle, it just didn't seem as prestigious. Besides, it wasn't for himself he shelled out two grand—it was for Audrey. This was her opportunity. If an appointment to a judgeship resulted, then his money was well spent.

By the time all the speeches were made and he and Audrey were crossing the Brooklyn Bridge back into Brooklyn, Kyle had only one thing on his mind, and that was peeling off Audrey's clothes one layer at a time to get to the bare essence of her scent. All night he kept getting whiffs of her Tresor. And now closed up in the car with her, he was drunk with the smell of her and she knew it. She had her hand right on top of the bulge pressing against his zipper.

"That hand is gonna get you in trouble," he said.

She cuffed his bulge and squeezed it. "You promise?"

Kyle shifted in his seat, but he kept his eyes on the road ahead as he turned onto Myrtle Avenue heading toward Clinton Hill. "Can you handle what's in there?"

"For the man who may have just gotten me an audience with the mayor, I can handle anything he has to offer."

"Okay, if you're sure. Because if you've never had a whopper, you might be intimidated."

"Baby, I'm a girl who tosses little fish back in the water, and I've never found cocktail franks to be filling. If there isn't a whopper inside these pants, then we have nothing to talk about."

"Oh, we have plenty to talk about."

"Then let's see if your whopper wants to come out to play."

Keeping his eyes on the road and his hands steady on the steering wheel, Kyle felt himself swell even more as Audrey expertly unzipped his pants and pulled him from the bonds of his black silk Calvin Kleins.

Audrey held onto Kyle as if she were holding onto a baton. "Whoa, big daddy! You do wanna come out to play, don't you?"

"Yes, ma'am." Kyle smiled smugly as Audrey began to slowly slide her hand up and down the length of his shaft. "So what game do you have in mind?"

"H'm, I don't know, but I'm sure something will come to mind."

Pressing in closer to Kyle, Audrey continued her slow, sensual massage of Kyle's whopper while he kept both hands firmly planted on the steering wheel and his eyes glued to the dark streets up ahead. He drove like that, at twenty miles an hour, all the way to Audrey's brownstone on Washington Avenue, and that's when Audrey immediately slid back into her seat and left him pointing toward the windshield. All he could do was look at her with that self-satisfied smirk on her face.

"Proud of yourself?"

Her smug smile said it all.

Kyle sat double-parked next to a tight empty spot in front of Audrey's front door, holding himself, looking pleadingly at Audrey. He couldn't begin to maneuver the car back and forth in order to park, he was painfully stiff, which Audrey thought was funny.

"Don't you think you should do something about this?"

"Not out here—my neighbors might see us."

"It's dark, it's late, who's gonna see?"

"One never knows," Audrey said, stretching her eyes wide.

"Audrey, you're cold."

"No, Kyle, I'm a lady."

"An ice lady."

"Ah, baby, come inside and let Momma show you how warm she can be." Audrey laid her hand atop Kyle's thigh.

He pushed Audrey off, and while she giggled like a schoolgirl, he dropped his head back against the headrest and closed his eyes—trying to will himself soft. If he had been with Dalia, she would have sucked on him like a lollipop until he exploded. She was nothing like Audrey—prim, proper, and a big tease. Dalia was younger than Audrey by twelve years, but Dalia could have shown Audrey a thing or ten. Hell, thoughts of Dalia weren't helping a bit. At this point, nothing would, except maybe his nightmare about being pulled into the toilet by his—that worked. He let out a sigh of relief.

"All better?"

"I wouldn't bother me if I were you."

"Oh, so you're not coming in?"

Forcing himself inside his pants, Kyle took his time zipping up. Hell yeah, he was going inside. A hand job was like that stingy ass $1,000-a-plate dinner—a teaser. He was way past ready for the main course.

Chapter
6

As weird as it was, as was his norm, Kyle awakened exactly one hour after he'd dropped off to sleep. It was three A.M. Kyle's internal alarm clock was on the money. He awakened refreshed and eager to take a hot shower to cleanse himself of the remnants of the lovemaking that had exhausted him, yet gave him the euphoric high that he needed like a junkie needed a fix. His mother was right, although he'd never tell her that she was—he was a sex addict. Sex was his drug, and he let every woman he was with know that. They all knew he liked it hot, heavy, and very often. Just that he neglected to tell any one of them that he also liked an eclectic mix of loving from an eclectic mix of women, which is why if a woman couldn't keep him satisfied, then she had no right to stop him from getting that satisfaction elsewhere.

Six years ago, Gail, his ex-wife, thought she could handle his fierce demand for sex. While they were going together, Gail was a champ, a contender. She put sexual moves on him that had him damn near crying uncle, especially when she role-played fulfilling his fantasies. Hell yeah, he married her, quick, fast, and in a hurry. But then, four short months after their wedding, Gail flipped the script on him. She started whining, "I'm tired. I'm sore. You're killing my vaginal muscles." Her vaginal muscles? Yeah, right! That wasn't it. What it was was that Gail had gotten him to the altar and figured her job was done. Well, she was wrong, but Kyle didn't sweat it. He went right out and got what he needed and had no qualms about it. A lot of screaming, a lot of tears, and not a single denial later, the marriage ended. It had lasted two years, long enough for Dawn to be born.

Three years after their divorce, after an initial bumpy start, he and Gail, because of Dawn, became pretty good friends. Dawn stayed with him every third weekend, and as much as he enjoyed having her around, he loved the single life and the freedom it afforded him—he never had to worry about a baby-sitter. Like tonight. He spent the evening with Audrey, and tomorrow night, he planned to spend the evening with Dalia Blake, the youngest of his paramours at twenty-four. Sweetest piece of ass he'd ever had. Dalia wasn't as sophisticated as Audrey, but that was all right. Dalia was a party girl. She—

"You're dressed," Audrey said, awakening. "Are you leaving?" She sat up and, in the low light, peered at the radio alarm clock on the nightstand—it was 3:15 A.M. "I thought you were spending the night."

"I have to get home." Kyle pulled on his jacket and tucked his bow tie in his breast pocket. "There's some work left from earlier in the day I need to look into."

"But, Kyle, it's the weekend. I had hoped—"

"Baby, in my business, weekends are like weekdays. The work has to get done no matter what day it is. But I tell you what," he said, preparing to lie, "I'll come back if I finish up early."

Audrey eased back down under the covers. "I won't hold my breath."

"I said I'll come back if I get a chance."

Twisting her lips in a cynical smirk, Audrey knew as well as Kyle he had no intention of seeing her again this weekend. Oh, sure, he might call and offer up his usual excuse—work—but he wasn't coming back. She may as well go on ahead with her plan to see Eric Bonner. Eric was making moves like he wanted a more serious relationship, why not see what he had to offer?

No matter how much Audrey sulked, Kyle refused to change his plans for the weekend. Most weekends he could spare only one evening per woman, and each was lucky to have that one day. He was a busy man. He'd see Audrey one day during the week for dinner, but for now, he was going home.

"Oh, by the way," Kyle said, remembering his discussion with the bank, "are you still using the MasterCard I gave you?" He already knew the answer, but it was the only way to broach the subject.

"Yes, aren't you getting the monthly statements?"

"Sure, but I just haven't had a chance to look it over." A lie. "I'm closing out the account with Chase and going with Republic." Another lie. "Did you use the card this past week?"

"I used it to buy the purse, the gown, and the shoes I wore to the dinner. You liked them, didn't you?"

Damn! That gown looked like it cost what he paid for the dinner. "Baby, you looked like a movie star." *Hell, she should, she spends money like she's one.*

"Oh, so you'll need my card back, or do you want me to cut it up?"

"Give it to me and I'll take care of it."

Audrey got out of bed and went straightaway, naked as the day she came into the world, and retrieved the credit card from her wallet. "Will you be giving me a new card?"

Hell no! Trying to impress your ass is killing me financially. "I should be getting new cards within two weeks. You'll get it then."

"Great. Thank you, sweetie." Audrey kissed Kyle meaningfully on the lips. She could more than afford to buy anything she needed and wanted, but Kyle's generosity was enabling her to double up on her mortgage payments. She could pay off her fifteen-year obligation in half the time. "I'll see you out."

Kyle left with the MasterCard burning a hole straight through his breast pocket into his chest. It's a wonder Audrey's hand didn't catch fire every time she touched the damn thing. He had told her, Dalia, and Lorna that they could charge $200 a month for essentials—gas, lunch or dinner if they were out, perfume, little things. In the beginning, they had done just that, but in the past six months, Audrey and Dalia both had lost their minds and started spending like the card had no limit. Lorna was the only one sticking to the original arrangement. If Kyle didn't know better, he'd swear Audrey and Dalia were in cahoots to bankrupt him; but that was impossible, they didn't even know each other—

at least the last time he checked they didn't. Whether they did or not, he was taking back his cards and burning them.

As soon as Kyle got home, he crawled into his bed, spread eagle on his back, comfortable with no one clinging to him. Truth be told, he preferred sleeping alone in his own bed. He didn't dream, and most importantly, he didn't have any nightmares. He might have slept well past eleven if the incessant, head-pounding squawking of the door bell hadn't awakened him. If it was those damn Jehovah's Witnesses ruining his rare late Saturday morning sleep, he was going to curse them to kingdom come! Snatching his bathrobe off the foot of the bed, with just his boxers on, Kyle pounded down the stairs to the front door, angrily yanking it open, immediately feeling the early March chill.

"Get the fu—"

"Be careful what you say, brother, you might have to eat those words one day."

"Carole! Why the hell are you laying on my damn bell like that?"

"Well, good morning to you, too, brother dear." Carole stepped around Kyle into the house, pecking him on the cheek as she passed.

Slamming the door, Kyle yanked his bathrobe tighter and walked away from Carole, leaving her at the door.

Somewhat amused, Carole followed Kyle through the front hallway into the kitchen at the back of the house.

"Laying on my damn bell like that . . ." Kyle mumbled.

"Maybe if you'd answered the door the first two times I rang it like a human being, I would not have gone ballistic."

"Excuse me! But didn't you think I might possibly be sleeping?"

"It crossed my mind, but did it matter?" Carole pressed her finger to her temple as if thinking. "No. Since when do you do much of that, anyway?"

Kyle took a deep breath, readying himself to run a string of curse words at his little sister, but the twinkle in her eyes and the spreading grin on her lips dispelled his anger with her. Begrudgingly, he began to smile himself.

"Give me a hug, boy. It's been a month since we've seen each other."

Obliging, Kyle hugged his little sister. Carole was the only person who could have gotten away with waking him up like that and still get a hug out of him.

"I called you last night," she said, stepping back out of her brother's arms. "Got in pretty late, huh?"

"I went to a fund-raiser for Assemblywoman Heloise Horton."

Carole shed her heavy jacket, tossing it onto the back of a chair. "She's an insider. She has a lot of big names behind her."

"I saw some of them last night. I'm surprised you weren't covering the event."

"I'm not a political reporter, remember? I cover crime in the streets."

"Some might say politicians are criminals."

"They better not say it too loudly." Carole sat at the kitchen table. "So who did you take to the fund-raiser?"

"A friend." Kyle lifted the glass pot from the coffee maker.

"H'm, okay. Don't tell me. I see you're still not staying over for breakfast. What's up with that, brother? Trying not to get caught again?"

Ignoring Carole's questions, Kyle turned on the tap and let the cold water run.

"So you're really not gonna tell me who you were out with last night?"

"No, *Mom*, I'm not," he answered, although he knew he'd end up telling Carole everything. He always did.

"Okay, I don't care. It was probably some chick too full of herself to notice that you don't really give a damn."

"I wouldn't say that. I think I care a lot, I'm just not the staying kind. Remember that song? 'I'm not the staying kind.' Who sang that?"

"That's way before my time, and probably yours, too. You better watch it, though. Most men can be caught no matter how slick they think they are."

"Is this what you came over here to talk to me about?"

"Well, would you believe that Mom called *me* yesterday?"

"Did hell freeze over?"

"No, she's just angrier at you this time than at me. You're in the doghouse big time."

Kyle began filling up the coffeepot. "What else is new in Hootersville? Coffee?"

"Where's my French Vanilla?"

"Same place it's always kept." Kyle emptied the pot of water into the automatic coffee maker reservoir, while Carole took the jar of fresh-ground French Vanilla beans from the cabinet and filled the coffee filter. Kyle was always glad to see Carole—she came around so rarely since he bought the house next door to their parents. Carole and Mom didn't see eye to eye on many issues, especially the issue of Carole's lesbianism. She was twenty-eight now, but she came out to their parents when she was nineteen, and they still weren't used to the reality of it. Carole was their beautiful, curly haired baby girl with the smile that brightened their world. Being a tomboy as a little girl was acceptable, and her growing into a beauty with a face and body that turned many heads was to their liking, but when Carole wasn't talking seriously about boys by the time she was sixteen, they became concerned. Kyle and Preston suspected way before Carole told it. Still, it wasn't easy for them to imagine their pretty baby sister making love to a woman in a way they couldn't fathom. That is, until Kyle went and rented a lesbian DVD—*Babes on Fire*. Wild! Kyle got a boner that wouldn't go down until he went rushing over to Keshia Robinson's apartment for a serious booty call that knocked him out for two hours afterward. Preston, on the other hand, if he tried to learn more about what Carole was into, he never said. The real problem for Carole came from their parents— all hell broke loose when she told them.

"You don't know what you're talking about," Betty said, shaking her head and wringing her hands. "You're confused. Men are gay, not women."

"Mom, I know you know better than that. I'm a lesbian, and you watch enough television to know what that means."

"Carole, you're not a lesbian, you just think you are because you don't date, because men aren't chasing behind you."

"Men aren't chasing behind me because I tell them up front I'm gay."

"Are you crazy? Why would you tell them that?"

"Because it's the truth. I don't wanna waste their time or mine, and I don't want them slobbering all over me trying to get me in bed to prove they can turn a lesbian straight. I'm gay, Mom, and I like being gay. That's all there is to it."

"No, Carole, I refuse to believe that you like doing vile things with girls. You're a beautiful girl yourself. You're supposed to have beautiful children. You should be with a man who'll marry you and make you happy."

"I am happy, Mom, and it's with another girl. I hope you'll accept that one day, because your grandchildren will have to come from your two sons."

That was an awful day for Carole. As ready as she thought she was to come out to Mom and Dad, she wasn't ready for the fight with Mom. Dad seemed to live in denial about Carole's revelation, but Mom voiced her very strong opinion whenever the need arose. She never accepted Carole's choice of lovers and never accepted that she was gay. In the beginning, she was always trying to set Carole up with guys from her church that Carole would boldly tell that she was a lesbian, embarrassing Mom until she finally stopped trying to get Carole to date men, but she never stopped trying to convince Carole that she should see a psychiatrist.

"In this day and time," Carole would say, "I find it hard to believe that you think a psychiatrist can cure a person of being gay. Do you think I'm gonna wake up one morning and have a serious craving for a man's dick . . ."

Betty gasped.

". . . because of something some shrink said to me?"

"If you gave yourself a chance with a man, Carole, you might want—"

"Mom, my sexual predilection," and Carole did say, predilection, "is not a mental condition or an illness. It's my desire, Mom. You need to stop stressing and just accept it, because I will not sugarcoat my life to make you happy. This is about me and my happiness. You have no say in the choices I make."

Betty wasn't backing down. "Since I have no say, then you don't need to be living under my roof."

Carole moved out and for a while lived with Preston, who voiced no opinion either way. Back then he was busy establishing his medical practice. While Kyle and Carole grew closer, it was eight months before Carole could bring herself to call Mom or Dad to see how they were doing. The stifled conversation lasted all of three minutes. Carole was hurt, but she moved on with her life. She got herself a series of jobs and put herself through college, and now she's a field reporter for NBC news. She and Mom aren't the best of friends, but they are on speaking terms, though clearly not about Carole's life.

The coffee was beginning to brew. Kyle took a half loaf of whole-wheat bread off the top of the refrigerator. "So, Carole, why is it that Mom's call brought you over this early on a Saturday morning?"

"Actually, I had planned on coming over anyway, which is why I called you last night. One of the things I wanted to tell you was to watch the eleven o'clock news. My story on the murder of that young Dominican couple up in Washington Heights aired, but you couldn't have caught it because you were, as usual, out doing your thing."

The fresh-brewed smell of French Vanilla coffee filled the kitchen with a heavenly aroma, reminding Kyle that he was hungry.

"Will it get you an Emmy or something?"

"A Mellon," Carole corrected, leaning back against the counter.

Kyle checked his refrigerator to see if he had anything besides eggs to offer. Carole didn't like eggs—said they were a chicken's unfertilized babies. Other than catsup and mustard, there was little else. "Want some toast with peanut butter?"

"I had breakfast, I'll just have coffee." She inhaled the delicious aroma of the brewing coffee, but she had something more immediate on her mind. "Kyle, when are you gonna settle down and see just one special lady?"

"Been there, done that, remember?"

"Seriously, Kyle. With HIV, and God knows what else out there, you can't keep—"

"Hey, I know what I'm doing. I'm not a kid, I know how to protect myself. So drop it." Kyle took out the eggs.

Carole quietly shook her head. "I have this theory. You wanna hear it?"

"No."

"Listen anyway. Kyle, I think your need for a variety of lovers is directly connected to the size of your penis, which—"

"Oh, hell no. I know you didn't say that."

"Which is directly connected to the size of your ego."

"Oh, shit. Carole, don't try to psychoanalyze me. I'm no different than most men out here."

"And that's the problem. You men wear your egos on the head of your penis. You feel the more women you can screw, the greater the *man*"—with her fingers, Carole indicated open and close quote marks—"you are."

"You got it wrong. The more women we screw, the more women we make happy."

"Kyle, you're delusional. Women don't like being one in a line of many. That's why polygamy has no place in this society. By nature, women are basically exclusive beings."

"Which is probably why we men are inclusive by nature. Y'all stifle us. Men like variety, Carole; we were born that way. When we cheat, we don't cheat for better, we cheat for different. And women need to accept that."

"No, we don't. We have choices."

"Oh, that's right, you most certainly do. How's that beautiful Sonji doing?"

"Kyle," Carole said, ignoring Kyle's question about her partner, "you're running around like a kid in a candy store. If you were a woman, people would be calling you a whore."

Kyle cut his eyes at his sister. "You most definitely spoke to Mom."

"That's her term for you, not mine."

"Good old, Mom. She has such good things to say about me."

"Oh, cut the hurt little boy act, Kyle. Neither one of us likes what you've been doing."

"Like I give a damn."

"Kyle—"

"It's my life, Carole. I wish both of you'd get off my back. In fact, let's talk about you. What's going on in your life?"

Carole sucked her teeth irritably. She hated it when Kyle shut her down.

Kyle persisted, "You and Sonji okay?"

"We're just fine. In fact, we're talking about making it legal next February."

"Legal as in a commitment ceremony?"

"No, as in a wedding ceremony."

That should not have surprised Kyle, but it did. The issue of same-sex marriages had been all over the news in the past three years, yet he hadn't thought once about it since it had nothing to do with him.

"Don't tell me," Carole said, "you're against same-sex marriages?"

"Actually, I was just wondering if it was legal here in New York yet. Is it?"

"Yes and no. The mayor of New Paltz, upstate New York, took a stand a few years ago and started marrying same-sex couples, and—"

"He stirred up a lot of controversy, too."

"That's for sure. Sonji and I will probably get married in Massachusetts, her sister lives there. Sonji and I can marry there and live here as a married couple—New York recognizes marriages performed elsewhere."

"You've done your homework, I see."

"Did you think I'd do otherwise?"

Kyle shrugged. "No."

"Good. Will you give me away?"

Kyle tilted his head thoughtfully. "Let me think about it."

"Kyle!"

"Oh, calm down. You know I'll give you away—with pleasure."

Carole went to Kyle and punched him lightly in the arm. "You've always been such a pest."

Both chuckling, Kyle and Carole hugged. They held onto each other for a long, sweet moment. It was Carole who pulled away first.

"Can I take this as a yes?"

"Nothing less. Of course, I won't be able to give Sonji the customary, 'You take care of my sister and don't lay your hands on her, or you'll have to answer to me' speech. I can't very well run over and kick her ass, can I?"

"You better not, but you wouldn't have to. Sonji is good for me, Kyle. We really love each other."

"Yeah, I know. Did you tell Mom and Dad, or is that a stupid question?"

"Stupid question."

"Don't worry about it, then." From the cabinet, Kyle took down two man-size gray mugs.

"I'm not. They'll know when they need to know. But back to you. For once, Mom's more angry with you than me."

"Do I look like I'm worried about it?"

"No, but Kyle, I must say, I agree with Mom—this time." Carole's eyes shot up at the ceiling.

So did Kyle's. "What are you looking at?"

"I'm waiting to see if lightning is gonna strike."

"If it doesn't, I'm going to strike your ass myself. Why in the world would you agree with Mom about anything that relates to me?"

"Because I don't feel that you should be sleeping with any of your employees either. You could—"

"I know, I know. I've been duly reprimanded. It won't happen again."

"I hope not, Kyle, because—"

"Carole! I said, I know. Let up!" Kyle quickly poured himself a half cup of coffee and immediately sipped it, burning his tongue. "Aw, damn!"

Carole rushed to the freezer to get a piece of ice. She handed it to Kyle. "Suck on it."

"I don't need it." He tossed the ice into the sink even though his tongue was stinging. "Pour yourself a cup."

"In a minute. I need to talk to you about Granddad."

"Save it. I already saw him," Kyle said. He expertly cracked three eggs into a bowl.

"I know. I saw him yesterday after you were there. Mom said the nurse told her you visited Granddad for about five minutes."

"What nurse? There was no nurse in his room when I was there."

"No, but his nurse saw you. She was there."

"Obviously spying for Mom. Look, before you come down on me, I had an appointment to get to and Granddad was out of it. He was on painkillers or something. He really was too weak for visitors."

"He has his moments, Kyle, but the pain medication knocks him out. He was all there when I got there, and he said he was glad to see you. He really misses seeing you, Kyle. Out of the three of us, it was you he was craziest about."

"Is that supposed to be my fault?"

"No, Kyle. I'm just saying you were his favorite, that's all." The gold turtle dangling from the gold chain around Kyle's neck caught Carole's eye. "I see you're still wearing that turtle he gave you. How old were you when he gave you that?"

"Who knows, I don't even remember. I still wear it because it's different." Kyle forgot most days that the little turtle lay on his chest. He couldn't even remember for what occasion his grandfather had given him the turtle. It just seemed he'd always worn it.

"Hey, Kyle, do you remember when Granddad and Grandma went to Spain?"

"Yeah, and?"

"Do you remember what he brought back for you?"

"How can I forget? The sword is hanging on the wall over my bed upstairs."

"Good, because it's a special sword."

"Why, because it belonged to some matador?"

"Kyle, that sword belonged to Manuel Benítez Pérez. It was signed. Perez was one of Spain's most famous matadors, Kyle. He's like royalty over there. Granddad paid four thousand dollars for that sword, and he gave it to you. How old were you? Fifteen? Sixteen?"

"Seventeen. It was my seventeenth birthday."

"Yeah, but—"

"Carole, don't beat me over the head about everything Grand-dad's given me. He gave me things because he wanted to. Yes, I appreciate the sword, although I never believed it was authentic. I think Granddad was robbed."

"God, I hope not. But, Kyle, here's the point. Granddad gave you something of greater value than he gave to either Preston or me. From that trip, Preston and I got some ten-dollar trinket that paled in comparison to that damn sword. We were both pissed and wanted to take that sword and bury it in the backyard somewhere."

"You all did."

"No, we hid it in the basement."

Chuckling, Kyle remembered fighting with Preston and Carole when they hid the sword from him. Preston was named after their grandfather and, as such, thought he should be the favorite getting that tasseled, beautifully etched silver sword, but it was Kyle their grandfather favored. Maybe it was because he looked so much like him—wavy black hair, rich dark brown skin, and high, strong cheekbones.

"I have to tell you, Kyle, it was no fun knowing that our grandfather loved you best and had no problem showing it in front of me and Preston."

"Now that I think about it, that was cold." Kyle could recall all the times he hung out with his grandfather without Carole or Preston. Whatever he wanted, his grandfather gave him.

"Yes, it was, but Grandma more than made up for it with all she did for me and Preston. You never got to go to Disney World with us when Grandma took us."

"And that's because I was sick, but I got to go to Tombstone for a week with Granddad instead when I got better."

Carole remembered how she cried when her grandfather said she and Preston couldn't go. "You know, Kyle, those two old people played a lot of games with us."

"That's because they were into one-upmanship with us, and that's because they were always fighting with each other, remember?"

"Yes, but they loved each other, and ever since Grandma died, Granddad's been real lonely. He's lost without her, and you not visiting him probably makes him feel all alone in the world."

"Stop exaggerating, Carole. Damn. Look, I'll try to go see him whenever I get a chance. I mean, I do miss hanging out with him, but damn, I hate seeing him so helpless, so feeble."

"We all do, Kyle, but he's old now."

"Tell me about it," Kyle said, remembering the times his grandfather used to pick him up under his armpits and swing him around so fast that he'd get dizzy and fall when he was let go. "Old age is such a bitch. I hope when I get to the point where I can't take care of myself and stand in front of a toilet like a man, that I drop dead from sheer will, or take my damn self out with a bullet under the chin."

"That's the coward's way out. You're no coward."

"No, but I'm scared to death of pissing in my pants. I ain't wearing any damn Pampers."

"But that only happened to Granddad because of the bladder cancer. If he hadn't—"

"Carole, I don't wanna talk about it." Kyle began whisking the eggs. "I'll go see him next week."

"Why not this afternoon?"

"Because I have plans."

"Kyle—"

"I said next week, Carole. Damn, give me a break. It was rough seeing him out of it like that."

Carole eyed her selfish brother. He was the spoiled one when she, being the youngest, never was, and she was the only girl. Go figure.

"Okay, Kyle. Do you want me to go with you to see Granddad?"

Relieved, Kyle answered, "Wednesday's good for me."

"It'll have to be after four in the afternoon. Earlier is no good for me."

"That'll work for me. Can we talk about something else now?"

"Sure. Sonji and I are planning to have our own baby."

Kyle quickly dropped his eyes down below Carole's waist and

just as quickly looked back at her face. "Is there something down there you've never told me about?"

"Don't be a wise ass, Kyle. I'm talking about artificial insemination. Besides, if I had one of those, you and I'd be scratching our balls and spitting out a bunch of lies about all the women we didn't lay."

"Damn, sis, that's cold. If you feel like that, are you sure you can raise a boy, that's assuming you and Sonji end up with a boy, without bias? Or are you only interested in having a girl? But then, you'd better be careful there, too. You wouldn't want to raise a man-hater."

"Oh, no, you didn't. You didn't say that."

"What? Man-hater?" Kyle suddenly realized that he'd put his foot in it.

"So you think I'm a man-hater, huh? Screw you, Kyle." Carole started to stand. "I thought you knew me better than that."

"What you getting so upset about. Carole, I didn't call you a man-hater. I said you wouldn't want to raise a man-hater."

"And what's that supposed to mean? That if I raised a girl, I'd raise her to hate men because I'm a lesbian?"

"Damn. Forget I said any damn thing. That's not what I meant. You're too damn sensitive, Carole."

"Sensitive, I'm not. As a lesbian, I can't afford to be. But, Kyle, I've gotten enough flack from Mom and Dad, I don't need it from you, of all people. Please, don't get tight assed on me like the rest of the family."

"I'm not, Carole. Sit down."

Carole sat, but she wasn't too relaxed and looked hard at Kyle as he sat across from her.

"Look, sis, I'm sorry if I said the wrong thing. I hope you and Sonji have a baby. You'll both be great parents."

"We will be, Kyle. Being gay isn't synonymous with being bad parents. I just need to know, or at least I hope, you'll be there for me. You will, won't you?"

Without hesitation, Kyle nodded twice, and Carole relaxed.

"So," Kyle said, going to the counter to get a cup of coffee for Carole, "who's gonna be the daddy?" He had to ask.

Carole smiled. "Stupid. Neither one of us. We're both women. We'll both be mothers."

"Oh." Kyle couldn't say he fully understood this. He had never thought about children when it came to gay people.

Carole checked her watch. "The coffee smells good, but I have to run. Sonji and I are driving up to Port Jervis to visit her parents."

"What's that, a three-hour drive?"

"Something like that. And yes, before you ask, Sonji is driving."

"Good, because you're a menace on the road."

"Not too much anymore. I'm driving better."

"Yeah, right."

"I am, seriously. Anyway, we're staying a few days. Kyle, please think about what I just said about me and Sonji having a baby and let me know your thoughts."

Kyle shrugged. "I'm happy for you, I'm there for you. What else do you need to know?"

"Just let me know your thoughts after you've had time to think about it. Kyle, Sonji and I want you to be a big part of our baby's life, so it's important how you feel."

"What, am I supposed to be the baby's godfather or something?"

"I hope," Carole said, gathering her jacket and hat to leave. She pecked Kyle on the cheek. "Oh, and, Kyle, please don't mention any of this to—"

He gave her a "Do I look stupid" stare.

"Okay, I'll call you Monday. Oh, and Dad's mad at you, too. He hurt his back trying to help Press move his piano."

Kyle didn't bat an eye. *What else is he going to get blamed for? The Knicks not making it to the playoffs?*

Carole let herself out while Kyle wondered who the dominant one in the relationship was—Carole or Sonji. He'd have to admit he's wondered before, but he thought it too weird to ponder on for too long, Carole being his sister and all. He didn't need to know how she did whatever she did. But every once in a while, he was curious.

Chapter
7

Dalia Blake—a vision in a thigh-length, clingy, low-cut, red knit dress showing off her round, tight ass; slim, narrow waist; flat stomach; and tits that saluted better than a battalion of marines at a graduation ceremony—was damn near every man's fantasy, at least she was Kyle's. From the moment he and Dalia hit the dance floor, guys with and without women on their arms were flashing glances or staring at Dalia shake her awesome behind in that snug-ass knit dress. Hell, he was looking and he was with her. Kyle didn't mind other men looking at what he had, he saw it as a compliment, not a threat. They had to be thinking how lucky he was—that, Kyle couldn't deny.

A little more than two years ago he spotted Dalia walking down Eastern Parkway toward the Utica Avenue subway stop. The girl was wearing a pair of jeans that she had to have oiled herself down to get in to. She was twitching her ass so hard, it was a wonder the earth didn't move. Like a man possessed, Kyle hurriedly found a parking space and raced down into the subway only seconds before the Manhattan-bound number 2 train pulled into the station. Foolishly, he jumped the turnstyle and sprinted onto the train, narrowly eluding a Transit Authority cop who was surely looking for him. He sidled up next to Dalia, started some small talk about the cool weather, and by the time the train pulled into the Atlantic Avenue station in downtown Brooklyn, he knew she was twenty-one years old, was living with her mother, and had dreams of owning her own hair salon. As the now-crowded train rolled through the tunnel into Manhattan and the crowd pressed them tight into each other, the swaying of the train intensified the sexual yearning of their bodies even more so after Dalia whispered her telephone number into his ear and teased him with the tip of her tongue on his earlobe. He never made it to his meeting in the city.

And now as he danced with her in her favorite club, The Lab, he felt out of place among teenagers and twenty-year-olds, many of whom still partied on their parents' money. Every once in a while, he hit the club scene to please Dalia. The fact that Dalia was young, sexually insatiable, and had a tongue that offered up a smorgasbord of foreplay on his genitalia that Kyle never imagined possible, had everything to do with why he was still seeing her. With Dalia, a man had to always keep his belly button and the other orifices of his body clean—one never knew where Dalia's tongue might end up on any given night. The girl was vicious with that tongue, and although he'd never tell anyone, Kyle got on the bone every time he thought of Dalia tonguing him until he whimpered like a kid being beat down by a bully after school. Dalia was a freak big time! He'd told her once, "You oughta register that thing as a lethal weapon," because damn if that wasn't what it was—she almost gave him a heart attack the first night he was with her. Who knew a woman could roll both balls around on her tongue like she was sucking on jawbreakers and jack a man off at the same time? Kyle didn't, and he thought he was going to teach Dalia a thing or two, her being twenty-one and him being a man touching up many a fine piece of ass since he was fourteen years old. How wrong was he? Dalia became the teacher and he her willing pupil, especially after the tongue roll, but when she wrapped her long, hard legs around his body like she was the wrapping paper and he was the present, he was Dalia's to do with as she pleased, and she'd been doing just that for more than two years—having her way and sending him home a happy man. Which is why, a month after he met her, he'd set her up in her own apartment and paid her rent the whole first year.

Unfortunately, beyond the sex, there wasn't a damn thing else happening between them. Dalia was totally all about herself. It seems most of her money and energy went into continually making herself look good. Besides her body, what Dalia worked hardest at was her hair, which was truly her crowning glory, whether she was wearing her own or what she bought from the store. Kyle had never been able to tell what Dalia's real hair looked like, she never wore the same style, the same length, or the same color for more than a week at a time. She was a chameleon, always changing her hair and her makeup to match. Tonight, she was a redhead, her hair full and long past her shoulders. Kyle hoped what Dalia had to lay on him later was as spicy as the color of her hair. Because again, the sex was all he was there for, and sex was all Dalia could offer.

Dalia was far from the brightest of the three women Kyle saw regularly. Her most animated conversation was about wanting Beyoncé to cut another album with Destiny's Child or the latest fab hairdo she created that day. Dalia was a hair stylist in a salon up on the Grand Concourse in the Bronx. Her dream, as she kept hinting, was to own a full-service hair salon offering facials, manicures, pedicures, and massages. A great idea, but not with his money. Dalia was too lazy to run a business. She barely managed to get up and go to work Tuesday through Saturday. In the two years that Kyle had known her, Dalia had been fired from six hair salons. Of course, it was never her fault, it was always the owners who were jealous of her—her skill, her beauty, her popularity with the clientele. Kyle had heard the excuses too many times before to care and didn't bother listening anymore. Tuning Dalia out was easy; all he had to do was nod every now and then while he made her favorite drink—Kahlua and ice-cold milk—and rubbed on those long legs until they opened wide for him to work his magic for a handful of minutes while biding his time until she was ready to go to work on him, which lasted a hell of a lot longer, which is as it should be. He paid well for the time and the pleasure. Last month, Dalia charged $1,300 on his MasterCard. Before the night was over, he was going to be confiscating her damn shop-till-you-drop credit card. The free ride was over. Of course, he wasn't going to mention the card until Dalia finished working her magic tongue. While he inhaled the fruity smell of her J-Lo perfumed bush, the scent of which clung to his slim mustache like

morning dew to grass, the mounting pressure in his body signaled that Dalia was only seconds from blasting him into orbit.

From Kyle came several explosive, deep-in-the-belly groans of
pleasurable release, and Dalia's mouth was still around him.
That's what he liked about Dalia, she wasn't one of those women
who pulled away just at that pivotal moment—she said it was
good for her skin. She wasn't wrong about that. From head to
beautifully pedicured toes, Dalia's skin glowed. But, of course,
she had that skin when he met her, so she'd been using that particular beauty cream for some time. He never questioned her
about it, he didn't want her questioning him in turn about his sex
life.

Dalia flopped onto Kyle's sweaty chest, kissing him full on the
mouth, tonguing him long and deep. This part he hated; but in fair-
ness, he couldn't pull away. That's why he carried mints—they
worked wonders for a sour mouth, but did nothing to destroy his
vision of Dalia going down on other men and swallowing their
juices. Kyle almost gagged.

Like a siren, Dalia went to rubbing herself atop Kyle. "Come
on, Daddy, don't quit on me now. I'm just getting started."

Kyle barely had energy to open his eyes. It was like this all the
time. He would do Dalia, then Dalia would do him, and then
she'd want to be done again. By now she had to know she had to
wait—he had to rest up a while before he could even begin thinking about rising to the occasion.

"C'mon, baby, you gotta let me catch my breath." Kyle easily
slid Dalia off of him.

Dalia lay on her back and planted her hand between her thighs.
"Ah, man, you gonna leave me hanging like this?"

"Baby, I'm no machine."

"You would be if you took some Ecstacy. I know guys that use
it and they can go all night."

"You speaking from experience or hearsay?"

"I just know, all right? I got some. You want it?"

Kyle gave her a suspicious look. "You messin' with someone
else?"

"No, I ain't. Do you want some or not?"

"I told you, I don't mess with drugs, not even for sex."

"But, baby, you gettin' old."

"Old? Girl, I'm far from old. I'm in my prime and can still hurt you."

Dalia mumbled, "In your dreams."

"What you say?"

"I said, by all means."

That wasn't what she said and Kyle knew it.

"Kyle, there's nothing wrong with using Viagra or Ecstacy to keep a man humpin'."

"I don't need it."

Yes, you do, Dalia thought.

"All I need is a little sleep and I can take care of your hot-ass tail just fine." Kyle rolled onto his side away from Dalia. He was breathing deep even before his eyes closed out the little bit of light in the room.

Dalia leaned across Kyle to get a look at his sleeping face. "Punk." She punched him on the shoulder, hard enough to wake most men, but Kyle didn't stir. He was out cold. Pushing off hard on his shoulder, Dalia sprang up off the bed and, with the telephone in hand, stomped off into the bathroom, slamming the door behind her.

"Old-ass man!" If it wasn't for the credit card Kyle gave her, she'd drop him like a bad habit. But that was all right, he'd wake up soon and run out of there like he was scared the bogeyman was gonna catch him if he wasn't out before the sun came up. But he wasn't ruining her Saturday night—she was going to get her itch scratched by the best, her main man, Jitu. She quickly punched in the number she knew by heart.

"Hey, baby, what's up?"

Chapter
8

Kyle surfed through every network and cable channel looking for something of interest but found nothing. None of the Sunday morning political talk shows held his attention beyond the first few minutes. The war in Iraq annoyed him; the rise in interest rates and oil and gas prices angered him and reminded him of his own financial situation. It wasn't lost on him that taking back the credit cards he'd given his women meant that he stood the chance of ruining his heady sex life. That scene last night with Dalia, after he asked for his credit card back, was a nightmare.

"So what am I supposed to use?" Dalia asked, quite upset. "How am I gonna pay for what I need?"

Kyle was dumbstruck. "Dalia, I didn't give you the card to live on. How did you pay for what you needed before I came along?"

"I was living at home, remember? You're the one who said I should have my own apartment. You're the one who stopped paying my rent a year ago, so I gotta use the credit card when I don't have cash."

Kyle could see how he got off on the wrong foot with Dalia—paying her bills, making her lazy and dependent. His best friend, Vernon, said he was a sugar daddy. Kyle had never thought so. At least he hadn't started out that way. He figured if he gave his special women a credit card with a spending limit, then they'd feel like they were special and treat him that way, at least be available to him when he wanted to be with them.

Dalia climbed onto Kyle's lap. She began massaging him, heating him up for a second course. "Don't you like being my sugar daddy, baby?"

"Oh, man." Kyle pushed Dalia's hand away. "That's what I am to you?"

"Look at you," Dalia said, taken aback. "Don't go getting mad. Man, I was just kidding. Why you looking like that?"

"You're not kidding. If I didn't have money, you wouldn't have me, would you?"

"Kyle, man, I said I was just joking. You know I love you." Again massaging Kyle, Dalia began giving him butterfly kisses on his neck."

"Yeah, right." Kyle all but pushed Dalia onto the floor as he moved her aside as he got up. "Sounds to me like you're in love with the guy you were talking to on the telephone in the bathroom."

Dalia inhaled a soft gasp. "You heard me?"

Kyle began putting on his shoes. "I need my credit card back."

"You're mad because I've been spending too much, right?"

"Get the card, Dalia." Kyle quickly tied his shoes.

"Kyle, just listen to me. I was talkin' to Jitu. He's just a friend, an old friend. There's nothing happenin' between us. I went into the bathroom to talk because you was sleepin' and I didn't wanna wake you up."

"How considerate of you. Get the card."

"Kyle, I promise, I won't spend so much anymore. I'll—"

"Dalia! Just get the damn card!"

"Aw, come on, Kyle. Please don't take my card."

"I have to go, Dalia. Please, get the card."

Kyle watched as Dalia, pretending to fumble around in her pocketbook, mumbled under her breath and came up with nothing. "I can't find it."

"Dalia, I don't have time for this. You have the card, give it to me."

"I said I can't find it!" Dalia thrust her pocketbook protectively under her armpit. "What you gonna do, make me give you something I don't have?"

Kyle snatched the pocketbook from Dalia's grasp so fast, she shrieked. Real quick, she tried to snatch the pocketbook back, but he kept it out of her reach by keeping his back to her. She pounded on his back, but he ignored the beating while he took out her wallet and riffled through it until he found the card. He tossed the wallet and the pocketbook onto the bed.

"Kyle, baby, please, please don't take the card." Dalia threw herself around Kyle's neck. "Baby, I'll do anything you want if you let me keep the card. I'll—"

"Why did you have to lie, Dalia?" He peeled Dalia off of his neck. "I might've given you another card in a few weeks when my business got straight, but now—"

"Kyle, I'm sorry. I didn't mean to lie. I need the card bad, Kyle. I'm not working. I need the card to—"

"Aw, shit. Dalia, I can't keep paying your way. Thirteen hundred dollars a month is a lot to come up with. I have a daughter to take care of, not to mention my own business and personal expenses."

"You're right, Kyle. I won't keep spending like that."

"That's what you said the last time."

"I promise this time, Kyle. For real. I'm supposed to start working in this new salon opening up in Flatbush in two weeks. Help me out until then, and I'll pay you back for what I charged last month."

"The bank's closed. You're too high maintenance, Dalia." Kyle grabbed his jacket and hurried out of the apartment, but he could hear Dalia hurling curses and damning him to hell all the way down the hall until he hit the stairs.

At five-fifteen in the morning, Dalia started calling, waking Kyle out of a sound sleep, apologizing and pleading to see him. He never spoke to her, he let the answering machine pick up her calls. He hadn't expected it to go as badly as it did last night, but it was just as well; he couldn't keep supporting Dalia while she sat back on her lazy ass or even screwed other guys behind his back while he kept giving her money like he was a fool, when he wasn't.

Riiiing!

Kyle waited for the answering machine to pick up the call.

"Hey, man. What's up?" Vernon said. *"We still on to watch the playoffs tonight?"*

Kyle picked up the phone. "Your place or mine?"

"Yours. Who you hiding from?"

"What time you coming over?'

"Around six. Who're you hiding from?"

"Dalia. I took my credit card from her last night."

"Man, I'm still trying to understand your reasoning for giving three women credit cards in the first place. That's crazy. If I ever did anything stupid like that at all, it would have been one woman getting my credit card, and that would have been my wife."

"Man, you aren't even married."

"Not yet, but I be-damn if I give a credit card to a woman that's not committed to me body and soul."

Beep!

"Man, I'm not trying to hear what you wouldn't do. I did it, it's done. I—"

"Kyle—"

Beep!

"That's my other line. I gotta go. I'll see you tonight."

Kyle hung up and let the ringing of the telephone trip the answering machine. "This is Kyle. You know what to do."

"Kyle, I know you're home, I see your car out front. Pick up—"

"Yeah, Mom. What's up?"

"The nursing home just called—your grandfather had a bad night."

"What, he couldn't sleep?"

"He was in a great deal of pain, Kyle. It doesn't look good. His doctor had him moved across to the hospital early this morning. The cancer . . ." Betty couldn't finish. She fought back the tears that threatened.

Rubbing his forehead, Kyle sighed heavily. This was the last thing he wanted to hear or deal with. "Granddad's a fighter, Mom. He'll be okay."

"No, Kyle, not this time. Your father and I are going over to the hospital. You—"

"Wednesday. Mom, I'm going to visit him on Wednesday, me and Carole."

"Wednesday may be too late. We have to go today."

Damn! I can't deal with this today, Kyle thought.

"Kyle, you need to be there, too."

God, how he wanted to say, "Hell no, I ain't going." He certainly didn't want to see his grandfather die.

"Kyle?"

"When are you going to the hospital?"

"In half an hour."

"Make it forty-five minutes. I'll drive."

A quick shower, a quick breakfast of eggs and toast, and Kyle walked out of his house at the same time his parents did. Spending his Sunday afternoon at the hospital wasn't his idea of a relaxing day, but one look at his father made him glad he volunteered to drive—his father was walking slow and very stiff with a slight bend forward at the waist. Carole said he hurt his back moving Preston's piano. Yep, his father was mad at him—he never looked him in the eye or said a word. They drove in silence the ten minutes to the hospital. Like a dutiful son, Kyle followed quietly behind his parents up to the Intensive Care Unit. Seeing his grandfather, drawn and sunken-faced, seemingly asleep, laid out on his back with a plastic tube snaking out of his nose while wired patches stuck to his bony chest connected him to a heart monitor, and IVs trailing from poles above his bed into the backs of both hands dripping fluids into his emaciated body, weakened Kyle's knees and tightened his throat. Granddad Preston looked even worse than he looked just a few days ago.

This is what Kyle feared. This is what he didn't want to see—his once strong grandfather reduced to folds of wrinkled skin covering a skeletal frame that for years carried a fearless fireman who was cited numerous times for heroism for saving lives in burning buildings from which many fled. Kyle didn't see the proud decedent of a Tuscarora Indian and an African slave who was once ashamed of his heritage but who embraced it when black fists raised in solidarity and pride at the Olympic track and field awards ceremony in Mexico City in 1968. It brought tears to his eyes. It was difficult to search for recognition in the time-worn, leathery mask of death that covered his grandfather's face and not find the man who bounced him on his knee and taught him how to swing a bat. Kyle started to move away from the bed, but his father caught him by the arm and stayed him with a firm hold, and with his eyes told him that his place was there at his mother's side.

Kyle stayed; he moved closer to his mother and put his hand on her back.

Betty's tears had started the minute she entered the ICU. Seeing her father, her tears now flowed freely as she tenderly stroked his arm. Although he tried, Kyle couldn't stop his own tears. He turned his face away and wiped his eyes.

"He knows we're here," Betty said softly. "Daddy?"

Kyle turned back just as his grandfather opened his eyes, but what he saw was not the clear brown, laughing eyes he knew, but blurry pupils that looked like they were covered with a film of dirty plastic.

Granddad Preston seemed to focus only on Kyle. "Is . . . that . . . you, boy?"

"Hey, Granddad." Kyle let his mother push him closer to the bed. "What're you trying to do? Scare us?"

Granddad Preston said nothing. He didn't even smile. Kyle watched as his eyes slowly closed again. Betty began to weep again. The monotonous sound of the heart monitor beeping reminded them that death was near.

"I got here as fast as I could," Preston said, coming up behind Kyle. He kissed his mother on the cheek and hugged his father. Preston and Kyle shook hands.

"He's not gonna make it," Marvin whispered.

"I know." Preston went around to the other side of the bed and laid his hand on his grandfather's forehead as if he were taking his temperature. With his thumb, he pulled back each of his eyelids. It was clear he didn't like what he saw. A glimpse at the monitors confirmed what he already knew.

"Mom, why don't you let Dad take you down to the cafeteria? Kyle and I—"

"I'm staying," Betty said.

Kyle didn't want to stay, but he wasn't about to say so. "Press is right, Mom. You shouldn't be here."

"This is my father. If no one else stays, I have to."

"Yes, but Betty," Marvin began, "we can—"

"Kyle," Granddad Preston said, his voice weak but loud enough for everyone to hear.

Betty immediately stepped back away from the bed and pushed Kyle into her spot closer to his grandfather.

"I'm here, Granddad." Kyle's heart quivered as his grandfather's left hand began to come up off the bed.

"Take his hand!" Betty urgently whispered.

Kyle took his grandfather's cold, bony hand. With both his hands, he covered his grandfather's hand, trying to warm it. But it was the unfocused look in his grandfather's eyes that tore at his heart and brought on the stinging in his nose and the tightening in his throat. He grit his teeth to keep from crying. No one said a word while they waited to see if Granddad had something to say.

"Boy . . . I . . . been . . . waitin' . . . on . . . you."

"I'm sorry I didn't get back up here sooner," Kyle said, hoping that his grandfather didn't hear the lie in his voice.

"You . . . still . . . got . . . that . . . turtle . . . I . . . gave . . . you?"

"Sure, Granddad. I'm wearing it right now."

"Show it to him, Kyle," Betty said.

Kyle quickly unbuttoned his jacket, stuck his hand down the neck of his sweater, and pulled out his gold turtle from its safe haven against his warm skin.

"See, Granddad. Here it is. Here's my turtle." Kyle held the turtle out to his grandfather.

His hand trembling, Granddad Preston slowly reached up and took the turtle in his hand. Kyle could feel the shaking in his grandfather's hand. He let him hold the turtle while he covered his hand and tried to steady him. Granddad Preston closed his eyes. He began to move his lips, saying words that none of them could hear.

"Daddy," Betty said. "Daddy, are you all right?"

Suddenly, Kyle was pulled downward. Granddad Preston had tightened his hold on the turtle. He was pulling Kyle to him. The gold chain around Kyle's neck was cutting into his skin.

"Granddad."

His eyes still closed, Granddad Preston said softly and

measuredly, "Boy, . . . you . . . got . . . to—" His words ended, his eyes closed, but his grip on Kyle's turtle was firm.

Beeeeeeeeeeeeeeeep!

"Oh God," Betty cried. "Daddy? Daddy?"

Marvin engulfed Betty in his arms. "I think he's gone."

Preston didn't wipe at the tears that welled up in his eyes. To himself he said a silent prayer.

Still bent over his grandfather's bed, Kyle continued to hold onto his hand, which still had a firm hold on his turtle. Kyle started to let his grandfather's hand down gently but realized his grandfather's hold on his turtle was solid. When he tried to ease the turtle out of his grandfather's hand and couldn't, Kyle became unnerved.

"Are you sure he's dead?" Kyle asked. "He's still holding on to my turtle."

"Let me help you," Preston said. Preston tried, too, to gently ease Granddad Preston's hold on Kyle's turtle. He was surprised that he couldn't.

"My God," Betty said, "Daddy has a death grip on it."

"Okay, Preston," Kyle said. "Get him off me."

Preston again tried, but he couldn't remove Granddad's hand without using more force, "This is very strange. It's almost like rigor mortis has set in already."

Gasping softly, Betty covered her mouth.

The hair on the nape of Kyle's neck stood on end. "Just get him off me!"

Betty took hold of her father's arm while Preston gave a firm tug and snapped the gold chain from around Kyle's neck, freeing him to straighten up and back away. Granddad Preston still had the turtle in his hand and the broken chain hanging from his fingers when Betty gently lay his arm atop his chest and kissed him lovingly on the forehead.

Kyle felt as if his own heart had stopped beating, like his chest was caving in on him. He rushed away from the bed.

The heart monitor alarm was shut off by a nurse who left as quietly as she had appeared.

Preston put his arm around Kyle's shoulder. "Are you all right?"

Kyle snapped hoarsely, "No, I'm not all right!"

"That was strange," Preston admitted. "I've never seen that before."

"Daddy didn't want to let go of you, Kyle," Betty said, forgetting her own anguish.

"It's like he wanted to take Kyle with him," Marvin said, perplexed by what he'd witnessed. "Maybe he did wanna take you, Kyle."

"That's not funny, Dad." Kyle had never felt so uneasy in his life. His heart was still pounding. More disturbing, this was the first time that turtle had ever been from around his neck since his grandfather gave it to him. He almost felt naked.

"I'm not joking," Marvin said. "That was most unusual."

"My God, Kyle," Betty said, "Daddy always loved you. It was like he was trying to hold on to you, like he didn't want to leave you."

"Will y'all stop talking crazy. I'm messed up enough as it is. Press, get me my turtle."

"Sure, Kyle. Give it a few minutes, his hand'll relax. I'll get it then."

"Mom," Preston continued, "is everything set?"

"All the arrangements are made," Marvin answered. "We just have to call the funeral home."

"Good. Mom, if you and Dad'll come with me, I'll help you take care of everything on this end."

"Well," Marvin said, "there's nothing more we can do here. He's on his way to a better place now."

Nodding her head sadly, Betty agreed as fresh tears emptied from her eyes.

Unable to pull his eyes away from his grandfather, Kyle was struck by how peaceful he looked, although he looked nothing like himself. He was so thin.

"Kyle," Preston said, "are you coming?"

"No, let him stay a while," Betty said. "He owes his grandfather this visit."

Kyle couldn't dispute his mother. He did owe his grandfather this visit, but as before, he didn't know what to say to him, and saying that he was sorry meant nothing now. It was too late. Maybe it was just as well his grandfather took the turtle from him, he hadn't done right by him in his last years. Hey, he didn't need the turtle anyway.

Chapter
9

Kyle had always wanted to know what there was about death that turned otherwise strong, intelligent people into weak-kneed simpletons? Admittedly, for the longest time, death did frighten him. The idea of going to sleep and never waking up was unfathomable. That is, until he was twelve and his grandmother, his father's mother, died, and when he was fifteen and a classmate drowned. Both times his grandfather explained that death was God's way of letting people sleep peacefully for eternity, that death was a friend for those suffering in life. Kyle understood that. His grandmother had an inoperable brain tumor, and his classmate, if he had lived, might have been a vegetable. Although Kyle no longer feared dying, he sometimes wondered where he'd end up after death; but he didn't worry too much about it, he figured he had time to walk the straight and narrow. Hey, if Jesus could forgive the murderer and thief crucified alongside him, then in his hour of death, God shouldn't have a problem forgiving him his minor indiscretions.

If anything disturbed Kyle now, it was how his mother was using her father's death as an excuse to wimp out and act downright helpless, which was so unlike her. If she wasn't crying, she was whining about how much she was going to miss "Daddy." What she didn't realize was that the daddy she knew had long since died. The old man they all saw take his last breath was only a shell of the man she called Daddy. If Mom allowed herself to understand that, she'd stop whining and return to the take-charge person Kyle knew and loved, instead of using him like he was her servant. She acted like nothing could get done unless he had a hand in getting it done. From the moment his grandfather died, his mother and father commandeered him as if he had no life, no business, no say.

"Kyle, drive us to the funeral home . . . drive us to the nursing home . . . drive us to the florist . . . drive us to the supermarket . . . Kyle . . . Kyle . . . Kyle."

He wanted to tell them both, *Damn, stick a prod up my ass and make me dig the grave, why don't you?*

He was bone-tired from running errands and seeing that his mother had something to eat. He hadn't been able to spend more than thirty minutes at a time in his office before being summoned by either his father or mother. Hell, in case they forgot, he wasn't an only child. He had to remind his mother of that.

"Why don't you ask Preston or Carole to take you, I have a business to run?"

Betty sat even straighter in the Queen Anne chair where, for two days, she had planted herself, holding court to receive family and friends. "Kyle, are you so darn selfish you can't think about anyone but yourself?"

"How can you call me selfish? I've been at you and Dad's beck and call for two days."

"If we need you for twenty more days, you shouldn't mind if it means making sure your grandfather is put away proper. He loved you, Kyle! It's you he left everything he owned in the world."

He didn't leave money.

"I think you can afford to spare some of your precious time to help make funeral arrangements. You owe him that much."

"So for a pair of gold cuff links, an eclectic array of souvenirs from around the world, and some useless Indian artifacts, I have to give up my personal and professional life, while Preston and Carole, who weren't left anything, get to continue living their lives?"

"For one thing, even if your grandfather left you a toothpick, you should be grateful. And secondly, Carole is on her way back from Port Jervis and won't get in until later. evening; Preston had surgeries scheduled that he couldn't cancel. And neither one, by the way, live next door."

"Lucky them," he said, standing at the open door. "I guess I need to get a new career and a change of address."

He stormed out of the house back to his own house and went straight up to bed and didn't answer his door or answer his telephone if he heard his parents' or Preston's voice on the answering machine. He also didn't take Dalia's or Audrey's calls; he knew what they wanted—money. Carole's call he answered; she was calling from her cell phone.

"Stop pouting, you're a big boy now," she teased when Kyle came on to the line.

"Don't start with me, Carole, I'm not in the mood. Where are you?"

"Home. I just got in from upstate. I took the rest of the week off. I'll be over tomorrow to help out. Seems Granddad couldn't wait till Wednesday, huh?"

"Apparently not. You speak to Mom?"

"Yeah, and I guess I don't need to tell you that she's mad at you— again."

"Spare me."

"Kyle, please be nice."

"I'm always nice," he said flatly.

"If you say so. Oh, I heard what happened with your gold turtle."

"I don't wanna talk about it." Kyle didn't want to be reminded of his grandfather's death. Which is why he had no intention of ever wearing that turtle around his neck again.

"Well, just so you know, Mom gave it to Press to take to a jeweler to get it fixed."

"He can keep it. I don't want it."

"Kyle, I think in time you might. So—"

"Carole, I'm going to bed now."

"Kind of early for you, isn't it?

"Carole, can we talk tomorrow? I—"

"Okay, sure. Oh, and heads up. Press is next door with the folks. So don't be surprised if he shows up. Mom said something about giving him your key."

"She better not." Kyle slammed down the telephone and raced from his bedroom toward the stairs wearing only pajama bottoms. He needed to double bolt the second lock. But he was too late. He could hear the cylinder click as Preston let himself in.

"Man, don't just barge into my house like you own it, you could get yourself shot!"

"Where's your gun?" Preston closed the door and flipped on the downstairs light. "Next time, answer your bell when I ring."

Kyle started down the stairs. "You know, you and Mom have lost your damn minds. I'm a grown-ass man. This is my house. I don't have to answer—"

"Cut the crap, Kyle! I'm not impressed by your bravado."

"Fuck you! Get outta my house."

Preston tossed the keys on the hall table and stood at the bottom of the stairs. "What's up with you, Kyle? Mom's having a hard time, she don't need you running around here acting like some put-upon child."

Kyle pushed past Preston who was half a head shorter than his own six-foot stature and fifteen pounds heavier. "Since I'm such a 'put-upon child,' why don't you be the adult for both of us and chauffeur Dad around and run errands for Mom like you're her kiss-ass gofer."

"You're proving yourself to be very immature, Kyle. If I had the time, I'd run errands without complaining."

"Oh, I forgot. You don't complain, do you, *Doctor*? Your time is extremely valuable, whereas mine isn't. I guess what I do for a living is child's play."

"Kyle, I am not going to allow you to pull me into a discussion about what I do versus what you do. You could have become a doctor if you hadn't yawned your way through college and had tried applying yourself."

"Fuck you, Preston. Take your condescending ass out of my house."

"Don't take your frustrations out on me, Kyle, or on Mom and Dad."

"Frustrations? I don't have any goddamn frustrations. I have a good life—one just as good as yours. I own this house and can buy whatever the hell I need and want. Contrary to what you might believe, I don't sit on my ass twiddling my thumbs all day."

"I never said you did. I—"

"Thanks for the respect, *Doctor Lawson*." Kyle made a beeline straight for the liquor cabinet in the living room.

Preston adjusted his wire-rimmed glasses and glanced back at the front door before following Kyle into the living room. He had told his parents he would talk to Kyle; he should have known it wouldn't be easy.

"I don't know what's going on with you, Kyle, but—"

"Not a damn thing." He poured himself a shot of bourbon.

"Kyle, your behavior is upsetting Mom at the worse possible time of her life."

"Oh, I'm the one who's upsetting her because I'm tired of being at her beck and call."

"Kyle, Mom just lost her father, our grandfather. She's taking Granddad's death very hard. Kyle, Mom needs all of us, including you, to be her backbone, to support her, not to be a burden—"

Kyle slammed the bottle of bourbon on the entertainment unit. "How the hell am I a burden to her or any of you? I've been taking care of my damn self since I was twenty-two years old. Yeah, Granddad died. So what? An old man, who had a full life, died. Yeah, I loved him, but the world didn't stop. I can't . . . No, we can't do another damn thing for him except put him in the ground and cover him up, and all the arrangements for that have been made."

"Man, Kyle, I didn't know you were so cold."

"Press, I call it being realistic. I loved Granddad just as much if not more than any of you."

"Coulda fooled me."

"No, I didn't go running up to see him every day, grinning in his face, pretending like I was happy to see him. Man, I wasn't. I was never happy to see him. I couldn't stand seeing him shriveled up and dying from some carnivorous disease that nibbled away on his organs like some starving piranha and sucked the life out of him with every breath he took. Hell no, I didn't wanna see him like that, and I'm not gonna let you, Mom, Dad, or anyone else make me feel guilty for feeling that way." Kyle tossed back the bourbon.

Exhaling deeply, Preston sat heavily in the armchair. He again adjusted his glasses. He didn't look up when Kyle slammed his glass down.

Kyle could feel the heat of the bourbon travel down his throat into his stomach. "Preston, Granddad was ninety-two years old. He had a long life—a good life. If we could ask him right now, what was the worst years of his life, I guarantee you he'd say the last year and a half after he was diagnosed with bladder cancer and was reduced to a bag of bones having to be taped into a diaper by women he might have flirted with when he was younger and healthier."

"He never complained."

"If you'd ever really listened to him, you'd know that he did. You didn't know him, Press, like I did."

"I think you got that wrong. He didn't let me get to know him like he let you."

"And that's because you never had time for him."

Kyle took some satisfaction in knowing how much it irritated Preston when their grandfather took him aside and shared his adventurous life as a fire fighter and as a world traveler.

"How ironic of you to say that. It was you who never went to see him."

"I have my reasons for not going to see him in that nursing home, and they're my business," Kyle said defiantly. "You don't know how he felt about getting old. I doubt if he ever told you."

"I know he accepted old age as part of the natural cycle of life."

Kyle sat on the arm of his sofa. "So, we all know that, but do you know what Granddad told me on his eightieth birthday?"

"I wouldn't know."

"Granddad told me if he ever got so old that he couldn't wash his own behind or hold his own dick, he wanted to be put out of his misery."

"He may not have meant—"

"Yes, the hell he did! Man, you're a urologist. You see patients with prostate cancer every day. You can't tell me none of them, men at that, never say 'I wanna die.' "

"Of course, some do, but Granddad had a full life and he—"

"He didn't like getting old and feeble, Press. And he most certainly did not want to be cut on. I tried to tell Mom how he felt, but she wouldn't listen. It was her call. How you and Dad, and even his doctor, let her override his wishes, I don't know. Granddad did not want to be operated on. He wanted to live out his life with some modicum of dignity."

"But the cancer was debilitating."

"And the aftermath of the surgery wasn't? Come on, Press, man. Granddad was miserable laid out on his back in that nursing home. Most days, he was out of his mind with pain and disgusted with not being in control of his own body. When I first visited him after his surgery, he'd be doped up on painkillers and wouldn't know I was there. Sitting with him was like sitting with the dead. When he was lucid, Granddad still couldn't converse or keep his eyes open."

"That's expected after surgery."

"Well, that's not what he expected for the end of his life. I stayed away because I couldn't stand to see him suffer like that. God forgive me if Granddad didn't understand that."

"That's the sad thing, Kyle, I don't think Granddad ever did. I think he felt like you deserted him."

"Well, there's nothing I can do about that. Look, man, what do you want from me?"

"Kyle, I don't want anything from you, but Mom wants you to act like you care."

"I'm sick of this." Kyle went for another shot of bourbon. He didn't feel a damn thing from the first shot. "Anything I do would be wrong. I'm done trying to please anyone around here. And there's nothing else that needs to be done, anyway. I had extra chairs delivered this afternoon. The funeral is Thursday. All we have to do is show up and make sure Granddad's buried."

"Well, Mom wants to know if Aunt Agatha, Uncle Otis, and Cousin Helen and her two children can stay over here."

"Five people?" Kyle had heard his parents discussing sleeping arrangements for family coming in from out of state, and he knew he'd have to let someone stay in his house, but five people? Naw. "Who's staying with you?"

"I don't have the room."

"Goddammit!" Kyle spiked the shot glass on the carpeted floor. It didn't break. It hit with a dull thud and bounced a foot away. Put upon? Damn right, he felt put upon.

"You know what, Press? You tell Mom she can have my whole goddamn house. I won't be here. I'll—"

"Kyle, you can't do that."

"I'll be at the funeral home on Thursday morning—on time. You have the key, let them all in. I don't give a damn."

"There you go, acting immature again."

"Big surprise, huh?" He started toward the stairs.

"What about your staff?"

"Mom's the office manager. Tell her to notify the employees."

"That's why I don't bother with you, Kyle. You've always been irresponsible and selfish."

With his foot on the first step, Kyle halted. "Then you can get the hell out of my house, can't you?"

"Your response doesn't surprise me, Kyle. It speaks to the level of your maturity."

"Keep pushing that immaturity bit, hear?"

"Kyle, I can see why you're no further along in your life than you are."

Kyle whipped back around to face Preston. "You're no Dr. Ben Carson, you pompous-ass bastard."

"No, but I'm no typist either."

There was a piercing stab in Kyle's left temple.

Preston continued, "And unlike you, I know what it is to stick to a course of study, get a degree, and work at a career, like a responsible adult."

Glaring at Preston, every muscle in Kyle's body tightened. "Get the fuck out of my house, man, before I kick your supercilious ass."

Preston stood his ground. "You've never been an adult, Kyle. You're still using training wheels and wearing a diaper. You need to—"

His fists clinched, Kyle rushed at Preston.

Preston struck a defensive stance—his right leg went back, his left leg was bent, and in front of him, his fists went up.

Kyle raised his fist to punch Preston in the jaw, but Preston threw up his left arm, blocking and deflecting Kyle's ill-thrown punch while ramming his right fist into Kyle's solar plexus, doubling him over into a gut-wrenching expulsion of air. Kyle felt the jarring pain all the way around his midsection. Straining, tears popped into his eyes.

"Aw, Kyle, I'm sorry. We shouldn't be doing this." Preston took Kyle by the arm and helped him onto a chair in the living room. "I didn't mean to hit you that hard."

Thrusting Preston's hands off of him, Kyle tried to catch his breath.

"Kyle, we don't need to be fighting amongst ourselves."

"Get the fuck outta my house."

"Kyle—"

"Get out!"

Kyle waited until he heard the front door close behind Preston before he slumped against the sofa back. *Goddamn, Preston!* He and Preston had both taken karate as kids, but Preston had continued practicing throughout college. He'd gotten as high as a second Dan, and it was obvious he hadn't forgotten a single thing. Preston could have beat his ass and he would have had only himself to blame for throwing the first punch. That's it, he wasn't hanging around for everyone to beat up on him. Nothing he did was right.

Kyle snatched the telephone and quickly punched in Lorna's number. He had been promising for more than a week that he'd get by to see her, and tonight was as good a time as any. He'd have to spend the night, but from Lorna he didn't have to run. She was already married. He'd shut down his office until Monday morning—he wasn't getting much done, anyway. What he needed to calm him down was some damn good loving from a woman who gave a damn about him.

Chapter
10

Lorna Renault, sweet as cotton candy, fine as aged wine, with long auburn-colored hair down past her shoulders and large hazel eyes that drew a man in and held him captive until he felt like he'd been kissed by an angel, was never demanding and was always willing to listen to Kyle lament about his troubles while she rubbed him down with baby oil until every hair on his body shined and his skin tingled. Lorna was Jamaican by way of France. To hear Lorna tell it, she'd lived in France all of her life; but in reality, she had only lived in France three years. She went there to study art at the famed Écoles d'art, and was quite disappointed when her instructors told her she didn't have the talent her teachers in Jamaica had convinced her that she had. Although overwhelmed with dejection, Lorna stubbornly hung in for two years, determined to improve upon her technique and skill, but she didn't do well enough to satisfy her instructors, a Madam Béranger, in particular, who told Lorna to stop wasting her family's money. After she dropped out, she stayed in Paris and enrolled in cooking courses, thinking that she might become a world-famous chef. That dream lasted a year until she started aching again to be an artist. She said something inside was driving her to paint. That's when she convinced her well-to-do husband to let her come to New York to study art. She moved in with her cousin, Mildred, in East Flatbush until she found her own apartment, and for the past year, she had been attending Pratt

Institute in Clinton Hill. Ten months ago, Kyle met her at the counter in Junior's Restaurant having lunch. Despite the diamond-encrusted wedding band on her finger, by the time their lunch ended, he had Lorna's telephone number and address and a date for that night. He could have had her social security and bank account numbers if he had asked for them.

"I don't have a lifetime to give," she said outside the restaurant, "but I can give you a hell of a night."

For Kyle, the gentle dart of her tongue in his mouth before she walked away ruined him for the rest of the day. He couldn't concentrate on a damn thing. True to her word, Lorna gave him a hell of a night that night and every night they happened to get together. She never talked much about her husband, who owned a construction company in Jamaica, or her six-year-old daughter, whom she said she missed and had seen only for a month each summer since she left home and at Christmas. As curious as he was as to how Lorna could leave her daughter behind, he asked no questions—his policy was to let people tell him what they wanted him to know, and in the beginning, Lorna wasn't telling much. If her husband called while he was there, she always went off into the bathroom to talk to him. That was all right with Kyle, he wasn't into breaking up happy homes, and that was just it, Lorna was far from home and wouldn't be living under the same roof with her husband for another two years. So Kyle never worried that Lorna's husband, whose name Lorna never mentioned and Kyle didn't care to know, would pay a surprise visit and catch him in his wife's bed where he was now.

He lay full inside her, moving slowly, arms and legs entwined, their bodies hot from the heat they were generating. This is what Kyle liked about being with Lorna—easy, undemanding. She never pushed him for anything. In fact, she had not wanted to take the credit card when he offered it to her two months after they met. She said she received enough from her husband to cover the rent and food, and her part-time job as a sales associate at Macy's department store paid enough to pay for incidentals. Bending his own rule, he asked her why she had to work at all if her husband was so rich?

"At times he get stingy," she answered. "He does not want me here."

"I thought he was all for you studying abroad."

"No, not at all. I fought long and hard to get him to agree to let me go to Paris. He did not want me to go, but I tell him, 'I will go with or without your approval. If I go without it, I will not come back.' "

"He fell for that?"

"He know I meant it. He marry me when I was an inexperienced 21 years old. I had a baby, his baby, before I finish my last year of college. I went back after the baby was born, but I did not get to do what I wanted most. I wanted to be an artist, and he know this before he marry me."

"So he let you go?"

"Yes, but he still not like it. When I did not do well at Écoles d'art, I tell him I want to come to America, and he scream that he would divorce me. I tell him go ahead. I will go to America anyway and marry another man that understand my desire to be an artist."

"So again he gave in?"

"He did not want to. He was very displeased with me. He give me enough money each month only to pay essentials. Nothing more."

"Then take the card. Use it in emergencies."

She did. From the monthly statement, Kyle didn't see where there were any emergencies, but three hundred dollars and sometimes a bit more was spent every month. Maybe he'd let her keep her card, she wasn't abusing it.

"Kyle, you're so quiet, is everything all right?"

"I was just thinking your husband must be crazy to let you live in another country."

"He trust me."

"Oh, yeah, well, he better rethink that."

"Kyle, this is the first I do a thing like this."

Kyle was a bit skeptical about that. "Lorna, as beautiful as you are, I can't imagine a hot-blooded Parisian not trying to get you into his bed."

Lowering her eyes, Lorna smiled the tiniest of knowing smiles.

Kyle tightened his hold on Lorna and pushed himself hard against her. "You're a very bad girl."

"Ooo, baby," she said, moving with Kyle. "Make me pay for being so bad."

Kyle did just that. He flipped Lorna onto her back, quickly entered her, and worked her until she screamed his name and came with him in a mighty exhalation of passion and fervor. Lorna's thighs were clamped so tightly around Kyle's body, he couldn't catch his breath. He reached behind, grabbed her legs, and pried them from around him.

Lorna giggled. "Aww, was I hurting you?"

Flopping onto his back, breathing hard, sweat pouring off his face, Kyle kneaded his left side. "I think you cracked my ribs."

"That is Tae Bo. It is making my legs very strong."

"Yeah, Billy Blanks is trying to make sexual killing machines out of you women."

"Men do Tae Bo, too. You should do it with me, Kyle. I have the advanced tape."

"No, thank you. My weight lifting and treadmill is all the workout I need, that is next to you." He drew Lorna full on top of him. Her skin felt like warm, soft butter flowing over his own skin. They began to kiss deep and—

Granddad Preston's face flashed in Kyle's mind abruptly ending their kiss, confusing Lorna, unnerving Kyle.

"What's wrong?"

"Damn," Kyle said, holding his hand over his forehead.

"Is it something I did?"

"No . . . no." He held Lorna close, her face lay on his chest. "It's my grandfather. I saw his face."

"Your grandfather? The one who just passed on?"

"Yeah, I saw him as clear as day."

"He must be worrying over you."

Kyle turned onto his side. "My grandfather is dead. He's not worrying over anyone or anything." Kyle got comfortable with his head nestled in the crook of his arm. He was going to sleep.

"Your grandfather is dead to this world, but, Kyle, he is not dead on the other side. His spirit is alive and well. For him to worry your mind while you are making love mean that he is concerned for you. I think he is watching over you."

"Hogwash. Let me get some sleep." He closed his eyes.

"What does hogwash mean?"

"Something stupid. I hope you don't believe in ghosts and voodoo."

"Actually, I do."

"Oh, shit." Kyle raised up and looked at Lorna. "Do you mess with that stuff—voodoo?"

"No, but I know people who do. Voodoo is not all bad. There is white voodoo, you know."

"I don't know and I don't care to know. I steer clear of any kind of hoodoo, voodoo, anything supernatural. It's all garbage."

"Well, I do not involve myself with voodoo either, but I do respect it."

"You sound like my grandfather. He used to say, 'Respect what you don't understand, and understand what you don't respect.' "

"He was a smart man, your grandfather. He had great wisdom."

"Yeah, he thought so. Before he got sick, he was some character." Kyle felt himself misting, surprising even himself. He shook it off.

"Are you all right?"

"You would have liked my grandfather—like you, he believed in spirits, holistic healing, ghosts."

"Was he born in the Caribbean? Because not too many African Americans believe in those things."

"My grandfather did. He was born in this country, down in North Carolina. In fact, he's part Native American."

"Indian?"

"Tuscarora Indian."

"I never heard of them before."

"The Tuscarora was a small tribe, probably less than ten thousand people at any given time, but they joined up with the Iroquois nation sometime in the early seventeen hundreds."

"Oh, I know about the Iroquois."

Talking about his heritage reminded Kyle of the many times

he sat with his grandfather listening to stories about his child-hood on the reservation. "The Iroquois were a powerful people who came from many other tribes or nations that joined the Iroquois to fight the white man. My grandfather's people, the Tuscarora, were the sixth nation to join."

"Then, Kyle, you have Indian blood in you."

"A lot of native African Americans do. During slavery, a lot of escaped slaves were taken in by Indian tribes, which is how my great, great, great-grandfather on my mother's side came to live with the Tuscarora. He married a shaman's daughter, so my grandfather came from a long line of shamans."

"That's like a voodoo doctor, correct?"

"Voodoo doctor, medicine man, holy man, witch doctor, take your pick, they're all the same. My grandfather lived on the reservation until he was about twelve."

"When was he twelve?"

"He was born in 1914, so he would have been twelve around 1926."

"So long ago."

"That's for sure. My great, great-grandmother's father wanted to school my grandfather in becoming a shaman, but his parents wouldn't hear of it because they wanted off the reservation. My great, great, great-grandfather hated living on the reservation, or in the 'Indian Woods' as the reservations were called. He thought the reservation was too confining, like a prison. It reminded him of plantation life, like he was still a slave."

Sighing reflectively, Lorna eased her hand across Kyle's chest. "This is too depressing, Kyle. I do not want to talk about slavery. It saddens me."

"Well, I was telling you about my grandfather because he be-lieved in spirits and natural healing, and that's because of his her-itage. If he had stayed on the reservation, he probably would have become a shaman like his forefathers."

"You know, Kyle, if your grandfather will not let go of your mind, maybe he had some sort of shaman power you didn't know about?"

"I said he believed in that stuff, I didn't say he practiced any ritualistic craft." Kyle felt a mounting irritation in his gut. "Look, baby, I need to clean up." He sat up. "I'm gonna go take a shower."

"Maybe I will take my shower with you—we can clean each other."

"I'd like that. I got nothing but time. In fact, why don't you play hooky tomorrow and keep me company."

"I must go to school in the morning, Kyle, there is a test. But I will not go to work in the afternoon."

Kyle didn't feel right staying the night, he'd rather be in his own bed, but he wasn't going anywhere near his own house if it meant putting up with his mother's intrusion in his life. He'd make the funeral as he promised, but until everyone cleared out of his house, he had no intention of stepping foot in there.

Chapter
11

As far as Kyle could see, spreading out wide across the horizon, a vast field of colorful wildflowers of yellows, oranges, whites, and purples surrounded him. High above, mountainous white clouds dotted the vivid blue sky. Kyle didn't know where he was or why he was in this field, but he was amazed at the brilliance of the floral colors. It was beautiful beyond belief, yet eerily silent. Kyle felt uneasy; he wanted to leave. He began looking for a path to lead him out of the field, but no path was visible. The knee-high flowers covered the ground like a thick, plush carpet; and as beautiful as the sight was before him, Kyle couldn't ignore the feeling of uneasiness and aloneness that swelled in his chest. He felt as alone as a man stranded on an island with no way off. Turning first one way, then the other, Kyle took in the vastness of the field, when out of nowhere, far off in the distance, he saw a tiny figure of a person appear. He watched as the person, dressed in white, came nearer, and his size grew big enough for Kyle to see that it was a man, perhaps a tall man— he swung his arms like a man with long arms. Still, there was no path on which the man walked—the flowers had not parted for his footfalls and had not fallen by the wayside. Kyle saw this and was as amazed as he was disturbed. He called to the man, "Hello!" The man did not answer, although he continued to draw near, near enough for Kyle to see that the man was not a young man. He had the determined, lumbering walk of a man who'd long since seen his youth. The way the man swung his arms, the way he led with his shoulders seemed familiar to Kyle. But it wasn't until the man got within several feet that Kyle recognized him. It was his grandfather—Granddad Preston!

Kyle was immediately struck by how different his grandfather looked. The skin on his old, time-worn face was tight, his eyes were clear yet quite reproachful. Granddad Preston looked as healthy and as strong as he did in his sixties. His thin gray hair was fuller, blacker, with only a shock of gray at each temple. The weight he had lost with old age and illness was regained and filled out the white shirt and trousers he wore.

"Granddad! Granddad!" Excited, Kyle hurried to meet his grandfather to embrace him, but his grandfather wasn't as close as Kyle thought. The nearer Kyle tried to get, the more constant his grandfather remained several feet away. Perplexed, Kyle stared at the grim look on his grandfather's face.

"Granddad, why can't I get close to you?"

His grandfather did not respond. He slowly shook his head.

"Granddad, it's me—Kyle. Are you all right?"

Granddad Preston fixed his gaze on Kyle's eyes.

"Don't you know me?" Kyle asked.

Granddad Preston raised his hand and beckoned Kyle to follow him.

"You want me to follow you?"

Beckoning no more, Granddad Preston turned and began to walk away.

At first unsure, Kyle took a few tentative steps before hurrying to catch up with his grandfather, who seemed to always stay well ahead of him. Looking back over his shoulder, Kyle saw that the flowers through which he trudged remained tall and untrampled, leaving no path to show that he passed through. Again, he was amazed, but he didn't stop to wonder why—his grandfather was moving farther away. The vast field of bright, colorful flowers quickly fell behind Kyle, and he found himself at the mouth of a large cave, which miraculously appeared, into which his grandfather disappeared.

Kyle pulled up short, stopping outside the cave. "Granddad! Where're you going?"

There was no response from the darkness within.

Anxious, Kyle called again, "Granddad!"

Again, no response from the blackness that filled Kyle's eyes. Kyle stepped back from the cave as he sensed the intensity of the air closing in behind him. Slowly looking back over his shoulder, Kyle saw the field of wildflowers slowly fade into a great wall of darkness that chilled his heart and turned his blood cold. The only light was the spot of daylight that eerily hovered over him. It was clear to Kyle that he could not go back, yet he did not want to go forward into the unknown of the cave.

"Grandson," Granddad Preston said, his voice suddenly rising up out of the darkness, "you must trust me."

Hesitating at first, Kyle finally answered, "I trust you, Granddad, but—" He cringed at the cave entrance. He was too afraid to enter and began stepping back, when suddenly, a vein-etched, bony hand with red clawlike nails shot out of the mouth of the cave like a striking cobra—catching Kyle's breath in his throat, stopping his heart—and grabbled Kyle by the front of his shirt with all the might of an 800-pound gorilla! Kyle screamed. He tried to break free, punching and chopping at the hand. The hand was unrelenting and could not be budged, pulling Kyle as if he was going along without a fight. Fear gripped Kyle's throat, making it hard for him to breathe. Digging his heels into the dirt, Kyle tried to tear his shirt free but couldn't. He was being dragged into the dark cave despite his resistance. With his fist, he started pounding on the hand, hurting himself, but not the hand that—

"Kyle! Kyle!" Lorna struggled to pin down Kyle's flailing arms. "Kyle, it's me—Lorna! Wake up!" She threw herself atop Kyle.

With a mighty shove and a loud grunt, Kyle threw Lorna off him onto the floor. She screamed, waking Kyle from his nightmare. He bolted upright in the bed and in the near darkness, breathing heavily, frantically searched for something familiar. There was nothing, until he was drawn to Lorna's voice.

"Kyle, you were having a terrible dream." She got herself off the floor and turned on the lamp next to the bed onto which she sat. "You threw me onto the floor!"

Kyle fell back against the pillow. Trickles of sweat rolled from his face onto the pillow. "Damn."

"You were striking out. You hit me in your sleep, Kyle. It was frightening. What did you dream?"

"I think I saw my grandfather. It felt so real."

"Oh, he visit you. He's worrying your mind."

"Don't start that. Besides, it wasn't my grandfather that made me strike out. It was this, this *hand* that came out of this dark cave and grabbed me."

"Your grandfather, he lead you to the cave, right?"

Kyle raised his head. "How did you know?"

"It would seem so by your fear. But why would your grandfather lead you to such a cave and scare you so?"

Kyle didn't know and didn't have a clear enough mind to guess. The dream felt almost too real to be a dream. He felt as if he were right there in the field with his grandfather, and at the mouth of the cave when that hand grabbed him, he almost peed on himself. Why, indeed, would his grandfather lead him to a dark cave for him to be jumped like that?

"You were close to your grandfather, were you not?"

"At one time we were real close."

"When was that?"

"All my life till a little more than a year ago when he got cancer and had to be put in a nursing home. I didn't see much of him after that."

"Could be your grandfather is angry with you, you think?"

"Well, damn, even if he were, he's dead."

"But, Kyle, dreams of dead people mean so much more than you think. My Aunt Yasmin, she know dreams. She interpret for many people. You should talk to her."

"What is she, a soothsayer or something?"

"What is that—soothsayer?"

"A seer, a fortune-teller."

"My aunt do see many things that we are unable to see. And she do tell people about their future."

Kyle smirked. "A soothsayer."

"No, Kyle, Aunt Yasmin is not like other readers. She has the gift."

"I bet she does—the gift of the con."

"No!" Lorna said, her agitation clear in her voice. "Aunt Yasmin does not con. She is a reader of tarot . . ."

Kyle said under his breath, "A scam artist."

"She sees many things in her cards."

"Look. I don't mess with psychics, clairvoyants, readers, seers, whatever you wanna call them. I don't even look at the horo-scopes, so forget about me talking to your aunt. I pass."

"But, Kyle, your dreams—"

"Lorna, the damn dreams don't mean a thing. I probably had that nightmare because I walked out on my mother tonight. She and my brother probably put a hex or something on me."

"See, you do believe—"

"No, I don't. It was a joke. Man."

Lorna laid her hand on Kyle's chest. "Well, if it was your mother who caused you to dream so badly, you should apologize to her. We must always respect our mothers."

"Aw, man." The last thing Kyle wanted to hear was a damn lecture about how he was treating his mother. "Lorna—"

"God do not like us to mistreat our mothers."

"Let it go, Lorna, I'm not having this discussion."

"But—"

Kyle punched his pillow and, hugging it, flopped over onto his stomach facing away from Lorna. From the pillow he inhaled the strong scent of jasmine and orchids—Lorna's Red Door per-fume, which she sprayed all over the sheets and pillows. She always did that whenever she knew that he was coming over.

Lorna stared at the back of Kyle's head. "Are you angry with me?"

He didn't answer.

She began to lightly rub Kyle's back.

He hugged the pillow tighter. It was just his luck that Lorna was not only superstitious but a nag when it came to family, which was ironic when she was cheating on her husband. She didn't have a problem doing that, but she did have a problem with him disrespecting his mother. Her own mother she probably called more than she called her husband, and respected her more. Go figure.

Lorna snuggled up against Kyle's side and laid her arm across his back.

That was more like it. Lorna's warm body and her sweet essence of jasmine was all he needed to relax and get back to sleep, but Lorna had other plans. Her hand slid down Kyle's back to his naked, firm buttocks, which she began to gently knead and stroke. Sighing, Kyle relaxed even more as Lorna wrapped her leg around his leg, but after that dream, he wasn't in the mood for making love even when Lorna tantalizingly eased her finger down the crack of his ass, making him clinch his cheeks and shift his body to relieve the swelling pressure on his budding erection. Still, he wouldn't turn over.

"Is the baby pouting?" Lorna teased.

"No," Kyle grumbled, which was true. It was the dream that was still disturbing him. Why the hell did he keep having dreams about a woman's hand trying to pull him into some damn godforsaken hole? A toilet? A dark-ass cave? What was he? A damn mole? He'd had plenty of bad dreams before, but what the hell was it with this hand? And his grandfather? Why in the world would he have such a horrible dream like that and see his grandfather, too?

Nimbly straddling Kyle, Lorna began rubbing herself atop Kyle's buttocks.

Kyle was having a hard time pretending that he wasn't aroused or interested. But his grandfather and that damn hand kept floating around in his mind. He had to get that vision out of his head and replace it with something good, something sexy. Kyle squeezed his eyes shut. At once, Lorna, Dalia, and Audrey all flashed in his mind. All three were bare-ass naked and all over him like Lorna was at that very moment. Now that, he could get with. Wouldn't it be something if he could make love to all three at the same time? Yeah, he could most definitely get with that.

Slowly turning onto his back as Lorna slid around onto his front, Kyle let her take him full inside her while he gripped her hips and forgot all about the serpentine hand of his nightmare.

Chapter
12

Every nerve in Kyle's body ached to get him up out of Lorna's bed and out of her apartment. It was not where he wanted to be, nor where he needed to be, but the alternative—home—was no less inviting. In the past few days his mother had become more of a pain in his ass than usual, and if he had to listen to her lecturing him about his so-called disreputable lifestyle one more time, he'd seriously consider suicide; it would be a lot easier than packing up and selling his house. The truth was, he lived his life no differently from a lot of guys his age who had their pick of women. Hell, if he was so bad, he wouldn't be able to hold onto one woman much less two or three. Like he told his father, he wasn't hurting anyone. In fact, he treated his women damn well—wining, dining, credit cards. What woman could complain about that? But with or without the credit card, Dalia, Audrey, and Lorna were going to stick around—he was a good thing and they knew it. Of course, he knew that Audrey was serious about commitment; that Dalia seriously needed a sugar daddy with deep pockets; and that Lorna's need was sexual but definitely temporary. At some point she was going back home to her husband and her life as a well-to-do Jamaican woman. She made no bones about liking her life in Kingston; she was treated like royalty as the wife of a wealthy man.

Riiiiing!

Lorna stirred. Kyle dared not answer the telephone. He nudged her.

Riiiiing!

With her eyes closed, Lorna reached for the telephone on the rattan and glass nightstand. Sleepily, she answered, "Hello?"

"Hi, Mommie!"

All grogginess completely left Lorna as she sat up. "Hi, baby. Good morning."

"You up, Mommie? Daddy said you would not be up."

"Daddy's right. I'm just getting up. How's my baby?"

"Fine. Mommie, Daddy say we will come visit you soon. Can we come tomorrow?"

"Tomorrow?" Lorna glanced down at Kyle looking up at her. "No, Cindy, your daddy will have to apply for visas for you and he. It will take some time, you know, like before."

"But, Mommie. I want to see you. I miss you." There was a tiny whimper.

"Oh, baby, I miss you also. I will see you soon, I promise."

"Will you buy me a present, Mommie?"

"Of course, I will. Cindy, why are you not in school?"

"I am at work with Daddy. I am helping him, Mommie."

Lorna's back stiffened. Throwing back the cover, she sprang up off the bed. "Cindy, let Mommie speak to Daddy."

"Okay, Mommie. Here, Daddy."

Without covering herself, Lorna started from the bedroom.

"Good morning, my love."

"Why is Cindy not in school?" Lorna asked brusquely. She closed herself off in the bathroom with a slam.

Kyle lay back with his arms under his head. The fact that Lorna was obviously upset didn't faze him. As far as he was concerned, that's the way it was with married people—men fuck up, women bitch. He wanted to know nothing about Lorna's disagreements or disputes with her husband, they had nothing to do with him. *Beep . . . beep . . . beep . . .*

Kyle quickly turned off the alarm clock. Six o'clock. Lorna had to go to classes and to work later. Hiding out in her place was perfect, he'd have it all to himself, but he had no intention of hanging in all day. What he'd do, he had not a clue. Maybe he'd sleep late and then—Then what? He wasn't about to lay up and wait for Lorna to come home and pat him on the head.

Kyle retrieved his cell phone from the pocket of his jacket hanging on the back of Lorna's closet. Maybe he could talk Vernon into playing hooky today. Back in high school, they skipped out often enough to warrant their parents being called in for a conference with the principal. That didn't stop them for long, but being threatened with being left back in their senior year did. Being labeled super seniors wasn't their idea of being cool.

"Hey, man, what's up?"

"*Nothing but the rent. What's up with you calling me this damn early?*"

"I wanted to catch you before you left for work."

"*I'm going in late, if I go in at all. My big-screen television is being delivered this morning—I hope—and I couldn't get my dumb ass brother over here to wait on the delivery.*"

"How much did he want?"

"*Fifty dollars, and that's after I talked him down from a hundred.*"

"Damn!"

"*Broke-ass brother. After all I did for him, he should do it for free.*"

Kyle couldn't agree more. Vernon's older brother, Dennis Price, had a B.A. in computer science and a Ph.D. in alcoholism. He graduated Brooklyn Technical High School a year ahead of Preston, then went on to New York University, where he met his future wife and got married. Dennis was doing good, everyone thought, until one day it was all over the six o'clock news that Dennis had stepped off the platform into the path of an oncoming train at Hoyt and Schermerhorn downtown Brooklyn. What do they say about God looking out for babies and fools? Dennis lost his right leg clear up to his hip, but he lived. Seems his wife had left him because of the drinking that only she knew about. They all knew that Dennis drank socially, they just didn't know that he couldn't get going in the morning without a drink, and that he carried his poison with him everywhere he went, including onto the job that paid him well enough for him to send his two children to a private school and for him to own a Benz and an Infiniti and a house up in Spring Valley. He lost everything and now lived on the streets.

"*I refuse to keep throwing money Dennis's way. He spends his whole SSI check on booze,*" Vernon said. "*He needs to get his ass dry and get up off of it and get a job; he didn't lose his hands. Or his brain!*"

"No, but he's not about to give up his addiction of choice. He—"

"*Kyle, man, I don't wanna talk about Dennis. The way I feel, I might drown his ass in a tub of rot gut if I get my hands on him. What time is your grandfather's funeral?*"

"Ten o'clock tomorrow morning."

"*I know you're missing the old man; he was all right. I wish he'd been my grandfather.*"

"Yeah, he was cool. Look, I'm not doing anything today, I'll come your way and wait for that delivery with you."

"*You closing down the office?*"

"Yeah, family's taking over my house."

"*Out of towners, huh? Bring me some of your mother's muffins.*"

"I'm not home. I'll see you in a few." Kyle ended the call just as Lorna came back into the room. He could see by the tight set of her lips and the angry glint in her eyes that her conversation with her husband hadn't gone too well. He watched her slam the telephone down on its base.

"My husband is coming." Lorna flopped down onto the bed.

"That's good." Kyle busied himself looking for and finding his underwear. This was as good a time as any to take a shower. "He obviously misses you."

"But I do not want him here."

"He's your husband, Lorna. You can't tell him not to come."

"I can if I tell him I want a divorce."

Alarms went off in Kyle's head. From outside the bathroom, he turned back. "Why would you do that? That's not what you really want."

"It is. Perhaps I should let him come so that I can tell him in person."

Oh, hell no! "Lorna, you need to think about this. Maybe you should go home and—"

"No, I should tell him here."

Kyle felt his stomach tighten. "When is he coming?"

"Maybe the end of next month, if he can."

"Well, that's plenty of time for you to think this through, Lorna, before he gets here."

Lorna was silent.

"How long will he be here?" Kyle asked.

"Perhaps a month. He has business to tend to."

It's time to end this. "Is he bringing your daughter?"

"Yes, but I do not want her here either."

"How can you say that, Lorna? That's your baby."

"This is true. But I do not want her to see her father and I disagree."

Kyle really wasn't liking what Lorna was saying. "Look, I think you'll feel differently once you see your husband and your daughter."

The "I don't think so" look Lorna gave him made Kyle widen his eyes. "I thought you missed your family, especially your daughter." Kyle went and sat on the bed.

"Sometimes I do, but I much rather my daughter stay in Kingston. This city is not the best for a small child such as she. Perhaps when she is older she can visit with you and I here."

Oh, shit! Alarms were clanking loud in Kyle's head. He nervously scratched his chin.

"That would be okay, Kyle, would it not? My daughter can play with your little girl, they can be like sisters. And who knows, maybe one day they can be big sisters to the baby we will have together."

Oh, hell no! I'm not in it like that! Kyle's heart was actually thumping, loudly. "Your husband might not like that."

"He will not have any say. I will not be his wife."

"Lorna, you're moving too fast. You should let your husband come. You need to see him. You've been away from home a long time. You might feel differently once he's here."

"I do not think so. I have thought long about this. I like my life here with you without them."

I gotta end this.

"You want me here with you, don't you, Kyle?"

Hell no! Kyle again scratched his chin. "Here? Lorna wanna know the truth? I'd go to Jamaica in a heartbeat to relax under that hot, Caribbean sun." Kyle was trying to sound lighthearted, but he was nervous as hell. This wasn't what he bargained for.

"And Lorna, after being in all this cold, I know you miss that beautiful beach house of yours in Kingston."

"Yes, I do, but it is not where I want to be if you are not there."

The back of Kyle's neck began to burn. Even touching it warmed his hand.

"I want to stay here, Kyle." Lorna lay across her bed in a seductive pose, her left hand slowly moving up from her stomach to her breast.

Even the bed under Kyle felt hot. He started to get up, but Lorna caught him by the arm.

"I want to be with you, Kyle."

"Lorna, when we got together, this wasn't what we discussed. I'm not into breaking up marriages."

"You are not to blame for the breakup of my marriage, Kyle. It has been over for a very long time. I just did not know it."

"Yeah, but do you really know that now? Lorna, you should really think about this, you might be wrong."

Lorna took Kyle's hand and laid it on her breast. "I'm yours, Kyle. My body belong to you. I belong to you."

Leaving his hand where it was, Kyle followed Lorna's hand to her nipple where she began to gently swirl her finger until her nipple hardened and stood erect like he himself was beginning to do. Never taking her eyes off Kyle, Lorna began licking her lips as she slid her other hand down between her thighs and started fingering herself, arching her back, making Kyle almost forget that he was in a hurry to get the hell out of there.

"You're bad," he said, covering himself with his underwear while pressing his erection down onto his thigh and holding it there. This was not the time to kick back and get stupid.

Lorna opened her thighs for Kyle to see how deep her finger was inside her body. He felt the pressure under his hand. *Whoa, boy. It's a trap.*

"Don't you want me, Kyle?"

"You're gonna be late for school." Kyle started backing away. "I don't wanna make you late."

Lorna stopped playing with herself. She pulled herself upright. "You want me to stay in America, don't you, Kyle?"

"Lorna." Kyle began shaking his head. All desire in his groin dissipated; he no longer had to hold himself down, even though Lorna's hand tried to make him respond again. He held her hand still.

"Lorna, you have a family."

"You said you love me, Kyle, You do love me, don't you?"

"Lorna, I care about you, but you have a husband who obviously cares more for you. You and I—"

"But I no longer love my husband. I love you. It is you I want to be with."

Kyle again shook his head. *I don't love you.*

"I will divorce my husband. He will not stand in the way of us being together."

Oh, shit! This wasn't supposed to happen like this. "Lorna, I'm not going to be the cause of your marriage breaking up. I think you should think about what you're saying."

"I know what I am saying, Kyle. I love you. I want to be your wife, not Stanley's. I have not loved him for a very long time. When I am with you, I forget that he exist in my life."

"But you have a daughter with your husband, Lorna. I know you're not trying to forget about her."

"No, no. I love my daughter. She will be taken care of no matter with whom she lives—her father or I. I will always be in my daughter's life, but I want to have a new life with you. This can be, can it not, Kyle?"

Oh, man! How the hell am I gonna get out of this? I never told you I wanted you. Hell, I don't love you. Why can't a woman be with a man without needing to tie him to her ring finger? The hell with taking a shower. Kyle pulled on his briefs.

"Look, I gotta go. Let's talk about this another time."

"Kyle, please say you—"

"I have to use the bathroom." He went quickly into the bathroom and was about to close the door—

"I have already told my husband I have met someone I want to be with. I told him that you want to be with me also."

Kyle opened the bathroom door wide. "You told him about me?"

"Yes, I—"

"Why did you do that?" Kyle stepped back into the bedroom. "You told him my name?"

"No . . . no. I did not tell him your name. I just told him I met someone who wants to be with me. I owed him the truth, Kyle."

"But that's not the truth, Lorna. I can't make a commitment to you. For one thing, you're still a married woman, and . . . and I'm still a married man," he outright lied.

Lorna's eyes widened. "But you told me you were divorced."

"I told you I *filed* for divorce, but my wife had contested it. My divorce isn't final yet, but even if I were free, I wouldn't let you destroy your marriage because of me."

"But—"

"No, Lorna. If you were already divorced, it would be different," he lied, "but you're not. If you left your husband because of me, you'd only end up hating me later if it didn't work out between us."

"But it will work out between us, Kyle. I know it. I feel it in my heart. I love—"

"Lorna, wait a minute. You're confusing love and freedom. You love your freedom away from your husband and child. You love having a different life from what you had at home. Lorna, you really don't know if it's love you feel for me. Right now, I'm just a distraction. Look, I gotta go. My grandfather's funeral is tomorrow and I have to run some errands."

"I will come with you." Lorna scooted off the bed.

"No!"

"You don't want me to come?"

"It's not that. You can't. A funeral isn't the place to meet people you don't already know. Look, I have to go. I have to be with my family." Ignoring the hurt look on Lorna's face, Kyle quickly gathered up his clothes. He dashed into the bathroom, slamming and locking the door, just in case. Coming to Lorna's wasn't such a good idea, after all. If she was planning to divorce her husband so she could marry him, then he needed to stop seeing her ass altogether, like right away.

Damn. Where did she get the idea that I'd marry her? No way! It was okay to hit her ass whenever he wanted some, but on a regular and permanent basis, he wasn't down for that. Hell no. For sure, it was time to let this one go.

Chapter
13

Vernon's voice boomed from the intercom, "Man, I thought you said you'd be here in a couple of hours. Can't you tell time yet?"

"Man, just open the damn door."

"Hold up a minute."

Kyle glanced back at the street as if he wanted to make sure that Lorna hadn't followed him. Damn, that was messed up. For damn sure he didn't want her to end her marriage and hang around hoping that he'd marry her. He left Lorna wrapped up in her bathrobe, sitting in her living room, her legs tucked under her body, her arms crossed high and tight across her chest, a pained expression on her face as she looked right through him when he said, "I'll call you later." What else could he say? He had no intention of calling her ever again, but it would be awkward to actually say that.

Finally buzzed into the building, Kyle bypassed the two elevators and sprinted up the six flights of stairs to Vernon's Eastern Parkway apartment across from the Brooklyn Museum of Art. Vernon did pretty well for himself as a New York City deputy engineer. As a teenager, Vernon had always wanted to live up on Eastern Parkway's grand roadway of towering, pre–World War II apartment buildings with bold, original molding–trimmed, spacious rooms, art deco lobbies, and uniformed doormen. Vernon's building no longer had a doorman, but he was satisfied all the same.

Vernon didn't bother to lock the door behind Kyle, he simply pushed it closed. He pulled on the strings of his baggy gray warm-up pants and tied them tighter around his trim waist. "What's up? You couldn't sleep?"

Kyle saw that Vernon's broad, muscular chest was glistening with perspiration. "You were working out?"

"You could say that." Vernon flexed his rock-hard biceps. "How am I looking?"

"Man, don't ask me, I'm not a woman."

Vernon gave Kyle a quizzical look. "What's up with you this morning? Who you running from?"

Kyle tossed his jacket across the arm of the sofa and headed for the kitchen. "Why do I have to be running from someone to stop by here?"

"Because of the hour—you're usually down in your office this early. What's up?"

"More than I care to talk about." Kyle suddenly sneezed, loud and hard, making him squeeze his eyes shut. Before he saw what was in his hand, he felt it—mucus.

Vernon covered his own nose and mouth. "Man, don't be bringing your germs up in here! I can't afford to get a cold. I have an important meeting tomorrow."

"Like I can." At the kitchen sink, Kyle washed his hands with dish detergent, and as soon as he dried his hands, he felt another sneeze coming on. With his finger, he pressed the side of his right nostril until the nagging urge to sneeze subsided.

Vernon uncovered his nose and mouth. "So what's really up with you?"

"Not a damn thing."

"Tell that to someone who doesn't know you. Who were you with last night?"

Vernon knew him too well. "I was with Lorna." From the cabinet over the counter, Kyle took a glass.

"So you pulled an all-nighter, huh? You need a splint for your johnson, man?"

"Hell no, I can handle Lorna." He rinsed the glass and sat it on the counter. "Then again, maybe I can't. Man, that woman just told me she wants to marry me."

"Isn't she already married?"

"She's talking about divorcing her husband and marrying me. If she know like I know, she better hold on to what she got—I'm not marrying her."

"Did you tell her that?"

"Hell yeah!"

"Then you better stop seeing her. If she's talking marriage, she's gonna ride you till she gets you. Man, she's gonna use every trick in the book to get you to the altar."

"No, the hell she isn't. I won't give her the chance. You can bet your ass on that. I'm done with Lorna. She scared me so bad, my balls drew up."

Vernon chuckled. "I bet they did."

"Forget her. What you got to eat?" Kyle opened the refrigerator.

"Rice Crispies if you brought your own milk."

In that instant, out of the corner of his eye, Kyle caught sight of a cockroach climbing up out of the toaster. "Man, if I had a gallon of milk in my back pocket, I wouldn't eat a single Rice Krispie in this place—I could be eating roach eggs."

"That's cold, man. How you gonna insult me like that?"

"How long you gonna let these cockroaches share your crib?"

"Man, they're not my roaches." Vernon retrieved a can of roach spray from under the sink. "They're coming from next door. I get this place exterminated every month, but that old lady next door won't let the man in to exterminate her place. Where did you see the roach?"

Kyle pointed to the toaster. "Must be real funky next door. I'd have to talk to that woman."

"And say what? Keep your pets inside your crib?" Vernon pushed the toaster aside. There was no roach. He picked up the toaster and brought it down hard on the counter. No roach dropped out. He sprayed along the back of the counter anyway. The strong, sickly pesticide smell immediately filled the large kitchen. No roach appeared.

"Everyone on the floor's been complaining, but the management company can't get her to comply. I keep getting these roaches, I'm gonna throw a fumigator bomb through her window and get her and the damn roaches."

"I would've done that a long time ago. I hate those things, " Kyle said, looking through the sparsely filled refrigerator containing only a few white cartons of half-eaten Chinese food and uncovered stale pizza. "Man, you're worse than me." Kyle closed the refrigerator door.

"If my mother lived next door to me, I'd have food in my house, too."

"At this point, I'd rather starve than have my mother living next door to me."

"Let me guess." Vernon followed Kyle back into the living room where they sat across from each other. "You and your mother are at it again."

"Actually, she's on my ass for screwing one of my employees who quit on me afterward."

"Damn, man, you still doing that? Who was it? Was it that fine ass, Grace?"

Kyle confirmed Vernon's guess with a silent look of "Who else?"

Vernon chuckled. "Well, I guess I can't blame you too much."

"Yeah, right."

"For real, man. Any fool could see that Grace had it bad for you. I think she wore those tight-ass clothes just for you." Vernon lowered his voice. "Shoot, I don't blame you. If she was always looking at me the way she looked at you, I would've hit it, too. She quit for real?"

"Yeah, I blew that, and I knew better."

"Since when did that stop you?" Vernon asked, impressed still with Kyle's ability to get almost any woman he wanted.

Kyle thought about it. "Never."

"Remember when we were in high school and that girl . . . What was her name? Oh, yeah, Toni. You were seeing Toni, and her little sister came in as a freshman and you wanted to get with her. Remember that? Man, you had sisters fighting over you."

Kyle remembered. All the guys in school were patting him on the back for that one. "Well, this isn't high school. Grace was my best transcriber. I'd never tell my mother, but she was right. I should have never touched that. I'm messing with my own business."

"Yeah, that was dumb."

"Aw, screw you, man." Kyle looked around the room. "Where you gonna put that big-ass television? You should—" Kyle heard a pair of heels clicking on the hardwood floor behind him. He looked toward the back of the five-room apartment just as a good-looking, wide-hipped woman with long brown, ropelike locks framing her face down to her chest sauntered up the hallway carrying a large overnight bag.

Vernon hurried to his woman, taking her bag. He put his arm around her. "Baby, this is my boy, Kyle. Kyle, this is Jennifer, my fiancée."

Stunned, Kyle threw Vernon a puzzled look. *Fiancée?*

Jennifer smiled. "I've heard so much about you, Kyle. Nice to finally meet you."

Maintaining his cool, Kyle went to Jennifer, shaking her hand. "I wish I could say the same," he said, punctuating his remark with a hard look at Vernon.

Vernon grinned sheepishly. "Well, we've all been so busy."

"Yeah, right," Kyle said, annoyed. "I guess us *best friends* were *too* busy to tell each other about important things like engagements."

Letting out a loud sigh, Vernon glanced down at Jennifer, just as she hit him in the stomach, making him grimace and cough.

"You didn't tell Kyle we were getting married?"

"Baby, that hurt."

"He didn't tell me you even existed," Kyle said.

"Vernon!" Jennifer again hit him in the stomach, this time harder, doubling him over.

"Best friends, huh, Vernon?" Kyle couldn't hide his hurt. "Look, Jennifer, I don't wanna run you off. I'll leave you two alone. I have to be somewhere."

"Oh, no, Kyle. You're not running me off. I have to get to work. You stay and talk to your friend here." She took her overnight bag from Vernon. "He and I will talk later. Kyle"—she again extended her hand—"it was nice meeting you."

"Yeah," he said, holding Jennifer's hand and making it a point to inhale her scent. "Nice perfume. Whisper?"

Vernon shot Kyle a hard, smothering glare.

"You have a good nose," Jennifer said, impressed.

Although there was a threatening tingle in his nose of an unwanted sneeze, Kyle was proud of his ability to call the name of Jennifer's perfume. He locked eyes with Vernon. "Vernon, your wife-to-be has excellent taste in perfume."

Vernon didn't bat an eye.

Jennifer slipped her hand out of Kyle's. "Okay, you guys, I have to get to work." She rubbed Vernon's hard stomach where she had hit him. "Tonight?"

"No doubt." Vernon walked Jennifer to the door where he took her coat from the hall closet and helped her into it.

Kyle sniffled and wiggled his nose in an attempt to forestall a sneeze. He looked away when Jennifer and Vernon tongued their good-bye, but fixed his eyes on Vernon as he stood in the doorway watching his woman walk down the hall to the elevator. The way Vernon was smiling, the way his eyes literally twinkled, said he was stupid over this one, for real. But if Vernon was that far gone, to the point of being engaged, how was it that Kyle didn't know a thing about it? Annoyed, his gut tight, he turned away from Vernon. He couldn't discern whether he was feeling embarrassed for interrupting whatever Vernon and Jennifer were doing before he barged in, or if he was ticked off because Vernon had never told him about Jennifer. Since high school they told each other about their women, about their conquests. Since when did Vernon flip the script?

Vernon waited until the elevator door closed before he closed his own door.

Kyle let out a whopper of a sneeze! His eyes watered.

"Damn, man," Vernon said. "What you doing about that cold?"

Kyle pressed his finger under his nose. "Does she come as pretty as she looks?"

Vernon glared hard at Kyle. "Don't go there."

The threatening look on Vernon's face surprised Kyle. "What the hell you getting upset for?"

"How my woman come is none of your damn business."

"The fact that you have a woman is none of my business, too, huh?"

"Man, we're not kids in high school. Jennifer isn't a piece of ass I met at a bar. I'm gonna marry her."

"If that's the case, how come you've never told me about her?"

"I thought I had." Again, both Vernon and Kyle sat.

Kyle glared hard at Vernon. "You'd lie in my face like this?"

"No, man, I thought I had."

"Vernon, don't play me for stupid. You know damn well you never told me about that woman. And what's worse, man, is that I'm beginning to think you didn't tell me or introduce me because you didn't want me to hit on her."

From the black brass trunk he used as a coffee table, Vernon picked up a copy of *Sports Illustrated.* "Tell me, Kyle. Would you dangle a piece of meat you wanted to eat in front of a lion's mouth?"

Kyle stared at Vernon. Was Vernon saying that putting a woman he wanted in front of him was tempting fate?

Vernon flipped through his magazine, unfazed by Kyle's smothering stare.

Kyle shot up off the sofa. "Damn! You think I'd do that to you?"

Vernon tossed the magazine at the trunk, it slid across the top onto the floor. "Your memory's bad, Kyle. Did you forget about Francine Hawkins?"

"Who the hell is Francine Hawkins?"

"A girl I was interested in back in college that you laid the same night I introduced you to her."

Stumped, Kyle rubbed his stubbly chin. He'd been in such a hurry to get out of Lorna's apartment, he hadn't showered or shaved, but one thing he knew for sure, though, he'd never messed with any girl Vernon was interested in.

"I'm not surprised you don't remember Francine, Kyle. You hit it one time and never called her for seconds."

"You're wrong, Vernon. I've never been with anyone you went with."

"I never got a chance to go with Francine, Kyle. You got to her first."

"Then I didn't take her from you, you weren't going with her."

"But I told you about her. I told you I wanted to get with her."

"Vernon, not only do I not remember that, but you need to listen to what you're saying. You're saying that you never went with her, that you *wanted* to get with her."

Vernon leaned forward, pressing his right elbow into the top of his thigh. "Yeah, but I told you I was liking Francine and that I had taken her to a movie."

"Let me clue you, Vernon. Taking a woman *out* isn't the same as going *with* her. I know you know—"

"Man, fuck that! You don't go after the girl your best friend is liking. That's off-limits. That's respecting the friendship, which you didn't." Vernon's heart was pumping hard.

"*If* I disrespected our friendship, it would have been because you didn't make your intensions clear."

"Clear!" Vernon was breathing hard, his muscles tight. He shot up off the sofa. "Did I have to wear a damn sandwich board on my fucking chest, or burn my name into her forehead? The bottom line, man, you shouldn't've touched her."

Kyle couldn't believe the depth of Vernon's anger. "Think about it, man. I would not've been able to touch her if she didn't want to be touched."

"You were wrong, Kyle! You were my friend. You never gave me a second thought once you got a hard-on for Francine."

"Man, this is crazy," Kyle said, feeling no guilt for what he didn't remember. "If you were this fucked up about it, why didn't you say something back then!"

Clinching his fists, taking deep breaths, expanding his chest, Vernon tried to calm himself down. "We were boys, Kyle. We were tight, man, just like we are now." He went to Kyle and held out his fist for an affirming fist-to-fist knuckle tap.

After a pause, Kyle obliged with a sound tap. "I swear, man, I don't remember being with a Francine Hawkins."

"Hey, don't sweat it. That was years ago. Besides, I figured even back then, if Francine could spread that easily for you, then I didn't need to be with her."

"So why did you bring her up?"

"You asked me why I hadn't introduced you to Jennifer."

Kyle drew back. "You really think I'd—"

"Look, man. When you're on the bone, your brain disengages. I wasn't sure what you'd do."

"Damn."

"I just know you're just as much a hound dog now as you were back in high school and college."

"Aw, shit."

"Hey, man, I'm being honest with you. Think about it. In the last few years, what woman have you met that you didn't think about getting into your bed?"

"I could name a hundred."

"And that would be a hundred that didn't interest you. Man, I know how Jennifer looks—she beautiful, and she smells good."

"My compliments. You finally got a good one."

"Fuck you, man. I've had more *good ones* than you could ever imagine. You just never met 'em because you don't know how to control that goddamn dick of yours."

"Oh, shit! Vernon, you think that little of me? You think I'd jump on your women and rape 'em?"

"Man, I didn't say that. I just know how quick you get a woody. Friendship and scruples be damned when you're around a good-looking, good-smelling woman."

"But you weren't going with Francine, Vernon! You can't blame—"

"No, but the coach was married to his wife. I know you didn't forget about that victory dinner we had after winning the eastern division and you started encroaching on the coach's wife on the dance floor, and y'all ended up in the bathroom with her bent over the sink and your meat rammed up her ass. . . ."

"You blame me for that? She came on to me."

"You're lucky it was me that walked in on you and not the coach. You like to say, 'if there be pain'; you would have had pain that night. The coach would have stomped and kicked your ass raw that night. You would have been screaming, 'No more pain.'"

"I would've handled it. If I can't take the pain, I don't need to be in the game."

"That's not the point, Kyle! You were wrong, man!"

That, Kyle couldn't deny. The vision of himself screwing Coach Grant's wife in the hotel bathroom was quite vivid and unforgettable. Looking back, maybe it was a dumb thing, but it was a serious high. Although they had gone to a bathroom on the other side of the building far away from the conference room the team was in, they still could have been busted by anyone. Luckily, it was Vernon who had come looking for him. Mrs. Grant wasn't the least bit fazed, she was good and grown and definitely knew what she was doing. Her perfume was as seductive a come-on as the cleavage-revealing dress that clung to her curvaceous body. She knew she was hot that night, and being that she had to be at least ten years younger than the coach, she was probably horny as hell for some young, hard dick. All night she had been pressing up against him when they danced, and before he knew it, she was hiking her dress up and putting her ass in his face. He went for it and thought about the coach afterward, but he wasn't taking all the blame.

"So you're gonna hold what I did back then against me for the rest of my life?"

Vernon shook his head. "Let me ask you something, man. Would you trust you if you were me?"

A self-conscious smirk was Kyle's response. He had to admit, maybe he wouldn't trust himself if he were in Vernon's shoes. But damn, was he really that bad, that much of a dog?

"Kyle, man, after all these years, I know your shit. I know what you like and I know how you are, which is why I haven't introduced you to any woman I've been serious about since I was twenty years old."

"Damn!" Kyle couldn't believe what he was hearing.

"And that's because of Francine Hawkins and the coach's wife." Vernon went to his dining table sitting just outside of the kitchen. From a large center bowl, he took a small stack of menus.

Kyle couldn't believe how bad he felt. "That's foul, man, you could've told me how you felt."

"Hey, I said it's done. I'm hungry. Let's order breakfast from around the corner."

No longer hungry, Kyle searched for words to defend himself, but there were none. He couldn't defend himself because there was nothing to defend. He still didn't know who the hell Francine Hawkins was, and Mrs. Grant was more the seducer than the seducee. All these years, Vernon had been holding those acts over his head, not trusting him. He never realized that Vernon hadn't been introducing him to some of his women. He thought Vernon just wasn't seeing many women, that he couldn't get many women. As men go, Vernon was an all-right looking dude with a good job, but he always thought Vernon too slow with the rap, and definitely not as good with women as he was.

"How about some bacon and eggs?" Vernon asked.

"Fuck bacon and eggs. Man, you don't trust me!"

Vernon shrugged. "I trust you with my life."

Kyle exhaled his anger. "But not your woman, right?"

Vernon didn't answer, nor did he look up from the menu. He already knew what he wanted more than breakfast—this conversation to end.

"Let it go, man."

Kyle couldn't. "I thought you knew me. I wouldn't push up on anyone you're interested in. *If* . . ."

Vernon chuckled drily to himself.

"*If* I did what you said I did back in college, I apologize. I'm sorry. It was a mistake. I wouldn't do anything like that again. You believe me, don't you?"

Vernon continued studying the menu. "Yeah, sure. What do you wanna eat?"

"Not a damn thing." Kyle was still trying to digest the fact that Vernon thought he was that much of a dog.

Vernon dropped the menu back into the bowl. He'd lost his appetite, too. "Hey, there's going to be a Stop the Violence march along Fulton Street from Malcolm X Boulevard down to Franklin Avenue in July, in memory of Councilman James E. Davis. You hear about it?"

If he had, Kyle didn't recall, and right now he wasn't the least bit interested. "Vernon—"

"You remember Davis, don't you? Davis was shot and killed in City Hall by that crazy dude who wanted his council seat in Clinton Hill. Remember?"

"I remember Davis, Vernon. He was a good brother. I—"

"Yeah, he was. Look, I'm on the organizing committee for the march, which I also volunteered you for. I hope you can make the meetings. The next one is—"

"Vernon! Man, how can you call yourself my friend all these years and not come clean with me?"

Riiiiing! Kyle touched the cell phone on his belt, but he was looking at Vernon, waiting for him to answer the question.

Riiiiing!

"You should answer that," Vernon said, "it could be important."

That was just it, most early morning calls were important, but Kyle was in no mood to deal with whatever the caller was calling about. He checked the caller ID on his cell phone. It was Carole. He breathed a sigh of relief—whatever Carole had to say could never be too bad.

Chapter
14

"Hey, sis. What's up?"

"Where the hell are you?"

"Why? What's wrong?"

"Where are you, Kyle?"

"I'm where I won't be harassed and maligned." He avoided looking at Vernon. "What's wrong?"

"Dad's in the hospital, or don't you care?"

"What the hell happened? He was fine when I left last night." Concerned, Vernon moved closer to Kyle.

"He has a blockage in his colon."

"Aw, sh—"

"He's having emergency surgery this afternoon."

"What hospital?" Kyle looked around for his jacket.

"Brookdale."

"Is surgery a must?"

"Who?" Vernon asked.

Kyle mouthed, "My father." He started putting on his jacket.

"What do you think, Kyle? He's not in the hospital for elective surgery."

"Goddammit, Carole, what the hell is the attitude for?"

"A better question, Kyle. Do you think this is the opportune time for you to call yourself running away—like you always do?"

"What the hell are you talking about? I've never run away from anything."

"I think your ex-wife and daughter might have something to say about that."

Kyle glanced at Vernon. "Screw you, Carole."

"I haven't cursed you, Kyle."

Vernon pulled Kyle by the arm. "Man, what're you doing? You're talking to Carole. That's your girl."

Kyle yanked his arm free. "At least I had a marriage."

"Yeah, but for how long? A minute?"

Kyle wanted to snap his phone shut but didn't. "I guess I was wrong about you, huh, Carole?" Again, he glanced at Vernon— the closet player-hater. "You don't think no more of me than Mom and Dad."

"Kyle, cut the 'woe is me' crap and get your ass back home. Mom needs you at the house."

Clinching his jaw, Kyle felt like throwing his cell phone against a wall. "I don't know why. She has you and Preston."

Vernon left the room.

"Damn, Kyle, Mom's here at the hospital. She and Dad have been in the ER since three this morning. I got here thirty minutes ago, and Press is on his way. As difficult as it might be to comprehend, Kyle, you need to do your part."

"And my part is at the house and not the hospital?"

"Kyle, do you even know what's going on? We have family coming in for Granddad's funeral, remember? Someone has to be at the house. Of course, if you wanna come to the hospital, then Sonji and I will go to the house and take care of business there. And speaking of business, what about your business? Press says you're closing down your office until after the funeral."

"So?"

"Kyle, that's your livelihood. Your staff can run the office, at least the work that's in-house while you and Mom take time off for the funeral."

"Let me worry about my business, Carole. When are people gonna start coming in? This afternoon? This evening?"

"I don't know, which is why someone should be at the house. Besides, Kyle, aren't people going to be staying at your house as well?"

"I didn't invite anyone."

Carole sucked her teeth.

"Well, I didn't."

"Kyle, you really do need to grow up."

Ever aware of Vernon somewhere in the back of the apartment, Kyle said calmly, "Great hearing that from you, Carole. I won't forget it."

"I hope you won't, and maybe that's just it. Maybe it's time you heard it from me, Kyle, that you need to stop walking around like you're God's gift to women. You—"

"I never said I was, but maybe I am. Think about it, Carole, I could probably get your woman."

"Damn, Kyle. I didn't realize how fucked up you were. Life's not all about you."

"I never said it was." He looked for any sign of Vernon in the hallway. There was none, but surely he was back there with his ears wide open.

"Everyone doesn't march to your beat, and certainly every woman on God's green earth isn't dying to get laid by you. The sooner you realize that, Kyle, the better off you'll be."

Kyle felt sick to his stomach. He couldn't believe all the animosity Carole had been holding against him. Of all the people in his family, he thought Carole was the one he could trust to be in his corner.

"You're a fraud, Carole. You don't understand a damn thing about me, and you care even less."

"I have much love for you, Kyle, and you know it, but—"

"Keep it. I don't wanna hear any more of your shit."

"Well, Kyle, that's too damn bad, because I have a whole lot more to say. You're a self-centered, selfish man, Kyle. And please, please don't pretend like you don't know that about yourself. You told me yourself that you're numero uno, mack daddy. But I have to pull your coattail, brother. In your own mind you are, but not to everyone else. You're a number one asshole. You're—"

"And what are you, Carole, but a woman wanting to be a man fucking a woman. Could it be you turned to women because no man would have you and because you were the one with the biggest dick!" Kyle snapped his phone shut and slam-dunked it onto the sofa where it bounced and hit the floor. Breathing hard, his chest heaving, Kyle repeatedly punched the palm of his left hand until pain shot into his wrist.

"Kyle!" Vernon said behind Kyle. "What the hell's going on? Man, that's your damn sister. How could you talk like that to her?"

Kyle couldn't stop punching his hand. "Fucking bitch."

"This is crazy. You and Carole are tight."

"Not anymore."

Riiiing! Kyle glared at his ringing cell phone on the floor. It was closer to Vernon than him, so Vernon snatched the phone off the floor.

Kyle lunged for it. "Don't answer it!"

Vernon snatched it out of Kyle's reach and flipped it open. "Hello?"

"Kyle, you lowlife son of a bitch—"

"Whoa! Carole, it's me, Vernon!"

"Vernon, you put that bastard back on the phone!"

"I don't think Kyle—"

Kyle snatched the phone. "Get off my back, Carole!"

"Kyle, you—You know what? I'm gonna take the high road."

"High or low, it doesn't matter to me."

"Obviously."

"Then leave me alone."

"Kyle, you know the worst thing Mom and Dad ever did for you was send you to Richmond to live with Grandma and Granddad for those two years. They spoiled you rotten. When you came back, you were a terror, especially when Mom and Dad couldn't lavish you with the same kind of attention Grandma and Granddad did."

"I never asked them for anything."

"Not in words, Kyle, by your insane behavior. The world didn't revolve around you at home, and you didn't like it. You made life miserable for all of us when you didn't get your way."

"I was no worse than you or Preston."

"Oh, yes, you were. Neither Press nor I took Dad's car and crashed it into three parked cars."

Kyle was fifteen then and wanted to impress his new friends

in his new high school. He hadn't made very many friends after returning from Richmond, and being able to sneak his father's car keys out of the house and take the car was a coup. His grandfather had taught him to drive while he was in Richmond, so handling that old Buick was a breeze. He drove a group of guys, including Vernon, up to the Bronx for a party, had a great time, and got high on a couple of beers and a joint. He made it back into Brooklyn okay; it was on Bedford Avenue, a few blocks from home, where he crashed. He got a twelve-month stint of community service and a year on juvenile probation. No one was happy about that but him; he made some friends, and Vernon was one of them.

"You were greedy for attention, and when you didn't get it from Mom and Dad, you sought it from other people. You had to be adored, looked up to. Maybe that's why you have to have so many women fawning over you now. Kyle, if any of your women ever got to know the real, selfish you, they'd leave your ass alone."

"Are you finished castrating me?"

"Just get your ass home, Kyle, and act like a responsible adult, and don't worry about my sex life and if you ever talk to me like that again, I will beat your ass."

The silence in his ear after Carole abruptly ended their connection made Kyle jerk his own phone from his ear. His jaw tight, he snapped the cell phone shut and tried to crush it in his fist. He wanted, again, to throw the phone, but it had cost him three bills. He jammed the phone back into its case on his belt. He wished that he'd never answered the damn thing. He began to pace.

"I gotta get the fuck away from my family."

"Carole jacked you up, huh?" Vernon asked, coming back into the room, this time fully dressed.

Kyle clinched and unclinched his fists, like he wanted to punch something. Everyone in his family was turning on him. Why? Not counting the car incident, he had never done anything to any of them.

"Man, you wanna talk about it?"

"I have to go." Kyle went out into the hallway.

"I'll stop by after work," Vernon said.

"Your woman is coming by tonight, remember?" He began jabbing at the elevator button.

Vernon could hear the motor of the elevator bringing one of the two cars up to the sixth floor. Vernon extended his hand. "Man, you know I'm here for you."

Kyle ignored Vernon's hand. "Slow-ass elevator."

Kyle bustled over to the brown stairwell door and, ramming his shoulder into it, slammed it up against the wall where it made a thunderous clap, just as another sneeze exploded from him. Hurrying down the stairs, the thought of a cold didn't disturb him as much as realizing that Vernon didn't trust him, or even more than Carole saying that he was being selfish and irresponsible. Now that pissed the hell out of him. If he was so fucking irresponsible, how was he running a successful business? He didn't need to ask for a damn thing from anyone in his family. What was so irresponsible about that? No, it wasn't him. It was his mother. She was angry with him about not visiting his grandfather and about him screwing Grace. His mother was the one who had everyone up in arms against him. He wished it were she laid up in pain in the hospital instead of his father.

Chapter
15

Brooding and sulking was never Kyle's way, he never let anything
get him down—for long—that is, until this morning. In his short
drive home he couldn't shake Vernon's angry words or Carole's
reproachful assault. If he didn't know better, he'd swear something really toxic had to be in the water for both Vernon and
Carole to turn on him the way they did. His mother always had
something negative to say about whatever he did, but not so with
Vernon and Carole? Those were the two people he had always
counted on, always trusted, always respected. But what did that
get him? A kick in the ass and a rude awakening. God knows why
Carole was beating up on him, her life was going the way she
wanted—her and Sonji were getting married and were planning
for a baby, and Vernon had unveiled his true face, that of jealousy.
He never would have thought Vernon a jealous dude, not after all
these years, but then again, hadn't Kyle heard somewhere that to
trust blindly is to be stupid? Stupid he had been. Hell, who
needed friends? Kyle didn't, not if it meant having to explain to
Vernon that he'd never make a move on his woman.

For the first time in a long time, Kyle wished he could sit down
and talk to his grandfather, but he was gone, wasn't he? *Granddad
never judged me or criticized me.* Sure his grandfather used to tell
him to respect himself and the women he was with, but he would-
n't lambaste him like he was an idiot child. More importantly, his
grandfather always had time to listen to him when he needed to

talk. Kyle missed their long talks, the sharing of stories. His grandfather's stories were always great—that is, until he got sick and the pain scrambled his thinking and disturbed his mind. In the beginning, Kyle felt bad that he couldn't bring himself to visit his grandfather and would call him to talk, but when it seemed his grandfather started talking out of his head, incoherent at times, Kyle couldn't deal with it and started calling less and less until he stopped calling altogether. That really upset his mother and she let him know it with her tongue-lashings, but Kyle wouldn't let her browbeat him into witnessing his grandfather's descent into senility. No one in the family but Carole and Vernon understood that—at least they'd said they did.

His body washed, his face shaven, Kyle scrambled up three eggs while listening to Robin Roberts update the morning news on Channel 7. He shook several stingy droplets of hot sauce onto the eggs with the hope that the hot sauce would open up the stuffy nose he was beginning to get. He topped off his breakfast with two slices of dark, crunchy toast and a glass of ginger ale just as the doorbell rang.

"The office door was closed," Diane said. "Aren't you opening up this morning?"

"My mother didn't call you last night?"

"No, was she supposed to?"

Damn. Exhaling his annoyance, Kyle stepped aside for Diane to come in. Since she was there, he may as well open up the office. There really was no legitimate reason why his staff couldn't do their work.

"Do me a favor. Go down through the back hall and open up the office for me.?"

"Is everything all right? I mean besides your grandfather dying? You sound nasal."

"Yeah, I started sneezing this morning, but I'm fine. My father's in the hospital, though."

"My God, is he all right?"

"He has a blockage in the colon. I think he'll be going into surgery this morning."

Kyle began walking Diane toward the back hall stairs leading to the basement office.

"He'll come through fine, Kyle, I know he will. What hospital?"

"Brookdale."

"Dr. Charles is on staff there. Did you call him?"

"No, I'm sure Dad'll be fine." The truth was, Kyle hadn't thought about Dr. Charles, who was an excellent gastroenterologist. He should have called him first thing this morning. By now, it was probably too late.

"I'll say a prayer for your father. Are you going over?"

"No, my brother and sister are there with my mother. We have family coming in from out of town, so I'm hanging around to let them in."

"Kyle, I'll let them in if you wanna go to the hospital."

Yeah, he could go to the hospital . . . but his mother would have a fit if he wasn't here to let his aunt and the rest of the family in. "Thanks, Diane, but you won't know when someone's ringing the bell at my parents' house, and I'm not sure if any of them know to ring my bell. I'll have to keep an eye out for them. Thanks, anyway."

"Okay."

At the top of the stairs to the basement, Kyle switched on the light, illuminating the basement. "Other than some transcription, there shouldn't be much else to do. If you'll go over the Gibson medical report and get started on the Jones transcription, I'd appreciate it."

"Okay."

"I believe Lucille and Nadine already have work on their desks. If they finish early, today's mail should bring in more work."

"Okay." Diane started to go down the stairs but turned back to Kyle. "Is Grace coming in today?"

"Ah, no. I don't think so."

"I wonder what's her problem. Anyway, Kyle, you know I'm here for you."

"I know, thanks." He coughed several times.

Diane put the back of her hand to Kyle's forehead. "Do you need me to get something for you? You have any cough medicine in the house?"

Annoyed, he eased her hand away. "Diane, I'm all right, don't worry. I'm sure I have something around here."

"If you need anything, Kyle, anything at all, just ask." Full on the lips, open mouth, tongue leading the way, Diane kissed Kyle, taking him by surprise.

He immediately pulled back. "You're gonna catch my cold."

"I doubt it. I'm so full of vitamin C and cod-liver oil capsules, a cold would be afraid to invade my body. I can't tell you the last time I had a cold."

"I guess I better get me some C's and nasty cod-liver oil capsules." What could he get to keep her from coming on to him? A kiss from Diane was as far from his mind as California was from the Atlantic Ocean. With all that was on his mind, Kyle wasn't in the mood for a quick piece, and at that moment, he decided that he wasn't ever sleeping with another one of his employees. He hadn't slept with Diane as much as he'd slept with Grace, but they had rolled around on his office sofa and did the desk hump more times than he could recall. Diane was married with three children, and at the age of thirty-four was frustrated that her husband was no longer touching her up like he used to. Kyle could empathize with her knowing how hot she was, but she couldn't count on him to scratch her itch anymore. She was going to have to whip her husband into shape or get herself another man. Yet, he hoped he wasn't going to lose Diane like he did Grace when he called it quits. His business couldn't take it.

He watched Diane descend the stairs. "Take messages for me. Call me only if it's important—a new client or an urgent request."

"Okay."

As soon as Diane was out of sight, Kyle closed the door, but he didn't lock it—his employees didn't have a run of the house upstairs. He returned to the living room just as the telephone started ringing.

"Hello?"

"Dad's in surgery," Carole said.

"Who's the surgeon?"

"A Doctor Bernardi."

The name was not familiar. "How long will the procedure take?"

"Depending on what the doctor finds, two hours or more. Kyle, cancer is a possibility."

"Let's not dwell on that right now. Let's see what the doctor finds. Where's Mom?"

"Press took her to breakfast. Anything happening there?"

"No."

There was an awkward silence from both ends of the line.

"Kyle, when this is over, we have to talk."

"Carole, tell Mom to call me when she comes back." He hung up the phone and went to the window just as Lucille was entering the yard. Her black wool hat was pulled down over her forehead like she was trying to hide from old-man winter. Lucille didn't like the cold, she was from Houston. Kyle never understood fully why and how people from hot climates can relocate to a city like New York, where the winters can be brutal, and then they whine and complain about being cold, yet don't pack up and get their ass back home on the fastest thing flying. Whatever was holding Lucille here, Kyle didn't know, she didn't appear to be happy here. Anyway, he was glad that Lucille was on time for a change. There was plenty of work to keep her busy as well, but he'd go down around noon to make sure everything was okay. He had work to do himself, but he didn't feel like being bothered.

Ten-fifteen. Kyle doubted if any of his family would be arriving this early. He changed from Channel 7 to CNN, the all-news cable channel, to see what the country had to worry about today besides the war in Iraq. Kyle could feel his tiredness coming down on him. He began to slowly roll his neck from side to side, releasing some of the tension from his early morning arguments, and then stretching his arms wide, he pushed them back, expanding his chest, feeling the pull that relaxed him a bit more. What he needed was a nap, especially after banging Lorna a few times last night and that awful dream that had awakened him. Yep, sacking out on the sofa was the best thing he could do for himself.

As soon as Kyle lay back, his body was embraced by the cushions. Two sleepy bats of his eyes—he was gone.

The curtains sailed open. Kyle was sitting in the mezzanine, front row, aisle seat center of a huge theater looking down on an empty stage.

Below him, the orchestra seats were full, on either side of him the seats were empty. In fact, all the seats in the mezzanine were empty. Kyle was not disturbed by the empty seats around him, he was comfortable. He looked again at the stage. A young actor appeared on stage wearing a pair of black suspenders over his bare chest that were attached to a pair of black boxers. On his feet, the actor wore a pair of white high-top sneakers. Kyle snickered at the actor's outfit, yet he was aware that the actor had no discernable features to identify him. The actor began to dance, moving his body comically to a tune only he seemed to hear. The sight tickled Kyle, he felt himself laughing, but not on the outside, only in his head. He looked around and saw that he was still sitting alone but he was no longer in the mezzanine, he was now sitting in the center of the orchestra quite a number of rows back from the stage. All the other seats that were once occupied, were now empty. He looked up at the mezzanine, but he could not tell if the seats were empty or not. He was puzzled. He looked left to right, right to left, and suddenly, Carole was sitting next to him, her attention on the actor on stage.

Focusing again on the stage, Kyle saw that the actor was still dancing when suddenly, a woman—naked on top, clad in matching black boxers on the bottom—materialized on stage. Her breasts were large and full, they hung down between the straps of the suspenders. Like the actor, the woman's face was indistinguishable. The woman began dancing around the man. The man continued to dance, seemingly unaware that the woman was there. The woman began tapping the man on the shoulder; he did not turn to face her, he closed his eyes, ignoring the woman. The woman took off her suspenders, wrapped one end around her hand, and started whipping the man, hitting him with the metal-teethed clip ends of the suspenders.

Inexplicably, Kyle began to jerk away from the stinging lashes of the metal clips. He realized that he was no longer sitting in the orchestra, he was now on stage, naked on top wearing suspenders attached to black boxers. The woman was beating him; she was brutal, she was hurting him. Kyle tried to cry out; he opened his mouth to scream, but he was voiceless. He took off running about the stage, trying to escape the woman's wrath. He could not escape, the woman was right on his heels. In the center of the stage, out of breath, he dropped to the floor, cowering, covering his head with his arms. He didn't see, but he knew that he was bleeding from the welts and cuts caused by the metal-teethed clip ends of the suspenders.

Abruptly, the beating stopped. Kyle wondered why, but he was too afraid to uncover his head. In his agony, the sound of applause, an audience clapping louder and louder penetrated Kyle's ears. He peeked out and saw that the theater was full of people, standing, applauding as if they had just seen a great performance, as if he had just performed. Right in front, he saw his mother, his father, his sister, his brother, and his best friend, Vernon. All the people who were supposed to care about him were applauding and doing nothing to help him. Kyle couldn't believe it. He peered up at the woman and was startled to see that the woman, whose face he couldn't distinguish before, was his great-grandmother. Her wide, high-cheeked features were prominent and clear. Her long, black, braided hair lay on her shoulders down to her waist. Her eyes were sad; her lips were rigid. Fully clothed, she was handing the suspenders, which were now broken—the clips were missing—to someone. Kyle looked to see whose hand was taking the suspenders. His eyes widened when he saw that his grandfather, again dressed in white, had the suspenders in hand, and in slow motion, raised them above his head, but in a blink of an eye they were no longer suspenders but two long bands of rawhide, looking to Kyle like a riding crop. His grandfather whipped the rawhide down across Kyle's face, opening up a long, ugly gash across his right cheek. In agonizing pain, Kyle flopped onto his belly, clawing at the floor trying to crawl away but the unrelenting sting of the rawhide stayed with him. The sound of applause echoed loudly throughout the theater.

Writhing in pain, Kyle started to holler, "Granddad! Granddad! Why are you beating me?"

His grandfather's mouth did not move. He struck Kyle harder with each determined descent of the rawhide.

"Stop! Stop! Stop!"

"Wake up, Kyle! Wake up!"

Hands were all over Kyle. He tried peeling them off, but someone was holding both his arms down while someone else had him around the neck, choking him.

"Kyle!" Lucille slapped Kyle hard across the face.

Gasping, Kyle's eyes sprang open! He locked eyes with

Lucille. What the hell was she doing there? Yeah, he was definitely in a nightmare.

Lucille shook Kyle. "Wake up, man!"

"My God, Kyle," Diane said, "you scared us to death. We thought someone was killing you up here."

The arm around Kyle's neck had not slackened, he was gasping desperately.

"Nadine, he can't breathe," Diane said. "Let go of him."

"He might—"

"Let him go!" Lucille said. "His eyes are about to pop out of his head."

Nadine quickly removed her arm. "You better be careful, he might lose it again."

"He's awake," Diane said, wiping the sweat from Kyle's forehead with her own hand. "Get him some water."

Nadine rushed off to the kitchen.

Kyle strained to get his breathing under control. His throat was dry and scratchy, and he felt groggy. This was a bad one.

Diane gently ran her finger along Kyle's jawline. "You have an ugly welt on your face. It wasn't there earlier."

Feeling the long, tender welt for himself, Kyle remembered the slash of the riding crop across his face in the dream.

"He probably scratched himself in his sleep," Lucille said, looking at Kyle's well-manicured nails. "Babies do that all the time."

"Well, I'm not a baby." Kyle used his elbows to get Lucille and Diane off of him. The only thing that felt scratchy was his throat.

Diane began rubbing the nape of Kyle's neck. "What were you dreaming about?"

He brushed Diane's hand away and said brusquely, "A pigeon-toed ballerina."

"He's awake now," Lucille said, stretching her eyes.

"Can I get you something, Kyle?" Diane asked.

"No." He didn't like that Diane or any one of his employees had seen him acting like a punk over a stupid dream, and he certainly didn't like them fussing over him.

"It must have been horrible," Lucille offered. "My heart almost stopped when you started screaming."

"Mine, too," Nadine said, coming back into the room carrying a glass of water.

Taking the water, Kyle put some bass in his voice. "I didn't scream." He drank the whole glass down in one long gulp.

"Oh, you did scream," Nadine said, "and you screamed loud."

Kyle slammed the glass down on the coffee table. "I did not scream!" He pushed himself up off the sofa and hurriedly got himself from in between Lucille and Diane. "Don't you all have work to do?"

Lucille looked from Diane to Nadine. "I guess we're no longer needed up here." She got up off the sofa.

Kyle looked at Lucille. *For damn sure you're not.*

Nadine smirked. "We were working, boss man."

"Yeah," Lucille said, "we came up here to rescue you."

"I didn't need rescuing! Get the hell back to work."

"Excuse me." Lucille put her hand on her hip. "Who are you talking to like that?"

"I'm talking to you. You wanna get paid, get your ass back to work."

Diane sprang to her feet. "Okay, we're getting carried away here." She nudged Lucille away from Kyle. "Lucille, let's go back to work."

"He can't talk to me like that. I'm not a child. I don't have to take his shit."

Kyle faced her. "You're right about that, Lucille. You don't have to take my shit. Get the fuck outta my house. You're fired!"

"Kyle!" Diane shrieked.

"No fucking problem," Lucille said. "I don't like working here, anyway."

"Then get the fuck out!"

Lucille stormed from the room, leaving Diane and Nadine stunned by what had just transpired before them.

"I never liked her, anyway." Kyle went to the front door and opened both the wooden door and the outer glass storm door, inviting in the cool, invigorating March air. Soon it would be summer. He'd remove the glass in the storm door, replace it with the screen panel, and leave the wooden door open and have fresh air and light streaming in all the time.

"Kyle," Diane said, "Lucille was only trying to help. We all were."

"I didn't need any help. I told you I was fine."

"But—"

"Come on," Nadine said, taking Diane by the arm, "we have work to do."

"Watch that woman," Kyle said. "She is to take nothing of mine out of here."

Diane shook her head, but Nadine gave Kyle an ugly glance. She was going to quit a whole lot sooner than she had planned. She didn't like working for a man who screwed his employees.

This time, Kyle locked the door at the top of the stairs leading to the basement. From now on, when he wasn't down there, he'd always lock it. Back on the sofa, he tried to make sense of the dream. What the hell was it with the suspenders and boxers, and why was he being beat with first the suspenders and then the riding crop? It made no sense, he couldn't figure any of it out. He dropped his head back and closed his eyes. His dreams were getting worse. If it was like Lorna had said, his grandfather was worrying about him, then he wasn't liking the way he worried. Better he didn't worry at all, he was messing up his sleep. It seemed more like his grandfather wanted to hurt him.

Kyle gingerly touched the welt on his face. There was no question that he scratched himself while he was dreaming that he was being beaten by his grandfather. There was no other explanation. He would be insane if he believed otherwise. But even in a dream, why would his grandfather want to beat him like that? Could it be like Lorna said? Could there be something to that shaman thing?

Chapter
16

Kyle felt miserable. His nose was stuffy, yet it kept running like a leaky faucet. His eyes were tired, watery, and red, and he wanted to close them in the worst kind of way, but sleep was the last thing he wanted to do. He pushed up the volume on his stereo while Gerald Levert passionately promised his woman a night of loving she'd never forget, which quickly grated on Kyle's nerves, so he quickly skipped to the upbeat, head-bobbing, pulsating Mary J. Blige CD, but it only made his head pound and failed to obliterate the haunting vision of his grandfather—dressed in a black suit and tie and a bright white shirt, laid out in his casket, still as a mannequin, his face chalky from a bad makeup job, with a long-ass white eagle feather in his hands atop his chest—from Kyle's mind. Nothing was working for Kyle, not even talking to himself about all he had to do. He couldn't stop thinking about how he stood frozen at the side of his grandfather's casket, staring at him, feeling that at any moment his grandfather would open his eyes, sit up, and point his long finger of damnation and reproach at him.

Although it was questionable, Kyle knew he wasn't losing his mind. He was quite cognizant that his grandfather was dead, that it was in his dreams that his grandfather was so disturbingly alive, and it was those dreams that were scaring the hell out of him. They seemed too real, too three-dimensional, and they were fucking with his sleep. He hadn't slept since yesterday morning when Diane, Lucille, and Nadine woke him up from his nightmare. There was no shame in his game, but he would never tell a living soul that as tired as he was, he was scared to close his eyes. Sleep was his nemesis, a siren's call, and Kyle had no desire to willingly succumb to its alluring embrace.

What kept coming to mind was the day his grandfather died. His grandfather had died clutching his hand, and Kyle remembered his father saying, "It's like he wanted to take Kyle with him." As stupid as those words sounded then, they were far from stupid now. After the dreams he'd had, it was as if his grandfather had indeed tried to take him with him just so he could kick his ass in the afterworld. If Kyle didn't know better, he'd think that his grandfather died angry at him for not visiting him more in the nursing home or at the hospital. Hell, if that was the case, then a whole lot of people were being jacked up by dead parents and grandparents.

Earlier, at the funeral, everyone must have thought Kyle was overwhelmed with grief when he had to be helped back to his seat after reading his grandfather's death song. He remembered when he wrote the death song, he was so much closer to his grandfather.

My grandfather, Preston White Cloud Howell, was a wise man, a quiet man, a spiritual man. He was at peace with himself, because he knew he lived his life to its fullest and for the love of his family. If you ever had the honor of knowing my grandfather, then you knew that he was blessed with the kindest heart and the humblest soul. He was a brilliant man blessed with native intelligence. He was smarter than any man I've ever known. He was not college educated, he was life educated. My grandfather was a highly decorated New York City fireman for 25 years. After he retired he became a successful businessman who started a hardware store with two thousand hard-earned dollars and parlayed that little bit of money into a million-dollar business. He was never one to let a little word like "can't" stop him from fulfilling his dreams.

Granddad, you have always been my rock. You have always been my best friend. Never was there a time when I couldn't count on you or know that you would selflessly put my wants above yours. You were that way with everyone you loved; you cared most for the lives you brought into this world. We, your children, Granddad, will never forget you; you're forever a part of our souls. We will miss you, but we know that we were blessed to have had you at all. Our love for you, Granddad, burns eternally.

Those words choked Kyle up a few times, but he didn't cry or show any kind of distress—although his nose kept running from the cold and his eyes were watery and drawn—until he had finished reading. He turned to look at his grandfather's casket and, for some reason, was drawn to it. He wanted to return to his seat, but he stood staring at his grandfather's closed casket, unable to pull himself away. It was as if some force kept him there, his feet planted, his mind frozen. He felt the snot on his upper lip, but couldn't raise his hand to wipe it away. He couldn't even bend to pick up the death song when it slipped from his hand to the floor. It was Preston who came up to him and whispered, "Are you all right?" and tugged at him to get him moving. Everyone watching might have been thinking they understood what he was going through, but none had a clue, and it would remain that way. He hated that blowing his nose and coughing kept everyone looking his way.

Since returning from the cemetery, after he'd gotten rid of Vernon and his girlfriend, Kyle had been hiding out in his basement office while overhead, people, mostly strangers, shuffled around his house, more than likely scuffing up his hardwood floors and snooping in his closets and drawers. A sudden thump made Kyle clench his jaw to suppress the urge to bolt upstairs and kick everyone out. His Aunt Agatha and Uncle Otis had gotten in just after four yesterday afternoon along with their daughter, Helen, who brought her two children—Francine, who was a well-developed thirteen-year-old, and Raj, a fifteen-year-old thug in training. Raj wore all of his clothes three sizes too big for his gangly frame. His baggy jeans hung off his narrow ass and bellowed over his spotless tan boots, while his triple X sweatshirt ballooned around his scrawny body and his shiny black do-rag hugged his head like a skull cap. The boy needed to be schooled that looking like a thug wasn't for everyone, especially when he wore horn-rimmed glasses, a mouthful of plastic-tracked braces, and didn't have an inch of clear, unscarred acne skin on his face. Kyle almost wanted to pull the boy aside and talk to him himself, but he wasn't up to getting involved with any of his family. He had no relationship with any of his out-of-town kin and wanted to keep it that way. It was hard enough dealing with his parents constantly nipping at his heels, Carole's bossiness, and Press's condescending superciliousness at every gathering. All were a pain in his ass and always had something to say about the way he lived his life, which was none of their damn business. Christmas shopping this year was going to be a breeze, he wasn't buying a damn thing for anyone, not even his employees. They would be lucky if they got a Christmas card.

Yesterday afternoon, just before Diane and Nadine—neither of whom were speaking to him—left for the day, Kyle apologized for raising his voice at them and asked Diane to call Lucille and ask her to come back to work. He desperately needed her; the work was starting to back up and Kyle wasn't of a mind to pound on a keyboard his damn self. He wouldn't know until Monday if Lucille accepted his apology. He closed the office down until then, and that's where he'd been tucked away since his relatives started arriving. He'd locked the upstairs door to the basement, and neither the loud voices nor the door bell buzzing were reason enough to pull him from down there. Until those intruders left his house, in his office was where he'd stay.

Riiiing! Kyle checked the caller ID to see whose number would flash. It was Audrey's.

He answered, "Hey, baby, what's up?"

"Just called to see how the funeral went. How're your parents?"

"They made it through. You free tonight?"

"Actually, I'm meeting a colleague for dinner."

That wasn't what Kyle wanted to hear. He needed to get out.

"Perhaps we can get together on Sunday."

"Sure. Why not." He'd play it cool, but he was disappointed. He sniffled. "So who're you going to dinner with?"

"A colleague, Eric Bonner. Kyle, you sound nasal. You have a cold?"

"A slight one. Where're you going for dinner?"

"Actually, I don't know. I left it to Eric. Kyle . . . we need to talk."

Those were words Kyle never liked to hear from a woman, especially when she was avoiding his questions. "What do we need to talk about?"

"Us—you and I . . ."

Oh, hell.

"Kyle, I need to know where we might be headed in our relationship."

It wasn't like Kyle didn't know the day was coming when he'd have to dump or get off the pot, but this wasn't the time to decide either way. "I'll bite, Audrey. Are you having second thoughts about being with me?"

"Well, no, but after three years, Kyle, I think we need to discuss whether we want the same thing or not."

"Depends on what that thing is. What—"

"Marriage, Kyle. I want marriage."

How was he supposed to tell Audrey that marriage anytime soon, like in the next ten years, was out of the question. For now, she was at the top of the list, but who knew whom he might meet tomorrow.

"Let's talk Sunday," Kyle said, not necessarily meaning this Sunday. "So, any word on the judgeship?"

"Actually, I got a call today—"

Buzzzz!

Kyle glanced at the office door. Damn! He wished whoever it was would leave him the hell alone.

"From the Mayor's office—"

"Audrey, I have to go. Someone's at the door."

"Oh, okay. I'll—"

Wondering who was at the door, Kyle dismissed Audrey with the press of his thumb on the Talk button. Carole and Preston both knew that he had to be down in his office if they couldn't find him upstairs. He wanted to see neither, but it was probably one of them looking to get him to take his turn fawning over their mother and being her errand boy. With their father missing the funeral because he was still in the hospital, their mother was emotionally and physically sapping them all dry. Thank God for short hospital stays.

"Dad's fine, he'll be home Friday," Carole said yesterday evening. "The blockage was removed. There was no cancer, and he doesn't have to wear a waste bag for six weeks, which is what he feared most."

Buzzzz!

As much as he hated to, Kyle opened the door.

"Want some company?" Gail asked.

Relieved, Kyle pecked Gail on the cheek and got a faint, spicy whiff of oriental flowers. "You smell good. Eden, right?"

"You have a cold, how can you smell my perfume?"

"Easy, you're wearing a lot of it."

Gail playfully punched Kyle in the stomach. "I am not!"

Laughing, Kyle held his stomach. "You've never worn Eden before. I like it."

"I've been wearing Eden since our divorce, so it's not for you I wear it. I wear it for me and my husband."

"Damn, don't be so cold."

"I'm just setting you straight."

"Excuse me, Mrs. Serrano. So you don't like Shalimar anymore?"

Gail gave Kyle a ho-hum look. "Shalimar is the past, Kyle. For me, there's no allure anymore. It doesn't go well with my chemistry."

Kyle wasn't stupid, he got Gail's message, but he flirted anyway. "Maybe I can put a little spark in that chemistry we used to have between us." He went to take Gail into his arms.

She slapped him away. "Boy, when're you gonna get over yourself?"

Laughing, Kyle kissed Gail on the cheek anyway. "The day before I die. Where's Dawn?"

"With Carole. You know how they get along."

"Yeah, like Tinkerbell and Peter Pan."

Chuckling, Gail looked around the office. "I see you have a new copier—nice."

"It handles the volume." Sneezing, Kyle continued on into his office where there was a love seat. "Want something to drink?"

"No, I'm fine, but you need to take something for that cold.

You sound terrible, and look even worse." Gail sat and so did Kyle. "Don't sit so close to me, I don't want your cold." Gail widened the space between them. "What're you taking, anyway?"

"My mother's next door," Kyle said, annoyed.

"Yeah, and? Answer the question, Kyle. What are you taking for your cold?"

"Man, you've gotten bossy. I feel sorry for Luis."

"Luis is a happy man—he has me."

A slow smile spread across Kyle's lips. "Is that right?"

"Stop playing with me, Kyle. What are you taking for your cold? You were never good about taking care of yourself."

With a heavy sigh, Kyle answered, "Ginger tea with honey and lemon."

"Kyle, you need to take cold tablets. Ginger tea with honey and lemon isn't going to break a cold."

"I'm not coughing as much as I was."

"Wait till you go to bed tonight. That's when the coughing starts."

Checking out Gail's long, shapely legs in her black stockings, Kyle seductively licked his lips. "Come to bed with me."

"Kyle!"

"Seriously, Gail. Your being here has already cured my headache. I'm sure making love to you will do wonders for my cold."

"Too bad your making love to me didn't do wonders for our marriage."

"Oh, that hurt," Kyle said, putting his hand over his heart.

"Kyle, stop playing. Get over yourself. Besides, I'm immune to you now. So be serious. How have you been?"

Kyle couldn't help but smile at his failed seduction. Yeah, Gail was well over him. For almost a year after separating from Gail, he could still seduce her into sleeping with him, and having sex with her post marriage was just as good as their premarital sex. But then Gail got religion. "It's not right. We're divorced. I've met someone. I don't cheat." Boy, he hated the first guy she hooked up with—he felt like the guy stole Gail from him. He could admit it now, he was angry with her for closing up shop on him. For the longest time, he wouldn't go around to see Dawn. That's when Carole stepped in. She popped him upside the head and scolded, "Grow up, Kyle! Being a father to your child isn't conditioned upon her mother's vagina being open for you to plug up. Get over it; that hole is closed to you." And, indeed, it was, but it took a while for him to get used to seeing Gail without wanting some. Two years ago when she remarried he didn't attend the wedding, he couldn't handle it. Of course it didn't help that her new husband, Luis, turned out to be not such a bad guy. Luis was a good stepfather, Dawn seemed to love him, and Gail never looked happier or better.

"Everyone's worried about you," Gail said.

"I don't see why. They're worrying for nothing."

"Are they, Kyle? You have dark rings under your eyes, you look a little thin, and Mom says you've been real testy. Are you getting any rest?"

Subconsciously, Kyle touched his stomach. It was hard and flat as it should be. He hadn't been eating very much, he wasn't hungry. His mother and Gail had remained close after his divorce, which he didn't mind, but he did mind that his mother talked about him to Gail. He could only hope that she didn't tell Gail about Grace.

"I have a cold, remember? No taste for food. And you can blame my irritability on my cold also, in addition to my busy schedule."

"That's been your excuse lately when you're supposed to be taking Dawn. She misses you, Kyle."

"I stop by to see Dawn at least once a week."

"For an hour, Kyle? You need to see her more."

"I have every intention of seeing my daughter on a more regular schedule as soon as my workload lets up. In fact, let's plan on Dawn spending the second weekend of next month with me."

"April? "Kyle, how are you gonna plan for a weekend four, five weeks away?"

Kyle went to his desk. "By putting it on my calendar." Which he did. "I can't help that I'm so busy."

"Don't play games, Kyle. Dawn'll be very upset if you stand her up."

"Don't worry, I won't." He returned to the sofa. "So what's new in your life?"

Laying her hand on her small, round belly, Gail lovingly patted it.

A sick feeling hit Kyle in the pit of his stomach. Pulling back, he looked at Gail's hand on her not so quite flat stomach. He hadn't noticed its roundness.

"I'm four months."

"Wow." What else could he say? Another man had gotten his wife—his ex-wife—pregnant.

Smiling still, Gail nodded.

Kyle tried to smile, but he didn't feel like his lips budged. "So Dawn finally gets a playmate."

"Yes, and she's very excited about it."

A strange feeling of sadness settled on Kyle. The thought of Gail having another man's baby left a sour taste in his already tasteless mouth.

"You're happy for me, aren't you, Kyle? You know I always wanted another baby."

"Sure, I'm happy for you." Kyle got up. He took a sip of his cold tea. He frowned.

"Eww. That must be nasty."

"Look, congrats to you and Luis."

"I'll tell him. He's really happy. He's been wanting a baby, boy or girl, it doesn't matter."

Coughing, Kyle didn't know what to say to that. He could remember wanting Dawn like that. For sure now he was going to have to spend more time with Dawn, Luis might push her aside once his own baby was born. Kyle blew his nose and tossed the tissue at the wastepaper basket six feet away, making it.

Buzzzz!

Kyle asked. "Doesn't your husband trust you with me?"

Gail rubbed her stomach. "Implicitly."

"He's stupid. We used to do it when you were pregnant, remember?"

"I do now, too."

"Gail, I didn't need to know that." Kyle went to answer the door.

"How long are you planning to stay down here?" Carole asked as soon as Kyle opened the door.

Kyle blocked the doorway with his arm. "What do you want, Carole?"

"I see your mood hasn't improved." She gave him the once-over. "Do you mind?"

Kyle stayed put. "Where's Dawn? She's supposed to be with you."

Gail came silently into the outer office from Kyle's office.

"Dawn should've been with you," Carole said, "but she's with her other daddy."

"Do us both a favor, Carole. Go back next door."

With her shoulder, Carole shoved Kyle aside. "Get outta my way."

"Next time, knock him down," Gail said.

"You're wrong, Carole. If I had pushed you back, you'd be bitching about me manhandling you."

"Damn right. Don't you ever put your hands on me."

"You tell him, Carole. I think you're the only woman he's ever been afraid of."

"That's because she's mean," Kyle said, remembering how when they were kids and Carole, always the tomboy, would fight him as hard as any guy when he picked on her, even if she couldn't win. She'd end up crying not because he hurt her, which he never did, but because she couldn't beat him.

Carole boldly put her hands on her hips. "What's going on with you, Kyle? Whomever or whatever has jammed that thorn up your ass we need to talk about, because I can't take much more of your attitude."

Kyle slammed his office door to the darkness and chill that touched his back. Seeing Gail over Carole's shoulder stopped him from jumping all over Carole. Gail would come to her defense. He didn't need both of them flapping their lips at him.

"Carole, is there a reason you're down here busting my balls?"

"Gail," Carole said without turning to face Gail, "Luis is ready to leave."

"Good, so am I," Gail said. Passing Carole, she kissed her on the cheek. "I'll call you tomorrow."

"Get home safe."

"Aren't you leaving with her?" Kyle asked Carole.

"No."

At the door, Gail paused. "Carole, find out what's wrong. He didn't tell me a thing."

As with his mother, it never bothered Kyle that his sister and ex-wife still got along so well, it did bother him that they often ganged up on him.

Gail pecked him on the cheek. "Take some cold tablets."

"Go boss your husband." Kyle closed the door once he saw Gail reach the stoop of his parents' house.

"You were stupid to let her go," Carole said.

"What do you want, Carole?" Kyle sat behind Lucille's desk. The picture of her son and daughter was gone. Unless Diane could convince Lucille to return, he was going to have a horrible Monday. Again he blew his nose and tossed the tissue, this time missing the basket.

Carole sat in the chair alongside Lucille's desk facing Kyle. "Vernon looks good. He seems to be totally smitten with his girl-friend. What's her name?"

"Jennifer, and I don't wanna talk about her or Vernon."

"No skin off my nose. Look, everyone's starting to leave. Mom needs you next door."

"Why? Are you leaving too?"

"Soon. I'm going with Sonji to drive her parents back up to Port Jervis. We may stay over."

"We don't have to go into you not getting behind the wheel, do we?"

"For one thing, smarty, Sonji's father is driving Sonji's car back, but I might drive us back on Saturday. And FYI, I'm a much better driver than I used to be. I've been practicing highway dri-ving."

"Well damn, Carole, after ten years of pretending to drive, it's about time you got the hang of turning your head, moving your eyes, and using your hands and your feet all at the same time."

"So I've never been especially well coordinated, sue me. I probably drive just as well as anyone else out here."

"You got that wrong, sis. You drive worse than anyone else out here. If people know like I know, they'd get off the road when you get behind the wheel."

"Geez, thanks, Kyle. Thanks for sinking my confidence."

"No, I'm just trying to save your life, and a lot of innocent people, Carole, know your limitations. Don't drive going or coming from Port Jervis, it's too risky."

Her feelings hurt, Carole said, "I'll keep that in mind, big brother. Hey, but wasn't it nice of Sonji's parents to come to the funeral?"

"Yeah, I guess. You will be part of the family soon." It always amazed Kyle that Sonji's parents never seemed to miss a beat in accepting that Sonji was a lesbian. Carole said they cried, but they never condemned Sonji or gave her ultimatums. Kyle always found that interesting, especially since Sonji was second-generation Pakistani. As a people, he didn't know they were so liberal.

"Anyway," Carole said, "Aunt Louise and Aunt Tess are staying with Mom till Sunday. Aunt Agatha and Uncle Otis are leaving tomorrow morning, but Helen is flying out tonight with her kids; she has to work tomorrow night. Press is taking them out to LaGuardia, but he has to go on home from there; he has a scheduled surgery tomorrow morning."

"And Mom wouldn't wanna interfere with Dr. Lawson's schedule, would she?"

"Kyle, you need to get over your anger with Press; he hasn't done a damn thing to you. He told me what happened the other night, and Mom told me why Grace quit."

"So everyone tells you how bad a boy I've been. Am I supposed to be scared of you or something?"

"There you go being childish again."

Kyle could feel his annoyance level reaching its peak. "That's it. Get the hell outta my house, Carole, before I throw you out."

"That's a real good way to handle this, Kyle. Throw me, and

everyone who tries to tell you that you have a problem that you're not addressing, out of your house."

"Everyone should mind their damn business and leave me the hell alone."

"Is that what you really want, Kyle? Will us leaving you alone get you to straighten out your life any faster?"

His headache was back with a vengeance. "Goddamn it, Carole—"

"Stop it! Don't you even start."

Kyle instantly clammed up.

"Kyle, I'm not down here to go toe to toe with you. Mom needs you right now. You're gonna have to go up and be with her in case she needs something. And tomorrow, you need to go pick up Dad. Can you do that, Kyle? Can we depend on you for that?"

"I don't know, Carole. If I were you, I wouldn't depend on me. In fact, if I'm such a no-account deadbeat, why would any of you depend on me for anything?"

"That's just it, Kyle, at one time you were very dependable. The question is, what changed you? Is all that pussy rotting your brain?"

Kyle slammed his hand down on the desk and shot up out of his chair, sending his achy head spinning. He had to close his eyes for a second to let the pain in his head settle in one spot.

"Kyle, you have got to get it together. You have to make some changes in your life. You have to—"

"Speaking of change, Carole. As I see it, you've changed."

"Oh what are we doing, Kyle? Tit for tat? Now you're gonna tell me how I've changed?"

"That's right. Since you were promoted to senior field reporter—"

Carole gasped.

"Perhaps looking down on me pushing papers around this little office from your high perch makes me look less than respectable."

"You can't be serious!"

"I don't have the high-profile jobs—the prestige—that you and Press have. I'm the black sheep—"

"That's the biggest crock of crap I've ever heard you sputter." Carole turned in her chair as Kyle walked away. "I've had this position for three years, and the only thing that's changed about me is my paycheck. Kyle, don't take out what you feel is your shortcoming on me or Press. If you don't feel good about what you're doing, then you need to close up this business and get yourself into something you can be proud of, because—"

"I'm damn proud of what I'm doing." His head was banging. God, he needed to lie down.

"Then why are you harping on what Press and I do for a living? If you feel like a failure, then—"

"Failure! I ain't no goddamn failure! My business is doing damn well. I earned well over half a million dollars last year. I think that qualifies me as a certified success, and I don't have to punch a clock in someone else's office."

Carole folded her arms. "Well, bully for you, Kyle. Since your business life is such a success, then surely it must be your personal life that's warping your mind and screwing you up, and by the way, that is the consensus. It seems the more women you date, the more screwed up you become. One of them or all of them must be filling your head with lies about your prowess, because you seem to be all about yourself these days. You don't give a damn about this family."

"Oh, so I'm selfish because I don't jump through hoops when Mom tells me to, or because I won't let Dad tell me how to live my life? I'm a grown man. I—"

"Kyle, you're a selfish man. You don't strain yourself to go see your daughter, your only child, more often than you go to see those broads you're screwing—"

"I see my daughter! You don't know—"

"Your father, our father, was rushed to the hospital and you didn't know because you were at some woman's house twisted into a pretzel up her ass. Kyle, you couldn't spare a minute to visit an old man, your grandfather, who worshipped the ground you walked on, and you're selfish because you don't care that your mother was scared out of her mind that she might lose her husband when she had yet to bury her father."

Kyle had no quick retort, no words to explain anything he was accused of. Folding his arms, he sat on the corner of Lucille's desk, wishing that he had a place he could escape to. He quickly snatched several tissues from the box on Lucille's desk and blew his nose, hard, but there was no relief in his clogged nose or stuffy head. He really did need to take something, but he didn't want to fall asleep from the drugs.

Carole went and sat shoulder to shoulder with Kyle. He tried to lean away from her, but she pressed her shoulder into him.

"I'm not angry with you, Kyle. You know I love you—a lot. But in truth, I'm a little disappointed in you. You're messing up, brother, and I don't know why. And what's worse, I don't know how to help you."

Kyle fixed his tired eyes on the large water jar in the corner when it inexplicably burped and its center gulped. He almost laughed, but not at the water. It was strange that Carole should choose to say that she was disappointed in him. She was his little sister. She was younger than both he and Press. And above all, she was gay, which disappointed their parents. How ironic that she would be disappointed in him.

"It's obvious that something's wrong, Kyle. Whatever it is, you can tell me. Talking is what you and I always did best, let's not lose that."

Kyle moved away from Carole and sat in the chair. What was he going to say? *Financially, little sis, I'm in trouble, can you bail me out? Or, I'm having these terrible dreams. Granddad is kicking my ass, can you make him stop? And yes, I may have one too many women who want me for the money I don't have. Can you help me make better choices in women?*

"Kyle—"

"Carole, aren't Sonji and her parents waiting for you?"

Carole gently pushed her long curly brown hair back behind her right ear. "Like Gail said, Kyle, take care of that cold. I'm going. You know my number."

Carole was barely an inch on the other side of the door when Kyle shut the door, double bolting it. He wasn't letting another

living soul in tonight to annoy the hell out of him. He'd had
enough. Every nerve in his body was fired up, and the only way
he could think of to alleviate the stress and open up his stuffy
head was to hump until he was too tired to think and too exhausted to dream. He knew who to call.

Chapter
17

"Hello?"

Kyle quietly clicked the Talk button, anonymously disconnecting his second call in fifteen minutes to Lorna before she figured out that it was him on the other end. It was a good thing she didn't have caller ID or *69. On one hand, he knew damn well he didn't need to complicate his life any more by being with Lorna or Dalia, for that matter, both of whom had their reasons for wanting more of him than he was willing to give. It was quite obvious Dalia wanted him for his deep pockets, where as Lorna might really be in love with him. Of the two women, Lorna was pushing him the hardest for a commitment. The truth was, he didn't want to be with any one of the women beyond the bedroom. He really wasn't in love with any of them and had been thinking about curtailing his visits with them. But tonight his need for one or the other was pressing. Tonight, he needed someone to keep him up in more ways than one so the dreams that haunted him would not find him. Dalia more than Lorna would—

Riiiing!

A quick glimpse of the caller ID box gave Kyle pause. *I be-damn!* It was Dalia. Maybe it was a sign. He let the telephone ring once more.

First coughing to clear his throat, he answered, "Yeah."

"Hey, baby, how you doin'?"

"The best I can, Dalia, what's up?"

"You, baby. I wanna see you."

The sound of heavy footfalls overhead made Kyle look annoyedly up at the ceiling. His cousins were gone and he thought Aunt Agatha and Uncle Otis had gone to bed. It was almost eleven o'clock, and as late as it was, he figured he could go upstairs without bumping into them.

"Why? You got something for me?"

"Me. Baby, don't you want some of me tonight? Don't you want me to suck you like a big, juicy Popsicle?"

"What man wouldn't?" While he said the words, Kyle wasn't feeling his own words or Dalia's. That surprised him, especially when only a minute ago that's all he craved, and usually all it ever took to get on the bone was to hear Dalia say what she was going to do to him. Kyle touched himself, but nothing in his pants moved.

"I'm wearing your favorite—a red satin G-string."

"Are you?" Kyle tried to imagine Dalia in nothing but that G-string, lying on her bed on her back with her thighs wide open. Nothing. He couldn't even begin to picture her in his mind. Maybe it was the cold. Maybe he was sicker than he thought. Maybe he had pneumonia.

"Hold on a minute." Putting the telephone down, Kyle blew his nose, not once but twice. He then drank the rest of his cold, bitter tea. He really wasn't feeling Dalia.

"Dalia, it's kinda late. We buried—"

"It's not late, Kyle! I'm wide awake and really hot in my ass for you. I wanna be with you, baby. I'm horny!"

"Well, damn. Is it like that?"

"Hell yeah! My hand ain't doin' a damn thing for me. I want your hand up my ass."

"Goddamn." It wasn't Dalia's blatant words that surprised Kyle. That was her, that's what turned him on, usually, about her. It was the fact that he wasn't responding to her that surprised him. Nothing was happening in his pants or in his mind, and that really troubled him. He sat heavily behind his desk. If he couldn't get it up just thinking about what Dalia was doing with her hand or what she wanted him to do, then he had a problem, and that was a problem that he'd never had before.

"Are you coming, Kyle? How soon will you be here?"

Kyle started coughing. "Baby, I have a bad cold. I can hardly breathe."

"Believe me, I got a cure for that."

"I bet you do, but I think I better stay home."

"Kyyyyle! I wanna see you, baby. I wanna see you tonight. I'll come to your house, okay? Let me come over there."

That wasn't happening. All kinds of alarms were going off in Kyle's head. Dalia was pushing too hard for this to be just a booty call. "Dalia, we buried my grandfather today. I have family staying over, so it's not—"

"Then come over here."

Yeah, much too hard. "Not tonight, baby. Why don't I come by on Saturday?"

"Saturday's too late, Kyle. I need to see you tonight, all right?"

Dalia's panic level had risen. "Dalia, why is Saturday too late? Are you gonna dry up by then?"

"I'm horny tonight, Kyle! I wanna see you tonight!"

The earsplitting shrillness in Dalia's voice made Kyle pull the telephone from his ear. Yeah, something was up. "Okay, Dalia, what's the real deal? And don't tell me you're so horny you just got to see me because of my special charm. Why do you *really* need to see me this night?"

Dalia said nothing.

"I don't have all night. Spit it out."

"I need a thousand dollars, okay? And I need it tonight. Can you give it to me, Kyle? I'll pay you back. I promise I will."

Of course, it was the money. Hadn't their relationship been based on how much money he gave Dalia from the first day when she asked for one hundred dollars to pay her cell phone bill just minutes after he pulled out of her. Hadn't he kept their lascivious relationship going by giving her cash and a credit card? Damn right she was horny for him. She needed him to stoke her pussy with a handful of large dead presidents.

"Kyle, please. I'm behind in my rent. I need to give my landlord some money tomorrow. If you lend me the money, Kyle, I'll give it back to you in two weeks. So can I come over—"

"I don't have it."

"Kyle, I said I'd give it back to you. I will. I promise."

"Dalia, I really don't have it. If I had it, I'd give it to you. My cash flow has been pretty one-sided these days. I'm strapped. I'm sorry."

"You're lyin'!"

"I don't have it. I can't give you what I don't have."

Dalia clicked off her phone, leaving a dead sound in Kyle's ear. He clicked off his own phone. "Good night to you, too."

Now breathing through his mouth, Kyle closed his eyes and lay his head back against the back of the love seat. God, he was tired. He didn't feel bad about Dalia hanging up on him, she did him a favor. He could no longer afford to be her sugar daddy. At least if he had been able to get it up, he would have gotten his money's worth, although that would have been some expensive pussy that he could no longer afford. Oh, hell, he may as well stay home. Besides, one of his heads was clogged, and the other was down for the count.

Buzzzzz!

"Now what!"

Buzzzz!

"Oh, hell no. I'm not answering it." Kyle got up anyway and went to the window. He carefully peeked out.

Damn! It was his mother and she wasn't wearing a coat. *Damn!* She stood with her shoulders hunched up to her ears and her arms tightly crossed. *Damn!* As much as he wanted to, he couldn't ignore her. He opened the door.

"It's about time." Betty hurried inside.

"Mom, what are you doing out at this hour and without a coat?"

"I'm only staying a minute. I brought you some cold tablets and some cough medicine."

He reluctantly closed the door. "You didn't need to. I'm fine."

"Kyle, you have a bad cold."

"And it'll run its course. I said I'm fine."

Betty filled a paper cup from the water cooler in the front office. "Take this." She held two large green gel capsules in her hand.

Kyle stepped back. "I don't need it." What he didn't need was to fall asleep. Isn't that what cold medicine made people do?

Betty thrust her open hand out toward Kyle. "Take them."

Betty and Kyle locked eyes. Betty's clear eyes were uncompromising; Kyle's watery eyes wavered. "Now, Kyle, I'm not leaving until you swallow both of them, and if you don't take them, I'm going to tell you how I feel about how you've been behaving."

Practically snatching the capsules from Betty's hands, Kyle slammed them into his own mouth. If he had to listen to her bitch, he might kill her. And maybe if he did fall asleep, he'd sleep deep enough not to dream. Taking the water, he quickly downed the capsules, while Betty poured a capful of dark red syrupy cough medicine into a small plastic cap.

"The capsules are enough. I don't need that."

"Drink it."

"Mom—"

Betty thrust the full cap against Kyle's chest, almost spilling the thick, syrupy elixir on his shirt. "Take it."

It was either take it or stand there and argue with her and Kyle had no desire, feeling as bad as he did, to butt heads with his stubborn mother. He snatched the cap and slammed it down on his tongue, banging it three times on his tongue to empty it completely.

"You happy now?"

"Kyle, I'm too tired to fight with you. You're a grown man. I shouldn't have to reprimand you or tell you what to do for your own good."

"Then don't. I'm tired of telling all of you to get off my back and to stop treating me like some mindless adolescent who can't discern right from wrong or up from down."

Betty arched her brow. "You said it, I didn't."

Taken aback, Kyle felt like a fist had just been rammed into his gut. "You know, Mom, my mistake was moving next door to you. You've beat Dad down, now you're trying to beat me down." The hurt look that flashed in his mother's eyes made Kyle immediately regret his words. "I meant—"

"I know what you meant, Kyle. You think because I'm always

on your father that I've beat him down, henpecked him so he's less of a man. You'd see it that way; you've always been down on me for so-called bossing your dad around. Well, I'm here to tell you you're wrong. What goes on between me and your dad only we understand. But let me tell you a little something about our relationship. Your father has always been and he always will be a procrastinator. He's in the hospital right now because he didn't do what he was supposed to do, and that was to get a baseline colonoscopy years ago when he turned fifty, and even one four years ago when he turned sixty. I tried to make him go, but did he? Oh, no, not him. He was too macho."

"Well, Mom, I guess I can understand how Dad felt about getting the procedure. I know how important it is, but I'm not real eager to get a colonoscopy either when I'm due."

"Then both of you are silly. If your father had gotten the colonoscopy, he would have avoided this painful episode of diverticulitis. Me? I take care of myself, and that means going to the doctor for routine tests and examinations. I . . ."

"That's because you're perfect," Kyle mumbled.

". . . never wait to the last minute to do anything," Betty said, not hearing what Kyle said. "Your father waits to the last minute to do everything, and a lot of times, he misses out on important things because he forgets. I'm the ribbon around your father's finger, Kyle. I'm the pushy woman who stands behind him, behind you, and this whole family."

Kyle let out a long, heavy breath. "Mom, please—"

"Your father is a good man, Kyle; but like so many men of his generation, he wasn't raised to run his household, he was raised to run his wife, and I wasn't having it. So if you think because I'm always on your dad about something that I'm beating him down, think again. And the next time you think about opening your smart-ass mouth about what goes on between me and your father, don't."

There was nothing Kyle could say. His mother was right. His father was a procrastinator, and they all knew it. How many times had he waited until the last minute to get his car inspected and ended up forgetting the date altogether and getting a ticket.

"Next time—"

"Okay, Mom, I got the message. But you do beat down on me all the time."

"That's because you always give me reason to, Kyle. Now take your smartass to bed, and tomorrow morning, take two more of these capsules after breakfast."

Betty thrust a small box of cold capsules in Kyle's hand.

At the door Betty turned back. "Oh, and in the morning, Kyle, show your family some Lawson hospitality. You were taught manners—act like it. Believe me, your grandfather wouldn't like the way you've been behaving. You're—"

"How am I behaving, Mom? What have I done that's so wrong?"

"Everything, and it's sad you don't know it."

"How could I not know? I know I'm not hurting anyone, killing anyone—"

"That you know of. Maybe—"

"I'm done. You're not making any sense."

"Not to you, but who's surprised? Oh, and I have your gold turtle. I'll get it fixed for you if you want, although I don't think you're deserving of it anymore."

"Then I tell you what. You keep it, or better still, give it to Preston. I'm sure he's most deserving."

Betty leveled a pitying gaze on her middle child. "You truly don't get it, do you, Kyle? Your grandfather thought you were most deserving. But then again, he's the one who spoiled you. I wish he could come back and slap you upside the head and knock some sense into you. He was the only one you'd ever listen to as a child."

Kyle felt his heart actually quiver. If his mother only knew. Suddenly he felt sick. That syrupy cough medicine had begun to make his empty stomach churn.

"What's wrong with you? You look like someone just walked on your grave."

"Why would you say something like that to me?"

"Something like what?"

"Dead people, Granddad, coming back to mess with me. I mean, could that happen?"

"Boy, stop talking nonsense."

"Is it nonsense if I dream about Granddad like he was still alive."

Betty studied Kyle's troubled eyes. "You've been dreaming about Dad?"

Kyle scratched his head. If he told her, she would go off on some tangent about his grandfather haunting him.

"You have, haven't you? So Dad's paid you a visit. I haven't dreamt about him yet. He hasn't visited me once, but I wish he would. I've been waiting. Has he said anything to you? Is he okay?"

"Is he supposed to say something to me? And what's this about a visit? What does that mean?"

"Exactly what it sounds like—a visit. Someone who's passed on who doesn't want to or can't let go visits someone they loved very much in their dreams. It's called a visit. Right after my mother died, she used to visit me all the time. Daddy, too. After a while she stopped coming. I miss her."

"Were they good dreams?"

"Beautiful dreams. She came to let me know that she was okay. She also came when Dawn was born. In fact, she came when each of Preston's children were born. Are your dreams with Dad good? How do you feel when you wake up?"

Kyle couldn't tell her the real deal. No telling how she'd interpret his dreams.

"They're just dreams, Mom."

"But what happens in the dreams?"

"Nothing. Look, I'm tired. Mom, please, please go home."

"Okay, so don't tell me. I expect to see you at breakfast at eight o'clock sharp?"

"And I have no say about that, huh?"

"Sure you do. Just say it after breakfast."

Staring at the door through which his mother had gone, Kyle clenched and unclenched his jaw. He hated that she always made him feel like a kid. It seemed in his mother's eyes he had never grown up. She never treated Preston or Carole like that, and that really angered him about her. But, on the other hand, he felt like a fool. No matter how angry his mother was at him, she still cared enough to take care of him. In his anger at her, he had avoided her and hadn't been very cordial to anyone else. All his relatives probably thought he was a selfish bastard, and they had probably been talking about him. He certainly didn't relish sitting and eating breakfast with any one of them.

Yawning, his eyes tired and heavy, his head weighing a ton on his shoulders, Kyle yearned for his bed, but he didn't think he could get his legs to carry him up two flights of stairs. Again locking his office door, he dragged himself into his office and collapsed on his love seat, one leg hanging over the arm, the other stretched out on the floor. Even before he blacked out, he felt his head spinning and his body floating up off the sofa. Sleep was a frightening but welcome release.

Chapter 18

His sight blinded by the cloth tied around his eyes, Kyle felt the sensual butterfly touches of the soft hands that grazed his bare buttocks, chest, back, shoulders, and arms. Kyle stood. His feet bare, his toes wiggling in what felt like soft, cool sand. He slowly turned and reached out, trying to touch whomever was touching him. He smiled as his fingertips brushed the soft skin of an elusive woman who would not let him catch her in a firm hold. He couldn't hear her laughter, but he could feel her flirtatious playfulness as she gently held his hand to her naked body and guided him to the place she wanted him to lightly touch. Even blindfolded, Kyle knew the feel of a soft, round breast and the nubbiness of a perky, suckable nipple. Another pair of hands alighted on his back and drifted down to his buttocks and lightly squeezed him. There was more than one woman—oh, there was yet a third pair of hands on Kyle's chest.

Kyle was liking this game of reach out and touch. He liked being touched, and he liked touching. His seasoned hands expertly discerned the roundness of a palmable ass, as well as the voluptuous curves and the flat, tight stomach of a taut, toned woman, each different from the next in some deliciously subtle way that his mind intuitively surmised. With every touch of his own hands and the hands that touched him, a feeling of sexual energy surged through Kyle's own body, speeding up his heart, heating up his skin, hardening and elongating him until the heaviness in his groin drew his hands to hold on to it to support it, to lovingly stroke the great extended length of it. Kyle wanted to see with his own eyes what he held in his hands, and he wanted to see the women who teased him mercilessly. He raised his left hand to remove the blindfold, but was stopped. Hands grabbed at his arm pulling his hand away from his face, keeping him from seeing what they had the pleasure of beholding. Kyle started to wrench his arm free when a pair of soft hands caressed his penis, stroking it, making it throb. He could smell her, the woman in front of him in whose hands he was massaged. She smelled of jasmine and orchids. She smelled like Lorna. Oh, yes, he was in for an erotic treat.

From behind, a warm body pressed up against Kyle, gently grinding him, while arms encircled his waist. His own arms dropped to his sides, his head rolled back as someone began kissing him on his back. Where Lorna's hands had been, now what had to be her tongue—wet and warm—began tonguing him, slowly drawing him into her mouth, wide and ready. Kyle smiled and completely gave himself over to her and to the other women to have their way with him.

In the next instant, Kyle was no longer standing. He was flat on his back, his eyes still covered, his body resting on something furry and soft. He was being kissed, massaged, and sucked off like he'd never been before. He wanted to see these women, he wanted to see if, indeed, Lorna was one of them. But each time he made a move to lift the blindfold from his eyes, hands stopped him. So he relaxed and let his mind and body enjoy the pleasure of what was being done to him. When a woman straddled his face, he did not hesitate to use his own tongue to relish her as if she were the finest of crème brûlée. And that's when a faint smell of musty lilacs and apricots filled his nostrils. He recognized that perfume—Tresor—it was Audrey's favorite. It pleased Kyle that it was Audrey he was enjoying, she was always as succulent and strong tasting as her perfume. She . . . suddenly the smell of lilacs and apricots grew heavy and bitter, gagging Kyle, putting a nauseatingly sour taste in his mouth. He tried to turn his face away, but Audrey's thighs held his head steadfast as she pressed herself into his mouth and nose, suffocating him. Kyle tried to rise up, but couldn't—Audrey's body atop his shoulders and her legs and another's hands held his arms penned to his sides, while someone lay on his right leg. The sour taste in Kyle's mouth, as well as the stiflingly burning sensation in his throat, was at odds with the intense arousal he was still feeling in his groin. The mouth that no longer felt like Lorna's but more like Dalia's was sucking him hard, drawing him deeper inside, pulling him into a full-blown Fourth of July ejaculation.

Kyle wanted to breathe, he wanted to relish completely the blow job he was getting. He struggled harder to free himself, and with a mighty bucking of his body, he threw Audrey off the top of his shoulders and as well freed himself of the hands that restrained him, but the mouth that sucked on him held fast, it was still there. He had to see who it was who had not been shaken off. Quickly removing the blindfold, Kyle could not believe his startled eyes. His jaw dropped, his heart stopped. He gawked in disbelief. He was horrified to see his penis in the mouth of a giant black snake! Frozen in fear, he was unable to move, unable to think as he watched the snake, coiled around his right leg, wrap its tongue around the length of his penis. Totally transfixed and totally conflicted, he was filled with terror while getting the best blow job he'd ever had. He was close to exploding. Then as if the snake realized that it was being watched, it stopped tonguing Kyle and looked at him with the beadiest, blackest eyes Kyle had ever seen. His huge penis instantly shrank inside itself—away from the snake's tongue—no longer eager to expel the nectar that would have brought forth a mind-numbing explosion of pleasure. Kyle's breath caught in his throat as the snake, its black eyes fixed on him, reared up, readying itself to strike. Pulse-pounding fear gripped Kyle.

Screaming, Kyle fell back onto his elbows and pushed off with the heels of his feet, scooting frantically backward, trying to get away from the snake just as the snake—mouth wide open, fangs bared—lunged at him. Recoiling into a tight ball, his head tucked against his chest, his eyes squeezed shut, Kyle clamped both hands protectively around his shriveled penis and balls. He couldn't stop screaming as he waited for the pain to come . . . he waited . . . he waited . . . none came. Curious but cautious, still coiled up as tight as a fist, his heart pounding in his chest, Kyle peeked warily out at where he knew the snake to be—above him. Again, his eyes bugged. There was no snake, there was no Audrey, there were no women in sight at all. Standing in front of Kyle—his arms akimbo, his legs apart, his head held high, his eyes as black as the beady eyes of the snake that was coiled around his leg—was his grandfather.

Kyle sat bolt upright, gasping for air, his throat tight, his tongue dry, his face, his body drenched with sweat. Deep, undulating waves of pulsating pain shot through Kyle's head.

Grunting and grimacing, he closed his eyes and pressed the balls of his hands to his forehead to try to still the pain in his head. He stayed like that for almost a full minute, breathing through his mouth, aching, and remembering the dream. In his delirium, Kyle looked anxiously around the room. A sliver of bright light from the side of the window blinds bounced off his eyes, sending a shock of piercing pain into his eyes and head. He quickly closed his eyes, and when he opened them, first one eye, then the other, he shifted out of the path of the ray of sunlight. He was in his office sitting on the floor. How the hell had he gotten down on the floor? Last night, he had fallen asleep on the love seat after taking those green cold capsules his mother had forced on him. They were probably spiked with some kind of mind-altering drug to kill his sex drive or castrate him altogether. Maybe that's what the dream was about.

That dream! God, that dream was awful. That snake! Kyle grabbed for his crotch. Thank God, he was all there. What in the world was that dream about? How could he be getting a blow job from Lorna one minute, at least he thought it was Lorna—he never got a look at her—and be sucked off by a big, black-ass snake the next? It was crazy. The whole damn dream was crazy. And his grandfather? Why in the hell was his grandfather popping up in his dreams? How did he get to his grandfather from the women and the snake? He could understand the connection between the women and the snake—they were both slippery and dangerous—yet nothing about that dream made sense. Why had he been blindfolded? Why couldn't he see the women who enticed and tantalized him? And the perfume, it was awful. How he could smell something so clearly in his dreams befuddled him. Just thinking about that smell made him want to throw up even now.

What could it all mean—him being blindfolded; a big, black-ass snake on his dick; the women? He might not have wanted to know before about his dreams, but he sure as hell needed to know now. These freaky-ass nightmares were happening too frequently and were messing with his head in more ways than one. In fact, Kyle's head was killing him. Maybe if he blew his nose he could relieve some of the pressure in his sinuses and his head. He took a deep breath and blew his nose into the tissue he took from his pocket. Again, he had to squeeze his eyes shut to try and quiet the pain that shot through his head. It didn't work. Turning clumsily onto his knees, Kyle leaned briefly against the seat cushion of the love seat before using it to lamely hoist himself up off the floor, but he quickly flopped down onto the love seat and slouched back, his achy head resting against the back. It felt like the veins at the front of his head were near to bursting. Kyle didn't know if his headache came from the cold or from the nightmare. Maybe Lorna was right. Maybe he needed to talk to her aunt—whatever her name was. Lorna was the last person he needed to be calling on, but somebody had to tell him something about what was going on in his sleep. Maybe he could catch Lorna before she left for work.

Lorna answered on the second ring, *"Hello."*

"Hey," Kyle said, holding his head.

"I was just on my way out."

"You all right?"

"What do you think, Kyle? I am very hurt."

"I'm sorry you feel that way, Lorna, but when we met and you said you were married, we both agreed we wouldn't let ourselves get too serious."

"Yes, but that was some time ago, Kyle. Do you think I could be with you and not fall in love with you?"

Kyle rubbed his forehead. Big mistake.

"Do you not care anything for me, Kyle? Did you make love to me and not care?"

Damn! "I care, Lorna. I care for you a lot, but I don't think we should be talking marriage while you're still married." Kyle felt boxed in. "I can't see you anymore if you're gonna—"

"Okay, okay, I won't talk marriage until I am divorced."

Damn, what are you, stupid? I'm not gonna talk marriage to you even then.

"Okay, Kyle?"

"Cool. Look, let me tell you why I called. The other day, you mentioned you had an aunt who interprets dreams."

"Yes, Aunt Yasmin. She is my mother's sister. She was born with the gift."

"So does that mean she's for real? Because, Lorna, I don't have time to be hoodwinked. I—"

"Kyle, Aunt Yasmin is for real. She does not pretend. She—"

"I need to meet her."

"You had another of those dreams?"

"I need to meet with your aunt today, Lorna. Can you arrange it?"

"Kyle, Aunt Yasmin is not home in her house here. She do not like the cold."

"So where is she?"

"She is with her daughter, my cousin Ella, in her Florida home."

"So can she do her psychic thing over the telephone like they used to do on the Psychic Hotline years ago?"

"I do not know about the Psychic Hotline, but Aunt Yasmin will not read for anyone on the telephone. She must be in the presence of the one she reads for. She say the essence is strongest in person."

"Okay. So if I flew down there, do you think she'd see me?"

"People come from all over to see Aunt Yasmin, no matter where she is."

"Then call your aunt, Lorna. Tell her I need to see her. I can fly down to Florida today."

"I thought you did not believe, Kyle."

"I don't."

"Then why are you asking to see my aunt?"

"Look . . . I have no choice."

"It is that bad?"

"If I'm entertaining the idea of seeing your aunt Lorna, what do you think?"

"Okay, Kyle, I will call her, and I will go with you."

"No . . . no, Lorna. I can do this. You don't need to go, besides you have work and school."

"I will take off, Kyle. You will need me to introduce you to my aunt."

"Why? Can't I meet her without you?"

"No, my aunt will not take an audience with a stranger. Each of her clients is a referral."

"Okay, so when you call, tell her about me so she'll know who I am when I show up."

"Kyle, it is best I go with you. My aunt is very particular about new people who come into her house."

Whether that was true or not, Kyle didn't know. Lorna was probably lying just so she could be with him, but the truth was, under the circumstances, it might be best she be with him when he met her aunt. This wasn't a social call.

"Look, you can go with me, but you can't be messing with my head talking about marriage and divorcing your husband. I can't handle that right now."

"I will not worry your mind about me."

"Good—"

Beeeep! The call waiting tone signaled in Kyle's ear.

"Because this trip isn't about us."

Beeeep!

"I have another call. Call me as soon as you talk to your aunt."

"I—"

"Kyle pressed the Flash button, disconnecting Lorna. "Yeah."

"We're waiting breakfast for you," Betty Lawson said.

"You all go on ahead, I'm not hungry."

"Come anyway."

Betty hung up before Kyle could say another word.

Kyle's first thought, *I'm not going!* His second thought, *Damn!*

His mother's nagging tongue was worse by far than his nagging headache. He may as well get it over with. Kyle went to the bathroom in the back of his office and, ignoring the tired eyes and puffiness he saw in the mirror over the sink, popped four ibuprofen tablets into his mouth along with two of the cold capsules his mother had given him last night and downed them with flat, warm water from the faucet. He didn't have to worry about falling asleep, he was too hyped. He headed next door without changing his clothes—why bother? He wasn't trying to impress anyone.

Chapter
19

Kyle hadn't allowed himself to be lulled by the airplane engine into the deep sleep he usually fell into on smooth-flying 747s. Although his eyes teared from his cold and from lack of sleep, he resisted closing his eyes. Twice he had to pop NoDoz tablets, but it seemed his need for sleep was stronger than the drug. And as soon as he convinced Lorna to wash off as much of her perfume as she could, he was able to breathe much easier—her perfume had been making him nauseous. Remnants of that dream were, disturbingly, still with him.

The two-hour-and-forty-minute flight to Jacksonville with Lorna, hugged up on his arm, asleep at his side most of the way, had given Kyle time to catch up on what little reading he could. On his way out of the house he'd grabbed *Trouble Man* by Travis Hunter off the bookshelf. He'd had it for more than two years and until now had never gotten around to reading a single page—he'd been that busy. By the time Kyle landed in Jacksonville, he felt a kinship with Jermaine Banks and the troubles in his life. Like Jermaine, Kyle was beginning to see that he just might have to make some changes in his own life. However, unlike Jermaine, Kyle was about to step outside of the real world in which he was so well rooted and into a world that was best left to ghost, goblins, and soothsayers. His mother and father would have a stroke if they knew that he was going to see a fortune-teller, they'd be calling him every kind of heathen, which is why, after he brought his father home from the hospital, he quickly excused himself without telling anyone where he was going or why. He'd packed an overnight bag and carried it out to his car in a big, black garbage bag—just in case his mother was looking out the window. After he and Lorna saw her aunt, they could hang out and enjoy some of Jacksonville's nightlife. That is, as long as she didn't pressure him, he could relax and enjoy being with her. He'd be back by Sunday evening—no one the wiser that he had even left town.

Three hours after landing, Kyle sat, stiff-necked, ass tight, thumb tensely twiddling in the large crowded front room of Lorna's aunt, Yasmin Rabb, impatiently waiting his turn for an audience with "Lady Yasmin," as she was known by her loyal clientele. Mentally ticking off the number of people waiting—seventeen—Kyle was reminded why he hated having to go to the doctor—the wait. He'd read once that most doctors schedule three patients for the same half-hour appointment just in case one or more of the patients didn't show up, so they'd still have someone to see at any given time. Kyle believed that, because no matter how early he always tried to be to the dentist or to his family doctor, he inevitably had to wait, minimally, an hour before he was seen. And now, even though Lorna had connections, hell she was Lady Yasmin's favorite niece from New York, he still had to wait his turn.

If it wasn't for the warm weather, Kyle wouldn't believe that he was in Jacksonville—it was seventy-eight degrees. He'd left New York wearing a heavy leather jacket and hadn't thought of putting it back on until he'd sat over an hour waiting to see Lorna's aunt. There was no question that the air conditioner was working—it felt like forty degrees in the waiting room, even with all those people giving off body heat. Kyle never would have imagined that he'd be sitting in a room with a bunch of strangers waiting to see a fortune-teller. Damn, how strange was that? Him seeking the advice of a fortune-teller, who would have thunk it? Even stranger that he came all this way, and that was because he didn't know where else to turn. He couldn't see himself walking blindly up a flight of stairs, over some bodega on Amsterdam Avenue in Washington Heights, not knowing a soul, trying to ask strangers about his dreams. At least Lorna knew Lady Yasmin, and that counted for something. Her cousin, Ella, told her that she and Kyle could wait in another more private section of the house, but Kyle wanted to wait with everyone else. He wanted to see people's faces after they'd been with Lady Yasmin.

Every time someone exited the red door, Kyle tried to determine whether he could see in their faces, in their eyes, some mystical revelation that whatever they sought from Lady Yasmin was realized. Most of their faces were as blank as when they passed through the red door. He wanted to see what was on the other side of that red door, but at the angle at which he sat, Kyle could see nothing beyond the opening and closing of the door. What if he came all this way and all he got was a trough of hogwash? What if he was proved right that fortune-tellers were nothing but scam artists? What if he didn't like what Lady Yasmin had to say? What if—

"Relax," Lorna said, returning to her seat next to Kyle after talking at length with her cousin. She patted Kyle on his knee. He had been shaking it a mile a minute. "There are just three people ahead of us now."

Kyle inhaled deeply and took his time letting his lungs deflate. Strange, he hadn't sniffled once since landing in Florida. Besides the warm weather, maybe all that medicine had finally kicked in. Then again, maybe his head had cleared up because he was nervous as hell.

"Do not worry, my aunt will put your mind at ease."

He said softly, "For what she charges, I should hope so."

"She will. Trust me."

Kyle felt the look of indignation from the lady sitting across from him before he actually saw it. She probably didn't like the remark about the charges, but what did he care. Fortune-telling was a business and money was a big part of it. The question was, what was he going to get for his one hundred dollars?

"You told her all about me, right?"

"No, I told you, she would not let me tell her about you. She knows nothing of your dreams. She said she do not want to be tainted by what I might tell her. I told her only that you need help. She said to bring you."

Again, Kyle looked around the room. They were sitting in the front room that had to be the living room of the house. There were two bright, large, floral pattern sofas, each holding four people squeezed next to each other, and chairs, some folding, some fixed, were placed in every available spot in the room. There was no coffee table or end tables, no lamps, but every white-trimmed sky blue wall had a picture of a tropical scene—beach, palm trees, idyllic sunsets. Now looking at the people waiting patiently to see Lady Yasmin, he saw that most of them—young, middle-aged, old as dirt—were women, all running their mouths, talking about nothing at all. The three men besides himself that waited seemed to be asleep, their eyes were closed, their heads were down. Maybe they felt as he did, out of place at a gathering for a bunch of hens, but Kyle didn't dare close his eyes for fear that sleep would seize him and snatch him deep into a dark tunnel of horror.

Kyle whispered to Lorna, "Why can't you tell me what she looks like?"

"Because it is best you see her for yourself and not through my eyes."

It frustrated Kyle that he had not been able to get Lorna to tell him much about her aunt beyond her ability to read dreams. Why the mystery?

"I need some air." Kyle went outside and stood on the front porch. He inhaled a lungful of fresh air. Clasping his hands behind his back, Kyle pulled his arms up high in line with his shoulders, pulling hard, stretching and easing the stiffness in his shoulders and chest. Feeling better, he resigned himself to waiting a bit longer to find out what it was his grandfather was trying to tell him.

An hour later, after two more people had left the house, Lorna came outside. "My aunt will see you now."

Chapter
20

As soon as Kyle stepped on the other side of the red door, so many things assaulted his senses—he inhaled the strong, redolent smell of burning incense, while his eyes slowly adjusted to the smoky haze that filled the dimly lit room and focused on the flicker of several white candles placed throughout. He immediately noticed that the room, shrouded in yards and yards of sheer red fabric, ceiling to floor, covering every wall and every window, giving the room the feel of an Arabian tent, was warmer by far than the waiting room. But it was Lady Yasmin who commanded Kyle's full attention.

He stood with his back to the closed red door as Lorna and her aunt kissed each other's cheek and embraced warmly. Since Lorna would tell him nothing, Kyle didn't know what to expect. He was enthralled by the woman he saw. Lady Yasmin was no spring chicken, she was at least in her mid-sixties, but she was a good-looking, regal-looking woman. She stood at least six feet tall, and perhaps she appeared so tall because of the long white embroidered caftan she wore. Whether she had high heels on her feet underneath, Kyle didn't know, but somehow he figured she might be barefooted—she looked to be the type of woman who was more comfortable when her feet were bare. Most striking about Lady Yasmin was her long, gray, ropelike locks snaking down her back to where Kyle had yet to see, but if the two ropes of locks that draped over her shoulder down the front of her caftan were any indication of the length that reached down her back, then her locks were nearly to the floor.

And what amazed Kyle, with all that gray hair, not a single wrinkle marred Lady Yasmin's glowingly unblemished ebony skin. She was a beautiful black woman who had to have been a mesmerizing beauty in her youth. Kyle wondered what kind of body lay hidden under her full-flowing caftan.

"Lorna," Lady Yasmin said, releasing her niece, "you and I must also talk."

Kyle noticed the low, melodic timbre of Lady Yasmin's Carribean accent.

"I am okay, Auntie Yasmin. Everything is well with me."

"I am not so sure of that," Lady Yasmin said, touching Lorna's face. "I feel something in your essence that we must talk about. How is your husband?"

"He is fine, Auntie Yasmin." Feeling a mite uneasy, Lorna turned to Kyle. "Kyle, this is my Aunt Yasmin. Aunt Yasmin, this is my friend, Kyle Lawson."

"Kyle," Lady Yasmin said, extending her hand just a few inches toward Kyle, forcing him to move closer to her to take her hand.

Kyle realized that Lady Yasmin didn't so much shake his hand as let her hand lie in his as if he were expected to bow or kiss the back of it. Unsure if he should, Kyle decided not to.

"Thank you for agreeing to see me. I've been having these—"

"I am always available for those who need me. Welcome to my home."

"Thank you." Again uncertain as to when he should let go of Lady Yasmin's hand since she didn't pull her hand back, Kyle continued to hold it. It was then, in spite of the burning incense, that he got a faint whiff of Lady Yasmin's savory perfume. It was a scent he didn't know. It was a scent that didn't nauseate him.

"I like your perfume. What is it?"

Lady Yasmin said nothing as she looked steadily into Kyle's eyes. Kyle was unnerved by the hard stare and the hazel brilliance of Lady Yasmin's eyes. With such dark skin, light-colored eyes was the last thing he expected. But then he wondered if those eyes were hers from birth or the magical transformation of colored contact lenses.

Trancelike, Lady Yasmin quietly took hold of Kyle's hand with both of hers. She began to hum a song that was spiritual in sound, that was, like her perfume, foreign to Kyle. Her hold was gentle at first, but then her grasp tightened and her stare grew more intense as her breathing deepened. Kyle looked anxiously from Lady Yasmin to Lorna. He was taken aback by the worry he saw on Lorna's face.

"It is bad," Lady Yasmin said, closing her eyes and holding firm to Kyle while she continued to hum her spiritual.

Kyle could feel the strain of his own breathing. He wasn't liking this. "What's she doing?"

"She is getting in touch with your aura."

"Leave us," Lady Yasmin said, speaking to Lorna.

"No, I want her to stay."

"My aunt knows best," Lorna said. "I will wait for you outside." Lorna hurriedly left the room.

Alone with Lady Yasmin, Kyle tried to ease his hand out of her grasp. She held him firm.

Lady Yasmin opened her eyes. "You were right to come. Your aura is troubled."

What was he supposed to say to that? Of course he was troubled, that's why he was there. He didn't need a fortune-teller to tell him that—anyone in the waiting room could have told him that.

"Look, I don't know about this aura thing. I just need you to—"

"You are not a believer, but that changes nothing for me. I get paid no matter your belief. I will read what I see."

Kyle was beginning to feel like he was about to be swindled, but he had come this far, he may as well see what her game was. "Miss Yasmin—"

"Lady Yasmin," she corrected, still holding on to Kyle's hand. "Come." She led him to the small white marble table sitting in the center of the room upon which sat a single large white burning candle and a square of white silk atop a small mound. With a grim nod, she indicated that Kyle should sit, and once he did, she let go of his hand. Then sitting across from him, Lady Yasmin lifted the square of silk revealing a brand-new deck of tarot cards that she'd already ordered the way she wanted them to be. With both hands, she picked up the cards and began to slowly shuffle them. She didn't look down at the cards, she looked instead into Kyle's eyes.

"Lady Yasmin, I need you to—"

"Shh." Lady Yasmin pointed her long, manicured, white-nailed finger at Kyle. "Do not disturb the spirits." Lady Yasmin continued to methodically shuffle the cards with expert hands. She shuffled a long time, testing Kyle's already short patience. Finally, she set the stack of cards on the table in the center, closer to Kyle.

Instinctively, Kyle knew to cut the cards. That done, he watched as Lady Yasmin fanned the entire deck, face down, out in front of her. When she did that, Kyle was reminded of the game of high/low he played as a boy to see who'd get the lowest card and would have to take the dare that would usually get the taker in trouble. Was he going to get in trouble now?

"Choose," Lady Yasmin said, her voice low and sultry. "Choose your fate. Choose seven cards."

Feeling cocky, Kyle quickly slid the first card out and was about to pick it up.

"You must leave it as it is, unturned, on the table."

Unfazed, Kyle quickly chose six more cards. Now he settled back, skeptical that anything could be read in the cards that would remotely touch on his life. More and more it dawned on him that he had wasted his time and money coming to Florida.

Lady Yasmin fixed her gaze on Kyle as she began to daintily float her right hand back and forth a few inches above the cards Kyle had chosen.

Kyle exhaled his annoyance with the theatrics and with Lady Yasmin for not letting him tell her about his dreams. "This is a mistake," he said, starting to stand.

"Sit!" Lady Yasmin ordered. "You will disturb the spirits."

"Look, I didn't come all this way to—"

"You must sit, or you will not hear what must be said."

"Why won't you let me tell you why I'm here?"

"Because, like you, I already know why you're here. I'm here to tell you what you don't already know, and that is a whole lot. Do you want me to continue or not?"

A strong feeling of doubt overwhelmed Kyle, but he sat anyway under the stern, reproachful glare of Lady Yasmin, who then picked up the card second from her right. She lay the card faceup in front of Kyle. The word "Justice" was written across the bottom, and a woman wearing a crown sat high on a throne.

Sitting back, Kyle looked quizzically at Lady Yasmin. *Yeah, and?*

"Justice. Justice is not pleased with you. You have done much in your past to warrant her wrath. You—"

"I don't know what you're talking about. I—"

"This is not the time to speak. You must listen and allow the spirits to right the wrong in your life."

Kyle frowned. Was he paying to be reprimanded like he was a kid? He could have stayed home and let his mother do that for free.

"Justice is stern. She punishes those who deserve punishment. You have been selfish . . ."

Oh, shit.

" . . with your love. You have harmed those you profess to love."

I haven't done a damn thing to anyone.

"The wrongs of the past have come to the present to exact retribution for the harm you've caused to the hearts of others."

"This is bullshit! I haven't done anything to anyone!"

Lady Yasmin remained focused. She turned over another card, taking it from the far left. This time, by the soft glow of the candle, Kyle saw what looked like a number of cups filled with trinkets.

"Seven of Cups," Lady Yasmin said. "The women you say you love you use, you take for granted."

"I haven't made anyone do a damn thing they didn't wanna do. It's not my fault women are attracted to me. I've made promises to no one."

Lady Yasmin continued, "You do not respect many, not even your mother. You—"

"Wait a minute. I respect my mother. I—"

"Your words are not necessary. Your words cannot alter what the cards tell me. Your life is in danger. You need to let the cards have their say."

"My life is in danger? What are you talking about?"

"Be still or I cannot go on. I will not be able to save your life."

Kyle's heart thumped. He leaned toward the table. He grimaced. With his eyes, he tried to again ask, *What the hell are you talking about?*

"What you have enjoyed for a night bears bitter consequences for your future. I see three women. They are your lovers, but one is not true. There is one who truly loves you. There is also one who wants you for the promise of the life you offer, and there is one who wants you dead?"

"One of them wants me dead? Are you serious?"

Lady Yasmin ignored Kyle's question. "This lover is very angry with you."

"That must be Dalia. I didn't give her the money she wanted. I can't believe she'd want me dead for that reason."

Leveling a reproachful glare on Kyle, silencing his, Lady Yasmin went on, "This woman wants you for herself alone. If you do not end it with her, she will take your life."

Oh, shit! Dalia wants to kill me! "It's Dalia, isn't it?"

"Her name is not revealed to me. The danger she represents is what I see." Another card was turned. "Five of Wands. You are under attack. Those closest to you are unhappy with you. They are demanding that you become a man of honor, a man of merit."

Kyle's leg went to shaking. *I didn't tell Lorna about my arguments with Carole, my mother, or my brother. But this is crazy. I can't believe Dalia wants to kill me over not giving her any more money. That's crazy.*

"Many are not pleased with the way you live your life. You are rebellious, you do not heed their counsel. You push all aside. You do not think you are wrong in your actions."

I'm not. Everyone needs to mind their goddamn business. My mother . . . What am I doing? This isn't about my mother or the women I see. This is bullshit! She's guessing. She doesn't really know.

"The Five of Wands demand repentance for wrongs. You have inner conflict. You will have no peace until you repent. Repenting will save your life." Yet another card was turned. "Three of Swords."

Kyle didn't like the image of the three swords piercing the blood red heart, not when the woman was talking about someone killing him.

"You have much pain that you will keep inside. You have lost the mother of your child to another. She has rejected you. Your heart is heavy. Oh, I see you have lost a powerful ally, a family member, an older man . . ."

Coincidence. She really doesn't know.

"They both loved you, but you were not worthy. The old man is angry, from the other side, he is scolding you, yet . . ."

Kyle felt the hair stand up on the nape of his neck.

". . . even now, he watches over you to protect you. The old man's love is strong, yet he causes you much pain." Lady Yasmin quickly flipped another card. "King of Cups. It is clear. The old man is your grandfather. He is wise. He is noble. He is holy."

Kyle's throat felt scratchy. His nose stung. It had to be the smoke from the incense that seemed to thicken around him—it was snuffing out his air. He felt his heart racing as the warm room began closing in on him.

"Your grandfather disapproves of your behavior. I see him, the old holy man. He is but a shadow, but he stands behind you."

His chest tight, his head stiff, Kyle didn't turn around, although his eyes shifted sideways trying to see if, indeed, someone was behind him. Of course he knew his grandfather could not be standing behind him, he was dead and buried way up in New York City. Besides, he didn't believe any of Lady Yasmin's voodoo malarkey. Lorna lied to him. She had to have told Lady Yasmin about his grandfather. That's the only explanation. This woman must think she's going to play him, but he wasn't that gullible.

"So what does he look like?" Kyle asked sarcastically.

Lady Yasmin did not hesitate. "Your grandfather's eyes are sharp. His mouth is pressed tight and turned down. He is not happy with you."

"Big surprise."

"Your grandfather is wearing a headdress, an Indian headdress. He carries an old medicine bag."

Kyle wouldn't let himself believe what he was hearing. "Lorna told you about me. She told you about my grandfather, too, didn't she?"

Lady Yasmin fixed an indignant glare on Kyle. "My niece has told me nothing. What I reveal to you is in the cards. Be still and listen, and watch how you speak to me, I do not put up with impudence for long."

Kyle was through, too. He couldn't believe this woman. She was treating him like a kid in first grade. Well, he wasn't putting up with that. "Look—"

Lady Yasmin raised her long, threatening finger, warning Kyle to speak no more.

He didn't and he didn't understand why he didn't. He quieted his tongue, but his mind was screaming, *Get the hell out of here!* If Lorna didn't tell her aunt about his grandfather, how could she know that he was an Indian? This was a scam. Lorna was in on it. It was probably about money. Lady Yasmin was probably going to charge him more for this bogus reading. Well, he wasn't paying more than the hundred dollars Lorna told him about earlier.

Lady Yasmin laid her right hand over her heart. With her left hand, she turned over the sixth card. Kyle saw that nine swords lay in a row atop each other behind a woman sitting up in bed crying into her hands.

"Okay, now this is what I'm here about. This woman looks like she woke up from a bad dream. That's why I'm here. I need to know about my dreams—about the snake, the hand, the cave. I flew all this damn way to find out what my dreams mean."

"You are very difficult," Lady Yasmin said evenly, "and you are very strong-headed. Continue to speak and I will not read further."

Kyle hadn't come all that way to not get something for his money. "Lady Yasmin, I'm not trying to be difficult, so please forgive me. I'm sorry if you think I am, but I haven't been able to sleep because of my dreams, and really my nightmares. I absolutely need to know what these dreams mean, if they mean anything at all. I need to know Lady Yasmin if I have something real to worry about. Lorna told me that you interpret dreams, that you could help me."

"I do not know how Lorna could tell you this. I do not interpret dreams. Most dreams mean nothing. Very few mean anything of consequence. There are some who say dreams are messages from the beyond. I say they are the subconscious revealing what is deepest in our thoughts, things that we put there ourselves. You say you dreamed of a snake?"

"A big-ass black snake. It was on my ... my ... my private part. And there were these women, three women, but I think I know who they are. I didn't see them, I smelled them, their perfumes, and they were doing things to me, you know, sexual things. Things I ... I really ... anyway, I opened my eyes and the snake was there. It was about to bite me when—"

Lady Yasmin held up her hand, stopping Kyle. Then closing her eyes, she touched the center of her forehead with her middle finger. Musingly, she gently traced a tiny circle on her forehead.

Leaning forward, Kyle asked in a hushed voice, "Can you tell me anything? Can—"

"Treachery. Deceit. Bad things happen when snakes are near." Lady Yasmin opened her eyes and lowered her hand. "You do not need me to interpret your dreams. A snake is never good. This has been so since the time of Eve. The bigger the snake, the worse your problems. Three women. Any man who has three women is asking for trouble. Hand in hand, a snake and three women can only mean the worst. Only pain can come from such a union. Is that what you wanted to hear?"

Sitting back, Kyle marveled at how easily Lady Yasmin told him that his troubles were of his own making. Again, his fault.

"Let's see what more the cards have to say." Lady Yasmin touched the edge of the card she had turned minutes before. "Nine of Swords. You are on a journey. Your grandfather is your guide, your spirit guide. He comes to you in your dreams. These dreams—"

"Nightmares," Kyle corrected.

Lady Yasmin held up her hand to quiet Kyle. "Your dreams are of another world, yet they are of this life. You fear the old holy man, you should not."

"That's easy for you to say, he's not jacking you up in your dreams."

"No, I am not the one he guides. Did you fear the old holy man when he walked the earth?"

"Of course not. He's my grandfather."

"Then, do not fear him now. Welcome him. He visits you for a reason."

"Well, I can do without his visits."

Lady Yasmin looked again at the Nine of Swords. "Your dreams frighten you. They wake you with their horror. Awake, they feel real. It is the old holy man. He cannot rest until you are right. You must let the holy one guide you. You must not question him. It will not go well for you otherwise."

"And what is that supposed to mean?"

"Your dreams can and will harm you."

The back of Kyle's neck bristled. "This is crazy."

"You do not sleep, your eyes tell me that. You are afraid of the terror that awaits when you succumb to the sleep you are desperate for."

Kyle could feel his soul quiver.

"But you won't be able to escape; you have lessons yet to be learned."

"What damn lessons?"

Ignoring Kyle's question, Lady Yasmin turned the final card. A man in armor rode a mighty white stallion. That card never surprised her. "Death."

Fear gripped Kyle's heart. A bead of sweat rolled down his forehead onto his nose, yet the chill he'd felt in the waiting room suddenly popped goose bumps on his arms. He had pulled the death card. Was Lady Yasmin again about to tell him that he was going to die?

"We must all, eventually, leave our earthly bodies. It is but a transition to another state of being in another world. Transition can also mean change on this earth. You must make changes in your life. Your transition must be spiritual, it must come from within. But transition cannot come if you do not right your wrong, or if you do not see that change is necessary for you to find peace. Your grandfather will not leave you alone if you do not do what is right. If you do not make amends, you may lose your life in this world. That is your warning. That is your reading. Go in peace."

Numb, Kyle stared at Lady Yasmin. This woman had just told him that he could die if he didn't fix whatever the hell was wrong in his life. And just like that, "That is your reading. Go in peace." Hell, he was more messed up than when he came. He didn't have to come all this way to be told that his grandfather was going to keep haunting him. But it was outrageous that Lady Yasmin had said that he was going to die if he didn't start respecting women. He respected women! He treated all women well—he gave them money, he gave them presents, he made love to each like she was the only one in his life. How much better could he treat them?

Lady Yasmin started gathering her cards. "You may leave your gift in the bowl, there at the door."

"How much?"

"I do not discuss money. You leave what you will." Then, as was her routine, Lady Yasmin focused on ordering her cards, readying them for her next reading—her niece. She had gotten bad vibes from Lorna when she embraced her. Lorna should not be with this man, she was a married woman. It was clear they were lovers, and that should not be.

Kyle didn't know if he was supposed to thank Lady Yasmin for fucking up his day or tell her to go to hell. He was at a loss for words, not that Lady Yasmin would let him speak if he had words to say. She had dismissed him, she was done with him. He started to stand and was surprised at how rubbery his legs were. This wasn't happening. He was no punk, he was a man. He squared his shoulders and held his head high. Sure, what Lady Yasmin said about Dalia wanting to kill him and about his grandfather hurting him caught him off guard, but he wasn't stupid. The best con artists could make a man believe he could walk a tightrope across Niagra Falls. And it appears that Lady Yasmin was the best, especially with Lorna's help. Lorna was behind this scam. She had told her aunt all about him. It was a scam, and no one could convince him otherwise.

"By the way," Lady Yasmin said just as Kyle dropped a C-note in the tall wicker basket sitting to the left of the door. "It is not perfume I wear, it is vanilla oil, and my eyes are mine from birth."

Kyle was suddenly afraid. What was real, he could not deny. It was true, he had wondered about Lady Yasmin's perfume and about her eyes. How had she known his thoughts? What if she was for real? What if what she said about his life being in danger was real? Was Dalia really going to kill him?

Stepping out into the brightness and coolness of the waiting room, Kyle had only one thing on his mind—getting the hell out of Florida.

Lorna quickly stepped up to Kyle. "You do not look good. What did my aunt say to you?"

"You lied."

"About what?"

"Your aunt does not interpret dreams."

"But she reads much in her cards. She—"

"Let's get outta here," Kyle said, taking Lorna's arm.

She pulled back. "I am next to see my aunt. We cannot leave yet."

"Well, I can." Kyle was about to walk away when Lorna pulled him back again.

Lorna glanced at the people waiting to see her aunt and was not surprised to see that they were looking intently at her and Kyle. She lowered her voice.

"You will not wait for me?"

"I have to get outta here—now."

"But, Kyle, I will not be long. We can leave as soon as my aunt is done."

Speaking no more, Kyle pulled his arm free with ease and headed for the door. After a second's hesitation, Lorna took off behind Kyle and was right on his heels when he stepped out onto the porch.

"Kyle, my aunt has asked to see me. It will take only a few minutes."

Kyle whipped out his wallet. "Take your ticket. I'll get your luggage from the car."

Lorna gasped. "You would leave without me?"

Kyle held the ticket out to her. "You're a big girl, Lorna. You can get on the plane by yourself."

"Why are you so cruel, Kyle? You are angry with me. I've done nothing to anger you. Did what my aunt tell you upset you so? What did she say?"

"Don't worry about it. I have to get back home, so I'm leaving. You don't have to leave. You stay and visit with your aunt. Call me when you get back." Kyle started off the porch.

Undecided, Lorna glanced back at the door. "Wait!" she said. "I will leave with you. Just give me a minute to say good-bye."

Kyle started down the steps toward his rental car. He had no desire to hang around Florida or around Lorna.

Just as Lorna started back inside, Ella opened the door. "Mother is asking for you."

"Ella, tell Aunt Yasmin I could not stay. Tell her I will call when I get back to New York. Kyle has to get back."

"But—"

"I have to go." Lorna embraced her cousin. "I will call."

Hurrying to catch up to Kyle, Lorna barely closed her car door when Kyle pulled out, heading straight for the airport. They had never checked into the hotel, their luggage was still in the trunk of the car. He would lose money on his tickets, but what the hell. He had to get home. He had to set Dalia straight.

Chapter
21

The grim set of Lorna's mouth and the hard look in her eyes all the way back to the airport told Kyle how angry she was with him, and that was fine with him. Maybe she'd keep her mouth shut all the way back to New York. Once there, he was going to sever any contact with her, anyway, so it was quite apropos that they didn't have adjoining seats—although the aisle seats right across from each other were much too close. Kyle closed his eyes as soon as the plane started taxiing down the runway, feigning sleep, keeping his head turned to the side away from Lorna. As the plane lifted smoothly into the air, Kyle felt his head lighten, and then, unexpectedly, minutes after the plane reached cruising altitude he fell into a deep, blissful sleep. He awakened as the plane touched down, keenly aware that he had not dreamed and that he had not stirred. Surprisingly, his sleep had been sweet enough to soften the hateful glare Lorna flashed his way. Closing his eyes again, he closed her out.

Even more surprising, Kyle slept in Atlanta while waiting for his connecting flight to New York, and slept, too, on that flight, nightmare free. Sleep was a welcome mistress that seduced him and lured him into her sensual boudoir with the gentlest kiss Kyle had ever had. He grumbled irritably when Lorna nudged him awake to try and find out what it was her aunt had said, but he growled at her to let him sleep and, begrudgingly, she did. He awakened minutes before touching down at LaGuardia, and for the first time in days, he felt rested, his head wasn't clogged, and that dreaded fear that had settled in his chest had dissipated.

It was one A.M. on Saturday when Kyle pulled up in front of Lorna's apartment building. Their short ride from the airport had been chillingly quiet, and he hadn't done a thing to try and thaw the wall of ice he'd built up around them. He double-parked the car and went immediately to the trunk to get Lorna's bag.

Lorna got out of the car but she stood standing in the street with the door open. "You are not going to park?"

Kyle closed the trunk and set the luggage upright on the sidewalk. "I have to get home."

"But . . . but we were to spend the weekend together."

"That was in Florida."

Leaving the car door open, Lorna headed around the car to the sidewalk. "But it is still the weekend, Kyle. Can we not still spend the weekend together?"

"Can't." He went around and closed his car door.

"What do you have to do, Kyle? You had nothing to do when we were to be in Florida. Did my aunt's words frighten you so that you cannot stand to be with me?"

"Lorna, it's late. Go upstairs. I have to leave."

"Kyle, I want to be with you."

"Not tonight. Now go inside before I pull off," he said, getting into his car and closing the door.

Leaving her bag on the sidewalk, Lorna hurried back around the car and got back inside.

"Damn! C'mon, Lorna, I have to go. Get out, I'm not going upstairs."

"Please, Kyle. If you leave, I feel you will not come back."

How perceptive of her. Looking at Lorna, as pretty as she was and knowing how well she could work her ass, Kyle had no desire to make love to her tonight or any night at this point. He may as well get it over with, once and for all.

"I think we should stop seeing each other."

Lorna's lips parted as she stared incredulously at Kyle.

"We can still be friends. We can talk, if you want, but we can't see each other intimately anymore."

"Did my aunt say something about me?"

"No."

"Did she tell you to leave me, to stay away from me?"

"Your aunt didn't even mention your name, Lorna. What she said was that I had problems and that I had to do something about my life."

"Am I the problem in your life, Kyle? Am I the one who cause you to dream—"

"Look, Lorna. I decided we had to stop seeing each other before I saw your aunt, way before I started having those dreams."

"But why, Kyle? Why must we end? What did I do wrong?"

God, he hated this part of breaking up. "This isn't about what you did or didn't do, Lorna. This is about me. There are a lot of things I have to work through, and I can't do it when I'm spreading myself thin."

"What do you mean *spreading yourself thin*? I have not—"

"Lorna, my life is very complicated. I can't be who you want me to be in your life. I can't . . . I can't give any part of myself to you when I have so many problems to deal with on my own."

"But, Kyle, I will be able to help you."

Kyle went to shaking his head.

"I will not burden you with any of my wants. I will help you in any way I can to—"

"You can't help me, Lorna! You're married—"

"But I intend to divorce my husband. I will be free to—"

"Look! I told you before, don't divorce your husband because of me." Even in the duskiness of the car, Kyle could see tears roll down Lorna's cheeks, but he had to get it over with. "Lorna, listen to me. I can't be with you. I—"

"But you have to be with me. I'm in love with you. I'm about to have your—"

"Dammit! Lorna, I never told you I loved you. I never told you I'd marry you or spend my life with you."

"But you made me think you loved me, Kyle. You made love to me like you loved me."

"So am I to be punished for that? I'm supposed to marry you?"

Lorna gasped at Kyle's cruelty. "Kyle!"

Kyle hit the steering wheel with the side of his fist. God, he hated this! He should have known Lorna would try to crawl up his ass if he let her go to Florida with him. Damn those dreams!

"Lorna, let's be real. We were never a couple. We got together for sex and sex only."

Tears slipped down Lorna's cheeks.

"I'm trying to be honest with you, Lorna. You were never my woman—"

"But . . . but you gave me a credit card like I was your woman!"

"My mistake. And by the way, I need that damn credit card back!"

Lorna drew back. Kyle you gave me that card. Why must you take it back?"

"The truth? I can't afford it, and we're done."

"No, Kyle. Please—"

"Lorna, you're married. Stay married. You got involved with me because your husband wasn't around. When we first got together, you and I both agreed it was temporary. You said you loved your husband, that you were going back home once you finished school. If you had told me otherwise, I wouldn't've gotten involved with you. I'm not into breaking up marriages."

Crying, Lorna scooted closer to Kyle and tried to put her arms around him, but he quickly pulled her arm from around his neck and, holding her wrists, pinned both her arms to her own body, her hands in her lap.

"Look, I don't have time for this drama. It's over."

"Kyle, please, I love you. I need to be with you. I—"

"Don't do this, Lorna. You don't need me. We saw each other, what, once a week most weeks for the past ten months, and that was exclusively for sex. We never did anything else. We never went out, except maybe to my place late at night a few times, but mostly, whenever we got together, we stayed in your place and screwed. How could you think our involvement was anything but what it was?"

Lorna stopped struggling and relaxed. Kyle released his hold on her. Looking at Kyle, she slowly laid her hand on top of her stomach and began to gently rub it. Kyle never looked at what

Lorna was doing. He had looked away from the pain in Lorna's eyes and the fresh tears that flowed.

If Kyle felt anything, it was annoyance. He had told Lorna just days ago that he wasn't going to be with her. Didn't she think he was serious? Not only did he not love her, but he'd never be able to trust her. She had been seeing him, screwing his brains out, while her husband probably thought she was being faithful to him. Nah, he could never marry her.

"Lorna, it's late. I have to go."

Lost in her anguish, Lorna cried into her hands.

Kyle wanted to kick himself for not speeding away before Lorna jumped back into his car. God, he couldn't take this drama. He reached across Lorna and opened the door on her side and pushed it open.

"Go inside, Lorna."

Lorna continued to cry.

Kyle got out of the car, slamming the door with a loud thud. He then fell back against the car. "Dammit," he said, hitting the door with the side of his fist. This was exactly what he didn't want to deal with—a crying woman bent on putting a noose around his damn neck. He walked away from the car. He looked from one end of the block to the other. Thank God, Lorna wasn't a wailer. If she had been, even with the windows of his car rolled up, in the stillness of the night, her cries might have carried and brought curious eyes to windows above. Kyle checked his watch—one thirty-five. If Lorna didn't hurry up and calm her ass down, he was going to drag her out of his car and not give a damn about the ruckus she made.

As if she knew what Kyle was thinking, Lorna suddenly got out of the car. Although she sniffled, she was no longer crying. Kyle watched as she wiped away the last of her tears before coming around the car to her bag. He said nothing about her leaving his car door open again. He hurriedly closed it himself.

By the time he came back around the car, Lorna had taken her bag and was walking toward her apartment building. She didn't look back, and Kyle thought it was only fitting. He didn't want her to say anything, he wanted it to end right then and there. He'd miss getting it on with Lorna, but he wouldn't miss the pressure.

It was only after he'd driven to the corner and was stopped at the light did he realize that he still hadn't gotten his credit card from Lorna. What the hell. There was only a $500 line of credit on it. What damage could she do? He'd cancel the card Monday morning and she'd soon be a distant memory.

Chapter
22

Kyle's better sense told him to go on home, but he felt driven to go see Dalia. As late as it was, he was wide awake and ready to face the person Lady Yasmin predicted was a threat to his life. Part of him didn't believe what she'd said about one of his women wanting him dead, that was just too far-fetched. Not that he didn't believe that a woman could kill; women were just as capable as men when it came to murder. He just didn't believe Dalia could be so angry at him for not giving her money that she'd want him dead. It was almost too bizarre to comprehend. And as for relationships ending, hell, people broke up every day, but rational people didn't kill each other, and he'd never thought of any of his women, including Dalia, as being irrational.

Taking a chance that Dalia might be home, Kyle entered her unlocked building, bypassed her intercom system in the foyer, and raced up the three flights to her apartment. In case Dalia was sleeping, after he rang the bell Kyle waited a minute to give her time to get to the door, but the sound of locks turning didn't come. He rang again, this time laying on the bell, the sound of which he could clearly hear through the door.

"Who the hell's ringin' my goddamn bell!"

His voice low, his face to the door, Kyle answered, "It's me, Dalia, Kyle."

"What the fuck do you want?"

"I wanna talk to you."

"I don't wanna talk to you."

Kyle glanced down the hall and hoped he wasn't disturbing any of Dalia's neighbors. "Dalia, I need to talk to you. It's important."

"Kiss my ass, Kyle! You don't give a damn about me."

"I care, Dalia, that's why I'm here."

"Bullshit, you didn't care when I asked you for help. You—"

Bang! Kyle slapped the door hard with the palm of his hand, sending the noise reverberating throughout the third floor. "Dalia, open the damn door!"

"Don't be hittin' on my damn door! You better stop all that damn noise out there before somebody calls the cops on you."

Kyle perked his ears, listening hard for any sound of people moving about inside their apartments. Hearing nothing, he pleaded, "Dalia, please, open the door."

"Why should I?"

"I wanna talk to you."

"You didn't listen to me when I was trying to talk to you."

"Look, I'm sorry if you thought I let you down."

"You *did* let me down, Kyle! I got a seventy-two-hour eviction notice because of you."

Kyle looked incredulously at the door. How in the hell was she blaming him for her eviction? Not paying her rent was on her and had nothing to do with him.

"You could've helped me, Kyle. You had the money."

Dumb ass! You could have helped your damn self if you were more responsible. "Okay, look, a lot was going on when you called. I didn't know you were in that much trouble."

"Well, I was and still am."

"Then open the door Dalia. Maybe I can help you."

No sound came from the other side of the door.

"Dalia, I can't help you standing out here in the hall."

Still, Dalia didn't answer.

Kyle pressed his ear to the door. He thought he heard a door close, perhaps Dalia's bedroom door. He knocked softly at the apartment door. "Dalia."

"I need a lot of money, Kyle. You gonna give me some?"

"Damn," Kyle said under his breath. If it wasn't for what Lady

Yasmin had said, he wouldn't even be here putting himself through this shit. If he didn't give Dalia the money, what could she do? Not a damn thing. But he was a good guy. A thousand? That was nothing. He could give that up without any pain.

"Okay, Dalia, open the door and we'll talk about it."

After the briefest of pauses, Dalia opened the door, though she didn't step aside to let Kyle inside. She stood with one hand on the door and the other on her naked hip.

An instant erection was Kyle's immediate response to seeing Dalia's nakedness under her short, open robe. Earlier, he hadn't wanted to be with Lorna, and just a day or so ago, he hadn't responded to Dalia's attempt to get a rise out of him over the telephone. But now, here he was not the least bit adverse to the thought of doing her. She looked mighty good.

"You trying to take a picture?" Dalia asked, her tone full of attitude.

"You gonna let me inside?"

Dalia smirked. "Inside my apartment, or inside me?"

Raising his left brow, Kyle leveled a "Is this a trick question?" gaze on Dalia. As hard as his johnson was, there was no question what it wanted to be inside of. It made him step close up on Dalia, close enough to touch that part of her body that it wanted to enter, but Kyle admonished, *Down, boy. That's not what we're here for.*

Dalia again smirked, she knew her power, she didn't back away.

Kyle noticed with mild interest that Dalia wasn't wearing perfume, but then she hadn't been expecting him. It had been a long time since he smelled her au naturel. There was a subtle, musky scent, like she had yet to bathe, which intrigued Kyle all the more.

Dalia let Kyle feel her heat long enough to want more, and then with a come hither look, she turned smoothly and walked away, leaving Kyle to close the door. He didn't see her glance at the closed bedroom door.

"You're a piece of work," he said, following Dalia into the dimly lit living room where she sat and crossed her long legs while letting her robe lay to the side.

"I'm me," she said, slowly rubbing her right leg atop her left, drawing Kyle's eyes to the shadowy slit in between her thighs.

Peeling off his jacket, Kyle tossed it across the back of the black leather sofa before he sat down next to Dalia. "Be serious. How are we supposed to talk when you're doing that with your leg?"

"Easy. Keep your eyes above my neck, which is where my mouth is," she said, although she began to sensually finger her left nipple, making it point right at Kyle.

"Keep your hands still and I'll keep my eyes where they belong."

"You mean like this?" Dalia opened her thighs and easily slipped her finger inside herself, but she did hold her hand still.

The throbbing heaviness pressing against Kyle's left thigh made him stretch out his left leg. Touching himself, he wanted badly what he hadn't come there for. Damn, Dalia would be the one to put him on the bone. No doubt, she knew how to get him, but he couldn't shake what Lady Yasmin told him.

Dalia pulled her finger out and extended it toward Kyle's nose.

He knocked her hand away, although he had sucked on that finger many times before. "Stop playing games, Dalia! Close your robe."

"No, I want it open." She wiped her finger on the hem of her robe.

"Hey, no sweat off my nose." Like hell it wasn't. "Did you get an eviction notice or not? You're still here, I don't see anything packed. Are you put out or not?"

"That's what the notice says. I went down to the court yesterday. By Monday, I gotta have the rent or I'm on the street."

"So do you have the rent?"

"No."

"Then how are you so laid-back?"

Dalia glanced at the bedroom door. "I ain't gotta stress until Monday morning. Why're you here, Kyle? You gonna give me the money?"

Kyle huffed. If he remembered correctly, Dalia's rent was $1,200 a month, and since she only asked him for a thousand, if she was three months past due, then she must have most of what she needed.

"A thousand right?"

"A thousand would help, but I need more than that."

"How much more? How behind are you?"

"Five months."

"Shit!" Kyle shot up off the sofa. "I thought you said three months."

"Five."

"Dalia, how the hell did you get five months behind in rent without trying to pay it off. You still have a job, don't you? And what about the money you got from me in the last five months. What did you do with all of that?"

"I had expenses."

"Yeah, like rent! Why didn't you pay it? That would have been the adult thing to do."

"Fuck you, Kyle, you ain't my damn father." Dalia quickly overlapped her robe, covering her nakedness. "Don't be giving me the third degree and dissing my ass up in here."

Again, Kyle sat. "Dalia, I'm not trying to be your father, but the truth is, not paying your rent for five months, especially when it's that high, is damned irresponsible. You're behind six thousand dollars. I'm surprised your landlord let you get that far behind. Didn't you get a notice before this one?"

Pouting, Dalia folded her arms across her chest and refused to answer.

"Dalia, six thousand dollars is a lot of money. I don't have six thousand dollars to give you."

"Then what the hell are you doing here, Kyle, waking my ass up, when you can't do a damn thing to help me out of this situation?"

"I care about you, Dalia," he lied. "Maybe I could've done something to help you months ago if you had told me you were in trouble. At this point—"

"The bottom line, Kyle. How much you gonna give me— now?"

Kyle scratched his brow. "Dalia, my money is tight right now. I'm close to filing bankruptcy my damn self. Six thousand dollars? Hell, I can't come up with that kind of money."

"Can you give me two or three thousand, Kyle? I can use whatever you can give me."

Kyle began rubbing the back of his neck. He could get his hands on a thousand or two, but he needed that money himself. He had wages to pay, he had an office to run, he had his own mortgage to pay. He had come up here thinking he could just talk to Dalia about being friends, about her not being upset with him. If he had known her problem was this major and her attitude was this stank, he would have taken his ass on home.

Again glancing at the door, Dalia suddenly got up and straddled Kyle.

He pulled back from her while holding her at arm's length. "What're you doing?"

Dalia started unbuckling Kyle's belt. "Kyle, if you lend me the money"—

Kyle gripped Dalia hands, staying her from unbuckling him all the way.

"I promise I'll pay you back, Kyle, I promise." Dalia kept trying to get Kyle's pants undone.

"Stop it, Dalia. Seducing me wo—"

Halting Kyle's protestations with her tongue stuck deep into his mouth, Dalia began grinding herself into him, trying to make him remember what making love to her was like. At first, half-heartedly, Kyle tried to push Dalia away, but her grinding was raising his temperature, boiling his blood, making him crave to free himself to taste of the sweetness he knew to be there. This was a guilty pleasure that he had no business indulging in, especially since he had no intention of giving her a dime. But what the hell, he was getting him some. In an instant, he gave in to the mighty tenseness that swelled his body and clamped Dalia to him with his powerful arms. He sucked on her tongue as deeply as she sucked on his. Yeah, he felt guilty, but there was nothing he could do about that now. He was too far gone.

Chapter
23

Kyle and Dalia never made it to the bedroom. The hardwood floor was rough on Kyle's knees, but he didn't feel a thing when he got into his zone. His chest was still heaving, he hadn't yet started to breathe normally when the reality of the moment hit him like a slap in the face—he'd just screwed a woman who desperately needed six thousand dollars. His mind groaned, while, in his ear, a little voice whispered, "Stupid!"

Dalia sat up. "We still got it, huh?"

"Yeah, I guess we do," Kyle said, trying not to look like he was in as much of a hurry as he was. He started pulling on his undershorts while still sitting on the floor, but he stood to put on his pants. "Where's my undershirt?"

"Is that what I'm sitting on?" From under her naked bottom, Dalia pulled Kyle's gray undershirt and held it out to him as she herself got up off the floor.

Kyle didn't even want to think about what might be on his undershirt—he rolled it up into a tight ball. His shirt and jacket would have to do. He found both.

"You leavin'?" Dalia asked, surprised.

"Yeah," he said, pulling on his jacket. "I'm just getting back in town, I haven't been home yet."

Dalia glanced at the door and said loudly, "So you're just gonna walk out? Just like that?"

"I'll call you—"

"Are you gonna give me the money?"

"Dalia, I told you, I don't have it. I—"

"Hold up! Hold up!" Dalia snatched on her skimpy robe and tied it tight around her waist. "You rolled up in here and screwed my brains out, and just like that you tippin'? You pullin' a wham, bam, thank you, ma'am, on me?"

"Dalia, you know damn well it's not like that. In the first place, I didn't come up here to do you. Let's call it what it is. You seduced me, and I let you. I hit it, and you let me. So let's not—"

"No. Uh-uh," Dalia said, her voice louder. She thrust her hands on her hips. "You tryin' to get away with screwin' me for free, but Kyle that ain't happenin'. I need some money, and you're gonna give it to me. You ain't gettin' out of here unless you do."

Looking down at all five foot four, 130 pounds of Dalia, Kyle knew that a good shove would get her out of his way.

"Dalia, don't take this where it don't need to go. I don't appreciate you threatening me."

"Believe me, baby, it ain't no threat."

Kyle stared at the cold glint in Dalia's eyes. What Lady Yasmin had predicted flooded his mind. Was this the threat on his life? If so, he wasn't the least bit intimidated by Dalia, but he wasn't liking the tight feeling he was getting in the pit of his stomach. Before Dalia's big mouth started wolfing, he considered giving up a thousand to help her out, but now, he wasn't giving her a damn thing.

"I think you better ask your family for the money."

Dalia shook her head. "Uh-uh. I don't have to. You're gonna give me all the money I need."

"Oh, you think so?"

"I know so."

From looking at Dalia, Kyle couldn't tell if she had been snorting something or smoking something, but the girl had to be on something to think she could make him give her money. Hell, she even had to be delusional to keep threatening him. What did she think he was? A punk?

"I tell you what, Dalia. I'm gonna do us both a favor. I'm gonna leave before either one of us says or does something we'll both regret." Kyle started around Dalia.

Dalia suddenly grabbed Kyle's arm. "Jitu! Jitu! He's getting away!"

"What the—" Before Kyle could give voice to his question, out of the corner of his eye he saw the bedroom door fly open and a blur of a figure came barreling out of the darkness toward him. Kyle barely had time to react before he was tackled and thrown into the sofa.

"Beat his ass, Jitu! Jack him up!" Dalia was jumping up and down. "Beat his ass down!"

Kyle's face was smashed on every side. In the low lighting of the living room, he couldn't see who it was that was beating him, and he couldn't defend himself—he was on his back and the person was on top of his stomach. Kyle's arms were useless, reminding him of his dream when someone had pinned him down. Like in the dream, he couldn't see who it was that was on him. Fear filled his gut and nearly paralyzed him. The taste of his own blood in his mouth nauseated him, and he could feel his eyes stinging. But what he heard, "Beat his ass! Beat his ass!" scared him.

Kyle knew he had to try and fight back. If he didn't, Lady Yasmin's prediction would come true—he'd lose his life. Reaching down deep and grunting loudly, Kyle pushed his body up off the sofa with his attacker still sitting on his stomach, throwing them both onto the floor. And then, quickly, Kyle tried to get his footing, but as soon as he did, he was being hit upside the head from behind. It was Dalia. She was repeatedly bashing him on the head, while her accomplice quickly got his footing and punched Kyle upside the head, knocking him down again. A raw, deep, primal scream tore from Kyle's throat.

"Shut him up!" Dalia ordered, switching on the overhead light, bathing the room in brightness. "I'll get his wallet. He don't wanna pay me, I'll take what's mine." She started patting Kyle down.

With his knee in Kyle's chest, Jitu tried to stuff Kyle's undershirt into his mouth, but Kyle, his sore jaw clamped shut, fought hard, holding on to Jitu's arm while trying to punch at the same time. But Jitu had the advantage, he was on top. He relentlessly slammed his fist into Kyle's face.

"Damn!" Dalia exclaimed, looking at Kyle while opening his wallet. "He's bleeding, Jitu. How we gonna explain how he got all bloody?"

"I ain't explainin' nothin'. I'm gonna dump his ass somewhere. You said this dude was rich. How much he got in there? He got a bank card?"

"He—"

BUZZZZZ! BUZZZZZZZZZZZ! "Open up! It's the police."

Gawking at the door, Dalia covered her mouth.

Jitu mimed, "Oh, shit!" He pressed his hands over Kyle's mouth.

Kyle began clawing at the brutal hand that tried to kill him.

BANG! BANG! BANG! "Open up! It's the police!"

Dalia began pacing frantically. "Oh my God, Jitu. We're gonna get locked up."

Jitu pushed off of Kyle and rushed to the window where he looked down on three red and white light flashing patrol cars. He immediately clutched his head and started pacing. "Goddamn! We're in trouble now!"

Kyle's head, face, and chest were killing him, but he called out throatily anyway, "Help!"

BANG! BANG! BANG! "Open up!"

Dalia threw Kyle's wallet at him, hitting him in the chest. "We could say he tried to rob us," Dalia said, wringing her hands.

"How you sound?" Jitu asked. "He ain't got no gun."

Kyle strained to get to his feet.

BANG! BANG! BANG!

"Help!" Kyle said weakly. The pain in his head was killing him. "Help me!"

"Shut up!" Dalia said, punching Kyle in the side, making him double over as she hit him in a spot where he was already sore. "All you had to do was give me the goddamn money. You had it. You could've just given it to me!"

"Open the door!" an officer again ordered.

Jitu flitted around the room, undecided as to what to do. "Man, I ain't goin' back to jail."

"Oh, God," Dalia said, "what're we gonna do?"

Kyle had to fight to keep his eyes open. He was close to blacking out. He couldn't believe that Dalia and her goon had tried to kill him. He got a good look at Jitu. No wonder he had overpowered him so badly. The man was at least 220 pounds of solid muscle. His bulging biceps were so big they looked deformed. He was about thirty years old, mean looking as hell, and as bald as a rock. And the whole time Kyle was boning Dalia, Jitu was hiding back in the bedroom, waiting to jump him.

BANG! BANG! BANG!

"Open up—now!"

"I know," Jitu said to Dalia. "Tell them he raped you and I happened to drop by and caught him."

"Yeah, I could say that. That's right. He did screw me against my will."

"That's a damn lie! I didn't rape you!"

"Shut up, man! I ain't done with you. I'll get you later. Dalia, go open the door."

Dalia tried to rip her robe, but the synthetic fabric wouldn't tear. On her way to the door, she pulled the robe off her shoulders. She opened the door to four patrolmen, all with their weapons drawn. Kyle had never been so happy to see a bunch of cops in his life. He stumbled toward them.

"He raped me!" Dalia said, suddenly crying.

Kyle fell back against the wall. "She's lying."

"You did, man! You raped her! I caught you." Jitu started toward the policemen.

"That's a lie!" Kyle said, grimacing from the pain in his jaw, in his head, and in his chest. He could feel his own blood oozing down his neck.

"Get down!" an officer said, pointing at Jitu.

"You got the wrong dude. He's the one that raped my girl. I came over—"

"Get down!" the officer ordered again. This time he and a second officer grabbed Jitu and threw him to the floor onto his stomach. Until he was handcuffed, they held him down with their knees in his back.

"Next time, dude," one of the officers said, "you wanna frame a guy for a crime, make sure no one can hear you. That door isn't soundproof. Your neighbors heard everything that went on in here, and so did we."

"Aw, shit!" Jitu said.

While an officer Mirandized Jitu, another officer forced Dalia's hands behind her back.

"What're you doing?" Dalia asked. "I haven't done anything. He—"

"Miss, you have the right to remain silent," an officer said, as he handcuffed Dalia's hands behind her back. "Should you give up the right to remain silent, anything you say may be used against you in a court of law."

"I didn't do anything. I swear, it wasn't me, it was—"

"Miss, do you understand your rights as they have been read to you?"

"Jitu, I can't go to jail," Dalia said. "This was your idea. You told me to let him in and try to get some money from him."

Jitu awkwardly raised his head up off the floor. "Shut up, bitch!"

Kyle slid wearily into a chair near the door. He couldn't believe he almost got himself killed for some pussy he didn't even have to have.

"Sir, EMS is on the way. We need a statement. Can you talk?"

Kyle's head dropped forward. Lady Yasmin was almost right—he was almost killed, but this was too close a call to be ignored. Maybe there was something to all of what she said, after all. Maybe—

Whatever revelations Kyle might have had were lost to the blackness that claimed him.

Chapter
24

The vast field of colorful wildflowers spread farther and wider than Kyle remembered. It surprised him not that he was in that field again, but with so many flowers around, he still wondered why he couldn't smell them. Even when a light breeze brushed the top of the flowers making them all sway lazily against each other, Kyle was in awe of their array of beautiful colors. The darkening sky didn't dim their brilliance, but the increasing breeze began whipping up around Kyle, intensifying, swirling, pushing him, making him brace himself against the wind that came out of nowhere. Then, suddenly, Kyle was caught up, snatched off his feet, and yanked backward out of the field into an opaque darkness, pulling him deeper and deeper inside, while outside the brightness and colorfulness of the field, shrank farther away out of Kyle's reach until it was completely out of sight. Moving swiftly backward, his feet not touching the ground, unable to see what it was or who it was who had a hold of him, Kyle began flailing his arms, trying to catch a grip on anything that his hands might happen to touch. He touched nothing. His hands thrashed about in open black air. Panicked, Kyle tried to scream but couldn't; his mouth wouldn't open. He tried to shut his eyes to the frightful darkness that engulfed him, but his eyes would not close. And then, just as suddenly as when he had been snatched up, Kyle was thrust to the ground, no longer a puppet in the swirl of winds. The absolute darkness that had surrounded him vanished into a dusky abyss of nowhereness.

Breathing in quick, short gasps, his heart pounding, Kyle swiftly jerked himself around to see where he was. Once his eyes adjusted, he saw that he was surrounded by a wall of rock. He was in a cave. High above the footing of the cave, seemingly coming out from the wall itself, was a flame of yellow fire eerily flashing amber hints of light in the dusk that didn't so much light the cave as suffuse it with scary shadows that chilled Kyle's heart. Rushing in the direction he had been pulled from, Kyle slammed into a solid, stone wall. Warily, with trembling hands, he felt along the rough wall for an opening that had to be there—but was not. How had he come through a solid wall, a wall that encased the small cave in which he stood?

Kyle's pounding heart thumped rapidly, but then it dawned, it had to be his grandfather and he was playing games with him. So what was he going to do to him now in this weird-ass cave besides make him claustrophobic? "Okay, shake it off." What did he have to fear? Besides, his grandfather would show up any minute now and either whip his ass or save him from some—

"Grrrrrrr."

The low, throaty rumble startled Kyle. He jerked around. He stretched his eyes searching the shadows around the cave, but saw nothing clearly to say if anything was there. Perhaps it was his imagination. Perhaps it was his fear. He went back to frantically flat-handing the wall trying to find an opening.

"Grrrrooowl!" The deep, threatening growl filled the cave.

Kyle could feel goose bumps pop on his arms. He pressed his back into the wall. He didn't know which way to move, which way to run. He didn't know where the growl came from. He didn't know what the growl came from. What it sounded like it could be, Kyle didn't want to think about. Then he heard the sound of something moving on the gritty dirt flooring. Kyle's heart quivered as he tried hard to widen his eyes to see what lay in the shadows. But then again, maybe he didn't need to see a damn thing. He was getting his ass out of there.

He began frantically feeling along the wall. There had to be an out. How else had he gotten in there? With his bare hands, Kyle began clawing at the rough, jagged rock wall, looking for a soft spot, an opening that had to be there.!

"Grrrrroowl!"

The thunderous growl shook Kyle to the core and weakened his knees.

He fell back against the wall, too stunned to hold himself up to face what suddenly appeared to walk right out of the wall beneath the burning yellow flame. A bear. A gigantic black bear—at least he looked black to Kyle—stood up on its hind legs, towering over Kyle, filling the cave with its bulk. Even in the shadowiness of the cave, Kyle could see the dagger-like claws and the menacingly sharp teeth.

"Grrrrroowl!" The bear lumbered toward Kyle.

Fear gripped Kyle. A lump in the back of his throat kept him from uttering a sound. Urine poured from his body, washing down his legs to his bare feet. Just as he sensed that he was entirely naked, a piercing cramp gripped his heart. Clutching his chest and gawking painfully at the massive beast above him, Kyle collapsed to his knees. Where was his grandfather? Why was he taking so long to appear?

The bear dropped down onto its front legs, its huge, snarling, gaping mouth a foot from Kyle's face. While his right hand clung to his chest, his left arm flew up to cover his head, and he went to screaming, "Granddad! Granddad!"

A booming silence filled Kyle's ears. Then—

"You shame me," Granddad Preston's voice said.

Unshielding his heart and his head, Kyle saw that the wide-open mouth of the bear was gone. Just a few feet away, his grandfather, again dressed in white, his face painted red, sat cross-legged on the floor of the . . . No, he was no longer in the cave. No longer was there a yellow flame casting shadows in the darkness of the cave. There was white light, but Kyle saw no source for that light. He looked around. He was in some sort of house, a long, narrow house. The floor was of dirt, the walls and low ceiling were framed of many small trees stripped of their branches and leaves and covered with many, many hides of animals long since dead. The house was empty except for his grandfather, and Kyle had never been so happy to see the man from whom he'd heard the stories of his Native American and African-American heritage.

"You feared before you were given cause to fear," Granddad Preston said. "The great beast meant you no harm."

"How can you say that? That bear was about to mangle me," Kyle said, realizing that he was still cowering against the wall of what was once the cave. He sat up.

"If that was so, then the bear was within you."

"That makes no sense, Granddad, and I'm not about to try and figure out what you're talking about." Kyle noticed that his grandfather's face was painted red. "Why is your face red?"

"Your fear is within, and it confused you. A warrior must never let his fear confuse him."

"Oh, so now I'm a warrior?"

"You cannot be a warrior if you are not yet a man."

Kyle knew he had just been insulted but had no words to defend himself.

"You have much to learn," Granddad Preston said, "and so little time to learn it."

"And what am I supposed to be learning that I don't already know? I'm not stupid, Granddad, and I am a man. I know you're trying to get me upset, but I'm cool." Kyle wasn't as cool as he was trying to put out. He was more uncomfortable than afraid. He didn't know what his grandfather was going to do to him.

"I asked you before, Granddad, why is your face red?"

"A shaman must shield his face from the light of day. It is the old way."

"Does the 'old way' have anything to do with me. Is that why I'm here?"

Granddad Preston beckoned Kyle to come closer.

Right away Kyle noticed as he began to crawl away from the wall to the center of the house where his grandfather sat that he was no longer completely naked—a loincloth covered his backside and groin. How his clothes had been removed from his body, he didn't know.

Granddad Preston beckoned Kyle to sit as he himself sat. Kyle did so, crossing his legs while looking into his grandfather's stern, unreadable face. Around his long, white, wavy-haired head he wore a strip of rawhide from which a long white feather hung to his shoulder. From a string around his neck hung a small pouch down to his chest. In his hand, he held a larger bag of brown hide covered in beads and dangling hide strips. At his side lay the bear shield that Kyle had last seen hanging over his grandfather's bed in his old house. What was it doing here?

"We don't have much time," Granddad Preston said.

"Time for what?"

"You will see."

"To tell you the truth, Granddad, I'm not interested in seeing anything. But what is this place? Why am I here? Why—"

"You are in the longhouse of the ancestors. You are in a sacred place in the woodlands of our people. My son, you have shamed yourself and the ancestors; you must be brought before them."

"Shamed! I haven't shamed anyone. What are you talking about?"

"You have dishonored your foremothers."

"Like hell I have. I haven't—"

"You use women as the white man used the maidens of our people generations ago."

"Is that what this is about? I don't rape women, Granddad. I don't use women as slaves who have no choice when I want to be with them. The women I see have free will."

"You abuse that will. You do not respect the daughters of man. You want only from them what pleasure you take. That is not honorable."

"I don't believe this." Kyle hit his thigh hard with his fist. "Even in my dreams people are accusing me of shit. Why is everyone getting on me? Granddad, I don't force any woman to be with me. How many times do I have to say this?"

"But you do, my son." Granddad Preston remained calm. "You force them with your charm, with your promises."

"That's bull. You know . . . Wait a minute. I don't have to listen to this. This is just a dream. You're not even real, Granddad, you're dead." I need to just wake my ass up that's all."

"Be still, my son. It is not time to return to your world. You must listen to my words—"

"But, Granddad, I—"

Granddad Preston put up his hand, silencing Kyle.

"You are of Tuscarora blood! You carry the blood of a proud people, a people of honor, a people of morals. The Creator did not give you life for you to shame your people. You must honor your ancestors, my son. You must honor your mother, your father; you must honor yourself. You must show respect for all people and do them no harm."

"Grandad, I swear. I've harmed no one."

"You have harmed many, my son. You have harmed yourself most. You will never be well in your soul unless you learn respect for all people."

"I do—"

Granddad Preston again held up his hand. "My son, you have a false pride, a pride that bares you shame and ignorance. A man of shame is worthless. His life is of little value to his people."

Dumbstruck, Kyle could only look at his grandfather. What was he saying? Was he telling him, like Lady Yasmin, that he was going to die or needed to die?

From his medicine bag, Granddad Preston took a small sack. From that he sprinkled fine particles of dried brown leaves into the small bowl of a long wooden pipe, which to Kyle seemed to just appear in his hand. Kyle chose not to question where the pipe came from, he was still having a hard time dealing with the fact that he was talking to his grandfather at all. He wanted desperately to wake up, but he didn't know how.

Kyle asked instead, "Is that a peace pipe?"

Granddad Preston packed the bowl. "It is a sacred pipe." Then lighting the pipe with fire that Kyle did not see ignited, he handed the smoking pipe to Kyle.

Taking the pipe, Kyle questioned, "Is this tobacco?"

"Hemp. Medicine."

"Medicine? Granddad, hemp is hashish. Hash. A drug."

"Smoke it."

"I can't believe you're giving me drugs." Kyle tried to give the pipe back to his grandfather. "I don't need this. I'm bugging as it is. I saw a big-ass bear that was about to chump down on my ass, and—"

"The bear harms only those who threaten him. Like all animals, he must be respected."

"Well, I sure as hell gave him his respect, I wasn't trying to get up on him."

Granddad Preston would not take the pipe back that Kyle still held out to him. "Smoke of the hemp."

"I told you, Granddad, I'm not smoking this stuff. I'm already on a trip that's blowing my mind. I'm sitting here talking to you and you're dead. I don't know anymore if I'm asleep or awake. This shit is bugging me out. I—"

"Do not disrespect me in this holy place! Watch your words and do as I say."

Kyle remembered what Lady Yasmin said, "You must let the holy one

*guide you, you must not question him. It will not go well for you other-
wise."* It wasn't that Kyle hadn't smoked hash or marijuana before, he
had done so many times and enjoyed the high he got. But the high he
might get from smoking this hemp, he wasn't sure of, just as he wasn't
sure what his grandfather had in mind for him—another flogging?

"No disrespect, Granddad, but why do I have to get high?"

"Time is very short, my son. You do not have time to follow the tradition. You do not have four days to fast, you do not have time to make
sacrifices of your body. You do not have time to sweat from your body the
bad things you've put in."

"Why would I have to do all that?"

"To prepare for your journey. You must seek your vision quest."

"Granddad, that's Indian folklore, that's not real. It's—"

"Speak not of what you do not know."

"I know if I get high, the only vision I'm gonna see is a naked
woman."

"Your words are ignorant, my son. Your mind has cursed you; it al-
lows you to say stupid things. . . ."

Kyle's mouth fell open.

"The mind learns when the tongue is silent, and your tongue is
never silent. Speak not again."

Kyle couldn't believe how demeaning his grandfather was being. His
words stung his pride and insulted his intelligence. They had always
gotten along. How could he talk to him that way? He needed to get out of
there before he said something he'd regret to his grandfather, although
the man was dead. God, above all, he really needed to wake up. Kyle
pinched himself hard on the thigh, hoping that the pain would wake him,
but there was no pain. He felt nothing. He pinched himself again, harder.
Why wasn't he feeling anything?

"In this world, my son, you feel only what the spirits want you to
feel."

Fear crept up Kyle's spine. "I don't wanna be here, Granddad. Let me
go."

"As a child, my son, you filled your mind with childish things that
consume you even now. To journey into manhood, you must fulfill your
vision quest. You never looked inward to find the man that you should
have become. You've only looked outward at the carnal pleasures that

you think make you a man. Your carnal prowess and your years do not make you a man. Principles, morals, courage, strength, and heart make you a man, my son. You must become a man before it is too late."

"I am a man damnit! I'm tired of this bullshit you're babbling. Granddad, I—"

"Silence!"

"But, Granddad—"

"Hold your tongue!"

Stung by his grandfather's rebuke, Kyle, slack-jawed, stared into his grandfather's blazingly angry eyes.

"Smoke the pipe, my son, and question me no more."

The look of unyielding rebuke in his grandfather's face moved Kyle to bring the stem of the calumet to his lips, and although at first hesitant, he dragged hard and long on the peculiar smelling smoke that immediately coated his tongue with a bitter, sharp tang and quickly filled his lungs with heat. Kyle would have thought that the high would have been slow in coming, but the light-headedness was swift and startling. His eyes rolled back in his head, he felt his body go limp, he felt his head lilting as if it wanted to float away on its own. As if in slow motion, Kyle sank to the floor onto his back, yet his eyes popped wide open.

"My son, your vision quest is now beginning." Granddad Preston closed his eyes.

The slow, steady beat of a deep-toned drum and the low, guttural singing of a tribal people began to fill Kyle's ears, but he saw not a drummer or a drum, or a choral of singers. Through the roof that was still on the long-house, he could see a large eagle . . . no, a buzzard, soaring over head, circling—coming closer. Kyle felt helpless—he couldn't lift his arms, he couldn't lift his head. He—

Chapter
25

"Mr. Lawson, Mr. Lawson. Wake up, Mr. Lawson."

Kyle was abruptly yanked from within the walls of the long-house.

"Wake up." The nurse continued to lightly shake Kyle's shoulder.

"Why isn't he waking up?" Vernon asked, shaking Kyle on the other shoulder. "Is he on something?"

"He's been given nothing. He's being observed." The nurse shook Kyle harder, bringing him out of his deep sleep. "He has a mild concussion. Mr. Lawson. Open your eyes, Mr. Lawson."

Kyle groggily opened his eyes.

"Hey, man," Vernon said, again shaking Kyle, "wake up."

At first unsure as to where he was, Kyle stared up at the brilliantly lit fluorescent ceiling overhead where no eagle or buzzard hovered. He could have sworn he had been sitting in the ancient longhouse with his grandfather, talking with him, and of all things, smoking hash, hearing primitive drums, but here he was, flat on his back in a hospital bed. He had had another one of those dreams. He should have been used to them by now, but they were just too bizarre. This time, talking to his grandfather, he could see how disturbed his grandfather was. When his grandfather was alive, he was never this upset with him. So why now? And about that vision quest—sure, he could remember his grandfather telling him, a long time ago, that he had to cleanse himself so that he'd be open to some great vision that would prepare him to be a man. He was around eleven then. His grandfather tried to make him fast, go without eating for four days, but his mother pitched a holy fit. She wouldn't hear of it, or of his grandfather trying to make him have a vision quest. Kyle truly didn't understand it then, and he really didn't understand it now. He was a man, no matter what his grandfather said. He didn't have to see some asinine vision to know that.

Turning his head slightly, Kyle looked at the petite, middle-aged Philippino nurse standing alongside his bed.

"Mr. Lawson, how do you feel?" she asked. "How does your head feel?"

Heavy-tongued and with a swollen jaw, Kyle answered, "I've felt better." He had a dull, throbbing headache that permeated his entire skull. Looking around the emergency room, in a fleetingly lucid moment in the ambulance, he remembered asking what hospital they were taking him to. Kings County Hospital he was told. Thank God he was too far away to be taken to Brookdale, which is where Preston worked.

"Hey, man," Vernon said, "what happened? Were you mugged?"

"I guess you could say that."

"So what happened?"

Kyle wasn't about to talk in front of the nurse or anyone, and fortunately, the emergency room was uncharacteristically sparse for a Friday night in Brooklyn. Perhaps the lingering chill of March was still keeping the riffraff off the streets and out of trouble.

The nurse checked Kyle's pulse. "I'll be back. Keep him talking."

"Sure." Vernon laid his jacket on the foot of the bed. "Are you gonna tell me what happened?"

Kyle frowned as he tried to get more comfortable in the narrow, overly used hospital bed. He was almost too embarrassed to tell Vernon the truth, but he might as well, he had the nurse drag Vernon out of bed to come to the hospital.

Kyle purposely lowered his voice. "Dalia and her punk-ass boyfriend jumped me."

"How the hell did that happen?"

"Man, don't talk so loud. What time is it?"

Vernon quickly checked his watch. "Six forty-eight."

Kyle gripped the side rails of the bed and slowly pulled himself into a sitting position. He was glad to see that he still had on his own clothes.

"Damn, man," Vernon said impatiently, "you're pissing me off. Are you gonna come out with it or not?"

Kyle gingerly touched his head. "I went to see Dalia after I got in from Florida—"

"When were you in Florida?"

"Yesterday. I flew in and flew out, but that's another story. Anyway, I got in early this morning, and on the way home I stopped by Dalia's to talk to her and got tangled up in her drama."

"You walked in on her and her boyfriend?"

"Yes and no. When I got there, her man wasn't in sight. He was there, but he was hiding."

"Hiding where?"

"In the bedroom, in the back. I was in the front room with Dalia."

"And you had no clue that her man was back there?"

"Nope."

"So what were you doing?"

"Talking," Kyle replied, fully aware of the half-truth he was telling. "See, Dalia had called me a day or so before asking for money. She was five months behind in rent, about to get evicted, and asked me for the money."

"How much?"

"Six thousand."

"Damn."

"I wasn't giving up six, but I considered giving her a thou, but then she started wolfing me, getting all loud, telling me that I was gonna give her the money like she could make me. Like I had no choice."

"Was she high?"

"I don't know, but I was trying to get my ass out of there when she called this big ass dude, who'd been hiding back in her bed-room, out to jump me."

"Man, he messed you up. Have you seen your face?"

"I don't need to see my face, I know how it feels." The pain in Kyle's head was making his eyes tear and his teeth hurt. He began to slowly roll his tongue around inside his cheek, making a sour face as he did.

"If there be pain, huh Kyle?" Vernon asked. "You sticking with that?"

"Man, this is different. The dude caught me off guard—"

"Like in football."

"He came at me so fast—"

"Like in football."

"I didn't even know he was back there, and when I tried to get my blows in, Dalia started hitting me on the head from behind with some hard-ass object—"

"Vicious."

"And telling the guy to beat me down."

"Sounds like she was trying to snuff you."

"No telling what would've happened if the cops hadn't shown up. I heard them say something about dumping me somewhere."

"Damn."

"And Dalia started going through my wallet looking for my bank card and credit cards. She was after whatever money I had."

"Damn, man. Dalia wasn't playing. And you used to screw her?"

"Never again." Kyle timidly touched his sore ribs. "That bitch. I was good to her. You know how much money I gave Dalia this past year? Thousands. And she'd turn around and try to snuff me? Me? She got some dude hiding back in her bedroom, laying to rob me. Man, when I get my ass up out of here, I'm gonna— "

"Wait a minute Kyle," Vernon said. "I'm trying to understand something. What kind of relationship did you have with Dalia? Was it money for sex, or did you have a real relationship with her?"

"Man—"

"No hold up, Kyle. I know you weren't exclusive with Dalia,

you had other women. So, what was it supposed to be between you and Dalia?"

"Does it matter, Vernon? Whatever it was, Dalia wasn't supposed to be trying to bash my head in and rob me."

"True, but what was up between y'all before this incident?"

"Sex, man. It was sex. Yeah, I gave her lots of money, but not money for sex. I was trying to be right with her."

"By giving her money?"

"Isn't that what women want? Vernon, I know you don't think you can be with a woman and not give her money or something."

"Yeah, maybe. But dinner, a movie, or a Happy Meal at McDonald's might've brought you less trouble then this."

"I wasn't giving Dalia diamonds, Vernon, but a few dollars could buy her what she wanted. I wasn't trying to be her sugar daddy."

"Yeah, but, Kyle, you started the relationship out like that, and Dalia obviously saw you as a sugar daddy from the get-go, so she had to expect that whenever she got behind the eight ball, she could turn to you. Man you almost can't fault her for how she was thinking."

"Like hell I can't. Dalia's dumb ass was trying to kill me for my money." A piercing pain in Kyle's head made him squeeze his right eye shut. First, his cold messed up his head and he seemed to have gotten over that, but now, this beating had messed him up even more. Damn, he was tired of the pain.

"Vernon, forget Dalia. I had ended it with her dumb ass even before this happened."

"And when did you do that?"

"A few days ago. I mean I had been with her, but I had taken back my credit card—"

"Were you with her last night? I mean, did you do her? No, that's stupid. You wouldn't've done that. Not with that dude there."

Kyle couldn't look Vernon in the eye. He glanced around the large room of hanging faded blue curtains, empty hospital beds, and IV poles pointing up at the bright fluorescent lights overhead. Several beds down, a woman lay moaning in her discomfort while a nurse and a doctor stood a few feet away discussing her treatment.

"Kyle, don't tell me you did Dalia while her man was hiding out in her bedroom."

"Vernon, I didn't know he was back there. And, man, think about it. The dude knew I was out in the living room. He knew I was doing her, he had to hear us. Why didn't he come out and beat me up then?"

"Maybe he's into voyeurism?"

"Hell no. He stayed back there because he wanted Dalia to screw me to get the money, but when I wasn't giving it up and tried to leave, that's when she called him and he jumped me."

Vernon shook his head in disgust. "Damn."

"They planned it, man. They set me up and—"

"And you fell for it, Kyle. Man, when are you gonna stop letting your dick dictate your actions? Kyle, you shouldn't've been there. You ended it with Dalia, you should've stayed away from her. You could've been killed, trying for a last one for the road."

Like in his dreams, Kyle couldn't defend his actions. Vernon was right. He had gone with the moment, knowing full well it was wrong.

"Man, you gotta get straight. If HIV don't catch up with you, someone's man will."

"Don't dog me, man! I know I was wrong. And I'm not totally stupid, I wear condoms."

"Yeah, but, Kyle—"

"I heard you, man!" Kyle gripped the side rails of the bed. "Damnit, I know I was wrong to go to Dalia's, but I'm done with her and Lorna. I'm done with the game."

"For how long, Kyle, a week? Or is it until your face heals, or will it be until you see another piece of ass you just gotta get with?"

"Man, I don't need you lecturing me!" Kyle's head was pounding. He pressed the balls of his hands to his temples and again squeezed his eyes shut.

"You okay?"

Kyle's eyes shot open. "Hell no I'm not working! Where's that nurse? I need some pain killers."

Vernon looked from one end of the emergency room to the other. "She must've stepped out. Want me to ask that other nurse down there?"

"Forget it. I'll wait. Look, man, I'm done with my old life, okay?"

Vernon gave Kyle a deadpan look.

"I'm serious, man, I mean it. But how you getting on me, Vernon? What about you? You're a player, just like me."

"I was never quite like you, Kyle. If I was with a woman, I didn't do anyone else out of respect for her."

Here we go with that respect thing again. "Have you been talking to my grandfather?"

"Huh?"

"Never mind." Kyle huffed quietly. "See, Vernon, I can remember when you did three girls at a time."

"When I was young and foolish, which I am not anymore."

Kyle grumbled, "Yeah, right."

"Kyle. Man, there's more to life than how many women we can hit before we can't ever get it up again. I want family. I want a wife that can look at me and know that she can trust me. With Jennifer, I'm about to permanently change my game."

"Is she pregnant? Did she set the baby trap for you?"

Giving Kyle a hard, long glare, Vernon turned and went to the foot of the bed. With his back to Kyle, he took in the quietness of the near-empty room. Kyle was his boy; they'd been friends since before he could remember. He'd never made a connection with another dude like he did with Kyle, before or since. He wanted to keep that special friendship they had, but if Kyle didn't or couldn't change his whoring ways, they weren't going to be able to hang out. He already knew that Jennifer wasn't the type to put up with him or his friends hanging out in clubs, picking up women, jumping from bed to bed. She'd said as much when they met. Jennifer wanted what he wanted—an honest relationship that each of them could depend on. And if he kept hanging out with Kyle, she would never trust him.

"Vernon, I didn't mean that, man."

Turning back, Vernon questioned, "Then you should not've said it."

"Yeah, but I thought maybe Jennifer pressured you—"

"No, Kyle, she didn't. I decided on my own that it's time to settle down. And maybe it's time for you, too, Kyle. At least time for you to be thinking about settling down."

"I did that once before, remember?"

"Kyle, you weren't ready when you married Gail, and I told you that at the time."

"Well, I thought I was ready." Ignoring his headache, Kyle tried to lower the railing on the side of his bed. He wasn't having much luck. "But this isn't about me and Gail. It's about you and me. You don't trust me, man."

"Should I?"

"Hell yeah. I've changed."

"Since this morning?"

"Or at least I'm working on changing. This is a wake-up call. I have to settle down or—"

"Or you're gonna get your ass killed." Vernon stood again at the side of the bed. He wanted to believe Kyle was on his way to changing but couldn't. He'd seen Kyle in action too many times.

Kyle elbowed the railing. "Lower this damn thing."

Vernon had no trouble lowering the railing. "Are you gonna press charges?"

"I already did. I'm not about to let Dalia or her thug get away with beating me down." Kyle touched one of the knots on the back of his head. The bandage wasn't doing anything to quiet the pain—his head was throbbing. It was a wonder Dalia hadn't cracked his skull.

"Did you call your parents or Carole?"

"I don't need them up in my business Vernon. Besides, if they get wind of this, I'll never hear the last of it." Kyle swung his legs over the side of the bed. "In fact, I'm getting up out of here—"

"No, no, no," the nurse said, hurrying toward Kyle. "You cannot get out of bed."

"I can if I'm leaving."

"Kyle, man," Vernon said, "you have a concussion."

"A headache. I'll take two aspirin at home." Sliding off the bed, Kyle landed squarely on his bare feet. "Where're my shoes?"

"Mr. Lawson, you must not get up."

"Where're my shoes?" Kyle asked again.

Vernon looked at the large white plastic bag at the foot of the bed. "They might be in this bag." He opened the bag. The shoes and Kyle's jacket were inside.

"Mr. Lawson, the doctor wants you to stay in the hospital for a twenty-four-hour observation. You should not walk around. You could black out."

"Nurse, I appreciate that," Kyle said, taking his shoes from Vernon, "but I have to go. What you could do for me is give me a couple of painkillers, that would help."

"I cannot give you anything. You are to be observed."

"I'll observe myself in my own bed—and everyone had better be out of my damn house." Kyle stepped into his shoes and left them untied. His head hurt too much to bend down.

"You cannot just leave," the nurse persisted, "the doctor must discharge you."

"I'm saving him the trouble." Kyle grabbed the plastic bag. "You have all of my information—bill me. Come on, Vernon. I need you to drive me to my car."

"Sir, you should not drive."

Ignoring the nurse, Kyle continued on toward the EXIT sign.

"What were you doing in Florida?" Vernon asked, pulling on his own jacket as he and Kyle hurried through the emergency room.

"Getting scammed. Have you ever heard of dead people coming back in dreams?"

"Yeah, but one better not come back to me. They have nothing to say that I wanna hear."

"That's the truth," Kyle said, thinking about his grandfather. Kyle began unwrapping the white bandage from around his head. "But suppose your Uncle Ray came back to tell you where he hid that winning lottery ticket that everyone swears he'd bought before he died?"

"Yeah, well, that's all he better say, because asleep or awake, I don't wanna see any dead people. They might wanna take my ass some place I don't wanna go—like to hell, and I don't mean where Satan is. I mean like to zombie land or nightmare land. I don't play that. I have enough problems dealing with the troubles of the living, I don't need the dead screwing up my life, too. That's probably why they have a psyche ward at most hospitals in this city—dead people driving folks outta their damn minds." Vernon looked at Kyle. "You dreaming about somebody dead? Your grandfather?"

"Hell no. I just asked." Tossing his blood-stained bandage into a garbage receptacle outside the hospital door, Kyle decided to keep his mouth shut about the dreams he'd been having—Vernon would think he was out of his mind. And actually, Kyle was beginning to think so himself. The dreams were feeling more real with each one he had. Why was his grandfather hell-bent on driving him out of his mind?

Chapter
26

Kyle refused to let Vernon drive him home, and rejected his offer to tail him to see him safely to his front door. Hell, he wasn't drunk—he didn't need a designated driver or babysitter. He had been driving since he was seventeen without a single accident, so a seven-minute drive home he could easily handle—or so he thought. He had a hell of a time staying awake and felt himself about to doze off twice. While he blasted his car stereo loud enough to vibrate his car and make his headache worse, he kept his windows closed so that his music didn't shatter the early Saturday morning tranquility of the Brooklyn streets he passed through. Still, it was sheer will that kept Kyle's eyes open. He had no desire to kill or be killed because of his foolish decision to drive himself home.

Finally pulling up safely in front of his house, Kyle relaxed his grip on the steering wheel and shut down the music. His head was killing him. If only he could get his hands on Dalia—he'd kill her.

Kyle looked up at his house. His Aunt Agatha and Uncle Otis should have cleared out by now, at least they better had, he wasn't in the mood for dealing with anyone, and although he had promised Vernon he'd call him when he got in, the way he was feeling, the only thing he'd be calling was hogs—that's how deep he'd probably be sleeping. That is, if he could make it to his front door without throwing up or blacking out. Self-consciously, he gingerly touched the back of his head. The knots and lumps were definitely there, and so were the stitches and patches of dried blood. He probably should have left the bandage on a few days more, but that was something his parents didn't need to see.

Just in case his mother was up and looking out her window, Kyle got out of the car like nothing was wrong and hurried into his house. The shallow sigh of relief he breathed as he locked his door with one hand and with the other clutched his head quickly turned into spastic gasps. With his jacket still on, he sat down heavily on the living room sofa and lay back. Upstairs in the bathroom, he had a bottle of ibuprofen, but climbing the stairs was the furthest thing from his mind as he sank into a dark pit of unconsciousness.

Through the naked tree branches overhead, Kyle could see that the eagle was no longer descending. It was soaring higher up in the sky, yet close enough still for him to see the great span of its majestic wings. Kyle couldn't take his eyes off the eagle as he felt like he, too, was soaring, like he was one with the eagle. Perhaps if he spread his arms wide, he, too, could fly high with the eagle and—

"Aaaaaah!"

Sudden searing, scalding pain in Kyle's chest made him contort his body, arch his back, and tensely strain the muscles in his neck as he cried out, awakening himself from his trancelike state of soaring with the eagle overhead. While his arms were outstretched to his sides, Kyle realized he was lying flat on his back with his legs spread just as wide as his arms. He lifted his head, looked down at his chest, and was horrified to see two ropes threaded through holes in his flesh just below his collarbones, on both sides of his chest, yet there was no blood. Coils of rope lay alongside his body. Aghast, Kyle went to grab for the ropes, but his arms wouldn't move. His heart racing, his eyes stretched, Kyle looked from one side to the other and saw that his wrists were tied to stakes in the ground. He tried to move his legs. They, too, were tied down. From deep in Kyle's throat, a bloodcurdling wail poured from between his lips as he tried to pull against the ropes that bound him to the stakes, but it was futile—he was bound tight. Every fiber of his body tensed with great agitation from the pain in his chest and the fear that consumed him as he looked down the length of his body and saw that he was completely naked, completely helpless. Panicked, he twisted his head from side to side looking for his grandfather. It had to be he who, again, was torturing him.

"Granddad!"

"I am here, my son."

Kyle dug the top of his head into the ground and rolled his eyes back in their sockets, straining to see his grandfather standing behind him.

"Granddad. Granddad, what is this in my chest? Why do you have me tied like this? What're you doing to me?"

"The tranquility of the field of flowers did not quiet your spirit or make you reflect. The obscure stillness of the cave did not calm your soul or give you pause."

"But how was I to know what I was supposed to do in those places? You didn't tell me anything."

"It is no man's burden to tell you what to do. You are no longer in diapers."

"No, but I'm not in the real world either." *Kyle strained to sit up but couldn't.* "This is a goddamn dream!"

"Are you sure?"

"Granddad, you're dead! You're not real."

"Are you sure, my son?"

"Oh, God," *Kyle moaned.* "This isn't real."

Granddad Preston looked upon his grandson with pity. "For some, my son, the passage to manhood is easy. For others, it is a difficult journey that eludes the unfortunate. . . ."

"I'm a man! I—"

"The solitude of a mountaintop will not bring you to look within. For you, my son, the okeepa, the sun dance, is your only chance. If you do not journey inward and find the core of your being, you cannot be saved. You will not fulfill the promise of your birthright."

"Give me another chance. I'll look inward. I'll—"

"You must change—"

"Granddad, listen to me! I'll change. I know what I've done wrong. I'll be a better person—I am a better person."

"Only in your own eyes."

"But, Granddad—"

"Silence your tongue!" *Granddad Preston ordered sternly.*

Kyle fell silent.

"My son, if it is in you to be a better person, we will soon find out."

"Granddad, please." Tears spilled down the sides of Kyle's face. "I'm in pain. Please let me go."

"True pain, my son, you do not yet know." Granddad Preston, his head back, raised his arms high to the sky.

To Kyle, the sun seemed to come out of hiding and shine brightly down on him, making him squeeze his eyes tight.

"Granddad, please. Please take these ropes out of my chest. Please don't put me through this. Untie me."

"The okeepa is of your choosing, my son. Your life's journey has brought you to this place." Granddad Preston dropped his arms and stepped back.

Suddenly, Kyle felt the coils of rope at his sides move and begin to rise above him. Hair-raising fear gripped him as the rope quickly grew taut and pulled at the flesh on his chest, stretching it like taffy. To his utter horror, Kyle was being pulled up off the ground toward the large naked tree branch overhead by the two ropes threaded through his flesh. His wrists and ankles were suddenly free of their restraints as his body lifted higher. Screaming from the mind-numbing pain, Kyle grabbed frantically for the ropes that tore at his skin, stretching it, pulling it from his chest. With all his might, he tensed every muscle in his body as he gripped the ropes in his fists and pulled on them while holding his stiff, dangling body in midair, trying to keep his weight off the ropes and off his flesh.

"Do not resist, my son. Open yourself to the Great White Spirit."

Kyle heard his grandfather through his screams, but he couldn't let go. He was too afraid that letting go meant tearing two large patches of his flesh from his body. He ignored the pain in his arms, he ignored the strain in his neck and back, he struggled to hold on to the ropes, but his struggle was in vain. The muscles in Kyle's arms urgently screamed from their own pain and began to shake uncontrollably. All the weight training he'd done over the years proved futile. He wasn't going to be able to hold on much longer. If this was the way he was supposed to go out, and he felt like, indeed, he was going to die, then what was there for him to do but let go? Fixing his eyes on the bright blue sky where the eagle no longer soared, Kyle gave up his struggle, gave up his screaming, and released his weak, shaky hold on the ropes.

Kyle's body dropped to within inches from the ground, but the ropes held him firm. The knife-piercing pain shooting through his body ex-

ploded in his ears, deafening him to the animalistic howls that gushed shamelessly from his throat. His body jerked and twisted in air, his arms flailed around wildly touching nothing, while his head bobbed and turned, disorienting him as to which direction he was facing. He couldn't see his grandfather, he could see no one. He was left alone to dangle from a tree that was as naked as he, but stronger by far to hold him against his will while he reluctantly gave himself over to the pain that racked his body. He could cry no more, his voice deserted him as a ghostly silence fell around him. He wondered how long it would be before the ropes tore the flesh from his body and released him from his torture?

What must have been only a few minutes felt like torturously long hours. Unable to stand the pain a second longer and feeling faint, Kyle let his head drop back, elongating his neck, pulling even more on his strained flesh. The weight of his body was killing him. It felt like his lungs and heart were about to be torn from his chest. The pain was unbearable. In his head, he pled for death. His useless arms hung languorous at his sides. Kyle closed his eyes on the bright sun above, but he was unable to close his mind or his mouth on the pain that branded his tense, pain-racked body. Somehow he knew he had to be deep in sleep in the real world in order to be so completely absorbed in this dream world. He was at his grandfather's will. There was no one to save him. Unable to save himself, Kyle dangled like a puppet waiting to be manipulated by some Great White Spirit of enlightenment.

Chapter
27

Riiiing!

Vernon could not know that neither the squeal of the ringing telephone nor Kyle's own voice on his answering machine could puncture the wall of Kyle's unconsciousness. He did not know that Kyle was deep in a place that no sound could penetrate, and even as Kyle lay on his living room sofa, the pain of his dream overshadowed the pain of his consciousness. Vernon had been trying to reach Kyle for the past forty-five minutes, and on this, his fourth call, Vernon decided not to leave a message and instead slammed down the phone.

"Dammit, Kyle! Why don't you ever listen to anyone? If you blacked your ass out in your house, I'm gonna have to go next door and get the key from your parents, and when they ask me why I want the key, I'm sure as hell gonna tell 'em that you got your stupid ass beat up by one of your women. Serves you right if they get on your ass."

As soon as Vernon pulled on his jacket, his telephone rang.

Vernon snatched up the telephone.

"Kyle!"

"No, baby, it's me," Jennifer said.

Vernon exhaled loudly.

"Oh, you don't wanna talk to me?"

"Baby, of course I wanna talk to you. I was expecting a call from Kyle."

"Do you want me to call back?"

"No, no. How you doing?"

"I can call back."

"No. What're you up to?" Concern for Kyle was quickly consigned to the far reaches of Vernon's mind. He'd check on his friend, as soon as he finished talking to the woman he loved.

The weight of Kyle's head on the back of his neck hurt terribly, but it was not nearly as bad at the excruciating pain in his chest. It hurt to breathe. Each breath was like shards of glass in his parched throat. Silent tears washed down the sides of Kyle's face onto his head, he couldn't cry out anymore—simply moving his mouth brought more agony to his maimed body. The burn in his thighs and ass muscles forced him to relax his muscles and dangle more loosely on the odious ropes that held him still. Kyle's mind told him he'd only been hanging for a few minutes, but to his body, it felt like a million hours. He had never known such horrific pain. It permeated every fiber of his being. Kyle tried hard to pray for death, but even in his mind, his words were jumbled. He couldn't focus, he couldn't think. Death didn't come to him, only more pain and a mind rendered blank of any profound revelations like a blackboard with nothing written upon it. And the nothingness, inside and out, was just as disturbing as the pain. There was nothing moving around Kyle—not even the kiss of a breeze from a butterfly fluttering its wings—and there was not a sound—not even the whisper of a cricket hiding in a bush. Whatever was supposed to come into Kyle's mind wasn't even trying to come, and it was angering him that he was helpless, that he was being punished for living his life, not by anyone else's rules, but by his own. And what was so wrong with that? If he died, and he hoped he would, from the tearing of his flesh and from the blood that would pour from his body, it would be his grandfather's fault.

For the third time Lorna pressed Kyle's bell and waited, hoping that he'd come to the door. She knew he was home, his car was parked right in front of his house. She'd taken a chance coming by, she knew Kyle might not want to see her, but what she had to say had to be done in person. Again, she rang the bell, pressing it hard and long.

"Hello? Can I help you?" Betty asked from her stoop.

Lorna was slow to turn toward the voice that called out to her. Kyle had told her that his parents lived next door and this could only be his mother. Who else would have the nerve to be so nosy? They'd never met before, and meeting Kyle's mother at this moment wasn't the best time. Not when Kyle had thrown her aside like an old pair of shoes after she told her husband she wanted a divorce. The timing was just wrong.

"Are you looking for my son?"

"If Kyle Lawson is your son, yes, I am looking for him."

"And you are?" Betty wasn't so sure she liked the look of this woman? She didn't look too happy, her face was too tight.

"I'm Lorna Renault, Mrs. Lawson, a good friend of Kyle's. Do you know if he is in? I see his car there, but he is not answering the bell."

"Kyle is probably sleeping—*with another woman.* When he wakes up, I'll tell him you came by."

Lorna checked her watch. "It is nine-fifteen. It is a little late to be sleeping."

"Actually, on a Saturday, it's still rather early. Kyle likes to sleep a bit late on weekends, but I'll make sure he knows that you were here."

She is trying to get rid of me. "Mrs. Lawson, I am a very close friend of Kyle's. I went with him to Florida yesterday. We—"

"Florida? Kyle wasn't in Florida yesterday."

"Oh, but he was. We flew there early yesterday, but we came back late last night."

"What in the world was Kyle doing in Florida?"

"He went to meet with my aunt."

Betty froze. *Oh, God. Don't tell me that stupid boy is going around meeting family members. Is this woman about to tell me that she and Kyle are getting married? If she is, I don't wanna hear it.*

"Miss . . . or is it Mrs. Renault?"

"It's Lorna."

Betty knew what that meant. "Well, Lorna, why don't I have Kyle call you as soon as he gets up?"

"It is very important that I see Kyle now." Lorna again pressed the bell, pushing it so hard her finger hurt.

It better not be that important, Betty looked hard at Lorna's stomach, but she was unable to tell anything through her loose-fitting jacket.

"Well, Lorna, if Kyle's bedroom door is closed and he's sound asleep, he'll never hear the bell. So, Lorna, when Kyle is up and about, I'll tell him to call you. It was really nice meeting you, Lorna."

Lorna again pressed the bell. There was no mistaking the sarcasm in Kyle's mother's words and the animosity in her glare. No telling what Kyle had said about her, that is, if he told his mother anything at all about their relationship. *The old bitty is acting like she does not want me near her precious son. Some women are so obvious in their jealousy of me. If this woman has her way, Kyle would probably still be in diapers, but Kyle is a grown man.*

"As you can see," Betty impatiently put her hand on her hip, "Kyle isn't coming to the door."

Lorna leaned back against the door. "I'll wait." *I have to see Kyle. I have to talk to him. He cannot push me aside. He cannot throw me aside, especially after I have told Stanley that I will divorce him, that I will start a new life in America with Kyle. But that was before Kyle said it was over between us, that was before I found out that I was pregnant. Kyle has to marry me. Stanley will not take me back, and I cannot go back to Jamaica pregnant with another man's child. My family will be disgraced.*

Betty couldn't believe the desperate women Kyle picked up. "Lorna, if I may point out, loitering is not permitted in this neighborhood. I suggest you leave before someone calls the police."

Now it was Lorna's turn to put her hand on her hip. She was used to bossy mothers—her soon-to-be ex-mother-in-law was bossy—and she knew well how to handle her. But then, perhaps this wasn't the time to handle Kyle's mother. She wouldn't gain any advantage with Kyle or his mother if she disrespected her.

"In that case, I guess I will leave," Lorna said, softening her tone. "Please, tell Kyle that I was here, and that it is vitally important I speak with him."

"I most certainly will," Betty said drily.

Pressing her lips tight, Lorna looked once at the door before leaving Kyle's stoop and going back to her car. *Nosy old bitty. I'll make sure Kyle sees very little of you.*

Until Lorna drove away, Betty didn't move an inch. *Kyle is going to hear my mouth as soon as he gets rid of whomever he's with. It's damn ridiculous that women show up on his doorstep while he hides up in his bedroom with another woman in his bed. That boy needs to grow up!*

Betty slammed her front door, shattering the early morning tranquility of her neighbors just beginning their day. She didn't have time for Kyle's foolishness. She had breakfast to cook for her sisters-in-law and a real man to take care of.

Kyle could feel the heat of the sun blazing down on his upturned face. Sweat and tears of misery pooled together as they continually weeped into his hairline, onto his scalp, and dripped to the ground. He wanted badly to wet his parched, cracked lips, but knew that his tongue was dry and that the effort to move any part of his body would bring him more pain. He had yet to open his eyes again, he didn't have the strength, and what was there for him to see but the blinding, scorching sun that showed no mercy on his sorrowful body? All the time, effort, and pride he'd devoted over the years to his well-muscled physique and his good looks he'd trade in a heartbeat for a glass of water and the feel of the solid earth under his feet. He thought about the vital fluid his body was losing but could do nothing about the sweating. He hated that he was reduced to tears like a weakling with no backbone, but that, too, he could do nothing about. He couldn't believe how submissive his body was to the pain and how quickly his mind scrambled to find a safe haven in the dark recesses of his brain, hiding, trembling in its fear that it would never find a way to free him. He never would have thought his body or mind, as strong as they were, could succumb so swiftly to the weakness of his flesh.

As Kyle's life's breath began to ebb, his mind began to embrace the darkness that protected it from the anguish of his despair. If only he could lift his head, maybe he could—

"Aaaaaaaagh . . ." *someone screamed!*

The scream shot through Kyle like a bullet. His eyes flew open and quickly shut against blinding sun. He tried to lift his head but couldn't, it was as if a stick was lodged in the front of his neck.

"Aaaaaaaagh."

Ignoring his pain, grimacing and squinting at once, Kyle again tried to lift his head; he needed to see who was screaming. It was a woman's scream; that, he knew. Straining against his pain, his teeth bared, his neck muscles tight and bulging, Kyle pulled his head up several inches; yet he could see not a thing below the horizon. Still straining, Kyle let his head drop slowly back. What did it matter? Even if he could see who it was that was screaming, there was nothing he could do to help.

"Aaaaaaaaaagh."

That scream filled Kyle's mind completely. It was as if the person were in his head.

"Help me! Oh, God. Please, help me."

Kyle's eyes popped open, but it wasn't the brightness of the sun he saw, it was the whiteness of the sky that spread before him. He stared unblinkingly into the whiteness as it dawned that he knew whose voice it was—it was Carole's. It was his sister's.

Chapter
28

"Please, let me go back to my family."

Kyle heard Carole's plea. And then as if a switch were turned on in his head, he saw Carole, he saw her as clear as day. He saw her naked breasts—nothing covered the top of her body, while from the waist down she wore a brown fringed rawhide skirt. Her long hair was wild all over her head, and her feet were bare. But it was her hands, bound in front of her, tied with rope, that startled Kyle. Carole was being pulled along behind a white man dressed as a frontiersman sitting tall on a horse—she was his captive. Kyle couldn't believe his eyes. Surely, it wasn't real.

Carole tripped. She fell to the ground. Heartlessly, she was dragged along behind the horse, her face in the dirt, her face and body scraped by the rough ground under her.

"Carole!" Kyle croaked, his body again tense, his fists tight, his jaw clinched as he strained with a throaty grunt to hold his head up.

The pain bowed Kyle's body into a horizontal arch. Every muscle in his body popped, holding him prone in midair, paralyzing him, rolling his eyes back in his head, but he quickly re-focused. He saw Carole as she was roughly grabbed up off the ground by the man who was no longer on the horse. Carole's tear-streaked face was scratched, bruised, and dirty.

The man brutally pulled Carole to him, and as dirty as she was, he began kissing on her, feeling her up, roughly pawing her breasts, making her squirm and fight to try and free herself. The look of fear and horror that masked Carole's face filled Kyle with pain greater than the pain he had been enduring.

Suddenly, it dawned on Kyle—he was no longer in physical pain. There was no pain in his chest or in his body anywhere. Amazed, he gingerly pulled against the ropes while pushing all the air out of his lungs and sucking his chest in. Nothing hurt, and although there was no physical pain, the memory of that awful pain lingered in his mind. How could his skin be numb to the pain when he was still hanging by his flesh? But it wasn't his flesh that he should be worrying about. What he'd gone through, what pain he'd suffered, wasn't important anymore. It was Carole who was in trouble and who needed to be rescued. He hated seeing his sister humiliated and hurt because of who she was—a woman. In his mind's eye, he could still see Carole, her wrists still tied, trying in vain to fend off her attacker, but she was overwhelmed, overpowered. Carole was thrown to the ground onto her back, and just as quickly, the man threw himself on top of her, forcing bloodcurdling screams to burst from her that sliced through Kyle like a knife.

"Oh, God," Betty said, hanging up the telephone.

"What's wrong?" Tess asked of her sister-in-law. "Who was that?"

"Sonji's mother. Carole and Sonji were in an accident."

"My God. Are they all right?" Louise asked.

"She doesn't know. They've been taken to the hospital. Sonji's parents are on their way there now."

"What hospital? Is it here in Brooklyn?"

"No, they're up in the Bronx—Jacoby. They were driving down from upstate, Port Jervis, and Carole was driving. They were on the Hutchinson River Parkway."

"Did Sonji's mother say how it happened?"

"She doesn't know much of anything. She just found out." Betty started taking off her apron. Lunch would have to wait. "I have to get to the hospital."

"I'll go with you," Louise said.

"No, no, I need you and Tess to stay here."

"You're gonna drive yourself to the Bronx?" Tess asked.

"Actually, I'm going next door to get Kyle. Tess, do me a favor."

"Anything."

"Call Preston. His telephone numbers are right there in that address book on the table. Tell him to meet me at the hospital."

"Right away."

"Oh, and, Louise, Marvin's medicine—"

"Betty, go see about Carole. We know how to take care of our brother."

"Okay, but don't wake him up. And when he does wake up, don't tell him about Carole until you hear from me. I don't want him to worry." Betty took her black jacket from the hall closet. "Oh, and about lunch—"

"Go on, Betty," Tess said. "We got this."

On her way out the door, Betty grabbed Kyle's house keys. She didn't have time to stand on his stoop ringing his bell.

With every fiber of his being, Kyle wanted to rescue Carole. He needed to save her from the bastard who was raping her, taking from her something she had not willingly given any man. With all his might, Kyle slowly drew his arms up and got a firm hold on the ropes that held him prisoner. Growling and grunting, calling on Herculean strength he never knew he possessed, Kyle pulled and pulled until the ropes snapped the very branch that once seemed stronger than he. He fell to the ground, but somehow it was on his feet he landed. With his fists clinched, his teeth bared, his eyes wide, Kyle turned in circles, searching for Carole, searching for her attacker.

Granddad Preston suddenly appeared. "You have freed yourself. It is good."

"Where's Carole? Someone's attacking Carole, Granddad. She needs my help. Where is she?"

"Does it hurt you to see your sister violated?"

"Damn right! I'm gonna kill the bastard!"

"You cannot kill that which you cannot touch."

"Where is he?"

"My son, has pain given you wisdom?"

Kyle circled his grandfather. "I don't have time for riddles, Granddad. I have to find Carole. Help me find her."

"Are you not worried about your own pain? Do you not worry about the holes in your chest?"

Kyle hadn't given a thought to the holes in his chest or to the pain he endured. He didn't glance down at his chest, which no longer held the ropes, or down past his waist, which was no longer bare. His thoughts were only of Carole.

"Granddad, help me find Carole. We have to help her."

"Sit, my son. Carole will be fine." Granddad Preston sank easily to the ground, crossing his legs as he sat.

"But Carole—"

"Do as I say."

Although he didn't want to, Kyle sat. His mind was racing just as swiftly as his heart. He hoped that Carole was okay, that she had not been violated. Or—

"Wait a minute, was what I saw happening to Carole an illusion? Is that because of the hash I smoked?"

"In Carole's past life, she was taken by the white man, just as he took our land. The people will remember for generations to come, but Carole remembers not. Her path in life has been dictated by her past life. The white man was very strong. You, my son, would not have been able to save your sister, and you could not save her now when your hands were unclean and bound by your own transgressions."

Ashamed, Kyle didn't try to hide the tears that slipped down his face. That some bastard would hurt his sister angered him. He cried out of rage that he couldn't help her and out of guilt that the way he'd been living his life was the reason he had been of no use to Carole.

"Carole's past is the history of many a mother's daughter," Granddad Preston said. "It is the duty of a father, of a brother, of a husband to protect the virtue of the maidens under his roof. A man cannot protect the maidens of his village if he cannot first protect the maidens under his roof. A maiden must be protected from harm and from misuse from the hands of strangers, and from the hands of loved ones. Without the maidens, man fails, man perishes. It is wise, my son, for you to remember that a maiden's mind and soul is just as important as the flesh of her earthly body. Honor this."

Giving some thought to the meaning behind his grandfather's words, Kyle wiped his face. He might not have taken any woman by force, but as his mother had said, he had seduced many women with smooth words, an alluring smile, and promises of a future he had no intention of honoring.

He had used women for the pleasure they afforded him, but for them, he sacrificed nothing. He never cared how a woman felt after he was done with her; he often left them after he'd gotten his fill. No, he might not have forced himself on any woman, but he had used them and callously tossed them aside so that he could take up with someone new. He wouldn't want anyone to treat Carole like that, especially knowing that when Carole was eighteen she had been hurt by a man who professed to love her. Hadn't she sworn off men because of that experience? Hadn't she told him that time and again? Wasn't he that same man she detested?

A cold feeling of shame washed over Kyle. He lowered his head. Carole had chosen an alternate lifestyle, but just the same, like most women, Carole was a daughter, a sister, and soon to be a wife to Sonji. Many more women were mothers, grandmothers, aunts, friends, and confidantes. Kyle wanted no one to harm his sister or his mother, in any way, physically or emotionally. And God forbid if someone should harm Dawn. Kyle didn't even want to think about it. He covered his face.

Granddad Preston said nothing, but he nodded slowly.

Kyle didn't like feeling that he had been no better than every other man who had no respect for women. He didn't like knowing that everyone had been right about him, but that's not how he wanted to live out the rest of his life.

"Granddad—" With his face still covered, Kyle hadn't realized that his grandfather had vanished. He was left alone to ponder the changes he had to make in his life.

Betty entered Kyle's living room just as Kyle opened his eyes. "Carole's been in an accident."

Instantly wide awake, his headache barely there, Kyle bolted up off the sofa. "Is she all right? Was she raped?"

That question gave Betty pause. "She was in a car accident, Kyle. Why would you ask if she'd been raped?"

Looking around the room, Kyle realized that he had again been dreaming. *Those dreams feel so damn real.* "Was Carole driving? Mom, you know Carole's a terrible driver. I told her not to drive." His heart was racing. "How bad is it?"

"I don't know. She's at Jacoby Hospital up in the Bronx."

Giving not a thought to the possibility that he might black out again, Kyle started for the door. "Let's go."

Betty started to head for the door but turned back. "You're dressed," she said.

"I hope so, Mom. I'm not going out of the house naked."

"Well, were you here earlier? Didn't you hear your bell ring?"

"Mom, can we just go?" Kyle opened the door. "We have to get to Carole."

Chapter
29

It had been a week since Carole's accident, and Kyle hadn't blacked out one time. The knots on the back of his head were gone, while Carole's swollen lip and two black eyes from being smashed in the face by the car's exploding air bag had healed considerably, and her broken nose and sprained wrist were still on the mend. Sonji had a dislodged shoulder and a nasty bruise on her forehead, and like Carole, she was healing also. If they had not been wearing their seat beats, albeit that Sonji had been wearing her shoulder strap behind her back instead of across her chest, no telling how bad off they could have been. As was suspected, Carole had been driving. According to Sonji, Carole had done pretty well until she got down in the Hunt's Point section on the Hutchinson River Parkway where cars merged into two lanes crossing over the bridge. That's where she lost control, collided with another car, bounced off, and rammed head-on into the bridge railing.

"That car was too close," Carole said in her own defense. "He came into my lane."

Of course, the driver of the other car said the same about Carole. The insurance company would have the last say.

Kyle was just glad to see that Carole and Sonji both were all right. He picked them both up from the hospital and squired them home and had been speaking to Carole at least once a day since then. He had yet to tell her about his dreams or what happened to her in the last one, he didn't think that would be something she'd want to hear. Besides, he was still trying to understand the connection between Carole's accident and his dream.

Each night since the accident, Kyle had gone to bed with some, no, with great trepidation, not knowing if he was in for another dream-scape, and dreaded the horrors his grandfather might visit upon him. But to his surprise, he slept through each night and dreamed about nothing. At first that was surprising, but then he surmised his grandfather had done what he set out to do—scare him to death.

After Kyle got back from the hospital that Saturday, and after checking on his father, he came home to take a shower. It was while he was showering he discovered two faint brown circular marks about the size of nickels on each side of his chest. Dripping wet, he had gotten out of the shower, water still running, to stand in front of the mirrored medicine cabinet. He stood gawking at the four spots that were never there on his chest before. He couldn't believe what he was seeing. With his washcloth, he scrubbed his chest hard trying to erase the marks that neither hurt nor could be scrubbed away.

"My God." Kyle glanced around the room. The twilight zone was supposed to be fiction, he wasn't supposed to be seeing things that weren't supposed to be or had no basis in fact. To him, a dream was a fantasy, an illusion, so what he was seeing on his chest couldn't be real.

Totally confused, still wet, still naked, the shower still running, Kyle sat on the closed seat of his toilet rubbing his chest. How in the world was he supposed to explain the marks on his chest when only in his dream had his chest been pierced? How could he ever explain this to anyone when he didn't understand it himself? Who would believe him? Who could he tell, anyway, who wouldn't believe that he was crazy? No doubt, if it was, indeed, his grandfather's goal to scare the hell out of him, he had more than succeeded. This was something totally outside of his realm of belief, but he wasn't interested in ever again meeting with a reader or psychic who might try to explain it. He didn't need to know any more than he already knew but didn't understand.

Riiiiing!

Startled by the ringing telephone, Kyle answered the phone even as his answering machine was picking up the call. "Yeah," he said once the message played out.

"Man, why didn't you call to let me know you made it home?" Vernon asked.

"Because I—"

"When you didn't answer your damn phone, Kyle, I had to go all the way to your house, and even then I had to hear it from your aunt that Carole had been in an accident and that you had driven your mother to the Bronx. That's foul, Kyle. You could've picked up the damn phone. You—"

"You're right, man. I was wrong." Kyle didn't feel like explaining that he had blacked out or that he had been tripping in the twilight zone. "I could've called"—*beep*, another call was waiting—"you're right. Man, I'm sorry"—*beep*—"Hey, I gotta get that—it could be Carole. I'll catch up with you later." Kyle clicked over on the other call, rudely disconnecting Vernon.

"Yeah?"

The line was silent.

"Look, I ain't got time—"

"It's me, Kyle, Dalia."

"I'm hanging up."

"Wait, Kyle! I know you're mad at me, but—"

"Dalia, you have nothing to say to me."

"I know, but I just wanna tell you that I'm sorry for—"

"Sorry won't get it, Dalia. You and that punk ass—"

"I know! I know, Kyle, but I was desperate. I needed the money bad."

"Then you should've gotten up off your lazy ass and gone to work and earned a damn paycheck like everyone else. I never signed a contract stating that I was your sugar daddy."

"You're right. I know I took you for granted. I promise I'll never do that again."

"You got that right. You won't ever have a chance to do anything to me ever again. You and I? Over."

"I understand, Kyle, I really do. I brought it on myself, but it wasn't my idea. It was Jitu. He said all I had to do was—"

"Dalia, I don't wanna hear it! The both of you can go straight to hell." He started to hang up.

"Kyle! Kyle, please. Please don't send me to jail. I can't—"

"Don't send you? I wanna know why your ass isn't in jail now?"

"They let me go, but Jitu's in jail. I have to go back Monday morning. Kyle, I'm so sorry. You know how I feel about you, I really like you a lot. I—"

"How lucky for me."

"It wasn't supposed to go down like that, Kyle. I was messed up. I'd shot a line—"

"I don't give a damn what you'd sucked up your nose, Dalia. Whether you were on something or not, you would've done the same damn thing. That's how you are, conniving. But do me a favor. Stay the hell away from me. Forget my damn number." Kyle slammed the phone down. He couldn't stand to hear another lying word from Dalia. He was cleaning house, and she was out with the trash. He had more important things to worry about than her stupid ass. As it was, he was still trying to wrap his mind around what was happening to him—in his dreams and in his reality.

Getting back into the shower, Kyle let the water beat down on his head. He stood like that for some time even after the water cooled and turned cold. Chilled to the bone, he tried to analyze every dream. What he came to realize was, as freaky as those dreams had been, they had meant something. Of course at first blush, not much made sense, except perhaps the okeepa—not the beating on stage, not the snake, not the hand that was always trying to grab him, not the bear in the cave—but after a while, en masse, he got the gist of most of the dreams. They were about his arrogance, about his disrespectfulness, about his immaturity, and about his lack of shame. He had been all those things and hadn't known enough to be ashamed. And now, a week later, after it had all sunk in, Kyle was ashamed. And as embarrassing as it might be, he had to try to make up for a lot of wrong he had done, even to Dalia.

His first call Monday morning was to the District Attorney's office. He dropped all charges against Dalia and her boyfriend. He felt no better about what they'd done to him, but he was a man and wasn't going to cry about it. He took his lumps, it was done. He'd never see Dalia again.

His second call was to Grace. It was his fault that she'd quit on him, but he needed her. The fact that she wasn't too happy to hear from him was expected.

"What do you want, Kyle? I don't work for you anymore."

"Forgiveness."

"On whose part?"

"Mine. I'm calling, Grace, to ask you to forgive me for taking advantage of you. I was wrong. I'm sorry."

Grace was silent, but she had not hung up on him.

"Look, Grace, I know you're still angry with me. I can understand that. I—"

"You used me, Kyle. You screwed me when you had no intention of being with me. I'm . . ."

"I'm sorry."

"I'm not a slut, Kyle. You can't use me like that. You knew I liked you, you knew I wanted to be with you. I even did a lot of work for you that you never paid me for—"

"You're right. I know I was wrong. Now if you're saying I didn't pay you for overtime, give me a list. Let's settle up."

"I can tell you now. You owe me twenty-five hundred dollars."

"Damn, that much?"

"So you're not gonna pay me?"

Kyle didn't see how it was that much, but if that's the figure Grace had, then who was he to argue when he didn't know. "Did you get another job yet?"

"I can't find a job. Are you gonna pay me what you owe me?"

"Grace, how about I go you one better?" Kyle said, crossing his fingers. "Tomorrow you come back to work for me and there'll be a check waiting on your desk."

Again, Grace said nothing, but this time Kyle was holding his breath. He needed Grace badly. He needed her to put a serious dent in the mound of medical reports that were piled up in his office since she left.

"Grace, do we have a deal?"

After a brief pause, Grace asked, *"You won't come on to me any-more?"*

Kyle almost laughed. Grace was the one who had come on to him, but this was no time to point fingers.

"From this moment, Grace, we're all about business and business only. Deal?"

"I'll be there in the morning. Have that check on my desk."

"No problem." Hanging up, Kyle dropped his head onto his desk. That call was hard as hell, but his mother will be happy—she liked Grace a lot. Of course, his grandfather would be pleased that he was making amends. He wished he could tell him, but more than that, he wished he could apologize to his grandfather for abandoning him. Only now he realized that instead of abandoning his grandfather in his infirmity, he should have been there holding his hand and making sure he understood that he was still a part of his life. In that Kyle had failed, but he had no intention of failing with Audrey. He called her and arranged to have dinner with her on Friday. He planned on telling her he was ready to settle down, that he wanted a future with her.

The one call he didn't make was to Lucille. He never liked her to begin with—she was too much of a grouch.

Kyle spent the rest of Monday catching up on his work, making appointments, and visiting with his father. He was trying not to make the same mistake twice—his father he would not abandon. By Tuesday afternoon, he was back in the routine of running his business, until he received his ninth call from Lorna. She had been leaving messages on his private home line since Saturday. She wanted to come over, but he wasn't about to allow that; he'd learned a valuable lesson from Dalia, and he wasn't about to set himself up like that again. What Lorna wouldn't tell him on the phone, he'd find out about in a public place and Junior's Restaurant, where they had met, was just as good a place as any to end it once and for all.

Chapter
30

Kyle told himself, and as well, he told Lorna, "This is the last time." He arrived on time—5:30—at Junior's to find Lorna already there. She had taken a table in the lounge section of the restaurant, away from the steady flow of early diners in the brightly lit seating area in the open restaurant. Several other tables in the lounge were occupied, but Lorna was sitting far in the back, alone, waiting for him with the grimmest of looks on her face. Kyle didn't get it. Why was Lorna not letting go?

Saying nothing, Kyle sat across from Lorna, who took up her glass and quietly took a sip of her drink.

A waiter slipped a menu on the table in front of Kyle. "Sir, would you like to order a drink?"

"No . . . Yes, bring me a beer." As soon as the waiter walked away, Kyle pushed the menu aside. "Okay, Lorna, what's so important? You have my full attention."

Lorna locked eyes with Kyle. "I'm pregnant."

Kyle's heart thumped. The back of his ears warmed just as his jaw tightened, but he didn't blink. He couldn't stop looking at Lorna, who hadn't blinked either. Kyle slowly sat back. He studied Lorna's face. Her expression hadn't changed, her eyes were steady. He knew what she was telling him, but he had to ask anyway.

"Are you saying that you being pregnant has something to do with me?"

A cold, accusatory glare was Lorna's answer.

Kyle was feeling sick. "I always wore condoms."

"I have been with no one else."

"And I'm supposed to take your word for it?"

"It is the truth."

Shaking his head, Kyle wasn't accepting her word as the gospel. "I'm not stupid, Lorna. I know how to protect myself. And I thought you knew how to protect yourself." Kyle's voice was low, but he lowered it even more. "There wasn't a time I didn't wear a condom with you."

"You're the only one I've been with, Kyle."

The muscles in Kyle's stomach knotted. "That's not true. You've been with your husband a few times at least since I've known you. He's visited you here, and I know you're not gonna sit there and tell me you didn't sleep with him any of the times he was here?"

"I have not—"

The waiter returned with Kyle's beer. "Are you ready to order, sir?"

Glaring at Lorna, Kyle flipped his hand at the waiter, rudely shooing him away.

"I will not lie to you," Lorna said in a hushed voice. "Yes, I did sleep with my husband. He is my husband, I am supposed to. But I did not get pregnant with him, I—"

"How do you know that, Lorna? How far gone are you, anyway? You don't look pregnant to me."

"Most pregnant women do not show until they are three months. I am late by three weeks, and I am never this late. And my husband was not here a month ago."

Kyle breathed a sigh of relief. He knew a little bit about pregnancy and the time line. "Lorna, your husband was here about two or three months ago. I remember because you couldn't go with me to Washington for the National Institute of Medical Reporting Conference because your husband was in town and I lost my money on your airline ticket. Remember?"

"Yes, but—"

"No, but. Because you're late by three weeks doesn't necessarily mean you got pregnant three weeks ago or a month ago. And have you considered the fact that your period could still come down."

"I know that, Kyle, I know that. But I'm always on time, and my husband used a condom and—"

"So did I!" he boomed, but he immediately lowered his voice again after quickly glancing to his right at the two thirty-something women seated several tables away. They were both looking their way.

"What are you trying to say, Lorna? Your husband's condoms worked and mine didn't?"

"You did not always wear a condom, Kyle."

"That's a lie," he snapped.

"There were times when we would do it multiple times and you had no more condoms."

"That's a lie, Lorna, I always had condoms. You're not putting your pregnancy on me. You better talk to your husband."

Her elbow on the table and her hand over her mouth, Lorna looked away. A tear slipped down her cheek. As inconspicuously as possible, she wiped it away.

Kyle picked up his beer but changed his mind about drinking it. He set it down again and, with a single finger, pushed it away. He didn't need this bull. He wasn't about to sit still and let Lorna railroad him into bearing the responsibility for her pregnancy. That wasn't happening. Not when he was trying to straighten out his life. Not when he had come to realize that it was Audrey he wanted to be with.

"Call your husband, Lorna. Tell him you're pregnant. Go home to him."

Lorna continued to wipe at the tears that flowed. "I cannot go home. I have asked my husband for a divorce."

Kyle couldn't believe how stupid Lorna was.

"I want to be with you, Kyle."

Kyle began shaking his head.

"I love you."

"Lorna, I told you when we got back from Florida that we were done. And that's another thing. If you thought you were pregnant, why didn't you mention it when we were in Florida or when we flew there and back. You had plenty of time to tell me."

"Kyle, you did not want to be bothered." Lorna took a deep breath to keep from crying. "You did not want to talk."

"Something like that you could have told me in half a second."

Lorna took a second to compose herself. "I wanted to be sure."

"Then what am I missing here? Since you've slept with me and your husband, how can you be sure until there is a paternity test?"

"I know I am pregnant with your baby."

"No. I don't think so, Lorna. You'd have to prove it to me. And telling your husband you want a divorce has nothing to do with me. I told you twice before this that we were done. If you asked your husband for a divorce, you did it on your own." Kyle pushed his chair back from the table. "I'm outta here."

"Wait!" Lorna quickly reached across the small table and grabbed Kyle's arm. "Kyle, please, I love you. You know I love you. I would not lie to you. This is your baby I carry."

To keep from making a scene, Kyle clamped his jaw shut. Again, he glanced to his right. The two women were boldly looking at him with the most hateful looks on their faces. *Nosy asses.* They probably could hear what he and Lorna were talking about and had condemned him without question. One woman looked down at her plate, but the other belligerently continued to glare at him. He gave her a loathsome sneer before cutting his eyes away and firmly, but placidly, pulling his arm free of Lorna's hold.

"Please do not be angry at me, Kyle. I did not set out to get pregnant."

All Kyle wanted to do was get away from Lorna. The tightness in his stomach and chest was making it hard for him to breathe. Standing, he tossed ten dollars onto the table.

"Lorna, you have two options. Get an abortion, go on with your life. Or, carry the baby to term and I'll get a DNA test. If it's mine, I'll do what's right."

Walking across the lounge toward the door, he could feel a hole being burned into his back by the searing hot glare of the women from the other table. He hadn't bothered to look their way, they didn't matter in his life. Lorna didn't matter either. That is, unless she was carrying his baby. Damn, this was the worst possible news he could have gotten. He had never ruled out having another child, he just hadn't planned on having a child with Lorna. He didn't love her. This could complicate his relationship with Audrey. He couldn't make a commitment to her without telling her about Lorna. What a mess. If the baby proved to be his, this was certainly going to screw up his life. Damn, he didn't need this. Lorna was wrong. He wore condoms every time he was with her.

Before he even got to his car parked at a meter up the street on Flatbush Avenue, Kyle could see the orange Department of Motor Vehicles envelope stuck on his windshield. A damn parking ticket! He looked around but didn't see the officer who wrote the ticket.

"Dammit." Kyle checked the meter—it had expired. He couldn't've been in Junior's a whole hour. It had to be a fast meter. He snatched the ticket and envelope off his car, tore it in half, and angrily balled it up in his fist. Defiantly, he tossed it into the back of his car. Eventually, he'd pay the ticket, but he'd never sit still for Lorna's trap.

Chapter
31

Neither the lingering pain in Kyle's head nor his god-awful dreams could be blamed for Kyle not getting much sleep—not this time. Kyle couldn't sleep because he couldn't stop thinking about Lorna's pregnancy. For two days he'd picked up the telephone to call her but never could go through with actually dialing her number. He wanted to know if her period came down, but it had been only a few days, so maybe it was a little soon to ask. He had been praying that blood would gush from Lorna's body and relieve him of the anxiety that she might be carrying his baby. He'd played this waiting game twice before in his life—the first time when he was seventeen and got his high school girlfriend Sandra pregnant. He couldn't eat or sleep for two weeks. If it wasn't for Sandra's parents not wanting her to have a baby while still in high school, he might not have slept another wink the remainder of his junior year. Sandra got an abortion, and they never got together again. From that point on, Kyle protected himself, that is, until he married Gail. Dawn wasn't planned, and while waiting to find out for a certainty whether Gail was pregnant or not, he gnawed his nails to the quick, but it was different—he loved Gail and his anxiety had everything to do with being an expectant father.

But this waiting, waiting for Lorna to let him know if she was pregnant was hell. He would never marry Lorna and didn't want children with her. What he couldn't understand was how she

could so easily risk so much—her marriage and her own child—
to be with him when he didn't want her. He could never be with
someone who didn't want to be with him, but that wasn't Lorna.
Lorna never talked much about her marriage, and from the moment they met, he'd taken her at her word that she was just here
to go to school and would go back to her husband. Being with him
could not have changed who Lorna's husband was or how she felt
about him. There had to be something more that she wasn't
telling, but hell, Kyle didn't care to know what it was. He could
only hope that if Lorna's period did come down, she'd be considerate enough to call and tell him immediately. It was a lot to hope
for, but he had nothing else to hang on to.

All day Kyle wondered how he'd tell Audrey, and now that he
was sitting across the table from her in his dining room, he was
still wondering. He'd done all the cooking himself, there was
nothing to throwing a couple of steaks in the oven and boiling a
box of garlic-and-herbs-flavored Rice-A-Roni in a few cups of
water. The steak had come out a little dry but was edible, while
the rice was just as it should be—good. He served a simple salad
with a bottle of red wine and he was good to go. Still, by the time
they'd finished eating and had settled on the living room sofa to
soft music and soft lights, he had not solved his problem or
brought up the subject of their relationship. Actually, there was no
rush, so he sat back and listened to Audrey talk about her ongoing
campaign for her judgeship. He enjoyed listening to her talk just
as much as he was enjoying the light new perfume she wore. This
one Kyle didn't know, and although its scent didn't nauseate him,
he couldn't forget the dream he'd had about the women and the
snake. A sour taste in the back of his throat made him want to
throw up. Sure, he hadn't seen Audrey's or the faces of any of the
women in his dream; yet, he could swear that it was Audrey who
had sat on his face, suffocating him.

Unexpectedly, Kyle retched. Hurriedly, he took a swig of wine,
gulping it down, emptying the glass.

"Are you all right?" Audrey asked.

Playing it cool, Kyle slid his arm around Audrey's shoulder as
he again settled back. "Yeah, just had a bitter taste in my mouth.

Normally, he would have mentioned her perfume, but figured as little talk and thought about perfume as possible would keep him from bringing that awful-ass dream to mind.

"It looks like you're a shoo-in," he said, referring to Audrey getting her judgeship.

"Believe me," Audrey said, leaning forward to set her glass on the coffee table, "I've campaigned hard. In a few months, I'll know if it was all worth it." She did not sit back.

"Don't worry, you got this." Kyle gently pulled Audrey back against his arm. "You can just cruise on in."

At the curb outside Kyle's house, a car pulled up.

"Not really, Kyle. I have to keep my name before the public and the powers that be. I can easily slip below the radar and my name could go unnoticed."

"Yeah, I guess you're right." Kyle drew Audrey closer, turning her face to him. "Hey, let's talk about us," he said, kissing her tenderly on the lips. He noticed at first that she didn't respond until he slid his tongue into her mouth.

Outside Kyle's living room window, prying eyes that should not have been there stared through the open blinds at Kyle kissing Audrey. Angry tears blurred their view, but the eyes continued to stare, unnoticed in the dark, into the house.

"I've missed you," Kyle said, sensually fingering Audrey's earlobe to get her in the mood.

Smiling uneasily, Audrey tilted her head slightly away from Kyle's hand. "That tickles," she said when Kyle went at her ear again.

But Kyle was persistent. Not knowing that spying eyes were at his window, he kissed Audrey again, this time longer. The eyes at the window backed away and faded into the night.

Audrey ended the kiss and held onto Kyle's hand to keep his finger still. "What's all this, Kyle? Other than the night of your grandfather's funeral, we haven't spoken in weeks."

"I know, and it's my fault. So much has been going on—my grandfather's death, my father's surgery, my sister's accident, and I've had problems with my staff I can't even begin to tell you about."

"I'm sure it's a lot to deal with, but, Kyle, you could have kept me in the loop, kept me informed. I was thinking you no longer wanted a relationship with me."

Kyle pulled back. "Baby, why would you think that? In fact, I wanted to talk to you about us stepping up our relationship, something more permanent."

Surprised, Audrey's eyes widened.

"Is something wrong with that?"

Audrey stood, moving away from Kyle, away from the temptation of his kisses and his body. "Why now, Kyle? When I wanted more from you, you couldn't give me more. After a while, I figured what we had was temporary. What's changed?"

Thoughtful, Kyle answered simply, "Me." He continued to sit.

"Meaning?"

"I'm no longer in free flight. I'm more grounded. I know what my priorities are, and you're one of them. I want you, Audrey. I think we can do great things together."

Audrey circled the couch sitting in the middle of the room. She went to the window and, seeing the blinds still open, musingly closed them to the darkness outside.

"Isn't this what you want?" Kyle asked, feeling not too good about Audrey standing with her back to him.

She faced him. "I'm seeing someone."

Kyle crossed his leg. That was the last thing he expected to hear. Rubbing his chin, he felt like a fool.

"I didn't think my being involved with someone mattered to you, Kyle. You were always so noncommittal, so otherwise occupied. Of course, it didn't help to know that I wasn't the only one in your life."

Kyle had no words to dispute her. "So how long have you been seeing—"

"Eric. Actually, I've known Eric for some time."

"Who is he—a judge?"

"Who he is isn't important, Kyle, but Eric is someone who's been waiting for me while I waited for you. I grew tired of waiting and so did he. I'm going to marry Eric."

"Then, Audrey, why are you here tonight? You could have told me this on the damn phone."

"I wanted to tell you in person. I thought I owed that to both of us."

Kyle chuckled low and dry. Wasn't that a bitch? Life was just too damn funny. Here he was ready to make all kinds of declarations to Audrey and here she was about to marry someone else. Too damn funny.

"I do love you, Kyle."

"Is that why you're marrying someone else?"

"No, I'm marrying someone else because it's highly likely that I'll be the only woman he touches."

Touché. The irony wasn't lost on Kyle. Somewhere out there, one of the women he'd screwed over was laughing at him. "Are you that sure?" he asked, trying to save face.

Audrey paused in thought. "Well, I don't think Eric will purposely set out to have other women in his life. But in your case, Kyle, I've known all along about you and all your women."

"What women?"

"Don't, Kyle. Don't try to play me for a fool," Audrey said cooly.

"I'm not. I just don't know what you're talking about."

"Oh, Kyle, let's not play games. It wasn't difficult for my investigator to get all the goods on you. Your life was an open book, if one cared to read it, and I did. I can't say I enjoyed all that I read, but I can say, knowing about Lorna and Dalia freed me to move on with Eric."

Kyle felt knee high to a midget. "So if you knew so much about me, why did you keep seeing me?"

"Because I had hope—hope that you'd think me special enough to only want to be with me."

"But that's what I'm doing now, Audrey."

Audrey shrugged. "It's too late."

"That's not what your kiss says."

"That kiss ended what never was."

Kyle remained calm, but he couldn't believe he was being dumped.

"Kyle, I really do love you. I just can't be involved with a man who loves himself and other women more."

Kyle went to Audrey, taking her hand. "But I've changed,

Audrey. I'm no longer seeing anyone else. I'm making a commitment to you. I wanna marry you. I want you to be my wife."

Stroking Kyle's hand once, Audrey smiled sadly. "I could never trust you, Kyle." She stepped back from him. "I'd always wonder, and I don't wanna live like that, wondering where you are or whom you're with."

"You won't have to. I've had . . . I guess you could say, a rude awakening. I know what's important—and that's the people I care about. I've learned to respect the women in my life."

"Oh, really? To whom or what do you credit this epiphany?"

"If I could explain it where it made sense, I'd tell you about it. Right now, suffice it to say, I've been reborn, in a way. Which is why I'm asking you, Audrey, to give me a chance to prove myself. If I—"

"I'm getting married, Kyle." Audrey turned a diamond engagement ring, which had been facing the inside of her hand, to the outside. She held her hand out for Kyle to see, but Kyle wouldn't look down.

"Be happy for me, Kyle."

"Yeah, sure," Kyle said flatly. He picked up Audrey's jacket.

Audrey kissed him softly on the cheek. "We can still be friends."

Kyle chuckled skeptically under his breath. "Let me help you with your jacket." He was still a gentleman, no matter what he was feeling.

"I'll never forget you, Kyle." Audrey said, buttoning her jacket.

"Yeah," Kyle said flatly. He went to the door and opened it. The night air was cooler than he expected, but he stepped out onto the stoop anyway.

Audrey came out behind Kyle. "I'm sorry," she said. She reached up to touch Kyle's face, but he drew back, stopping her.

For a painful moment, he held her gaze until the tightness in his throat forced him to look away. And as soon as Audrey stepped off his stoop, he went back into the house, not the least bit concerned whether she made it to her car safely or not. He could not stand there another minute and pretend that he wasn't hurt. Kyle hated that he felt like crying; it wasn't what he wanted to do.

And he wasn't going to allow himself to cry, he was a man, after all. He had to bear the responsibility for losing Audrey, it was his fault. What the hell, he didn't need anyone. Kyle hurried upstairs to his exercise room and stripped down to his briefs. He didn't waste time putting on exercise clothes, he picked up a set of fifty-pound free weights and began pumping hard and fast, popping his biceps. For an hour he tackled all his weights—shoulder-pressing two hundred pounds and curling a hundred pounds until sweat popped from his pores, cooling him down, dissipating his need to cry or drink himself into a stupor.

Playing the game his way, he had lost Audrey, he had been set up by Lorna, and he had been set upon by Dalia.

"Ah, man, the hell with it," he said. "I don't need any of 'em."

Now that Kyle thought about it, maybe it was a good thing he was free of the women in his life; they'd all sapped him—emotionally, physically, and financially. The sad thing was, if he was duped by any one of them, he'd brought it on himself. The game was his creation. He set the rules, he made the moves, but dammit wasn't he the one who ended up losing in the end? Wasn't he supposed to win something? But the truth was, going out with three women at the same time had him telling too many lies and trying to be too many things to too many people. He looked at his telephone book on the nightstand. It was full of numbers. He could just simply dial and get almost any one of the other women he knew to show up on his doorstep, but did he want that? Hell no. Not anymore. He was tired and he wasn't feeling it like that anymore. Maybe it was time he took a break and got his head together. What could it hurt? He could use the rest.

Chapter
32

For the first time in years, Kyle felt like a fish out of water. Again, he had no social plans for the weekend. Three months was the longest he'd ever gone without female companionship, that is, female of the opposite sex not related to him and older than four years old. Dawn would actually be five in July, just two weeks away, and according to her, she was good and grown. Things that were coming out of her little mouth could have come from a twelve-year-old—the little monster was that fresh.

Last weekend, in the sweetest little voice, Dawn asked, "Daddy, when can I have my own baby, a real baby?"

After he got over his initial shock, Kyle answered, "When you're thirty, have lots of money of your own, and have a husband."

Dawn thought about it. "I have lots of money now, Daddy."

Humoring her, he said, "Wow, you must have more money than me. How much do you have?"

"Five nickels and nine pennies."

Smiling behind his fist, Kyle had to press his fist into his nose to keep from laughing out loud. It took a minute to get control of himself. "That is a lot of money," he said as seriously as he could.

"So can I have a baby now, Daddy?"

"But you're not thirty yet."

"What's thirty?"

Kyle felt like he was digging himself deeper into a hole. "Have you talked to your mother about this?"

"Uh-huh."

"What did she say?"

"She said I can have a baby if I take care of it myself."

"She's right about that. You can't even take care of yourself right now."

"But I can take care of a baby, Daddy. I know how. I take care of Kelly all by myself."

"Who's Kelly?" Kyle wasn't ready for this kind of conversation with his baby girl. Wasn't he supposed to be talking about the Muppets or something?

"My baby doll," Dawn said, dragging her ratty-haired, barefooted, no underwear–wearing, brown-faced, ruby-lipped baby doll off the floor.

This time Kyle did laugh.

"Daddy!"

"Huh?" He quickly sobered up.

"How come you laughing at Kelly?"

"I'm not laughing at Kelly, baby." On the inside he was laughing hard, but looking into Dawn's big, bright, brown eyes, he couldn't begin to imagine her pregnant or any baby's mother. He also couldn't imagine anyone abusing Dawn's body, stealing her innocence, scarring her mind. He would never want any man like himself to walk into her life and use her like some paper cup he once needed to drink out of, but no longer needed once his thirst was quenched.

"I tell you what, Dawn. When you get married, you can have a baby." He popped a grape into his mouth.

"I have a husband and he wants a baby, too."

Kyle almost swallowed the grape in his mouth. Coughing, he cleared his throat. "How come I don't know about this? Who's your husband?"

"Jessie's my husband. He's in my class. We got married yesterday."

"Does your mother know about that?"

"Uh-huh."

Dawn's eyes sparkled like white Christmas lights on a cold,

dark night. Kyle never wanted to see the light dim in her eyes. He took Dawn onto his lap. "You're a bit young to be married, little girl. Maybe you should just wait until you finish school, and—"

"Preschool?"

Kyle chuckled. "No, baby. High school . . . no, college."

"Next year, Daddy?"

Kyle again chuckled. "No, twenty-two years from now when you look just like your mother."

Dawn's jaw dropped, her eyes widened, and Kyle had the best belly laugh he'd had in a long time. He'd been spending more time with Dawn and enjoying every minute of it. At times she made him laugh, at times she made him want to hollar with her willfulness and determination to do what she wanted to do. But he was enjoying her all the same.

This weekend he didn't have Dawn, and as he drove away from his last appointment for the week, he wondered why he hadn't heard from Lorna. It had been weeks, and although he was curious, he dared not call her—he didn't need to go looking for bad news. Maybe she went back to Jamaica, at least he hoped she did. On that thought, he crossed his fingers.

On the other hand, he hadn't given Dalia a single thought, while he had thought about Audrey a few times. He was kind of sorry he blew a future with Audrey, but hey, no use feeling sorry for himself or spending time wondering what-if. That would only annoy him and make him start talking to himself about his own stupidity. Still, it was Friday and he had nothing to do. It was coming up on five o'clock and he didn't have to call in or go back to his office to make sure the afternoon went well. Since Grace returned, he knew everything was running smoothly. His mother was no longer angry with him, and his father had returned to the hardware business Granddad Preston had built with a healthy outlook on life, "I'll outlive all of you," he said the day his doctor pronounced him well. He had plans for expanding the business so retiring was the furthest thing from his mind, and Kyle was behind him on that. Retiring was for old people looking forward to dying, and he wasn't ready to die either. He needed something to do tonight.

Thoughts of hooking up with Vernon were quickly dashed

when he thought about the last time he saw Vernon. He was with Jennifer, he was always with Jennifer. If he wasn't with Jennifer, he was on his way out the door to meet up with her or was expecting her at any minute. They had become inseparable. He'd never tell Vernon, but he was envious of what Vernon had with Jennifer. They were a loving couple and looking toward the future, while Kyle had nothing close to that on the horizon.

Kyle never thought he wanted to get married again, but something was missing from his life now that he was no longer running the streets or bedding every woman he could. Oh, he'd had some offers; after all, he still had it going on—he was good-looking, he was well-dressed, he was sophisticated, and his finances were looking better. Who wouldn't want to be with him? More than once he had been tempted to invite a particular young lady who worked at Brookdale Hospital out, but at the last minute, the sweet scent of a familiar perfume would waft from the soft curve of her neck or from the heat of her chest, tantalizing his senses, stirring up memories of all the women he'd been with. He'd hurriedly back off and go on about his business, committed to giving himself much needed rest. For a while there, he thought he'd lost his predilection for perfumes, but it seemed he hadn't completely. Yet every time he got close enough to a woman to smell her, thoughts of all that could go wrong in the relationship permeated his mind, not to mention that god-awful dream with the snake and Audrey sitting on his face, smothering him, taking his life's breath, gagging him with her perfume. After some pondering, perhaps the dream meant that Audrey would have stifled him if they had gotten married. Whatever it meant, Kyle didn't have to concern himself about it, Audrey was soon to be someone else's wife. Besides, he wasn't in the game anymore, but he'd be lying if he said he didn't miss all the sex. It was a pain waking up every morning and going to bed every night with a hard-on. In his mind he knew what he was doing was right, but his mind and body weren't in sync with what he was doing. What his body needed and desperately wanted, his mind had no control over and no say about. Cold showers weren't working, and neither were boring games of solitaire, which is why Kyle didn't want to go home.

Kyle headed to Carole's. Last night she said she had the day off. She and Sonji were buying a house together in preparation for their upcoming wedding. They moved their wedding day up and were getting married in less than a month. Originally, Kyle had been tapped to walk Carole down the aisle because their father had initially declined the honor. After his colon cancer scare, he changed his mind and was now looking forward to walking his daughter down the aisle. Seems something good can come from bad, and now that Kyle thought about it, that was going to be a crowded aisle. Sonji's father was walking her down the aisle also. That confused everyone but Carole and Sonji. Kyle had asked, "Isn't someone supposed to stand at the alter and watch the bride approach?"

"That's man's way," Carole said.

"The sexist way," Sonji added, chopping onions for the tomato sauce she was making. "We don't envision one of us walking down the aisle to meet the other who will be standing up front like she's lord and master. Carole and I will walk down the aisle together, hand in hand, approaching our new life as equals. Just as we are now."

Kyle had looked away then when Sonji and Carole kissed. He still wasn't that liberal.

He was going to the wedding with Gail and her husband. How ironic was that? He and Luis had been getting along quite well now that he went over regularly to pick up Dawn. Gail was right—Luis was a nice guy.

Pressing Carole's bell the second time, Kyle began to wonder if she was even home. Maybe he should have called. About to descend the stairs, Carole suddenly threw the door open wide.

"Just the person I need to see. Come right on in, my brother."

Chapter
33

In stunned silence, Kyle's mouth was still hanging open. Surely, he could not have heard right.

"Kyle, I don't know why you're so shocked. I told you Sonji and I wanted our own baby."

"But did you tell him that our baby would have your DNA and my DNA?" Sonji asked.

Kyle tried to grasp what they were talking about. "Are you asking me to get down with Sonji in order to make you a baby?"

"Of course not."

"No way," Sonji said, cooly disgusted.

"Then what are you saying?"

"Kyle," Carole said, "we're asking you for your sperm, your DNA, not your lovemaking prowess."

Wham! Kyle's mind hit a brick wall. He dropped the handful of peanuts he had been about to toss into his mouth five minutes before. He stared at Carole.

"Kyle, don't look so scandalized. You disperse a lot of sperm, anyway, and assuming that you use condoms, you dispose of a lot of baby makers."

Now he was disgusted. "I don't wanna talk about this with you two."

"Look, we're all adults here," Carole said. "We've all had Biology 101."

"Yes, but we're not all consenting adults about this subject matter. What I do or don't do is none of your business." Kyle took another handful of peanuts from the bowl on the table but popped only a few into his mouth.

"Oh, please." Carole sat across from Kyle. "Listen, even if you didn't use condoms, which I can't imagine, you deposit gobs of sperm into women who don't want children, so they use something to block or kill your seed, and eventually they wash everything away. So all we're asking is that you donate what you would have wasted anyway to Sonji, to help her get pregnant."

At that moment, Kyle had a visual picture of his sperm flowing from his penis and of himself washing it away.

"In other words, Kyle," Sonji said, "put some of your mighty men to good use and support the cause."

"You're serious?"

"Damn serious," Carole said. "Just think about it, Kyle. By giving us a baby that we'll love unconditionally and give the world to, you could redeem yourself for all the babies who might've been, and for all their mothers whose hearts you've shamelessly broken."

"Well, damn, sis. Rake me over the coals, will you."

"Oh, come on, Kyle. Your feelings can't possibly be hurt, not after all the women you've hurt. And really, there isn't anything incredible about what I'm asking you. It's—"

"It's insane."

"Kyle, Sonji is fertile and she's healthy. You probably wouldn't have to do it but one time."

"Do it?" That quick Kyle could see himself, and even feel himself, making love to Sonji. She was a beautiful woman, dark, smooth complexion, long black hair that was always flowing down her back, a tiny little waist, and curvy hips that he could grab on to and—

"Donate, Kyle. If you donated—"

Kyle irritably brushed peanuts off his lap, hoping that neither Carole nor Sonji saw that his imagination had a physical reaction. "I should have taken my ass on home."

"Like I don't know where you live," Carole said, "and I know how to get there."

"I'm moving."

"Please, Kyle. Before you say no, just think about it. I wouldn't ask if I thought it was wrong or immoral. This is something that siblings of gays do all the time. You'd—"

"Carole, I love you to death. In fact, next to Dawn, I'd give up my life for you. But—"

"Giving up your life isn't what I'm asking. I'm asking that you give me a child through my life partner. A child, Kyle, from your sperm, our shared DNA."

"Oh, man." Kyle sprang up off the chair and began to pace. "Carole, I don't know."

"Kyle, please think about it," Carole said, standing. "A baby with Sonji would be beautiful."

Again a lecherous thought crept into Kyle's mind when he looked at Sonji. Making a baby with Sonji would be beautiful. When he first met her, he did wonder what it would be like, and right now he had better stop thinking about it.

"I have no brother," Sonji said, "but if I did, Kyle, I would ask him the same thing we're asking you. Just think of it as a precious gift you'd give to your sister. A gift that would make her happy beyond measure."

"I can give her a Mercedes. That would make you happy, wouldn't it, Carole?"

"I can buy my own damn Mercedes, Kyle," Carole said, "but I can't buy a baby of our blood. Kyle, we could adopt, and who knows, in the end we just may. But for our first, Sonji and I would love to see our own faces in our baby."

Kyle stopped pacing. "Let me understand this. What you're asking me to do is father a child with your woman, through artificial insemination, right?"

"Yes, your sperm would be injected directly into Sonji via a syringe."

"Aw, man." Kyle got a funny feeling in his groin. "What women won't do to have a baby? A syringe?"

"I know that's foreign to you, Kyle, but sorry, you don't get the pleasure of impregnating Sonji the old-fashioned way."

"Oh, I'm real hurt about that, Carole. No offense, Sonji, but you're not my type." That lie didn't feel too bad.

"You're not mine either." Sonji winked impishly at Carole.

"So give me the 411," Kyle said, realizing that he had not said no outright. "How did you two decide that Sonji would be the baby maker?"

"For one thing," Carole began, "Sonji doesn't have a brother, so I can't do it. And since we decided to ask you, it's kind of gross for me to even consider carrying a baby whose DNA was put there by my own brother."

"Yuk," Sonji said, frowning.

Kyle shuddered. "I'd have to agree with you on that one. So, let me understand this. Technically, if I did this—and that's a big if—I'd be this baby's biological father, its biological uncle, and—"

"It's godfather," Sonji said.

"Oh, man. I don't know if I can do this."

"Kyle, you can. Believe me, there's nothing wrong with you donating sperm to Sonji."

Kyle shook his head. "I'm not feeling this, Carole. I understand what you're asking, but it just don't feel right."

"If you're worried about supporting our baby—"

He hadn't thought about that. "Will I have to? Legally, I might have to, right?"

"No," Sonji said. "Carole will legally adopt the baby and your name will never appear on the birth certificate."

"Carole! Carole, something has to be wrong with this."

"There isn't, believe me."

"Kyle," Sonji said, "if you wanted to be involved in our baby's life, of course you could be, you would be the uncle."

"But what if, when the kid grows up, he . . ."

"Or she," Sonji corrected.

". . . wants to know who the father is. What will you tell him?"

Sonji and Carole exchanged uncertain looks. "We haven't thought that one through yet," Carole admitted.

"Well, don't you think you should?"

"We will—eventually," Sonji said.

"The point is, Kyle," Carole said, "we have to get to that point. If you do this, whatever your role in the child's life is, you'll love him—or her—just as much as you love Dawn, and so will we."

Before Kyle's eyes flashed a big-bellied Lorna, pleading for him to marry her. "Loving a child isn't the problem, Carole. How that child comes to be is the problem."

"Come on, Kyle. Half the kids in the world are unwanted even if they come into the world under the best of circumstances. Too many are mistakes, and not enough are planned."

Kyle sickened at the thought of the baby he didn't want with Lorna.

Carole pressed further. "Kyle, donating your sperm isn't a difficult thing to do. All you need is a magazine and your fingers."

Kyle couldn't believe he actually grasped behind what Carole said.

"I'll buy the magazine," Sonji chimed in.

Kyle clicked his teeth. "You two are a joke. You should hit the clubs."

Neither Sonji nor Carole cracked a smile. Carole instead brushed away a tear.

"Please, Kyle, I want a child. I've never turned my back on being a mother, I just turned my back on being with men, but what I need, I can only get from a man."

Kyle tried not to look into Carole's eyes. "What about a sperm bank? You could go there. They're anonymous. And what about cloning? That's—"

"Don't patronize me, Kyle. I'm not in the mood for stupid questions."

"What makes it stupid, Carole? Because you don't wanna hear it?"

Carole clinched her jaw and looked sorrowfully at Sonji.

In that look, Kyle saw the magnitude of Carole's desire to have a baby, but he didn't think he could give her what she wanted. "Carole, I'm sorry but—"

"Please, Kyle. Don't say no right now."

"But, Carole—"

"Kyle, Kyle. Wait. Just hear me out. Please."

Backing down from what he was about to say, Kyle obliged his sister. He waited.

"Kyle, I want . . . no, I need you to be the donor. Besides being my brother—"

"Preston's your brother, too. Have you asked him?"

"I'm asking you, Kyle. Look, I thought you and I had a special connection—we've always been close. Am I wrong?"

What could he say to that? By his silence, Kyle acknowledged that Carole wasn't wrong.

"That's why I'm asking you," Carole said. "And like I started to say before, you're really a great person. You're smart, you're cute, you have a big heart, and other than being a shameless womanizer . . .

"I'm not like that anymore."

. . . you're really great with Dawn. Gail told me how doting you've become, and Dawn loves you to death. I want my child, boy or girl, to be like Dawn or a little Kyle, ah . . . minus the womanizing."

"He doesn't do that anymore," Sonji said. "Didn't you hear him?"

"Well, good for you, Kyle. So, if you'll give really serious consideration to what I'm asking you, I'll give you, without hesitation, a kidney when you need it."

The faux smile on Carole's lips belied the teary glint in her eyes. There was no doubt in Kyle's mind that Carole desperately wanted him to donate his sperm to Sonji. In truth, the idea was daunting. He'd heard of women donating eggs to other women or even to their own daughters, and occasionally, he'd read about grandmothers carrying their own grandchildren to term in their own bellies for their daughters, but he had never heard of men donating sperm to family members or to anyone other than a sperm bank. And knowing who it was that would be getting his sperm made Kyle uncomfortable.

"Kyle, you can't know . . .

"Okay, Carole—"

. . . how much this means to me. You'd—"

"Carole, listen to me," Kyle pressed.

"Let him talk," Sonji said.

Carole finally stopped talking, but her tears kept rolling down her cheeks.

"I'll donate a kidney, too," Sonji chimed in.

Kyle felt cornered. "So I'll have my own personal organ bank, huh?"

"Anything you want," Carole said. "Kyle, you know I'd give you a kidney anyway if you needed it, but I want a baby desperately. Sonji and I, both, desperately want a baby. We want to experience the joy . . .

"And pain," Sonji added.

". . . of bringing a baby into the world."

Sonji went to Carole and put her arm around her waist. They both stood waiting anxiously for Kyle to tell them he would make their dream a reality, but Kyle wasn't quite ready to give them a definitive answer. He needed time.

"Look, I gotta go."

"But, Kyle," Carole began, "you—"

"It's done every day," Sonji said.

"Please don't say no," Carole implored.

On the way home, Kyle wrestled with the idea of donating his sperm to his sister's girlfriend, fiancée, mate, life partner, whatever the hell Sonji was. So Sonji was going to be carrying the baby, and Carole would be the daddy in waiting. No surprise there. Carole was always a tomboy. Hell, she could outslug any boy on the softball team throughout high school. Oh, boy. Mom and Dad, especially Mom, was going to have a major stroke if and when she found out about this latest development. But that wasn't Kyle's concern, he was not going to be the bearer of this news, much less tell them that it might be his sperm responsible for the baby seeing the light of day. Damn, he sure as hell had to think hard and long about Carole's request. If he did donate his sperm, how would he ever explain to Dawn, who technically would be that child's sister and cousin, how her Aunt Carole was the child's mother, her daddy's sister, and Sonji's husband . . . or wife? Oh, man. Could his life get any more complicated?

Chapter
34

By Sunday afternoon, Kyle still hadn't made a decision either way as to whether he'd help Sonji get pregnant. Carole called once, but he didn't take her call. In fact, he didn't take any calls the whole weekend, choosing instead to work down in his office catching up on his own paperwork, paperwork that bored him and made him want to be off doing other things, one of which entailed being with Audrey. Since that wasn't going to happen, Kyle refused to dwell on it. Still, he felt closed in and wanted to be outside, away from his office, but where was he to go? When it came down to it, there was no where Kyle could go and be around people he knew, who wouldn't be able to look at him without a passing thought about how callously he had treated the women in his life. No matter what Carole said about wanting him to father Sonji's child, even she was mindful of his despicable history with women, and that bothered him. There was a time when Kyle would not have cared what anyone thought about him, and it wasn't like he lived and breathed for anyone's approval now, but strangely, he no longer wanted his family or his best friend to look at him with shame or disgust in their eyes. Wow! Granddad Preston would love to know he was thinking like that.

Kyle turned on the television in his office and while he plodded through finishing up a medical report, he half listened to the last game of the NBA finals, but not even the cheering crowd at every basket advantage or missed shot was able to draw his full attention. Actually, nothing much interested him these days, especially the work he was doing. Even while he yawned, Kyle was thinking that his medical transcription business wasn't cutting it anymore. Sure, he made money, but for him, that was the only positive thing about the business. He no longer felt like begging doctors and hospitals for work that always outlined in detail some poor soul's illness and reminded him of his own mortality. Perhaps it was just as well that he hadn't become a doctor, he really didn't have the stomach for it. He needed to find something else to do. Just what that something was, he didn't know, but he'd had enough of medical reports for a lifetime.

Again Kyle yawned. The sudden rumble of thunder outside his window made him feel even more lethargic. Staying up late watching television and still getting up at his usual early hour was taking its toll. Kyle was sleepy and although he fought it, he finally got up from his desk and went and sat on the love seat. Within minutes he had dazed off. He didn't dream, he didn't snore, he didn't hear a thing, that is, until the crowd cheering on his television woke him. Drowsily, he looked at the television but had no clue as to who the new NBA champions were, and the truth is, he didn't much care. On his mind, was the difficult decision he had to make. Maybe to Carole and Sonji it was no big deal, but to him, it was a big deal to donate his sperm to Sonji, someone he knew, who would be carrying a baby, who they say won't be his, while Lorna will be growing big with a baby that she is already claiming to be his. If it were up to him, he'd hand Lorna's baby over to Carole and Sonji the minute it was born—that would solve everyone's problem.

Seeing that it was well after midnight, Kyle turned off the television and headed upstairs to his bedroom. His phone hadn't rung all evening, and it was just as well. He wasn't in the mood for talking to anyone.

Just as he got to the top of the stairs—*Buzzzz!*

Kyle couldn't imagine who it could be at that late hour. Hurrying back down the stairs to the living room in the darkness, he peeked outside through a gingerly raised slat in the closed venetian blinds. It was still raining out. The wet windowpane glistened with droplets and streaks of water, making it difficult to see who was standing at the door. Kyle could barely make out the shape of the large black umbrella covering the dark figure.

Buzzzz!

Kyle could pretend he wasn't in. Whoever it was should have called first. Peering harder, he strained to make out the dark figure standing on his stoop. He couldn't. What if it was Dalia? No, it wouldn't be her, he had dropped the charges against her. Maybe it was her boyfriend. No, he was probably still in jail; he had violated his probation.

Buzzzz!

There was nothing for Kyle to be nervous about. Leaving the light out, Kyle opened the door—just enough to look out to see who had rung the bell.

"I didn't think you were home."

"What're you doing here? Do you know how late it is?"

"I had to see you."

Lorna was the last person Kyle wanted to see. "This isn't a good time. I was just on my way up to bed."

"Please, Kyle. It is miserable out here. I came all this way to see you."

"You should have called, Lorna. I'm not up to company tonight."

"It's important, Kyle." Lorna put her hand on the knob of the outside glass and iron door. "I won't stay long—I promise."

A crack of thunder boomed in the night sky making Kyle wish that he had ignored the bell and gone on into his bedroom and closed the door. He loved sleeping on a rainy night. A flash of lightning flared high overhead, brightening the sky but an instant, moving Kyle to unlock the outer door and let in his unwanted guest.

"Ten minutes, but then you gotta go." That sounded cold in Kyle's own ears, and although he regretted his coldness, he really didn't want to see Lorna. Until she had the baby he wouldn't know if it was his or not.

Wet despite her large umbrella, Lorna stepped inside and handed her open umbrella to Kyle to close.

"Didn't you ever hear that you're not supposed to have an open umbrella in a house?"

"No." Lorna took off her trench coat and handed it also to Kyle who, although he was still trying to close the umbrella, was struck by the flatness of Lorna's stomach in her body-hugging shirt and skin-tight pants. He let the coat drop to the floor.

"My coat, Kyle." Lorna picked up her coat and again handed it to Kyle.

"Dammit, I can't close this thing." Kyle thrust the umbrella at Lorna and reached inside the living room and flicked on the ceiling light.

With just a press of a button on the handle, Lorna collapsed the umbrella and leaned it against the hall wall, then went on into the living room, passing close to Kyle, who got a faint whiff of her perfume. She sat quietly on the edge of the sofa with her pocketbook on her lap, waiting for Kyle to come in. Out in the hallway, Kyle stuck the long umbrella in the umbrella stand at the door and draped Lorna's wet coat over it. He frowned at the rainwater on his hardwood floor, but he didn't bother to dry it up. Already he regretted opening the door, now he couldn't wait to close the door with Lorna on the other side.

"Is this about your pregnancy?" Kyle stood in the doorway of the living room with his arms folded tight across his chest, wondering why Lorna's stomach was so flat.

Lorna pushed her damp hair back off her forehead. She dabbed lightly at her face while she tried to find the words to explain why she was there.

Kyle said impatiently. "I have to get up in the morning."

Lorna lowered her eyes. "I am not pregnant."

Calm on the outside, Kyle was practically jumping for joy on the inside.

"I was just very late. I'm not pregnant."

"So you were never pregnant?"

"No."

Kyle felt like the weight of the world was lifted off his shoulders. He let his arms drop to his sides. He closed his eyes. *Thank you Lord.*

"Had you told your husband you thought you were pregnant?"

Her eyes still on her hands, Lorna said, "I had not told him that. I will go home at the end of the month. We will talk then about our marriage."

"That's good." Kyle felt like shouting, "Get the hell out!"

Lorna said nothing.

"Take it from me, Lorna. Do everything you can to save your marriage."

Still, Lorna was silent.

"If you think about it, you'll realize that you still love your husband. You've just been living away from him so long you lost sight of that."

Lorna began rubbing her hands together. "Perhaps."

Kyle glanced at the clock on the DVD. "Wow, it's twelve-fifty. It's late."

Lorna made no move to stand or lift her eyes.

"I have to get up in the morning, Lorna."

Still, Lorna sat while Kyle grew more anxious.

A clap of thunder broke the silence. "It's raining really hard," he said. "Do you need a cab or did you drive yourself?"

"You really want to get rid of me, don't you?"

Kyle again glanced at the DVD. In a minute he was going to unceremoniously help Lorna to the door. "I'm really tired, Lorna."

"You're still upset with me."

"Everything's cool. In fact, we're cool, Lorna. I hope everything works out for you and your husband."

Lorna slowly raised her head. "I love you, Kyle. I really—"

"No, Lorna, don't go there. Let's say goodbye without any emotion getting in the way. We had a good time together. I really enjoyed being with you. But now it's over and," Kyle shrugged, "we have to move on."

Lorna lowered her eyes. From her pocketbook she took the credit card that Kyle had almost forgotten about. She handed it to him.

Kyle looked at the card, front and back. Vernon was right. He had been trying to buy the women he saw. Maybe he was wrong, after all, to think he could buy genuine affection. All he'd bought for his money was a boatload of trouble and the wrong women. He pocketed the card. Later, he'd shred it.

Lorna stood. "I'll miss you, Kyle."

Kyle nodded, but he wasn't going to miss her. "I'll get your coat."

"Kyle."

He turned back.

For the first time, Lorna looked straight into Kyle's eyes. "Can I kiss you one last time?"

Looking at Lorna, her eyes sad, her pouty lips inviting, Kyle remembered what it was like to devour her mouth and draw from her the sweetest kisses in the world. He felt himself stir at the memory. That wasn't a good sign.

"Let's just say good-bye, Lorna."

"It is only a kiss, Kyle. What harm can it do?"

He chuckled. "No harm, but a whole lot of damage."

"Just a kiss." Lorna moved close up on Kyle, touching her body to his, pressing her pelvis into his, moving ever so slightly, tantalizing him, heating him up.

"Don't play with me."

"I'm not," she said, lightly kissing Kyle's neck.

Kyle closed his eyes. Damn, she felt good. He didn't move back, nor did he push Lorna away. He smelled her perfume, and although he didn't like it much, he didn't totally dislike it enough to make her stop.

Lorna put her arms around Kyle's neck. She pulled him down to her, she kissed him lightly on the lips—once, then twice. His kiss was just as light, but what he was feeling stirring began to press against her, reminding him that it had been a long time since he had been with anyone. Dalia had been his last encounter, and Lorna was reminding him how sorely he missed making love. She kissed him again, this time letting her tongue dart teasingly into his mouth. Kyle's tongue also responded and met Lorna's tongue in a tender embrace that soon heated into a passionate dance. It was just a kiss he said to himself, what harm could it do?

Chapter
35

Booming rumbles of thunder echoed outside Kyle's shuttered bedroom windows, closing him off from the torrential rain that beat down on his three-story limestone. Conflicting emotions of escalating moans and groans of passion clashed with his anger at himself for what he was doing. Even while his body lost itself in the throes of its pleasure, his mind chided him for backsliding and reverting to the dog he once was. He hated that he had so easily taken Lorna into his bed, forgetting so quickly that he was not supposed to let sex dictate his life. Totally conflicted, he was oblivious to the storm slamming outside his bedroom windows. Not even Luther Vandross crooning on the stereo ten feet away penetrated his mind. He was riding high on an undulating ocean of waves, while sitting on top of him, riding him, was the woman he had told time and again that it was over. He might regret sleeping with her one last time, but for now, damn, she was riding him like a champion on an iron horse.

"I love you, Kyle. I know you love me," Lorna said, gyrating her body sensually atop Kyle's manhood and gripping him even harder with her strong muscles. Lorna heard the thunder overhead, and usually she was afraid when claps of thunder sounded like bombs on a battlefield, but this time she didn't give a thought to the thunder, she was concerned only with the task at hand—rocking Kyle's world. Oh, sure she was enjoying the ride, what woman wouldn't, but she was doing this solely for Kyle. The mounting tension in her sweet spot confirmed for her that she was getting hers, so she knew Kyle was getting his—his body was no longer relaxed. Under her, she could feel the muscles in his thighs tighten and pop. She could only imagine that his buttocks were squeezed into hard rocks, because Kyle had pushed his lower body up off the bed with her, all 135 pounds of her, on top of him. His body was quaking, his teeth were bared, his eyes had rolled back in his head. Yeah, she had him. He was hers. He would never push her away now, not after what she could do for him.

Kyle grit his teeth harder, hating himself for what he was doing. He kept saying over and over to himself, *A hard head makes for a soft brain. A hard head makes for a soft brain.* That's what Vernon would be saying to him if he saw what he was doing and to whom. Why was it that he couldn't—

"Oh, damn!" Kyle exploded in a heart-pounding release of sexual ejaculation. He hadn't even tried to wait for Lorna, who moaned in her own release.

"Damn." Kyle hated that it felt so good.

Lorna fell atop Kyle's sweaty chest, out of breath, while sweet, spastic pulses continually erupted in her most private place. They were good together. The sex was always the best. No one else could do it for him like her.

Lorna kissed Kyle full on the lips. "That was good, wasn't it, baby? You liked that, didn't you?"

His breath shallow, unable to speak, his eyes closed, Kyle said nothing as he wiped his mouth with the back of his hand. He was disgusted with himself.

"I know you're not wiping away my kiss." Lorna kissed Kyle again.

Frowning, Kyle tried to turn his face away from Lorna's lips, but she stayed tight on him, clinging to him, irritating him.

"Damn, Lorna, let me get some air." He tried to push Lorna away.

Her feelings hurt, Lorna let up on her hold, but she still didn't let go. "What's wrong? Why are you talking to me like this?"

"You're suffocating me." Kyle pushed Lorna off of him and

onto the bed. "I knew this was a mistake." He started to sit up, but Lorna quickly pulled Kyle back down onto his back.

"Okay, I will let you breathe, but, Kyle, you know that we are good together. You know this."

"Don't start, Lorna. We're done. We're done."

After what she'd just put on him, Lorna had hoped that Kyle would change his mind and take her back. She couldn't lose Kyle. Kyle Lawson was everything she ever wanted in a man. He was educated, he was successful, he had his own home, he knew the right people, and he had money, lots of it. But more important, he made her feel like Stanley had never made her feel.

"Kyle, we just made love. We could not have made love like this if it was over."

Still on his back, Kyle closed his eyes. He was drained. Making love to Lorna always left him weak and sleepy. The last thing he wanted to do was have this discussion. Maybe if he ignored her, she'd get pissed enough to leave and let him go to sleep. He turned onto his side away from her.

Kyle's back didn't deter Lorna. "Kyle, we have to talk about this. Please. I love you."

Kyle didn't flutter a lash or flinch an inch. He couldn't believe that he had again taken himself down this brainless path. Knucklehead. That's what he was. That's what his grandfather used to call him when he was a kid and did stupid things. After all he'd been through, he should have known better than to fall back into the same pattern of behavior that had gotten him in trouble with his grandfather and with Dalia, just weeks ago. This was the absolute worst thing he could have done—continue to be a slave to a piece of flesh that was incapable of thinking about the consequences. Hadn't he learned anything after that Dalia disaster? Hadn't his weakness almost gotten him killed? How stupid was he? And after Lorna's pregnancy scare, the last thing he should have done was touch her. Thank God, at least he had taken the time to put on a condom, which reminded him of what Carole had said, "You dispose of a lot of good sperm." And here he was, indiscriminately and stupidly doing it again.

"Kyle, you love me, I know you love me. We could not have—"

"Dammit, Lorna! Get a clue." Up on his elbow, Kyle faced Lorna. "I am not in love with you. And for damn sure we're not getting back together."

As if she was hearing this for the first time, Lorna stared disbelievingly at Kyle.

"Come on, Lorna, we're done. Let's not do this. Damn."

"Then why did you make love to me, Kyle? Why did you let me in when—"

"Wait a minute. You talked your way back in here. You just had to see me, remember? You came through the storm to my house, I didn't go to yours, Lorna. I knew you were up to something with that one last kiss bit, and I fell for it like an idiot. It's my fault, I should have put you out, but I didn't. So, okay, you got what you wanted—you seduced me. You put it out there for me and I hit it like the dog I am. But I know I was wrong, we both were. Since we can't take it back, let's move on."

Fighting to keep from crying, Lorna's chin quivered.

"Go home, Lorna. Please." Kyle lay back down.

Chest-fallen, Lorna scooted to the edge of the king-size bed and got off. She balled her fists up into a tight ball at her sides. "You cannot just throw me away like I am trash. "

Kyle lay like a zombie. He wanted Lorna to disappear.

Before Kyle, Lorna stood without a stitch of clothes on. She wanted him to see fully what he was giving up, but he closed his eyes.

"Why are you so cruel, Kyle? I do not deserve this." The tears started. "Kyle, please—"

An explosive clap of thunder startled Lorna. Her eyes shot toward the window. The shutters were closed, yet suddenly, she felt naked. Shivering, she covered her breasts with her arms. She looked back at Kyle and was surprised by his hard, cold glare.

"You hate me, don't you?" she asked.

"Damn, it wasn't worth all this."

Kyle felt like shooting himself. He sprang up off the bed.

"Lorna, if I hated you, you could not've gotten back in my bed, which was wrong on my part. I apologize. Hey, blame it all on me, but believe me, it won't happen again. I promise you that."

Painful tears rolled down Lorna's cheeks. She hugged herself, but she continued to tremble, not from the chill, but from her anger.

"Don't do this to yourself, Lorna. Just get dressed and go home."

Lorna rubbed her shoulders trying to ward off the chill. "It is that other woman, isn't it?"

"Aw, man." Kyle snatched his boxers off the chair and yanked them on.

"I saw you with a woman here. You had dinner with her here, in this house. You kissed her, I saw you."

"What?"

"Do not deny it, Kyle. I saw you! You were downstairs with her on the sofa."

"You were spying on me?"

"You made love to her, didn't you? Why, Kyle? What can she do for you that I cannot? Just tell me what it is, I will do it." Lorna grabbed Kyle's arm. "Just tell me."

Kyle peeled Lorna's hands off his arm. "I should have never let you in here." He looked around for his pants.

"Please, Kyle!" Lorna tried again to latch on to Kyle. He pushed her away.

"Go home, Lorna."

"I am sorry, Kyle. I cannot stand to think that you made love to another woman. Look at me, Kyle." Lorna spread her arms wide, boldly exposing her nakedness to him. "I am a good-looking woman, a desirable woman. I am better looking than the whore you have chosen over me."

Kyle didn't look at Lorna's body. "Actually, you look no better, no worse. The difference is class. You're not showing any."

Lorna's tears brimmed and fell. "You bastard!"

"You're right, Lorna. I am a bastard and I've been one for a very long time. Don't get me wrong, I'm not proud of it. I used women—not for money, but for pleasure. I used you tonight when I knew better, and I'm sorry. We wouldn't be having this damn discussion if I had stuck to my decision to have nothing to do with you or any other woman. And if I had respected that decision, I would have called you a cab and walked you to the door. But I didn't. And I didn't because I am that bastard you called me.

All my life I put sex above common sense, above family, above respect, above practicality. You don't need a man like me, Lorna. You deserve a good man, most likely a man like your husband. Go home to your husband, Lorna. He and your daughter are what you need."

Kyle picked up Lorna's bra and held it out to her.

Lorna's tears stopped. She ignored the bra. "I hate you."

"You have every right to."

"I ended my marriage for you. I—"

"Lorna, I thought you said you were going home to talk to your husband."

"My husband wants nothing to do with me. He has filed for divorce and custody of my child. I will be left with nothing."

A deep rumble of thunder sounded overhead, sending a chill up Kyle's spine. "I'm sorry to hear that, Lorna, but that one is on you. I never told you to end your marriage."

Lorna glared at Kyle. "But you made me think that you loved me."

"I'm not dancing in this circle again, Lorna. It's over between us. I'm sorry about your husband." He picked up her pants and blouse.

Those, Lorna snatched. "I will never forgive you."

Kyle could live with that. He handed Lorna her panties. For a minute they stood staring at each other.

"I feel dirty," she said, "I need to wash myself."

Kyle stepped back and indicated with his hand that she knew the way. He watched her go off down the hall—her mouth shut, her tail tucked, her feelings hurt—to the bathroom. When she closed the door, he cursed himself as he sat heavily on the side of the bed. He was tired out of his mind, but this time, not just from the sex. He was emotionally whipped. He had brought this drama on himself and could blame no one. But for damn sure he was through letting his johnson control him. Hearing the shower come on in the bathroom, he grabbed a pillow and pulled it to the center of the bed, where he laid his weary head. Kyle was asleep before Lorna even stepped into the tub. He didn't hear Lorna curse his name or pound the tiled wall of the shower with her fist.

Angry tears washed down Lorna's face. The hot shower

cleansed away the remnants of sweat and the aftermath of their lovemaking, but the hot water did nothing to wash away her anger or temper the torrent of words that the running shower water muted. When the hot water made her already hot skin prickle, Lorna made the water cooler until she was taking a cold shower. The iciness of the water made her breathe deep and at times hold her breath, but she had to bring herself down from the boiling point. She had never been so angry. How dare Kyle talk to her like she was a twenty-dollar hooker he'd picked up on a street corner somewhere. Kyle was a cruel son of a bitch who did not deserve to live. If her brothers were in this country, she'd have them drag his ass into an alley somewhere and beat him to death. But they weren't, she was all alone. She was going to have to deal with Kyle in her own way.

The sounds of drums beat in Kyle's head. He looked around and was surprised to see that he was again in the longhouse. In the center a small fire burned. He went to the fire.

"Sit."

Kyle turned to see his grandfather enter the longhouse. "Granddad, I've been wanting to see you."

Granddad Preston sat before the fire. Kyle sat, too, and could see clearly the disturbed look on his grandfather's face.

"I know I messed up. I—"

Granddad Preston held up his hand, stopping Kyle from speaking. "You shame your people still. Did you not learn from your pain, from your wrongs?"

It didn't surprise Kyle that his grandfather knew what he'd done. He hanged his head shamefully.

"What do you say for yourself, my son?"

Watching the flames burn but not dance, Kyle raised his head. "Nothing. I don't seem to have control over my own body. It's like it wants what it wants and the hell with what's right. And it scares me, Granddad, because I don't think I can ever control it."

Granddad Preston slipped his hand into his medicine bag. From it, he took a smaller sack.

Kyle began shaking his head. "I'm not gonna smoke whatever you're about to give me."

Granddad Preston took a pinch of the gray powder from the sack and threw it onto the fire, flaring the low flame, sparking it only inches into the air.

"Why did you do that?"

"What is fire?" Granddad Preston asked.

Stumped by the inane question, Kyle creased his brow and looked stupidly at his grandfather.

"My son, is fire not heat?"

"Yeah, and light, too, I guess."

"Fire is anger, my son. It is explosive."

"Okay. And?"

"Fire is the soul of a woman, it is her passion. Fire smothers deep within the bosom of a woman and flares when she is scorned. A scorned woman becomes fire. She cannot be tamed."

Kyle thought of Lorna. Hadn't he scorned her? Was she now fire?

It didn't take Lorna long to dress, she had worn a tiny little blouse and a simple pair of tight black pants. She had planned to seduce Kyle, but she did not want to be obvious. Kyle could never resist the plunging neck line that revealed her beautiful breasts or the tight pants that clung to her every curve. Still, her body, her lovemaking wasn't enough to change Kyle's mind or get him to the altar, not when another woman held his heart. That other woman might think that she had won Kyle, but she was mistaken. Kyle was hers and no one else's.

Again, Granddad Preston threw a pinch of gray powder onto the fire. Again, the flames flared, this time a foot into the air.

Kyle reared back. "Are you trying to burn me?"

"Do you not see the dangers of fire? To play with a woman's soul is to play with fire. You, my son, have not learned yet to respect the soul of a woman. You must do so in order to control your flesh and to redeem your own soul."

"But I've learned from my mistakes."

Granddad Preston eyed Kyle skeptically.

"I swear, Granddad, this time I have. I know now never to use a woman for my own pleasure when I want nothing from her otherwise. I know that my promises are lies that can hurt a woman who really cares

about me. I would hate for my own daughter to be hurt like that. I've hurt a lot of women, and I'm ashamed of that."

"Is that what your heart tells you, or is it just your tongue that speaks?"

"It's my heart. I don't like who I am and what I've done."

"Then you must become the master of your body and not let your body master you."

"But how? I have tried."

"Not hard enough. You have never given pause before leaping. You have never considered the consequences before your deeds. You have never said no."

Kyle batted his eyes in astonishment. It was true. He had never said no to sex with any woman. He had always given himself over to the moment.

"But is it that simple, Granddad? A pause, a thought, saying no?"

"To do wrong is simple. To do what is right takes strength of mind and character. The question is, my son, are you now strong of mind and character?"

For the first time, Kyle realized he'd been weak all his life. The strength he needed now, he didn't know how to get.

"Don't worry, my son. You were born with what you need to strengthen you. You must look inward and search for the man who sleeps within. Awaken him, and you will be the man of your heritage."

For Kyle, it all made sense. He had to purge himself on the outside in order to get to the man on the inside. It was time.

Returning to the bedroom for her shoes, Lorna found Kyle sound asleep. For a minute she stood over him, wanting badly to curl up next to him to feel the warmth of his body, but knew that if she awakened him, he'd spew more ugly words at her. She hated him just as much now as she loved him. He had been cruel, he had hurt her. Slowly walking around the bed to the other side to get her shoes, she watched as Kyle slept like he had not a care in the world. He always went to sleep after they made love. Didn't that count for something? Didn't he think they had something special? Didn't he know that he'd never find another woman—an educated, sophisticated, sexy woman—like her? How could he just dump her like that? How could he be so cold to her? After she'd done things in bed with him she'd never done with any man, not even her husband, how could he just dismiss her?

While tears again slid down Lorna's cheeks, a rumble of thunder made her heart leap, and her hands tightened around the size-seven shoes in her hands. Kyle's peaceful sleep irked her. Chances were, the minute she left, that other woman would be replacing her in his bed.

Lorna stared down at Kyle, hating him more and more, yet loving his long black lashes, his perfect mouth, his chiseled jawline, even the vein pulsing in his neck. How could she want to make love to him all over again when she hated him so much? She could see herself smashing his face in with a baseball bat; he'd never think about another woman again.

Granddad Preston poured all the powder from his sack into the palm of his hand. Kyle eyed him suspiciously.

"Granddad, why are you—"

A crack of thunder exploded outside the bedroom window, again making Lorna jump. She dropped her shoes to the floor. Looking around the room, her eyes came to rest on the sword mounted on the wall over the head of the bed. Without a moment's hesitation, she went to the sword, drawn to it by some irresistible force. With both hands, she removed the heavy sword from its mounting. As if in a trance, she gripped the handle of the sword in her fists and held it up, its tip pointing at the ceiling. Even in the dim, low light of the bedroom, the sword reflected the faint light from the lamp and shone its long, sharp blade, mesmerizing Lorna. Turning toward Kyle, his head resting on the center of the bed, she raised the sword even higher as she circled the bed so that she could stand at the foot right across from Kyle's neck.

Kyle watched as his grandfather was about to throw the handful of powder onto the fire. "Grand—"

A flash of light, a mighty explosion slammed Kyle back against the wall of the longhouse, knocking the air out of him.

* * *

Gasping for air, Kyle's eyes suddenly opened, and what he focused on, high over his head and coming closer, was the long blade of a sword. He quickly rolled away but was nicked on the neck by the tip of the sword. Behind him he heard the swish of the mighty sword as it cut into the pillow where only seconds before his head had rested. He bolted off the bed and quickly looked back. He saw Lorna, with the sword clutched in her hands, its blade had cut the pillow in half. She was shaking uncontrollably.

"Oh, God!" Lorna dropped the sword and clamped her hands to her mouth.

A tingling sensation climbed up Kyle's legs into his groin, rendering him shaky on his feet. He started to sit down but thought better of it. He started to move farther away from the bed but again thought better of that, too. He grabbed the sword, his grandfather's gift to him from Spain, and rushed to the closet where he stood the sword inside against the back wall. He slammed the door shut. He turned up the lighting in the bedroom.

"I didn't mean it," Lorna cried. "I didn't know what I was doing."

Shaking, Kyle managed to pull on his shirt. He couldn't believe what had almost happened to him. Is that what his grandfather was trying to tell him in his dream—that Lorna was angry enough to kill him? Is that what Lorna's own aunt, Lady Yasmin, had been trying to tell him? Why hadn't he seen that himself? Lorna had been desperate to be with him. Her showing up tonight had proved that.

"I want you to leave now."

"Kyle, I'm sorry. Please don't hate me."

"Just get the hell out, Lorna!"

"Oh, God," Lorna cried harder. Her legs giving way, Lorna sank onto the edge of the bed as she cried pitifully into her hands.

Kyle slumped back against the doorjamb. A stinging on the side of his neck made him touch it. He felt the wetness. He looked at his finger. Blood.

"Damn" was all he could say. He had come close to losing his life—again—and so had Lorna. She would have lost her freedom because she had been caught up in his game. He had played her like he played all the others, but she, like Dalia, wasn't to be played with, and he should have known that. His grandfather was right. He had to become master of his body and inflict no further pain onto others. They couldn't handle the pain, and it seems, neither could he.

Chapter 36

For some knuckleheads, life's lessons are hard learned. For Kyle, his life's lessons were hard learned and long in coming. What he'd always known in theory—don't play the game if you can't stand the pain—he finally understood in actuality. What Dalia and her man had put on him had been bad enough, but what Lorna had been about to dole out to him would have been more than he could stand—if he lived. With the front door double-bolted at Lorna's back, Kyle cleaned the blood from his neck and shoulder, bandaged himself, then took a long, hot shower. Back in his bedroom, he looked at his rumpled bed with a bad taste in his mouth. How could he be so stupid? Getting that last one for the road, as Vernon would say, almost ended his life. Well, this time he learned his lesson. It would be a cold day in hell before he even thought about shaking hands with a woman he had no interest in or had no business being with. Never again. He was definitely closing this chapter of his life.

First thing, though, change the sheets. No need to have Lorna's scent wafting up his nose while he slept. Kyle lifted the demolished pillow that took the full blunt of the blade for him off the bed and was about to toss it when the slit in it opened up and in its white, fluffy innards lay a long, sparkling chain of gold. Puzzled, Kyle wondered how the chain got on the inside of the pillow. He hadn't been wearing one, so it couldn't be his, and

Lorna hadn't been lying on it when the pillow was cut. Strange. How could a gold chain be inside the pillow?

Kyle gingerly lifted the chain and slowly pulled it out of the pillow and was stunned to see, at the end of the chain, his gold turtle. How could that be? His mother had the turtle. How could it be inside his pillow? Maybe his mother . . . No, it wasn't his mother, it was his grandfather. Dropping the pillow, but holding on to his turtle, Kyle dragged a chair over to the window and sat down. He opened the shutters, pulling them back all the way. He sat in the darkness, fingering his turtle, watching the rain fall steadily from the sky. It had been raining for a long time. Tomorrow morning, the streets would be clean, and new grass will have sprouted on lawns. Kyle opened the window just enough to let in the cool fresh air. It had been a warm start to June, and it was quickly heating up to be a scorcher of a summer. The cool night air invigorated Kyle, waking him mentally, making him see even clearer that if he hadn't awakened when he did, Lorna might have cut off his head. It was still blowing his mind how his dream about his grandfather throwing powder, probably gun powder, onto the fire had exploded and had, in reality, startled him awake. All of his dreams about his grandfather and what his grandfather did to him in those dreams seemed so surreal, yet were all too real. How ironic that the only person he'd told about the dreams was Lorna, the very person who might've killed him, but he couldn't fault her for her anger at him.

In good conscience, Kyle couldn't sit back and point a finger at either Lorna or Dalia, or even call them crazies. The truth was, all the blame was his and it was time to stop being a knucklehead. It was time he grew up and did something else with his life besides screw women and run a clerical pool. Preston was right, he had never been disciplined enough to go after what he really wanted out of life—a career that challenged him. He just had to figure out what that career was; then maybe he could begin to plot the path he needed to set foot on. Maybe then he could become the man his grandfather thought he could be.

Epilogue

Every morning, the minute Kyle opened his eyes, he reminded himself that his grandfather was watching him. He hadn't dreamed about him in well over five years, but he lived his life as if his grandfather were spying on him, watching his every move, testing him, putting beautiful women in his path to see if he'd weaken and use them for his own pleasure. So far he hadn't and, in fact, had been celibate the whole five years. But now, for the past six months, he was seeing Nia, a tax accountant. He'd been seeing her pretty steadily, and no one else. He really liked Nia and could see himself settling down with her, but as yet, he hadn't gone to bed with her. He'd be lying if he said it was easy, it was hard as hell. In fact, it was the hardest thing he'd ever done in his life, but he took one day at a time, often glancing at a small picture of his grandfather that he kept in his wallet as a reminder. But then, of course, every time he undressed in front of a mirror, the inch scar on his neck and the circular scars high up on his chest were reminders enough, which is why he feared stumbling and falling back into his old ways. No telling what the old Indian had in mind for him if ever he did backslide.

So much had changed since that long ago night when Lorna came close to decapitating him with the very sword his grandfather had given him. He gave that sword to Preston for safekeeping, and he doubted if he'd ever take it back. He never told anyone about that night, he would have been a fool to. His mother would have said, "It would have served you right for being so trifling." Vernon would have said, "Man, don't you ever learn?" The truth was, he finally had. By the end of that long ago summer, his bags were packed, he'd turned the day-to-day running of his business over to his mother, and she and Grace immediately expanded, moving her and Grace's offices upstairs to the main floor. The top floor Kyle still used whenever he was in town, which was often enough to see Dawn and Brigette, Carole and Sonji's daughter. It was funny how much Brigette resembled Dawn, but it was no surprise, they shared the same paternal DNA. Strangest of all, he didn't look at Brigette as his daughter as he thought he would. He saw her solely as his niece and godchild. Still, he wondered when Brigette was older if she would wonder about the man who gave her life.

Everyone in the family knew who Brigette's daddy was, it was never a secret. Kyle told everyone himself because he had no doubt that he had done the right thing for Carole. Of course, it surprised no one that their mother, Betty, had a hard time dealing with how Brigette was conceived and Kyle's part in it.

"There must be something wrong with you being the biological father of your sister's baby," Betty said, throwing out any argument she could come up with to vent her disapproval.

"Mom, as long as Carole isn't the biological mother of the baby, then there's no problem. Technically, she's raising her niece, and that's been done by lots of people. Just accept the baby, Mom. She's a part of me, and she's a part of you. That's all there is to it."

It wasn't that black and white for Betty. She did accept the baby somewhat; she didn't ignore Brigette or refuse to touch her, but she held a part of herself back from truly accepting that Carole and Sonji were married and that, with Brigette, they were a family. Kyle didn't get to see Brigette or Dawn as often as he wanted since moving to North Carolina, but he made sure he came home as often as he could. And for sure, nothing kept him away from birthday parties and special events for either Dawn or Brigette.

It was at Brigette's fifth birthday party that Kyle watched from the sideline when his mother cornered Carole in the kitchen.

"She's a beautiful little girl," Betty said, teary-eyed.

"Yes, she is," Carole agreed, uncomfortable with her mother's tears. She took a bag of ice from the freezer.

"She's a beautiful gift," Carole said, smiling at Kyle across the room.

Kyle smiled back. He couldn't hear what Carole and his mother were talking about, but he crossed his fingers for good measure.

"I raised you the best I knew how," Betty said, stopping Carole from her task of filling the ice bucket.

"Mom, I have no complaints," Carole said. "Do you think we need more chips out there?"

"I tried to be a good mother. I don't know what I could have done differently."

The word "differently" gave Carole pause. "Mom, I hope you're not saying that you failed at mothering me because of the alternative lifestyle I've chosen to live?"

Betty's eyes watered. "Well, Carole, I must have failed you somehow. Why else would you choose to be with a woman over a man?"

"Simple, Mom, I prefer the gentle, considerate love of a woman over the hard, selfish love of a man. Hey, maybe you should take the credit for how I turned out. After all, it was at your breasts that I received the greatest comfort, and it was in your arms I felt the safest. Maybe that's why I choose to be with women."

Betty didn't know how to take that. She didn't know what to say.

Smiling, Carole kissed Betty on the cheek. "Thanks, Mom. Bring some chips with you."

Carole left Betty still trying to figure out if it was, indeed, her fault that her only daughter was gay because she showed her love.

Winking at Kyle, Carole went about being the perfect hostess to the mothers of eight energetic kids high on sugar running around her living room. From where he sat, Kyle could see the confusion on his mother's face. Perhaps it was time she got out all of her feelings about her only daughter being a lesbian. Who better to talk to than her son, the psychologist.

IF THERE BE PAIN

GLORIA MALLETTE

ABOUT THIS GUIDE

The suggested questions are intended to enhance
your group's reading of this book.

DISCUSSION QUESTIONS

1. This story, *If There Be Pain*, actually grew out of a true story of a man who was just like Kyle. He had everything going for him—a successful business, a caring family, his own home—yet he was a serious womanizer. Women were this man's Achilles heel. Unlike Kyle, this man was, indeed, killed by one of his lovers. Why is it that men like Kyle are never content to be with one woman?

2. Could Kyle's relationship with his mother in any way have affected his relationships with women?

3. What about Kyle's relationship with his father? Does the way a man treat the women in his life have any bearing on what he has seen his father or mother do in their relationship?

4. Could Kyle's need for many lovers be a cover-up for his fear of commitment, or is it simply an issue of no respect for women, or perhaps an issue of poor self-esteem?

5. Many old-timers believe in the "visit" from a loved one who's passed on. Is this belief more generational or cultural?

6. The haunting of Kyle in his dreams by his grandfather may seem fantastical, but is it plausible?

7. Nightmares are frightening. Can dreams or nightmares affect one's real life in any way? Should dreams be seriously considered or interpreted?

8. In Kyle's vision quest he sees the molestation of his sister, Carole. Like so many men, Kyle would kill to protect his

child, his sister, and his mother. Why do men like Kyle not see the women they use or abuse as daughters, mothers or sisters of men who feel as he does about his own family?

9. When Lorna realized that Kyle had no intention of marrying her, do you believe she attempted to kill Kyle out of love or greed?